DAMAGED HEARTS

*the **complete** series*

DAMAGED
HEARTS

the **complete** *series*

New York Times Bestselling Author
MONICA MURPHY

Damaged Hearts Series
Copyright 2018 by Monica Murphy

This book is a work of fiction. The names, characters, places, and incidents are products of the writer's imagination or have been used fictitiously and are not to be construed as real. Any resemblance to persons, living or dead, actual events, locale or organizations is entirely coincidental. The publisher does not have any control over and does not assume any responsibility for author or third-party Web sites or their content.

Published in the United States of America
www.monicamurphyauthor.com

Cover design by Shanoff Designs
Interior design and formatting by: www.emtippettsbookdesigns.com

HER
DEFIANT
HEART

Summer

They say the taste of revenge is sweet.

I don't know who *they* are, but I've heard that saying—or something close to it—my entire life. Revenge is sweet.

Sweet.

Let me tell you something.

Revenge isn't sweet. Not even close.

It's bitter and nasty and dark and vile. It chokes you, literally *chokes* you until you're filled with nothing but anger and sadness and despair and you can't even breathe, you're so overcome with emotion.

And the rage.

The rage is what drives you, despite the awful taste. And if you have enough rage inside you, then you will do your damnedest to get back at the one who hurt you the most.

You see, I know what revenge tastes like, because I am hell-bent on revenge against the one who did me—*us*—wrong. I'm going to destroy her, just like she destroyed my father. My poor, heartbroken father, who lost his will to live long before he actually died.

She tried to destroy me too, but I wouldn't let her. I couldn't. Someone had to be strong. Someone had to be able to withstand this and survive.

My father? He's gone.

Dead.

And now?

She's going to pay.

And she won't even know what—or who—hit her.

ONE

Fall

I watch him, the way he laughs just before he takes another drink from his glass, his hand braced, long fingers spread wide on the gleaming oak bar counter. Blue-and-black plaid sleeves rolled up to reveal glorious, carved-from-marble-but-not-really forearms that can't be real, yet are.

The black and blue on his shirt reminds me of bruises. I should want to see him bruised and battered, just like my heart, my freaking soul. But he's not bruised. Not even close. He seems happy and carefree, like he doesn't give a shit about anyone or anything.

Life is just that good for him.

I can't tear my gaze away from him, not that he notices me. Why should he? He's surrounded by so many girls, all of them focused only on him. His dark brown eyes light up when he smiles, bright and open and flirtatious, and he doesn't have to say a damn thing. They're all quivering with anticipation, hoping and praying he's flirting with them.

So. Pitiful.

The way the girls swarm him makes me think of flies, and he's the giant, steaming pile of crap freshly deposited on the ground. They buzz, buzz, buzz around him, loud with their laughter and their gestures and their ever-ready smiles, calling his name over and over again like that's going to magically make him respond.

He's not interested in any of them. When one of the girls touches him—the lightest press of fingers against his arm, his shoulder, even his chest—those glowing eyes of his dim. For the briefest, bleakest moment, I feel almost…akin with him. Like he and I, we could be the same.

No way is that even close to possible.

Tucking a wayward strand of hair behind my ear, I slump my shoulders forward, my posture closed off, though my gaze sharp, aimed directly at him. Rhett Montgomery. He's with a group of friends, his frat buddies with snotty names like Chip and Spencer, assholes who rule the campus and keep tallies of the girls they've fucked by carving dashes into their headboards with extra-sharp knives. They keep score sheets and compare notes like it's a great big laugh, how awful they are. How they use girls and toss them aside like a tissue they just blew their nose into.

Even though I've been on campus for only two months,

I've heard rumors. These guys are not my kind.

Especially Rhett Montgomery.

One of the girls laughs extra loud, an almost guffawing sound that reminds me of a horse. I lift my head, wincing at the offensive noise, and my gaze meets Rhett's. Locks with his.

Look away.

The voice is a harsh whisper rattling in my brain, and I usually obey it.

But it's like I can't look away.

He doesn't either. That glow in his gaze, I swear it intensifies the longer he stares at me. Like his eyes are lit from within, flickering candlelight that hypnotizes and draws me in, and when his lush mouth curves into a slow yet knowing smile, I finally do tear my gaze away from his, breaking the spell.

My heart is pounding furiously and I reach for my glass of water with shaky hands, the ice rattling against the sides as I sip. Once I swallow, I take a deep, cleansing breath, glancing out of the corner of my eye to find he's already distracted by someone else. Another one of his asshole buddies who's giving him a high five, God knows why. The slap of their palms is loud despite the multiple TVs hanging on the walls, the girls' laughter, the clink of glasses, the low hum of constant talking.

He looked at me. He seemed to look right *through* me, and I feel completely…

Unsettled.

That happened too soon. He wasn't supposed to notice me yet.

The thought flashes in my brain, like too-bright headlights in the darkest night, and I remember why I'm here. What I'm doing. Why Rhett Montgomery is involved. I've studied him for days. Months. He's never noticed me before until tonight. And I've been around. Lurking close by, on the sidelines like some sort of twisted stalker, which I suppose I am.

Really, I should've known he doesn't like obvious girls. And every single one of those girls surrounding him right now is obvious. Desperate.

I keep my distance on purpose, because I'm not ready. Eventually, I'm going to approach him. And when I finally do talk to him, when I finally become a part of his life, I want him to believe I'm a mystery, a code he can't crack.

"Hey."

I go completely still at the sound of his deep voice. Panic rises, making my throat clog with unspoken words, and I lift my head, our gazes meeting once again, his expression open. Friendly. A flood of helplessness fills me and I part my lips, but no sound comes out.

This isn't going as planned. At all.

"You're alone." His statement is obvious, and he does this soft laugh thing that could only be described as a "duh" sound.

I nod, still unable to speak.

"And you're in a bar, but you're drinking water." He tilts his head in the direction of my water glass, which I'm suddenly gripping with all my might. "That's downright sacrilegious."

How does he know it's water? "It could be something else."

"Like what?" Is he actually challenging me?

"Um…" My voice drifts. My father wasn't a big drinker, which, when you think about it is really surprising. So I don't really know much beyond beer is beer and wine is wine.

"Maybe vodka?" His rumbly voice knocks me from my thoughts. I need to focus.

"Not vodka." I shake my head. May as well confess my truth. "Actually, I don't like to drink." Correction: I don't like to lose control, and that was one thing my father told me time and again. Liquor makes you lose control.

It makes you do things you'll regret.

"Ah, so you do make conversation." His smile is full of relief. Sweet and intimate, nothing like that flash of teeth he was offering up to his overbearing harem earlier. "So why are you in a bar if you don't like to drink?"

Right. Why am I in a bar? Not like I can tell him the truth.

"I'm—meeting someone."

He lifts his brows. "Are they late?" I must send him a questioning look because he immediately says, "You've been here for a while. I couldn't help but notice. Beautiful girl sitting alone in a bar, giving off that 'I'm too cool for this scene' vibe…"

Wait a minute. Is he—flirting with me? Or insulting me? I slam back the rest of my water and rise to my feet, a trembling breath leaving me when I realize how close Rhett is standing. So close, I can feel his body heat radiating toward me, and I can smell his appealing—delectable—scent. *God.*

"I was just leaving," I say icily, my shoulder brushing against his broad chest when I walk past him. A scatter of tingles washes over me at first contact, electrifying my skin, and I try my best to shake it off.

That certainly wasn't supposed to happen either.

"Hey, I didn't mean to make you mad." He chases after me, pushing his way through the crowd as I head toward the door. I don't turn back, I don't acknowledge him or make a sound because I want him to think he made me angry.

And he did. He definitely made me angry.

So why does it feel like I'm trying to convince myself?

With an irritated huff, I push open the door and exit the bar, the sudden silence calming my racing heart as the cool fall air washes over my heated skin. I breathe a sigh of relief when I realize he didn't follow me outside. He must not be interested after all.

At least, for now.

A satisfied smile curls my lips, and I duck my head against the wind as I start to make my way home, my mind full of endless possibilities.

Maybe us meeting like that for the first time will work out for the best after all.

TWO

"Hey. You're the girl from the other night. The one who ran out on me."

Slowly I look up to find Rhett Montgomery standing in front of the table I'm sitting at, my eyes going wide with surprise when they land on his too-handsome face. Though I'm not really shocked to find him here. I've followed him long enough to know he'd be at the library. He meets with his study group every Thursday night at seven, and they're usually here for an hour or so. I deliberately planted myself at the table closest to the front door of the library and patiently waited for him to pass by.

I tilt my head to the side and narrow my eyes, contemplating him. Like I don't quite remember him. He takes a step back, seemingly affronted that I could possibly forget him—hard eye roll—and before he takes off, I snap my fingers like I just had a revelation.

"The guy who insulted me for being too cool at the bar," I tell him as I slowly close my Intro to Communications textbook.

His mouth pops open like I just punched him in the stomach. "I didn't insult you."

"From what I vaguely remember, it sounded like you did." I flash him a sweet smile to counterbalance the venom in my words.

"If you thought I was being rude, I apologize." He actually sounds sincere, which surprises me. But he's constantly surprising me so…

"You're forgiven," I murmur. I need to remember myself and stop being so rude to him.

He gestures toward the empty chair across from me. "Can I sit down?"

"Um, sure?" Oh God. I do *not* want him to sit down. I don't want to make small talk with Rhett Montgomery, not yet. I just wanted him to see me, catch a fleeting glimpse or maybe say something quick and then go about his night. Doesn't he have a party to go to or a girl to bang?

"You said it like a question." His brows are lowered, and he's frowning at me. "If you want me to leave you alone, I will."

Again with the serious tone. I believed him just now when he said that, even though I know I shouldn't.

"No, you can stay." I watch as he pulls the chair out and

settles in, dropping his backpack at his feet.

"Why'd you leave the other night?" Rhett asks.

My gaze meets his once more, noting the sincerity in his gaze. He appears genuinely confused. I'm tempted to confess everything to him, but I keep my mouth shut.

"I didn't want to stay there anymore," I say with a little shrug.

"You got ditched, huh?" He lifts his brows, his handsome face now full of sympathy.

The very last thing I want is for him to feel sorry for me. "No, I didn't get ditched," I snap. I immediately regret how mean I sound.

"But the person you were supposed to meet that night never showed up. Right?" He's almost scowling at me, he's frowning so hard. I suddenly remember what I said to him that night. "Hot date that didn't pan out, huh?"

"No," I say quickly. Too quickly. God, just talking to him makes me feel defensive, and that's not a good thing. Not at all. "I met him somewhere else."

"Oh, really?"

His questions are making me uncomfortable. So are his good looks. His thick, dark brown hair, his brown eyes, his perfect face and perfect body and sexy voice and the way he's watching me, leaning toward me like he might actually be interested.

I remind myself this is what I want. This is how I'm going

to worm my way inside, by using Rhett. I should be okay with his attention, should be thrilled that it's all happening so quickly.

But I'm not. I don't know why. Maybe because this scares me. *He* scares me. You can plot and plan and think your way through all the scenarios, but when reality hits and you're actually dealing with the person you're going to use, it's terrifying.

What if I screw up? What if he finds out my secret? What if he exposes me and ruins me forever?

I push those negative thoughts out of my mind and focus on the lie I'm about to tell him instead.

"I left the bar because I got tired of dealing with douchey frat guys," I finally tell him, with as much disdain as I can muster. Which is a lot, by the offended expression on his face.

"So now I'm a douchey frat guy."

I say nothing for a moment, and the wounded look on his face breaks me. "I'm not meaning you."

"Good to know," he says with a slight nod. He looks pleased with himself. "What's your name?"

I've been waiting for this moment for months. I've even rehearsed saying it out loud to him, just to get used to hearing me say it. Though I've become desensitized, since I legally changed my name just before enrolling here and all my professors call me by my new name.

Yet I'm still not used to it. Besides, I chose this name for

Rhett. Figured he might like it, that it sounds rich girl enough to appeal to him.

"Jensen." My voice is small, smaller than I meant it to be. Just being in his presence makes me nervous.

The faint smile curving his full lips is irritatingly appealing. "Jensen," he repeats, like he's testing it out. "I knew a Jensen once."

"You did?" Great. Some girl who probably blew his mind and blew his dick. I should've come up with a better name. But it was the closest to my actual name, and no way could I use that when I met him.

"Yeah, he was on the football team with me in high school. Jensen Graham. Big ol' lineman, probably weighed close to two-twenty-five, maybe even two-fifty." Rhett laughs, shakes his head. "We always called him Jenny just to piss him off."

Relief floods me. It was a *guy* named Jensen, not some hot girl with glossy pink lips from his past.

"Did it?" When Rhett sends me a questioning look, I continue, "Piss him off?"

"Oh, yeah. He seriously hated it when we called him that." The faraway look on Rhett's face tells me he's shifted into nostalgic mode.

"Sounds like you guys were kind of mean."

"You know how it is. Locker room talk." Rhett chuckles, but I don't say anything and when he realizes I'm not laughing, he stops. "You didn't ask what my name is."

I probably just bruised his massive ego and I didn't even mean to. "What's your name?"

"Rhett."

"Oh. Like *Gone with the Wind*?" I make a tiny face, as if I'm offended.

He winces. "Yeah. Tell me you've never watched that movie."

"I've never watched that movie," I say, my voice monotone. I'm lying. I've totally watched that movie. When I was a little girl, my father made me watch it, calling it a classic. I thought Scarlett O'Hara was a total bitch and Rhett Butler was funny-looking.

"Good." He smiles again, his cheeks the faintest pink. He's blushing? Damn it, I don't want him to be appealing or cute. "My mother is from the south."

"She named you?" We're already talking about family and we barely know each other. I thought this guy was a jerk. King douche of the douches. But he's being so nice right now. So... sincere.

I don't get it.

"Yeah." His tone is wistful, and I know why. His mother is dead, though I don't want him to tell me that. I don't want to feel sorry for him, but maybe he doesn't want me to feel sorry for him either so he's keeping that bit of information to himself.

"I should go." Before he can say anything else, I grab my

backpack from the floor and set it on the table, unzipping it and shoving my textbook inside. He stands when I stand, as if he's going to walk me out of the library like some sort of gentleman, and I'm not prepared for that. Nice, handsome, seemingly wholesome boys who want to do right by me. It's ridiculous, a myth, a fairytale in this harsh, cruel world. I know Rhett isn't nice or wholesome.

There's no way he can be.

"You live on campus?" he asks as we exit the library together. He even holds the door open for me, and I have to thank him because I'm not a complete bitch.

"No, I have my own place." It's a total shit-hole that's drafty and cold and in a scary part of town, but it's all mine.

"You parked out in the south lot?" When I glance up at him, he shrugs. "You probably shouldn't be on campus this late at night by yourself. I'll walk you to your car."

There's campus security who will escort you wherever you need to go—you just have to call or text. I guess Rhett wants to be my campus security tonight. "I don't have a car."

My dad's car finally broke down for good right before he died, and I haven't had one since.

"Do you walk home?" He asks way too many questions. Why can't he just say good night and we go our separate ways?

"I take the bus."

"I'll walk you to the bus stop then," he says, his words final, like I can't argue with him.

So I don't.

We walk side by side, him chatting me up, asking endless questions about school, what courses I take, how long have I been there. I give him vague answers, not asking anything in return. I pretty much already know everything about him, and any of those small, secret details he might reveal? He won't share those yet.

Finding out his flaws, his worries, his fears, will only make him more human. That's the last thing I want. I need to treat him like the bridge that will lead me to what I'm really looking for.

When I come to a pause at the bus stop, he glances around, his expression serious before his gaze meets mine. "It's dark here."

"I'll be fine." I shrug then smile, because I want him to leave. "Thanks for walking me."

"I'm staying here until the bus arrives."

"You really don't have to—"

"I'm staying," he says firmly, his gaze dark. "It's not safe here."

"I wait for the bus here pretty much every night."

"You shouldn't."

"I don't have a choice."

"You don't have a friend to give you a lift? Or to at least ride the bus with you?"

I shake my head, sending him a fierce look that says *don't you dare give me a bunch of sympathy because I have no friends.*

He doesn't. Instead he says, "You should take Uber. Or Lyft."

I scoff. Literally scoff. "I can't afford to take an Uber everywhere. I'm not rich like you."

He tilts his head to the side, contemplating me. "How do you know I'm rich?"

Panic races through my brain and I stand up straight, contemplating him right back. "Look at how you're dressed." I wave a hand at him, at his expensive Nike sweatshirt, at the track pants, the very expensive Nikes on his feet. "You're like a walking billboard for Nike. And that watch you're wearing." I point at his wrist and he shakes his sleeve down so it covers the thick silver watch. "Probably worth one year of tuition."

"Not quite," he mutters, looking irritated.

I almost want to laugh. "Close enough."

"You don't know me." His gaze locks with mine again, practically daring me to say something in return.

"You don't know me either," I say with a lift of my chin.

The bus chooses that moment to rumble up the street, stopping in front of us with a screech of brakes and the stench of exhaust. The doors whine as they swing open and a few people disembark. The driver—his name is Stan—looks at me, waves me on with a weary waggle of his fingers. "Don't got all night," he calls.

Without a word, I climb onto the bus and settle into my

usual seat at the very back, staring straight ahead. I can feel Rhett watching me and I want to look at him, but I don't. Not until the bus pulls away from the curb and we're inching our way to the stoplight do I glance over my right shoulder to see him still standing there.

Watching me.

THREE

Nine years ago

"I want my mama." I cross my skinny arms and tuck my chin into my neck, glaring at my father from beneath my brows. I do this when things aren't going my way, say those cruel words so I can watch him wince, witness his heart practically writhing in pain when he hears the word *mama* or *mommy* or *mom*.

I'm only twelve and I already know how to stick it to my father where it hurts the most.

His voice is reed-thin when he says, "You know she can't be here with you, Jenny. I've told you this time and again."

"I don't care." I cross my arms tighter, to the point that it hurts, and I relish in the pain. At least I'm feeling something. "Where did she go? Why doesn't she like me?"

"She loves you, sweetheart. She just…doesn't know how to show it."

"I don't believe you." I know he's lying. Why won't he tell me the truth? "Why doesn't she come see us? Come see *me*? Where is she?"

Daddy sighs. Shakes his head. Blinks at me like he's trying to bring me into focus. "Gone. Gone, gone, gone."

The thing is, he knows where she is. I know he does. I found a thin folder in his desk one Saturday afternoon a few weeks ago, when he was outside mowing the weeds in the front yard and I was supposed to be cleaning the bathroom. I got bored and started rummaging around in his desk, looking for clues. To what, I'm never sure.

I just know my life is a mystery and he's the one holding onto all the information.

I flipped through that folder with muted fascination, reading all the newspaper and magazine articles he clipped out, all about a woman named Diane. I picked up one glossy page torn out of a magazine, clutching the jagged edges tight as I stared hard at her face.

Her face sorta looked like mine, especially when she smiled. And when I saw that, I knew without a doubt she was a part of me. That I was a part of her.

"She's not gone," I tell him, feeling defiant. My voice is firm and my heart is beating so hard it feels like it wants to leap out of my chest.

"Yes, she is," he says wearily, rubbing a hand over his eyes. He's tired. He works hard but makes little. There's never much to eat, I don't have many clothes to wear and my shoes are too tight. I don't remember the last time I got a haircut and I need a bra but I don't have one, so I wear that old coat of mine all the time so the boys can't see my boobs. They're getting so big and sometimes they hurt, especially when I do P.E. But how do I tell Daddy that? He doesn't know how to get me a bra. He can barely take care of himself.

"No, she's not. And I need her. There's stuff a girl needs from her mom that her dad can't help her with," I tell him, lifting my chin. "We need to call her."

"We can't."

"Write her then."

"Can't do that either, Jenny."

"Then let's go to her fancy house and tell her I need her *help!*" I scream the last word, relishing in the pained expression on my father's face. I bet I shocked him when I said *fancy house*, because she lives in one. I know exactly who my mama is.

It's that lady in the magazine. Diane.

She doesn't have the same last name as us because she's married someone else, even though I thought she was married to my daddy. She's got some other rich guy who takes care of her. They have a family, kids and stuff—two that look my age, maybe a little older, and a younger one, a little girl who wears beautiful dresses and has pretty hair—and here I sit with just my daddy in a rotten old house with hardly any food in the fridge and nothing much to call ours.

I hate her for that. If she'd just come see me, if she would just help me, then maybe I could forgive her.

But I don't think that's ever going to happen.

"What do you need help with?" Daddy asks. "I can help you."

I shake my head furiously. "No, you can't."

"I can, Jenny. I'm here for you. I've always been here for you." The look he sends me is pleading. "Let me help you."

"I want my mama!" I sound like a baby, but I don't care.

Anger makes his face tighten up. I made him mad, but for once, I don't care. "*No.* She's dead to us," he spits out.

He hasn't said that to me in a long time. His words used to make me cry. I'd scream no and run to my room, crying into my pillow. I didn't like it when he said she was dead to us.

Now I realize it's the opposite. We're dead to her. She doesn't care about us. She can't. What mom would act this way? Why would a wife leave a man she's supposed to love? I don't get it.

"That doesn't mean she's really dead. I know who she is, Daddy." I drop my arms and stand right in front of him. My father is tall, but he's skinny. He's not very intimidating, what with that sad look on his face all the time. People know my daddy has a broken heart, but he doesn't do much to try and fix it. No one else does either. How can you fix a man who doesn't want to be fixed? "Let's go see her."

"No." He shakes his head, his eyes glassy. Like he might

start to cry.

I've seen him cry a lot. You ever watch movies or TV shows where the men say they don't cry? They've never met my daddy. He cries all the time. I used to cry with him.

I stopped doing that about a year ago. I'm tired of crying. I want to *do* something.

"Why not?" I grab his hands. They feel paper-thin and they're so cold. Like there's no life in him. "Please, Daddy. I bet if she saw me, she'd want to help."

"She left us a long time ago. She doesn't want to help us."

"Maybe she doesn't want to help you, but she might want me." That's the only thing that gives me any hope, that my mom doesn't realize how much I look like her, or how much I need her. Maybe she forgot about me. Maybe my daddy told her we didn't want her, but that's not true. I want her.

I want her in my life so bad.

He sighs again, more shaking of the head, more whispers of my name like I'm a hopeless, ridiculous little girl. I'm not. I'm growing up. Daddy might not see it, but it's true.

"It's not going to happen," he says firmly. "So for the love of Christ, *stop* asking for her like a little baby! She doesn't care about us, okay? She doesn't care about me and she definitely doesn't care about you."

His tone is venomous. Final. He's breathing hard when he finishes and I'm breathing hard too, tears streaming down my face, landing on my lips so I can taste the salt. We stare at each other, our chests heaving, our bodies trembling. Mine is at least, and I think his is too.

"I hate you," I whisper just before I turn and run to my room.

"You don't mean what you say," he calls after me as I throw myself on my bed. "You don't have anyone else, Jennifer Rae! And don't you forget it!"

I push my face into my pillow, trying to drown out his words, but I know he speaks the truth.

I know he's all I have.

I know my mama doesn't love me.

I don't know what I did to her to make her feel that way.

FOUR

T he only reason I'm at this college is because of him. How messed up is that? But it's true. Rhett is why I'm at this university, and while I'm taking courses and actually doing well, all of that comes second to my true purpose.

To get close to Rhett Montgomery.

He could go to any college in the world, I'm sure, considering his family is so wealthy. But he chose to remain close to home and go to a state university near where he grew up, which is surprising. His mother went here, though, and I even read a newspaper article online that quoted him saying that he came here to be close to her, or some sentimental bullshit like that. Any normal girl would say, "Aw, how sweet," but I don't get it.

What I do get is that I'm done with being scared. Hiding in the shadows for the first eight weeks of the fall semester is pretty damn stupid—and cowardly. I've wasted half the semester alone just following him around. But it took that long to even work up the courage to say something to him. Not that I was the one who approached him first. Of course, he had to notice me versus the other way around. The girl who pretended not to care about him, that's the one he wanted to talk to.

Not surprising though. I discovered pretty early that boys love a challenge. I lost my virginity when I was fifteen to my first serious boyfriend, a loudmouth guy two years older than me who could burp the alphabet after draining almost half a keg at the regular Friday night parties. All the girls laughed and thought he was so talented and funny while I merely rolled my eyes and told my one friend—Lyssa, who I miss terribly—that I thought he should be embarrassed by his so-called skills.

Turned out he overheard my rude comment, and then he chased after me for weeks. I kept telling him no. Finally, I relented, broken down by his constant texting and walking with me in between classes. At one of those infamous Friday night parties, he got me drunk, took me up to his parents' bedroom—they were away for the weekend, so it was his turn to hold the party—where he proceeded to kiss me all over my body and then take my virginity with a couple of swift pumps of his hips.

Once he got inside, it was all over in less than ten minutes. I was left with a searing pain between my legs, a wet spot beneath the mattress, and the dawning realization that I'd sacrificed my virginity to the boy who was popular for burping the alphabet.

Talk about lame.

But once it was over, it was over, and I could freely give away my body to any boy I might be interested in and not feel shame or guilt over it. It's weird, but it was like once the bridge had been crossed, I never looked back. Any attention is good, right? Better than none at all. I'm not ashamed of the list of boys I've had sex with, but I'm not necessarily proud of it either. Mainly because I never loved one of them. I can't even say that I cared for any of them. Not in a deep and meaningful way.

Does that make me callous? Probably. But sex is just sex. Love is for those who want to end up damaged for the rest of their lives. Look at my father, nursing his broken heart for years while the woman who ruined him for anyone else continues to live her life like he doesn't even matter.

Love is for idiots who want to hurt. Love is for suckers who think they need it in order to survive.

Love doesn't keep you alive. It bleeds you dry.

I can pretend to fall in love with Rhett, though. That won't be difficult. He'll take me right where I want to go.

This is why I'm hanging around the gross diner just off campus, the one I know he likes to frequent with his friends on a Saturday afternoon. The place smells greasy and I want to go home so I can take a shower, but instead I'm drinking a bitter cup of coffee and messing around on my laptop, scrolling Pinterest. Really, I should be studying, or writing the essay that's due Tuesday. But I'm too anxious, too keyed up thinking about seeing Rhett and what I might say to him to concentrate on anything meaningful.

I'm not disappointed when I finally spot him either. He enters the diner within twenty minutes of my arrival, surrounded by his frat brothers. My stupid heart trips over itself at seeing his dark brown hair wind-tousled and his cheeks pink with health, wearing a black sweater and jeans. He looks like he walked straight out of a goddamn Ralph Lauren shoot, the all-American rich boy who can do no wrong. I ignore the tingles of electricity I experience when our eyes lock, ignore my fluttering, nervous stomach when he slowly makes his way toward my booth, that giant smile on his face unabashed in his pleasure in seeing me.

"Why do we keep running into each other?" he asks, his voice warm, his eyes sparkling as he takes me in, as if I'm the best thing he's seen in a long time.

"Small town, I guess." I shrug with so much fake nonchalance I pray he doesn't realize what a phony I am. But he doesn't. He's too enthralled with me, which is unbelievable. I tried my best to look like the girls he takes photos with on social media, and I did it all on a budget too, while those girls probably spent way too much money on their hair, clothes, jewelry and whatever else they own.

Me? I sorta already looked like them. I'm a dark blonde, and if I had more money, I'd pay for highlights, but that's not going to happen. Instead, I bought a cheap curling iron at Walgreens and practiced and practiced until I got the waves just right. He seems to like girls with wavy hair. Subtle makeup. Sun-kissed good looks and big, toothy smiles. Luckily enough, my teeth are fairly straight—thanks, Dad—and I never had braces. I'm blue-eyed and pink-cheeked thanks to my mother. I'm pretty, and Rhett seems to like them pretty.

What a superficial asshole.

"I've never seen you here before," he says, that smile still curling his lush mouth. His friends are calling his name but he's ignoring them, completely focused on me.

"I'm usually here in the morning." This is a lie. Though my shift usually starts Saturday afternoon so normally I wouldn't be here no matter what.

"Well, lucky me that you're here right now." His smile grows and I find myself smiling in return. I almost stop, almost wear the scowl that wants to appear when he's around.

I *need* to smile, though, so I let go, offering him a quick one before I press my lips together, like I have to contain my excitement at his proximity.

We remain quiet for a moment, just staring at each other, and I'm not sure how this is happening but I go along with it. His friends are still calling his name, the waitress having already seated them at a nearby booth. They don't want him talking to me. They want to bask in his attention for a few hours more.

I'm starting to get the sense that everyone wants to bask in Rhett Montgomery's attention.

"Your friends are calling you," I finally say.

He glances over his shoulder, then returns his attention to me. "They can wait."

I'm surprised he's putting talking to me above wanting to spend time with his friends. "Well, my homework can't." I gesture to the open textbook by my laptop. "Nice to see you again."

"Nice to see you again? That's all I get?" He slides into the booth seat across from mine, leaning across the table like he wants to get closer to me. "I bet you don't even remember my name."

"I bet you don't remember mine either," I toss back at him, tacking on an annoying giggle after I say it.

He makes a face, like he knows I'm fake as hell. "Jensen."

"Rhett."

His smile is back, wider than ever. "You should come sit with us."

"No, thank you." My voice is prim, like a snotty rich girl's would be. Wouldn't they find it hilarious to know that I spent my teenage years living in a mobile-home-slash-trailer, in the decrepit old fifth-wheel my dad called our new home right before I started eighth grade.

One brow lifts. "My friends would love to meet you."

"I doubt that."

"It's true." He glances over his shoulder again, and they call out to him, a couple of choice words ringing in the air. The waitress glares, stomping over to their table to give them a lecture I suppose, and Rhett whirls around so he's facing me once more, his expression full of amusement. "Or maybe not."

"Go hang out with your friends," I tell him gently, wanting to give the impression that I am the perfectly understanding girlfriend. He might not have those types of serious thoughts about me—yet—but my good behavior can enter his subconscious, right?

"Jensen. I want to see you again." He reaches across the table and touches the top of my right hand, his warm fingers practically burning my skin. I snatch my hand away from his, my fingers trembling as I clutch my hands together in my lap.

One casual touch from him and I feel like I'm going to erupt in flames.

It's terrifying.

"I don't have a lot of time," I tell him, nibbling on my lower lip. Like it's a major dilemma, being asked out by the hottest guy on campus.

"What do you mean?" He's frowning so hard he's got wrinkles in his forehead.

"I'm taking a heavy course load." That's true. "Plus, I work."

Also true. "Part-time, but it's a lot to deal with." Okay, that's a lie. "And I just...I have so much on my plate." Not so much that I wouldn't use this guy to get close to the woman he calls Mom.

I can rightfully call her Mom too. Even more than he can.

Because here's my big secret. The reason I want to get close to Rhett Montgomery. My mother, the fancy lady I saw in the magazines and newspaper articles my father had stashed in his desk, is named Diane Montgomery.

She married Rhett's dad. He is my...

Stepbrother.

Talk about twisted.

"You gotta make time for fun, Jens." No one has ever called me Jens before. "What are you doing tonight?"

"Working." True.

"Where do you work?"

I do not want to tell him where I work.

"I clean offices at night, when no one else is around." Lie. A big, fat lie.

He's frowning again. "That sounds dangerous."

Is he for real right now? "How?"

"If no one is around, that means the parking lots are empty, the buildings are empty. Some creeper could totally attack you when you least expect it." My eyes go wide and he immediately leans back against the seat, shaking his head. "Sorry. I didn't want to scare you, but you know what I mean."

"I have a tiny bottle of mace on my keychain." And I keep a pocketknife in my purse. I deal with a lot of creepers at work. He has no freaking idea how many.

"Good." He nods, placated by my lame declaration. "You want my advice?"

"Oh, please." Like this pretty boy has ever had to defend himself.

"Kick them in the nuts if you're ever attacked."

I nod, trying my best to remain solemn. Serious. "Good advice." The best advice is go for the eyes and gouge them out if you can, but what does he know?

"Since you're so busy, being a big time working girl and all, you probably need a break. You should go out with me tomorrow then."

I'm taken off guard by his request. "But it's Sunday." What, like I go to church? Please, it's more like I sleep in till the midafternoon since I don't get home from work until late.

"So? Go to brunch with me."

Where I come from, we don't brunch. I don't think I've ever been to brunch. Sometimes we would have to skip a meal because there was no food in the house, but I don't think that counts.

"Um, what time?" I ask, trying to sound casual. Inside, I'm a bundle of nerves.

His smile returns yet again, flashing lots of shiny white teeth. "Eleven?"

"Eleven thirty?" I counter.

"Okay. Give me your number." He flicks his chin at my crappy old iPhone 5c and then pulls out his fancy new iPhone, opening it with a glance, his fingers poised over the screen.

I rattle off my number, noticing the way my voice shakes, how my knees are knocking together. Crap, he's making me nervous, and I told myself I wouldn't get nervous. He enters the digits into his phone and I immediately have a text notification pop up on my cracked screen.

Grabbing my phone, I read his message.

Tell me where you live.

Glancing up from my phone, I send him a pointed look. "How about you tell me where we're going and I'll meet you there?" I don't want him to know where I live. I really don't want him to know much of anything about me.

The less he knows, the better.

"I wanted to pick you up. Be a gentleman." He sounds sincere, which I find unbelievable. But maybe he is. Maybe Rhett Montgomery is too good to be true.

"It's easier if I can meet you. I have to work tomorrow afternoon." A lie, since I'm not on the schedule. Though if I wanted to go into work and catch a few extra hours, Don would let me.

Don's my boss. He'd let me do whatever I want if I would only spread my legs for him, but I won't cross that line. I might not take sex seriously, but I take having sex with my boss very seriously.

As in, I won't do it.

"I'll text you the restaurant's name and address. I still need to figure out where we're going." He slides out of the booth seat. "Talk to you later."

And then he's gone.

FIVE

So my job that I didn't want to reveal to the precious, perfect Rhett? I work at a dance club.

That's code for strip joint.

I'm not a stripper, though. I'm—oh my *God*—a topless server. Yes, it's so degrading, but the tips are amazing and the money allows me to live on my own. I may live in a shit-hole, but it's mine and I don't have to share it with a stranger who'll write her name on all her food in the refrigerator and have her slimy boyfriend stay over all the time.

Yes, I've got an overactive imagination, thank you very much.

I make good money, mostly in cash tips that go straight into my pockets, and my job allows me to go to school during the day and work at night. I have long, late hours, though. I come home past two in the morning, sometimes almost three.

I've been propositioned for lap dances, blowjobs and the like more times than I can remember. Plenty of men—and women—have touched my ass. Pinched it, slapped it, cupped it, caressed it. That's what happens when you walk around without a shirt on for hours at a time.

If my dear, lovely mother knew what kind of person I turned out to be, she'd probably freak the hell out.

Or maybe not, since she's never seemed to care about me anyway.

Did I mention that we haven't seen each other since I was a baby? Not even two years old? Maybe I was around seventeen months when she left? I don't know exactly—I can't remember that far back—but I've heard the story countless times. That one night when she ran out on my dad and me after a huge fight and never came back.

That was twenty years ago. It's pretty sad that she could forget me so easily. Raise another family—three kids who aren't even her blood—yet never acknowledge me.

God, I hate that bitch. I hate those kids she raised too. And one of them I'm going to have to fuck and pretend I actually like it. Like *him.* I'll deserve an Academy Award for my performance by the time I'm through.

"You're late," Don says as the heavy door slams behind me. Employees use the entrance in the back of the club so we don't have to deal with the customers. Guests, Don calls them. *Sounds classier*, he's always saying before he explodes with that phlegmy, gross laugh of his. Which then turns into a coughing fit, and I'm always afraid he'll hack up a lung.

"No, I'm not," I say as I check the time just before I punch in for my shift. I head for the employee lockers where I'll stash my bag and my sweatshirt, Don right on my heels.

"Fine, fine," he mutters. "So tell me. When you gonna jump on stage? You're starting to get more requests."

I jerk open the metal door, shoving my bag inside before I turn to face him. "Never."

His pale blue eyes fill with disappointment. "You would be perfect out there. You have a fantastic body."

I've become used to people analyzing my body, and I've only worked here for a little over two months. I moved to this town to attend the university and got the job before school started. I needed money, fast, and this was the ideal solution to my cash flow problem.

"I'm a terrible dancer," I tell the inside of my locker. No way do I want to turn and face Don. Since my encounter with Rhett, I've been feeling extra low about coming to work tonight. If Rhett knew what I really did to earn money, he'd probably be disgusted.

Shame washes over my skin at the thought of him finding me here, making me burn with embarrassment.

"I bet you're a better dancer than you think you are. You could probably really shake it on the stage." Don says this stuff to me pretty much every time I come into work. He doesn't know when to give up. "You'd look good on stage, Jen."

I tell everyone at work to call me Jen. It reminds me of who I really am. Sometimes I need that, so I don't forget where I came from, or what my purpose is.

"Just because I have nice tits doesn't mean I should be shaking them on stage." As if to prove my point, I whip off my sweatshirt, shove it into my tiny locker and slam the door before turning to face Don. I can tell it takes everything within him to keep his gaze fixed on my face and not let it drop to my chest. "I'm perfectly happy working as a server."

Don's gaze lingers on my breasts for a minute too long and I sorta want to slap him on the face for it. He's such a perv. "You know you'd make a hell of a lot more money if you stripped, doll."

Always tempting. He knows where to get me. I've never really had money, so I have no idea what that's like, to be comfortable financially.

No. No way. Keep your eye on your long-term goal. Stripping isn't it. Getting in good with the Montgomery family is where you'll find your fortune.

"I'll consider your suggestion," I say just to appease him, and he grins, his mouth opening like he's going to say something I don't want to hear. I start walking, heading for the bar so I can grab my tray and start taking orders. I came to work in my short, tight black skirt and high stiletto heels, wearing my favorite old gray sweatshirt temporarily so I can be semi-comfortable until it's show time.

And right now, it is definitely show time.

"You mean it?" Don sounds so hopeful, I almost wish I was telling him the truth.

"Sure," I say halfheartedly, speeding up so I can lose him, which I easily do. Don isn't the most physical guy, and we've all learned real fast that if you stay quick on your feet, you can outrun him most nights. The majority of us who work for Don want to outrun him as much as possible.

The club is packed, the music loud and the multicolored lights that flash are almost blinding. I weave my way through the thick crowds, chin up, gaze not meeting anyone's. I know they're looking at my naked chest, and I know if I make eye connection with any of them, they'll more than likely make a suggestive comment I'm not in the mood for.

I'm almost to the bar when I hear a friendly voice and I nearly sag with relief. "Hey, hooker."

I smile at my coworker who calls all of us hookers, almost like it's a term of endearment, which from her, I guess it is. Savannah is tough as nails and a college student like me, though she's a senior set to graduate in the spring. She's been working at City Lights since she was barely eighteen, and she's seen it all. But she sticks it out since she needs the money. She's fully funded her college education with her income and tips, and she plans on being a child psychologist someday.

"Don try to get you to strip?" she finally asks when I don't really say anything.

"Of course." I grab an empty tray but stay by Savannah's side. She's waiting for Chuck the bartender to make her drink order, and I should go start taking drink orders too since it looks busy tonight, but I'm not quite ready to face the crowds yet.

"You finally give in and say yes?"

"Of course not."

Savannah laughs and shakes her head. "That's my girl. Don't ever give in, or else you'll end up like that." She nods toward the stage, and we both watch the woman writhing on the floor in nothing but a see-through white G-string.

Candy Raine is one of the older strippers at City Lights, and one of the least popular because she's so old. And when I say old, she's barely thirty-five. That's not ancient, not by a long shot, but in the stripper world it is. Candy can't seem to do anything else. She has no other job, no other skills, and no ambition to get out of here either. Savannah always uses Candy as the prime example of what not to turn into.

"Seven more months," Savannah says as Chuck loads up her tray full of drinks. "Seven more months and then I can leave this hellhole once and for all and be done with this place. I cannot wait."

"I'm jealous," I say wistfully, though deep down I'm not. I won't be here as long as Savannah. I have a plan, one that's way better than working at a strip club for the next four years of my life.

"Just don't get dazzled by the big tips and you'll be fine. Keep your head on straight and eyes fixed on the end game. If you do that, lap dances and blowjobs in the back room won't be your fate." Savannah's evil laugh rings as she grabs her tray and balances it over her head with one hand. "See ya." She winks at me and then she's gone, off making her way toward her various tables.

"Better get on it," Chuck urges, his gruff voice making me turn to look at him. He's a good guy, not very affectionate, but you can tell he cares about us. He never gives me the creeps either, which makes me trust him more than any other guy that works at this club. "It's extra busy tonight."

For the tiniest moment, I'm tempted to turn around and run out. Just keep running and never look back. If I could, I'd head all the way back home.

I can't go back there, though. My home is gone. Dad is gone. This is my reality now. Going to school and stalking some guy I'm supposed to pretend to like. Working at a strip club where I serve leering perverts their drinks while I walk around topless. This is my world.

And I fucking hate it.

SIX

"You showed up," Rhett says when he catches sight of me slowly approaching the restaurant. He rises from the bench he was sitting on, his eyes lighting up when they land on me and I can't help but feel like there's a spotlight following me as I walk toward him. Like we're on a stage, putting on some sort of show for our invisible yet enthralled viewers, ready and eager to be tantalized by our burdening supposed-romance.

"I said I would," I reply, stopping just in front of him. He's dressed up in pressed khakis and a light blue button-down shirt, his sleeves rolled up to his elbows giving him a more casual air. Though I can tell by the way his clothes look that they're designer, more expensive than anything I own.

Me? I tried to dress up in my best jeans, a plain white T-shirt and a cute burgundy cardigan I got on sale. I'm not even close to designer. I can't afford anything expensive, unless it's some collab with a designer at Target. That's about as high end as I get.

"I'm glad you kept your word." His voice is a low murmur, heavy on the flirtation, and I remind myself that I can pretend to think he's hot, but deep down I have to remember that I'm using him. I'm not attracted to him, I'm merely *acting* like I'm attracted to him.

So I ignore the sizzle of awareness that zips through me at the sound of his sexy voice. Or the gentlemanly way he opens the door for me. And I definitely ignore the tingles that wash over my skin when he rests his hand on my lower back, guiding me into the restaurant. The very cute girl standing behind the hostess desk stands at attention when she catches sight of Rhett. She practically gobbles him up with her gaze as she checks him out, and I'm tempted to bare my territorial fangs and tell this bitch to back off, he's mine.

Yeah. That wouldn't go over so well.

Instead I smile politely at her as Rhett asks for a table for two. The hostess sends me a withering look as she grabs the tall, heavy-looking menus, and seems to put an extra swish in her step as she asks us to follow her.

Rhett doesn't even pay attention to her. His hand is still at my lower back, his fingers barely touching me, yet his body is so close to mine I can feel the heat radiating from him, smell his delicious, spicy-clean man scent. I'm not usually into this sort of thing, falling for a guy because of his scent or the way he touches me. I don't fall for anyone *period*, friends or family and definitely not men who claim they're interested in me. No one ever sticks around, you know? And the ones who do stick, usually need lots of help, like my dad.

Once we're seated and the hostess has left us alone, Rhett sets his menu on the table and studies me. "I really thought you weren't going to show up for our date," he confesses.

I almost didn't, not that I'd ever admit that to him. I'm surprised he'd tell me that. "I would never do that, though I'm sorry I was running a little late."

"You should've texted and let me know what's going on." He sounds like an overly concerned boyfriend. I don't know if I like that. His behavior should give me more reason to dislike him so I can cling to it. "I was kind of worried."

"I'm sorry." I don't sound sorry, though, and I think he knows it, so I try to soften my snide words with an apologetic smile. He smiles in return, his gaze sticking to mine for a moment too long before I finally tear mine away and start checking out the menu.

Dread fills me as I keep reading. The prices are outrageous and I try to find the cheapest option, though I'm starving. Like *my stomach is growling loudly and I'm afraid he might hear it* starving. And everything sounds so good, like dreamily, melt-in-my-mouth good. There's a buffet too; that includes unlimited mimosas. The alcohol sounds like a smart choice.

Something to numb me, loosen me up—but not too loose— and make it easier for me to fake this so-called date.

"I think I'm doing the buffet." Rhett shuts his menu and I do the same, mimicking his movements. I read somewhere once, maybe in *Cosmo*, that you should use the same body language as your date, because that tells him you're interested. "How about you?"

"I think I want the same." *Please God, let him pay for my meal.*

"It was the unlimited mimosas that got you, right?" The lopsided smile Rhett flashes me makes me smile in return, all while I try my best to battle the heat that washes over me. He's too quick with his smiles, with his seeming approval of everything I do. Makes me not trust him even more. "They're my mom's—well, my stepmom's—favorite part of the brunch menu here. She loves this place."

The heat is gone, replaced by icy cold tendrils of fury. My entire body seems to sag under the weight of his words, the implication, the oh-so-casual way he talks about *my* mother.

Not his.

Mine.

"Are you two...close?" It takes everything out of me to ask this question. My voice is strained, my throat burns and my eyes sting. I blink back the angry tears and shake my head once quickly, dismissing the emotion.

Rhett's smile is gone in an instant, and he seems to go

cold too. Dormant. "Our relationship isn't great. She's not my mom, and when I was younger I reminded her of that fact every chance I got."

Interesting. Everything I see on the Internet tells a different story. But then again, you can tell whatever story you want on social media. What happens behind closed doors is another matter. "Did she boss you around?"

"No. Well, yeah, I guess. She just—she tried to be my mom, and I didn't want her to do that. I already had a mom, you know? And then she died." His eyes go dark, his expression somber. He doesn't like talking about his dead mother, not that I can blame him. I don't want to talk to him about my dead father, so the feeling is mutual. "She overstepped her boundaries a lot, especially when she first moved in with us. Still does."

"Because she's always mothering you?" I practically spit the question out and I clamp my lips shut so I don't say something awful. Talking about her is difficult, harder than I thought it would be. How she can be a mother to him and completely ignore me my entire life, I will never understand.

"No, she doesn't try to mother me." He tilts his head to the side, like he's trying to figure out what she is to him. Or more like he's trying to figure out how to explain her to me. "Our relationship over the years has…changed."

"For the better?" *Don't act like you care too much. He'll wonder what's up with all the questions.*

"Not, necessarily." His gaze lifts, locking on our server. "Ah, there's our future mimosa angel."

I glance up to find a gorgeous blonde standing beside our table, holding a small tablet and a stylus. Her smile is slow and sultry, and I study her carefully, hoping I can…what? Pick up tips? What's up with this restaurant? Do they only hire beautiful women to work for them? "I'm guessing you two want the brunch with unlimited mimosas?"

"You're so smart." Rhett hands over his menu and I do the same, though the server isn't even looking in my direction as she takes the menu from me. Her focus is zeroed in on Rhett. Damn, that's rude. Even when there's a woman at the club— which is rare but still, it happens—I always make eye contact with her when I'm taking their drink order. Though most of the time they act embarrassed. Suppose I can't blame them since I'm the one who's topless.

"I try my best." The server is blatantly flirting. She even leans over a little bit, offering Rhett a glimpse of her chest via her deep V-neck shirt. "I'll bring out the mimosas. Go ahead and help yourselves at the buffet. There are two chefs on duty today, at the waffle bar and the omelet bar."

"Thank you," I murmur, though my words are pointless. It's funny, how I want to blend in and not be noticed, yet I'm offended when the waitress doesn't acknowledge me.

The server saunters away and Rhett's already getting out of his chair. "Ready to fix your plate?"

"But my purse…" I point helplessly at my cheap black bag sitting at my feet. Not that anyone would want to steal it. All I see are a fleet of Louis Vuitton, Chanel and Gucci bags. I might be broke, but one of my favorite things to do is read fashion blogs. I look at the pretty photos and dream.

Rhett doesn't even look at my pitiful bag, thank goodness. "It'll be fine. No one will take it."

If someone steals it, which I doubt, I know Rhett will replace whatever I lose, and that isn't much. Pushing my worry away, I rise to my feet and follow him to the buffet line, grabbing a warm plate and staring in wonder at all the food spread out before me. So much fruit, so many pastries. Bacon and sausage and hash browns and country potatoes. There are salads and thinly sliced deli meats, a bagel and toast section, and the chef at the waffle bar is beckoning me to come to him, so I do.

He prepares me a Belgian waffle and tops it with fresh strawberries and whipped cream. I quickly grab a few pieces of bacon and then I head back to the table, my shabby purse sitting right where I left it. Rhett hasn't returned yet, and I wonder if I should wait for him.

My stomach growls in protest at the thought.

"Here's your drinks." The server appears, placing our mimosas on the table. Her gaze lands on my plate and she wrinkles her nose. "You're really going to eat all that?"

I glance at my plate, wondering what she's complaining

about. This is the biggest meal I've had in weeks. Possibly in years, especially since I'm not through yet. "Yeeeaaah." I draw the word out, like *duh*. I don't know what her problem is.

"That's just—so many calories on one plate." Her gaze shifts to my body and she offers up a blatant perusal. "You must work out."

Running all over a strip club while carrying drinks and avoiding grabby-handed customers is about as much of a workout as I get. "Sometimes," I say with a shrug.

"Well, if you want my advice, sugar is the devil," she sing-songs.

My fingers itch to slap the smug smirk on her face. I bet she'd love to see me fatten up as I shove the food in my mouth. Picking up my fork, I puncture a whipped-cream-covered strawberry and bring it to my lips. "Didn't ask for your advice, but thanks anyway."

She shoots me a dirty look before taking off and I plop the strawberry in my mouth, the juicy sweetness exploding on my tongue. Wow, this is good.

I grab another forkful of strawberry and whipped cream and consume it, closing my eyes for the briefest moment. I haven't even got to the good part yet—the warm, crunchy, sweet waffle. I open my eyes and reach for the syrup on the table, pouring a light steam of it on top of my waffle just as Rhett returns and sits down across from me.

"Their waffles are delicious," he says.

I examine his plate—the one that's waffle-free. "Why didn't you get one?"

He smiles, seemingly embarrassed. "I'm training right now, so I can't eat too much junk."

"Training for what?" I know what he's in training for. I know everything about this guy that I could find in my extensive Google search and hardcore sleuthing on his social media.

"Basketball." He shrugs when I give him my best *ooh I'm impressed* look. "I'm just okay. I mostly play as a stress reliever. I won't go pro or anything."

"You really don't think so?" In some of my Rhett Montgomery research, the sports-related articles have mentioned that he has potential, but he's not what they consider tall enough.

"Nah. I'm not a giant like the rest of the pros." He shrugs again before he starts eating from his bowl of fruit.

"You're pretty tall, though." That was another thing I read in that online article about dating. Build them up. Be a fangirl. I'm not real good at that, but I can learn. This is a start.

"Not tall enough." He says it so matter-of-factly, I'm taken aback.

"And you're okay with that? It's not your dream, to play for the pros?"

"I'm just being realistic. I'm decent, but I'm not a superstar, and I'm not built like a superstar either." He stops eating to take a drink of his mimosa, his gaze never leaving mine. I can't look away either, which is unsettling. What is so enthralling about this guy anyway?

"Being realistic is no fun," I tell him with a mock pout, my lips pursed.

He doesn't smile or laugh, though. Just keeps watching me, his expression serious. "What about you? What are your dreams?"

I'm taken off guard by his question. A question no one has ever really asked me before. "Um…" My voice drifts and I realize my mind is void. Empty. I don't have any dreams.

Well. I do dream of taking down my mother in every horrible way possible, but I can't tell him that. He'll think I'm a total psycho.

"Come on." Rhett shifts in his seat, leaning forward, his hawk-like gaze still trained on mine. "There's got to be something you want. Something you hope for."

"I want to graduate college."

He dismisses my statement with a wave of his fingers. "Boring. Dig a little deeper."

"What's your dream?" I toss back at him, trying to change the subject. I don't want to talk about my hopes and dreams. I've lived pretty much my entire life without any. What's the point in starting now?

"Aw, come on. Don't dodge my question." He's smiling, but there's a determined gleam in his eyes that throws me. I don't like how intent he is on finding out my dreams. Maybe they're none of his damn business. "Tell me. You've got to have at least one dream. One wish for your world."

"Peace and harmony?" I joke, but he's not having it. Neither am I. In fact, I'm starting to get pissed. "Look, I barely know you. I don't feel comfortable sharing all of my secret hopes and dreams and fears with you, okay?"

"Hey, sorry." He leans back in his chair, seemingly shocked. I didn't mean to sound so hostile, but I can't have him trying to dig around and figure out what drives me to do what I do. I have to keep up my carefully constructed wall around me at all times when I'm with him.

I can't have emotional outbursts in front of him either, so I need to calm the hell down before he decides I'm not worth it.

Taking a deep breath, I exhale slowly and then say, "Look, I'm sorry. I didn't mean to jump all over you."

"No, I get it. It's okay. I'm sorry too. I forget that other people aren't like me."

Oh God. Please don't tell me he's going to give me a bunch of crap about how he's different than other guys and I'm supposed to fall for it. "What do you mean by that?"

"It probably seems weird, but I don't mind telling strangers my secrets." When I send him a look, he continues, "I'm serious. We don't know each other that well. Who are you going to tell my secrets to? If I confess all to someone I'm close with, then they'll blab to whoever will listen, mostly to people who know me. And that's usually people I don't want to know my secrets. I can't risk it."

He is oddly making sense to me. He's also admitting he has secrets. I want to know every single one of them—so I can use them against him when the time is right. "So what you're saying is, I'm not a risk."

"Not yet." His gaze warms when it drops to my mouth for the briefest moment. I go warm too, and I tell myself to get over it. "But you might be."

I hate what he just said. I hate worse my reaction to his words. He wants to keep seeing me. He's implying he wants me to become a risk. I should be thrilled. I've got him right where I want him.

Instead, I'm nauseous. My food doesn't sound so good anymore, and I can feel a headache coming on. I didn't expect to feel awful. To almost feel...sorry for him. And that's totally ridiculous, because I don't care about this guy. I can't care about him at all. He's the enemy. For years I've hated him, and at one point, I focused all my blame on him for taking my mother away from me. Stupid, right?

But this boy sitting across from me knows her. Grew up with her. Complains about her like he has every right to, when he doesn't. He so doesn't.

She belongs to me. She's *my* mother.

"I'll probably always be a risk to you," I tell him, using my knife and fork to cut into my waffles. Anger surges inside of me, reminding me that I'm pretty freaking hungry after all, and I've barely touched my plate. I happily shovel a forkful of waffles into my mouth, nearly moaning with pleasure at the taste.

"You're saying that we'll never get close." His voice is flat. Did I upset him? I suddenly don't care if I did.

I shrug. "Take it as you will."

"I'm taking what you said as a challenge." I lift my head up, my guilty gaze meeting his. "And I love a challenge. You'll find this out about me, I promise."

Great, he's determined. I shouldn't be surprised. This is exactly what I wanted. For Rhett to chase after me.

"I need more bacon," I tell him, shoving some in my mouth while he laughs at me.

That's okay. He can think I'm joking.

After all, I'll get the last laugh.

SEVEN

'm one of those weird millennials who doesn't like social media much, except when using it for stalking purposes. And fine, on occasion, I like Instagram. But I mean, let's be real—pretty much everyone in my age group is addicted to social media. The reason? They don't know how to live their life without it. Think about it. If someone took the Internet away, or their phones away, and threw them in a dumpster fire, or if the President of the United States banned all social media for life, I'm sure a ton of people in their early to late twenties would up and die. Just flat out not exist any longer.

I'm sure there would be a ton of people of *all* ages who would freak out and rather die than live without social media and/or their phones. That's how dependent our society has become.

I was raised differently. I know, I know I sound like that

typical girl who's all, "But I'm soooo different. Not like other people at all. I'm special." Like I just mentally accused Rhett of acting on our brunch date.

But when you grow up broke, when you don't have much food to eat in the fridge, cell phones and the Internet are a total luxury, one I never had until I was sixteen, the summer before my junior year. That's when I got my first crappy little phone with its crappy little plan, and I was so damn happy I thought I would burst. I believed my new phone would become my new best friend. The connection to a whole other world I was always seeking, yet somehow never realized it until now.

Then I discovered what a time suck my phone became and that it's really hard to function on social media when you're not very social.

As in, I didn't have a lot of friends. I still don't. Friends are hard to come by. I have one I can count on, but I don't talk to her that much. I'm too busy planning my revenge. She's busy living her actual life. We have different priorities right now.

Ha ha, I'm so funny, but you know what I mean.

Anyway, I have all the accounts I should. Facebook (never use it). Twitter (don't understand it, don't want to understand it), Instagram (my favorite), Tumblr (used to be my favorite, now I don't know what to do with it), Pinterest (biggest time suck in all the land) and Snapchat (half the time I don't know what I'm doing).

But you see, I don't want to share my life with anyone else, especially virtual strangers. No one cares that much about my pitiful life, am I right?

I was shocked to see Rhett followed me on Instagram the afternoon of our brunch date, and that he added me on Snapchat that night. I followed him back on IG, scrolling through his feed and immediately getting bored.

I've already scrolled through his feed before. Countless times. He has a public profile, which made it easier for me to stalk him. He shows off on IG, how great his life is, where he travels, all his friends, all the girls. We get it, your life is perfection.

I couldn't add him on Snapchat before we started talking, though, since it tells you every person who adds you and I couldn't risk it. I didn't want him to think I was some stalker set out to get his fine ass, like every other girl on campus who lusts after him.

But when he added me a couple of days ago, I went ahead and added him right back. Not that I could see much. Snapchat allows you to post on your story, and some people do it excessively, but not Rhett. There were no stories from him to look at, and he hadn't even snapped me back after I added him, for whatever reason, I don't know.

I'm not the kind to make the first approach, but in this moment, I decided to hell with it, and I sent him a snap. A selfie of me, making a face, my tongue sticking out. Below my face, I typed, **what are you up to?** and then sent it.

Rhett immediately snaps me back, a selfie of him and the words. **Not much. How bout u?**

I decide to tell him the truth, something I'm not used to. **Bored.**

He takes the conversation to chat. **Same. Though I should be doing homework.**

I should be too. One thing I shouldn't be doing is talking with him. Or…

Maybe I should. I keep automatically throwing up these walls, mentally listing all the reasons why I shouldn't talk to him or see him or spend time with him. When that's exactly what I *should* be doing—spending time with him. How else am I going to get closer to Rhett?

What I really need is for him to take me to Daddy and Stepmama's house so I can meet them. Look that woman straight in the eyes and silently defy her to not recognize me.

That's my ultimate goal.

My phone dings, letting me know Rhett said something, and I check it.

I want to see you again.

I stare at the words he just typed, unsure as how to answer. He's bold. He just asks for what he wants and isn't afraid of the consequences. I'm not used to that. My father was weak. He didn't know how to ask for what he wanted. If he did, I wonder if he'd still have my mother in his life.

Chewing on my lower lip, I wonder how I should answer

him. My fingers hover over the cracked screen, fingernails tapping. I'm sitting on the saggy couch in my living room, textbooks scattered around me, the sun slowly going down, making my shack of a house grow darker and darker. Reminding me just how alone I really am.

I'm pretty busy this week. This isn't a lie. I have class, I have to work Wednesday and Thursday nights. Friday night I'm off, but Saturdays are always busy, so I never get time off then.

Too busy to go out to dinner with me?

Maybe.

I add a winking emoji to let him know I'm flirting. Hopefully he takes the bait.

Come on. You need to go out and have fun sometime, right?

He adds a winking emoji right back.

Okay, good. He's flirting. This I can work with. It's a lot easier to do this over Snapchat versus in person.

But I do need to play hard to get.

You're so right. But I'm just really focused right now.

There. That answer should work.

Focused on having no fun? I smile despite my annoyance. He's persistent, I will give him that. **You doing anything Friday night? Or is your schedule too full?**

It's like he reached into my brain and saw my schedule for the week.

Actually, I'm free.

Not anymore. You're going out. With. Me. ☺

💙 💙 💙

There's been this ball of nerves resting in the pit of my stomach since my text conversation with Rhett on Monday night. Anticipation and dread about my dinner date with him on Friday. He's been consistently snapping and texting me since I agreed to go with him, and I respond dutifully. I've started to wait for his snaps, my heart racing every time the notification sounds.

Since I don't really talk to anyone else, those notifications are all from him. I've discovered a few things about Rhett Montgomery. Intimate, personal things I didn't pick up on when I did my online stalking.

One, he's very chatty. He will send me these long-winded texts and I respond to him with a *yeah*, or *sure*. I bet that drives him crazy. But it's like the guy has a lot to say, and it's not total bullshit either. He's…God, I can't believe I'm admitting this, but he's interesting.

He's also smart. I like talking to him. He makes good conversation, and he's never boring.

Protective. Always asking me if I'm okay, if I'm safe, like he actually cares. He doesn't even know me, but that doesn't matter.

Kind. Rhett's also kind, it complements his protectiveness. He's nice to the rude server at the restaurant, he talks about his friends and family in a way that I can feel his love for them. That sounds corny, but it's true.

Flirtatious. Very flirtatious. He says things that allude to his attraction toward me. He likes me. He's into me. I know this because that's exactly what he says. Plus, the last couple of nights, he's sent me photos of him just out of the shower, hair wet and no shirt on, his dark gaze smoldering as he stares into the camera. From what I can tell he has a broad set of shoulders and a nice body.

He's hot. There's no denying it.

It's hard for me to trust if all this flirtatious protectiveness is real, though. It feels too good to be true. Phony.

That's what I keep telling myself. He's fake. No one can be that sweet, that sexy, that interested in a girl he barely knows. It's got to be an act.

Got to be.

I had to break down and let Rhett pick me up at my house, after he kept telling me again and again he wanted to come get me.

You don't have a car. You'll have to ride the bus to meet me at the restaurant, he told me when I asked where he was taking me. *Let me come get you.*

I just told myself that when he arrives at my house, I have to meet him out front, so he can't come inside. Not that I have anything to hide—my true identity isn't obvious, I've hidden everything I own that refers to Jennifer Fanelli, not that he'd have a clue who that is.

And not that there's much to Jennifer Fanelli in the first place.

Truthfully? I don't want him to see my meager belongings and judge me for it (*he'd never judge you for it, he's the perfect almost boyfriend!*). Everything I own came from a thrift shop, Walmart or Target, and some of my furniture I even found on the side of the road, like the scratched-up coffee table and the dresser in my bedroom with the drawers that don't open all the way.

Thank God for Savannah. When I spotted the furniture, I called her up to meet me in front of the house with the dresser and coffee table waiting on the sidewalk. She helped me shove the furniture in the trunk of her car, the both of us laughing the entire time as we tried our best not to break anything.

She's my first real friend here, yet I'm not real with her. Not at all.

I go all out for the date, wearing my best jeans and an old pair of black slip-on Vans that still look decent. I splurged and bought a new black long-sleeved T-shirt. So simple, yet it looks pretty good on me—everyone looks good in black, right? Savannah recently cleaned out her makeup stash so I used some of the stuff she gave me, adding layers of mascara to my eyelashes and slicking on the berry-colored lipstick until my lips shine.

Checking my reflection in the mirror, I tell myself I look good. Good enough. I blew my dark blonde hair straight and I'm wearing the tiny diamond earrings my dad said belonged to my mom. They're not real—she got them on QVC or the Home Shopping Network, he couldn't remember—but she left them behind when she left us, and I've kept them with me my entire life.

For some weird, stupid reason, they make me feel closer to her.

By the time I hear a car pull up in front of my place, I'm already out the door and locking it, leaving the front porch light on, the dingy yellow glow better than complete darkness when I return home. It's cold out—a storm is supposed to move in tomorrow and I sort of wish for a coat, but it's too late now. No way am I going back inside. Rhett might follow me in.

"Hey." Rhett is already out of his sleek black car and jogging up the front walk toward my front door. "You're ready, huh."

"Why do you sound so disappointed?" I'm teasing him, but I also want to know his answer.

He stops just in front of me, tall and broad, clean and fresh. I can smell his soapy scent, appreciate his floppy damp hair, the appreciative glow in his eyes no doubt matching my own. There's no denying Rhett is attractive, and for the briefest moment, I wallow in his dreamy good looks. "I was hoping to meet your roommate."

I blink at him, trying to compute what he said until it finally sinks in. "I don't have a roommate."

He frowns, his dark brows furrowed. Damn it, he's extra cute when he does that. "Are you serious?"

"Why are you so surprised?"

"Everyone I know has a roommate."

"Including you?" I already know the answer to this question.

"Yeah, including me." He looks at my dark house, his brows still furrowed. "So you live here alone."

"I sure do."

"How can you afford it?" His gaze meets mine.

"Look at this neighborhood." I hold up my arms, waving at the houses nearby. My voice is full of amusement, but deep down inside, I burn with shame. "It's not the best side of town, so rent is cheap." Well, not that cheap, but definitely less expensive than his neighborhood, I'm sure.

"Looks dangerous." He sounds almost…angry. On my behalf?

Probably.

Like I said, too good to be true.

"It's not that bad." It's awful, but it could be worse. My neighbor is kind of shady, pretty sure he's a dealer, but I mind my own business.

Now Rhett's examining the neighbor's house, the street, the entire neighborhood. "I don't like thinking of you alone here, especially at night."

I'm so tempted to roll my eyes, but I keep myself in check. "You don't like thinking of me alone anywhere." I grab hold of his hand—ignoring the electricity that sparks between us when our skin touches—and we start walking toward his car. "You shouldn't worry so much."

He lets me lead him. "It sounds like you need someone to worry about you."

"I can take care of myself." I send him an irritable look, but it fades when I see the way he's smiling at me.

"I like this independent woman thing you've got going on, but it's okay to let someone take care of you every once in a while." His smile grows. "You should give it a try sometime."

"With you?" I raise my brows, trying to ignore the way my heart beats rapidly against my chest, or the hot flush that sweeps over my skin.

"Maybe." He winks, actually winks as he lets go of my hand and opens the passenger-side door for me. I climb inside the expensive sports car, the leather-tinged-with-Rhett scent enveloping me the moment he shuts the door.

It takes him maybe ten seconds to get into the car, but I'm already irritated by then. Saying I should let him take care of me, who the hell does he think he is? I refuse to depend on anyone but myself. I am the key to my own destiny, and I will never forget it.

"I hope you like Italian," he says as he starts the car with a push of a button, something I've never seen before. The engine purrs, he revs the car with a steady push of the gas pedal and then we're off, peeling down the street with a squeal of brakes, Rhett shifting the car into gear smoothly, like some sort of goddamn professional.

I'll look back on this night later and remember this is the moment I realize I'm in way over my head.

EIGHT

l Gabbiano is the finest Italian restaurant in town—at least, according to the sign outside the building, it is. Rhett opens my car door for me, taking my hand as we walk through the parking lot, his fingers warm and sure as they tuck around mine. I cling to him, his solid heat drawing me in, making me want to do and say crazy things. Instead, I focus on my upcoming performance, praying I'm wearing the right thing, scared I'm going to do something stupid to mess this up.

Being with him makes me feel insecure. Is it because I'm an imposter? Am I scared of getting caught?

Yes. A thousand times yes.

"Jensen."

His sexy deep voice knocks me from my worrying thoughts. "What?" My head snaps up to find he's watching me carefully. So carefully, I'm almost scared he can read my thoughts.

"Did I tell you that you look beautiful tonight?" He squeezes my hand as we approach the restaurant, slowing his pace so I have no choice but to stop with him.

My cheeks go hot. I'm not used to the constant compliments. They make me uncomfortable, especially when I remember what I'm doing. "Yes, you did. But thank you again."

He also told me I looked beautiful on the drive over, when I caught him staring at me while we waited at an intersection for the light to turn green. He'd seemed entranced with *me,* and let me tell you, that's heady stuff. No one ever seems to care about me. I just…move through life without affecting anyone.

With Rhett, it feels like he actually wants to be a part of my life. That he's so grateful I'm here with him. That should make me feel strong, right? Like he's giving me all the power and eventually, I can use it against him.

But I don't feel strong. His words and actions make me unsure. Make me doubt I'm doing the right thing, when I've never wavered from my purpose before.

I don't like it.

"You seem nervous." With his other hand, he pushes wayward tendrils of hair away from my cheek, his fingers a lingering caress on my skin. I can't stop the shiver that takes over me and he feels it, I know he can. Without a word, he leans in and I tilt my head back, his mouth hovering above mine. Right there in front of the restaurant where everyone can see us, he kisses me. The barest brush of lips, his kiss is the lightest touch that somehow grabs hold of my heart and strangles it until I feel like I can't breathe.

"This isn't a test," he murmurs after he lifts his lips away from mine.

I frown. "What do you mean?"

"I don't want you tense or nervous. I don't want anything from you that you can't give." There he goes again, seemingly reading my mind. "I just want to get to know you better." He taps the tip of my nose with his index finger. "A lot better."

His words throw me. I've always been someone's secret. My mother's. The boys I've been with…no one wants to admit they know me. Here's Rhett kissing me in front of a restaurant, holding my hand like we're a real couple, saying such sweet things that should make me wary but instead his words make me want to melt.

And I can't melt. I need to remain ice-cold. No feelings, no emotions. That way, no one can hurt me.

"Why me?" I blurt, snagging my hand out of his so I can step away from him. I need the distance. I know this isn't the best spot to have this discussion, but I'm seized with the sudden urge to know exactly why he's acting this way.

"Now I have to ask you what you mean." He scratches the side of his head, looking adorably confused.

"We see each other a couple of times and now you're taking

me to dinner and it feels like there are all these expectations—"
Stop talking, stop talking! "—and I don't know why you chose
me."

"I'm drawn to you. Isn't that a good enough reason?"

It's the answer my old self wants. It's the answer Jennifer is
immensely pleased with—and yes, I just referred to myself in
the third person. I set out to trap him and it happened quicker
than I imagined. Here he is, interested in me, taking me out to
an expensive dinner and most likely secretly hoping he'll be
peeling my panties off my body with his teeth by the end of
the night. Normally I'd give my body to him without question.
That was always the plan.

Instead, my insecurities come flying out, making me say
stupid stuff, just like I feared. Again, I'm about to blow it and
that's the last thing I need.

Stay. Focused.

"Yes." I breathe a sigh and nod once, to reaffirm my answer.
"That's a good enough reason."

"Great. Now that we've got that settled…" he says just
before he kisses me again, a quick one that takes me by surprise.
"Let's go eat," he murmurs, and all I can do is blink up at him,
trying to bring his handsome face back into focus. By the time
I recover, he's holding my hand again, leading me toward the
restaurant entrance, and I follow along blindly, nearly tripping
over the sidewalk.

As we enter the building, I'm immediately dazzled by the

stark white interior and the open ceiling with its crisscrossing rough-hewn beams. There are colorful flower arrangements everywhere, their lush, fresh scent lingering in the lobby, and I take a deep breath, savoring the smell. This place reeks of money. It's expensive, classy, like nowhere I've ever been before.

Two men clad in sharp black suits stand behind a high counter, and as we approach them I can see they're scanning an extensive list with fierce concentration. One of them glances up when Rhett says he has a reservation and offers his name. The one man stands a little straighter, calling Rhett *Mr. Montgomery* with a touch of awe and respect. He nods at his coworker before leading us deep into the restaurant, until we're at a table by an expansive window that overlooks the river that runs through town. Candlelight flickers in the pale gold votive resting in the center of the table, casting its glow upon the single white rose sitting in a crystal vase by the window.

My palms are sweating as the host holds the chair out for me, and I practically fall into it, shocked when he gently pushes my chair closer to the table. He takes the napkin from the plate and shakes it out before draping it across my lap, and I can only sit there, unsure of what to say or what to do next. I mutter a thank-you when he finishes, and my gaze cuts to Rhett, who's watching me with amusement, his mouth curled into a lopsided smile.

I both want to smack and kiss that smile off his face.

"You've never been to a place like this before."

My cheeks heat with embarrassment and I'm thankful for the dim lighting so he can't see me. "Guess I'm not used to strange men doing things for me," I admit. That's better than confessing I don't know how to function in fancy restaurants. I need him to believe I can be a part of his world, that I would fit in seamlessly, no matter what the situation is.

"The food here is fantastic." His change of subject tells me he must sense my nervousness, and he tears his gaze away from mine, cracking open the menu. "I'm starving."

"Me too." Not really. I'm too nervous to eat, too freaked out I'll screw something up and prove to Rhett I don't belong here. I don't belong with him.

"Do you have a preference for anything?" He skims the menu, his lips slightly pursed, a lock of thick hair falling over his forehead. I watch him instead of checking my meal options, captivated by his dark good looks, the way he sinks his teeth into his lower lip, as if he's concentrating really hard. This is all supposed to be pretend, but why does tonight feel so real? I'm barely in and I'm already taking it way too seriously. He's just so good-looking and charming and oh my God, what am I even *doing*?

Suddenly Rhett glances up, his gaze meeting mine, and his knowing smile tells me I've been caught staring.

My heart thumping out of control, I jerk my gaze back to the menu, squinting as I try to make out the minimal descriptions, trying my best to ignore the outrageous prices. Everywhere he takes me, I can't afford. I can't even understand what's on this stupid menu since it's written mostly in Italian.

Situations like this remind me that I'm completely out of my element, though I knew this from the very start. I somehow forgot, though, that the Montgomery family moves in a different stratosphere than mine.

I remember he asked me if I had any preferences and I finally answer him.

"Um, what do you recommend?" I can't say spaghetti, because that is my favorite Italian dish, but it's also the most common Italian dish there is. What in the world is antipasto? Some sort of appetizer? I can figure out *insalata*, and even *minestra*, salad and soup. Oh, I recognize fettucine alfredo, since I had that once at the Olive Garden. Dad took me there for my twelfth birthday, when things were better, and he was better too. When we had a little more money and we could splurge on special occasions, but that was it.

"Any of the risottos are good," Rhett says, and I nod. Okay, I can do that. I've watched *Hell's Kitchen* before—I actually know what risotto is, since Gordon Ramsey makes it all the time. My gaze jumps to the risotto section, and my eyes go wide when I see the prices. I can't believe rice costs that freaking much. "Plus, all of their pasta is homemade, and it's amazing," he continues.

"Nice." I nod, anxiety rising within me, making it even

harder to focus. I don't know what to get, and I'm afraid I'll say it wrong when I'm asked what I want. I'm not in the mood to make a fool of myself tonight either.

One tiny mistake could ruin everything.

Snapping the menu shut, I smile at Rhett when his gaze meets mine once more. "Will you order for me?"

He appears surprised by my request, but he rolls with it. He's so easygoing, it's downright unreal. "Sure, if you're okay with that. Are you interested in a particular dish?"

"I'm interested in whatever you think is good." I sit up straighter and stretch my lips into a closed-mouth smile, trying to look like an agreeable date so hopefully he'll want to see me again. God, it's so difficult, striving for perfect all the time. "Surprise me."

"Really?" He sounds excited and he raises his eyebrows. "You trust me enough to order for you?"

I don't trust you for shit, I want to tell him, but I don't. I can only imagine the hurt that would cross his face at my words. I get the feeling he's not used to insults. He grew up having an idyllic, carefree life with my bitch of a mother showering all of her affection on him while I didn't even get a scrap.

"I'm sure whatever you choose, I'll love," I say carefully, immediately wishing I could snatch back my use of the word *love*.

I don't throw that word around lightly. Love isn't a good or easy emotion. It's painful and hard and only ends up hurting you.

That's all love has ever done for me.

He points his index finger at me. "I promise you won't regret this."

I'm sure I will. I'm sure I'll regret everything that will eventually happen between Rhett and me. But there's no going back now.

I'm all in.

NINE

Five years ago

"Where've you been."

The sharp voice sounds in the utter darkness just after I shut the front door with a quiet thud. Gasping, I whirl around and the lamp clicks on, casting dirty yellowish light on my father, who's sitting on the sagging couch, clad only in a stretched-out white T-shirt and a pair of faded boxers.

"Out." I clear my throat when I hear the squeakiness of nerves.

He gives me that look, the one shrewd and full of distrust. "With who?"

"Friends." A boy. One my father wouldn't approve of, and that's what makes him extra exciting. After the Burper—my first sexual experience—I found someone else to be with. We're not in a real relationship or anything, we just like to fuck. His words.

He thinks I'm some sort of miracle girl brought down from the heavens.

"You sure you don't want a boyfriend?" Nathaniel asked earlier, right after he was done with me in the backseat of his car. He's seventeen, a senior, a bad boy, a smoker, a drinker, a fornicator. He is everything I am not, yet wish to be. And he's recruiting me over to the dark side, slowly but surely.

"Positive," I told him, my tone extra dry. And bored. Always bored. Boys get their rocks off and girls get a boy sweating and grunting while thrusting inside their body. This one doesn't care about my pleasure, just like the Burper. "Got a cigarette?" I asked him when I noticed he was staring at my tits.

He eagerly handed it over, probably hopeful I'd give him a blowie or a hand job, but forget that. He got what he wanted. He wasn't getting it twice.

"What friends?" Daddy asks, his vicious tone bringing me back to the present. "You don't have any friends."

I'm offended, more because he's right than by what he actually said. I don't have any friends beyond one, and Alyssa and I don't hang out that much. It's hard for me to get close to anyone. I don't trust easily.

"You don't know them—" I say, but he cuts me off with a look.

"Them. You're not referring to girls. More like boys. Or just one *boy.*" He spits the last word out. "Don't bother lying. I know what you do when you leave our home."

Our *home?* I almost laugh in his face. Where we live isn't a home. It's a shit-hole. A dirty, rundown trailer. We are the epitome of trash. I don't let anyone know where I live for fear they'd never stop teasing me about it.

"You don't know crap," I mutter, turning to walk to the back of the trailer, where my bed is. But the trailer is small and my dad is somehow extra fast, because next thing I know, he's stopping me from going anywhere, one hand on my arm, fingers pressing into my skin so hard I'm afraid I might bruise. I try to jerk away from his hold, but his fingers tighten.

Trapping me.

"I know more than you think," he rasps, his gaze narrowed, eyes full of disgust. "You look like a slut. That skirt barely covers your butt."

A gasp escapes me and my chest tightens. He's never called me anything so awful before. "Let go of me." I struggle to get away from him, but he only squeezes tighter.

"You've been with a boy. You smell like it." He leans in closer and sniffs, his lips curling. "You smell like sex."

I want to die of embarrassment. I want to punch him in the stomach, knee him in the balls, do something to cause him even a fraction of the pain he just inflicted on me with his horrific words. I can't even bother denying what he said, because he's right. I probably *do* smell like sex. Sex and cigarettes and Nathaniel's overpowering Axe cologne.

"You're just like her," Daddy says, giving me a little shake. My gaze meets his and I see all the anger and pain swirling there. This is a chronic problem. He's always thinking of her, never remembering it's me. "I couldn't keep her satisfied. I can't keep you happy either."

His fingers go loose and I take my opportunity, pulling out of his grip. The tiny back bedroom is only a few steps away, but the distance feels like miles. I run toward the room, shutting the door as hard as I can right in my father's face.

"Open the door!" He rattles the handle just as I turn the cheap lock to keep him out. He could bust right in if he wanted to, but he weakly shakes the handle for maybe another thirty seconds before he gives up and stomps away.

I push away from the door and go to my bed, collapsing on top of it with a muted cry. The room is small, and drafty, and I swear the walls are going to collapse on top of me when a slight wind picks up.

But it's all mine. My father gave it to me instead of taking it for himself when we first moved into the tiny fifth-wheel a couple years ago. He said I was a young woman who needed privacy and my own space, and he was right. I cried and cried when we got kicked out of our old house, when I had to leave my bedroom behind. I was a wailing, hysterical mess, and I swear he gave me the only bedroom truly to shut me up.

I've learned since then I'll do whatever it takes to get what I want.

TEN

"So tell me about your family." The wine is making me loose, both my body and my tongue. I picked at the antipasto plate, so my stomach is mostly full of wine as we wait for our dinner, which is taking for-freaking-ever.

Rhett keeps trying to get me to talk, but I dodge all of his questions, doing my best to turn them back on him. He wanted to know about my family, so I told him about my father, how he died, and how I'm now an orphan.

Sort of the truth.

He asked if I had any siblings and I wanted to say so badly, *I'm sitting across from one right now*, but I knew that wouldn't go over well, so I told him I had none.

Now it's his turn to answer my questions.

"What do you want to know about my family?" He raises

a brow and it's so sexy, when raised eyebrows shouldn't be that sexy. I don't even know what's the matter with me. I'm not acting right.

I blame the wine.

"Everything." I prop my elbow on the table and rest my chin on my curled fingers, shooting him an adoring look. It's not really a lie either, because right now, in the flickering candlelight, his lips stained by the fancy wine he ordered, he's adorable. "Do you look like your dad?"

"Not really. My older brother looks like my dad." He shakes his head, then pushes his hair away from his forehead with an impatient shove of his fingers. "I look more like my mother."

"Oh." I didn't want to bring up a sore subject, but here I am, blundering right into the topic of his dead mother.

"She died when I was five." He frowns. "Or did I already tell you that?"

"No." I shake my head. "You didn't. You just mention that she passed, but I didn't know you were only five." I pause, take a sip of my wine. "How awful."

"Yeah." He smiles, but it's weak. "I guess we have the dead parent thing in common."

I return the smile, my body tingling with triumph. That had been the plan all along. Finding common ground with Rhett about our dead parents. But I should probably change the subject. "Are you close with your brother?"

"Yeah, we're pretty close." His smile grows. "And there's my little sister. I'm really close to Addie."

It's like my brain short circuits at hearing her name. I always forget about the little sister. That's because I don't want to remember her. The daughter my mother stuck around for. The one who doesn't even belong to my mother, yet she raised her anyway.

"It must've been so hard." I swallow past the lump in my throat. "Your sister losing her mother at such a young age."

He tilts his head, contemplating me. "How did you know about that?"

My stomach drops. Oh God. Did I mess up and reveal too much? "I, um. I just assumed, I guess. Or does your sister belong to your stepmother? Is she your half-sister?"

My heart is racing and I pray I didn't say the wrong thing. I need to keep my mouth shut and let him feed me the information.

"My mom died after giving birth to my sister," Rhett says quietly, his gaze going turbulent. "Let's change the subject. I don't want to get depressed over dinner. Let's talk about you."

Yeah. That's a depressing subject. "You already know everything there is to know about me. There's not much else to tell."

"Uh huh." His eyes are sparkling as he studies me. "More like you want to keep up the mysterious air."

"You think I'm mysterious?" I'm truly shocked.

He nods, reaching across the table to grab my hand. "You

either dodge my questions completely or you give me short answers. You don't want to tell me anything."

He's so right. "That's not true," I lie.

"Whatever. It's cool." He squeezes my hand, and I swear he's amused by me. "I like mysterious girls."

My heart skips a beat at his words, at the way he's looking at me. His thumb is sliding gently over the top of my hand, and I'm caught up in the spell Rhett is casting over me. He makes me want to forget. About my fucked up life. About my plans for revenge. None of it matters if I can just sit here for the rest of the night and stare into his beautiful brown eyes.

"Have you always been so independent?" he asks when I still haven't said anything to him.

"I guess." I shrug, uncomfortable with how closely he's watching me. I'm not used to someone paying attention to me like Rhett does. "I've always had to take care of myself."

"No parents? You just magically appeared?" He's teasing me, but it rubs me the wrong way.

"My father is dead," I say bluntly. "And my mother left when I was very young." I clear my throat, so much emotion forming there it's difficult to speak. "Like, I-don't-even-remember-her young. I was practically a baby." I pause, checking on Rhett's reaction and he's enthralled. I continue. "My parents got into a terrible fight."

"Did he hurt her? Did he ever hurt you?" Rhett breathes. His nostrils flare and his eyes blaze with anger. He's squeezing my hand so tightly I have to carefully pull away from his grip before he accidentally hurts me.

"No, no. Nothing physical." I think of the few moments when my father did actually hit me, but it never amounted to anything. He was too scared, too weak. "My parents hurt each other with words. Or at least, my mother hurt my father with words. He claims he never did anything wrong."

He had to have, though. No one's perfect. And while it still hurts that he's gone, and his pain has become my pain, I know he was in the wrong sometimes too.

But my mother was worse. She never came back.

"Emotional abuse can be more painful than physical," Rhett says, and I'm tempted to scream at him, *What do you know about abuse?* But I don't.

"Words hurt." I offer up a grimace of a smile. "And I guess the words my parents tossed at each other that one particular night were spectacularly painful. My mother packed up a few things and left." Another pause, to let my words really sink in. "She never came back."

"Never?" Rhett sounds so doubtful.

I slowly shake my head. "I haven't seen her in twenty years."

"She's never tried to find you?"

"No." My voice is sharp and I clear my throat again. "Never."

"Have you tried to look her up? Seems like anyone can be

found through a Google search these days."

"Oh, I've tried, but I can't find her. There's no trace of her."
His question, the skeptical expression on his face, he's making
me feel stupid. Who wouldn't try to find her long-lost mother
via Google? "I believe she changed her name."

"What's her name?"

Nerves make my stomach flutter and twitch, the consumed
wine suddenly threatening to rise. Has she ever admitted her
true name to her current husband? Her stepson? Her new
family? "Why does it matter what her name was? That's not
her name now."

"Maybe I could help you." He leans forward, full of
eagerness. "I could do some extensive searches, maybe even
hire a private detective—"

I hold up my hand to stop him from saying anything else.
"I don't want to find her."

Rhett frowns. "But you just said you tried to find her."

"Years ago, in my early teens, I was *desperate* to find
her. She became almost…mythical to me, and I thought
she could, I don't know, rescue me. Like I'm living in some
sort of wretched fairytale and I need my long-lost mama to
save my life." I'm trying to make a joke, but Rhett's not even
cracking a smile. "But after all the searching and coming up
with nothing, I realized she doesn't want to be found. Not by
me, not by anyone."

"Do you think she scrubbed her name?"

Now I'm frowning. "What do you mean?"

"You can scrub your identity from the Internet. Pay someone to get rid of any and all references about you until… poof." Rhett snaps his fingers. "You don't exist anymore."

Oh. Right. I know about this, considered doing it myself, not that I had much of an Internet footprint. With no phone and no real social media trail, Jennifer Fanelli didn't have much of an existence. I didn't participate in any activities at school, I had no real friends…yeah. I'm like a ghost.

"That's probably what she did." With a sigh, I grab my wineglass and drain it. It's like I don't even care any longer. The "I need to be on my best behavior so he'll like me" veneer has been completely washed off by wine.

There's no reeling it back either. Even though I know I should. The panic races through my veins as I contemplate the nearly empty wine bottle sitting in the middle of the table. I want to lunge for it, bring the bottle to my lips and drink it dry. I know I need to restrain myself and play my part, but I can't. The alcohol has made me melancholy, the fact that this boy knows my mother yet we sit here and pretend that she's this fuzzy myth…

It's fucking with my head. My emotions.

My heart.

"So sorry for the delay." The stressed-out server is standing beside our table, a plate balanced in each hand, and he sets a plate in front of me before doing the same for Rhett. "It's extremely busy tonight. Do you need anything else?"

I think about asking for more wine, but Rhett answers for the both of us, telling the server we're fine.

"Very well." The waiter bows, like we're royalty, and then takes off.

"I'm sorry if I made you upset," Rhett says quietly. "I was just trying to help."

His apology throws me off guard. "I—no, it's fine. You didn't upset me."

"Clearly you're lying."

My heart threatens to explode from my chest.

"Because I know what I said about your mom made you upset," he continues, his expression pained. Like he hates that he hurt me. My heart swells and for the quickest moment, I wish this night, this date with Rhett, was real. "I just, I don't know, I wanted to help. And sometimes I overstep my place. So I'm sorry for that."

We both go quiet, choosing to start on our meals so we can avoid conversation. At least, that's what I'm doing. Maybe he's giving me time, space, whatever you want to call it, and I'm sort of floored. As in, I don't know how to react. He's just so nice. And respectful. He's unlike any other guy I've ever been with before, and I'm drawn to his polite manners and kind gestures. It doesn't feel fake.

The way he treats me feels all too real.

"Thank you for apologizing," I finally say, causing him to

glance up from his plate, our gazes meeting. "It means a lot to me."

"Honestly Jens, I didn't want to see you cry," he says, his voice tender, his brown eyes full of concern.

My eyes fill with tears at his words and I blink them away. I drop my gaze, concentrating on the plate of food in front of me, letting my growling stomach remind me that yes, I should keep eating. "You're too good to be true," I murmur.

Maybe he does actually like me. And God, maybe I… actually like him too.

That thought is too terrifying to contemplate.

ELEVEN

We go to the movies after dinner, and it's so normal, such a typical date, yet something I've never done with a guy before. Standing in line in front of the movie theater feels surreal. It's cold out and I'm standing close to Rhett, my side pressing against his and he wraps his arm around my shoulders, giving me a squeeze.

"I can feel you trembling," he tells me laughingly, and I laugh too, pretending that yes, I'm so cold.

My trembling is more from nerves. Just standing next to him makes me feel edgy. Scared. Excited.

Aroused.

I turn toward him, relishing his warmth, his scent. He smells amazing, woodsy yet citrusy, and I breathe him in deep. He has no clue his effect on me, and that's probably best. I don't want him to know the power he holds over me. How I have to work so hard to fight it, to remind myself why I'm with him.

Tonight, I don't want to remember.

I sneak a glance at his face. He's staring straight ahead, scanning the giant movie listings board, and I admire his sexy jawline, those defined cheekbones. He's got a rich boy face. It sounds ridiculous, but it's true. There's nothing soft about Rhett Montgomery. He's all sharp lines and moneyed features. He inherited his good looks from a long line of attractive rich people that goes back generations.

It's intoxicating, all that rich sexiness. It's not just his looks either, but the way he carries himself, how he speaks, the cut of his clothing, the silk of his hair, the tone of his voice. It all screams money. And as I've gotten to know him, I realize I want a piece of it, a piece of *him,* if only for this moment.

"Funny or scary?" Rhett looks down, catches me staring. I don't look away and neither does he. The pleased smile on his face tells me he likes that I was watching him. "What are you in the mood for?"

"Scary," I tell him. I can envision me hiding my face in his shoulder, him having to hold me close. Jumping in his arms every time I'm startled. I like the direction this is going.

"Scary it is then." He removes his arm from my shoulders when we're next in line to pay, and I feel hollow. That arm around me was like a public claiming, and I never thought I'd be the type to like that sort of thing, but I do.

Once Rhett pays for our tickets, we enter the main lobby,

and I may sound like a total idiot right now, but I'm dazzled. The lobby is enormous, lit up like I imagine Las Vegas is, and it's full of people. The concession stand has lines, the scent of popcorn lingers in the air and I watch a kid no older than eight haul away a bucket of popcorn and a cup of soda, both items almost as big as him.

"I want popcorn," I admit, and Rhett laughs.

"Same," he agrees, steering me toward the concession counter. We stand in line and I remain quiet, listening to the conversations around us, spying on people. Rhett checks his phone discreetly—I'm sure he doesn't want to seem rude on our date—but I don't mind. It gives me time to observe, to figure out how I should act.

The girl behind us is telling her friend how she saw the trailer for the scary movie we're going to see, and how she nearly peed her pants, it frightened her so bad. The couple ahead of us are also going to see the same movie, and they're both discussing the director, who's well known and respected in the movie world, so they expect this to be a decent movie and not trash, as the guy tells her.

By the time we're seated in the hushed quiet of the theater showing our movie, the giant popcorn bucket wedged between us, I'm feeling anxious. Why, I don't know.

"Are you regretting our movie choice?" Rhett asks, his voice low.

I turn to look at him, startled to find his face so close to mine. "What do you mean?"

"You're squirming in your seat and the movie hasn't even started yet," he says, his voice teasing.

"Oh, I guess I'm not the biggest fan of scary movies," I confess.

His brows draw together in seeming confusion. I love when he does that. "But you're the one who wanted to see a scary movie."

"I guess I liked the idea of you holding me close during the bad parts," I murmur.

His smile is knowing as he slips his arms around the back of my chair, his hand dropping to my shoulder. "I'm here for you. You want to jump in my lap, bury your face in my neck? I'm your man."

I laugh, shaking my head. "How kind of you to offer up your services."

"If a beautiful woman wants to throw herself at me in the middle of a movie, I'm not going to protest."

My entire body goes hot at him calling me a beautiful woman. It's dangerous, how easily I could get used to his compliments.

I part my lips, ready to continue our conversation, when the lights go dim and the screen flashes with theater-themed messages about turning the ringer off your cell phones and how we shouldn't talk too loud. Rhett removes his arm from the back of my seat as I settle into my oversized reclining chair and reach for some popcorn at the same time he does too.

It's downright intimate, our sharing the popcorn, sitting in the dark, our gazes glued to the big screen. I forget about everyone else sitting by us. All I can focus on is the man sitting next to me, his knee occasionally brushing against mine as he shifts around in his seat, like he can't get comfortable.

Once the movie finally starts, I realize quick the subject matter is a little too close to home. It's about a woman who's seeking vengeance on the man who killed her husband— and this man was her husband's business partner. I mean, my situation is totally different, but then again…it's not. Vengeance is vengeance, and as the story unfolds, I become more and more uncomfortable. She not only wants to destroy the business partner who was acquitted of murdering her husband for lack of evidence, but his entire family as well. His friends, his business…everything and everyone that means something to him, she wants to eliminate.

And I can relate. I really can. She's laughing and crying and trying to kill the man's wife, setting his home on fire, chasing after his precious dog so she can brutally kill him, for the love of God, and I'm still rooting for her.

I shouldn't be rooting for her. Not at all. But I understand her anger and how it drives her to do such horrible things. Things I don't think I'm capable of.

Maybe I am, though. Maybe we all are, if we're pushed hard enough.

I think of my mother. Does she ever think of me? Remember me? Would she recognize me if I met her on the street?

She better not, because that's why I'm here.

Just like that, I'm mad. Anger is all I've had left for so long, and I reveled in it. My anger fueled me, and I needed it like air.

Rhett suddenly takes my hand and laces our fingers together loosely. Lost in my own thoughts, the sweet gesture startles me, and I glance over at him to find he's already watching me, his lips curled in the faintest smile.

"This movie is crazy," he whispers, his eye wide in the darkness. "*She's* crazy."

My heart falls. If he thinks she's crazy…

What will he think of me?

TWELVE

R hett takes me home in his fancy sports car, zipping down the streets, passing the late-evening traffic with ease. The satellite radio is on low and I remain quiet, my head filled with thoughts of the movie, of what I'm doing, of what I'm going to do. He makes light conversation and I respond to him as casually as possible, hoping he doesn't catch the tremor in my voice that's been brought on by nerves.

Watching that movie threw me. Spending time with Rhett and actually liking him threw me even harder.

We make it to my house in what feels like record time, and he walks me to the front door like the gentleman that he is. "I had fun tonight," I tell him, pulling my keys out of my purse as we approach the door.

"I did too," he agrees, shifting closer to me. So close I can feel his breath on my cheek. I turn to find him invading my personal space, not that I'm protesting. I tilt my head back so I can meet his gaze and he smiles at me. It's an intimate smile, not the shark teeth he flashes at the pretty girls in the bar. This one is just for me, and witnessing it makes everything inside me go liquid. "Even though that movie was a trip."

My stomach sinks and slowly starts to churn. "You didn't like it?"

"Oh, it was entertaining, but that chick scared me." Rhett shakes his head. "She was hell-bent on ruining that guy."

"You didn't think it was deserved? He *did* kill her husband, and the justice system let him get away with it," I point out.

He tilts his head to the side, contemplating me. "True, but still. She was way over the top. Why not just take him out and be done with it? Why did she have to destroy everyone else in his life too?"

I'm compelled to explain her feelings and what drove her, not that he cares. I guess I do. Too much. "Because it hurts to see the ones you love suffer. If you're gone, then it's over. But if someone takes away the ones who matter to you, you're in pain for the rest of your life." Oh, it sounds so logical when I explain it that way. Simple.

Nothing in life is simple, though. I'm complicating everything right now just having this conversation with him. My sworn enemy. My stepbrother.

It's all so weird and twisted. I feel like I'm living in a Lifetime movie.

"You've been thinking a lot about this, haven't you?" Rhett's amused. He wouldn't be if he knew I was planning the same sort of thing.

"Maybe," I say with a careless smile.

Without warning he moves in on me, so I have no choice but to back up until my butt hits the front door. "You are unlike any girl I've ever gone out with before," he murmurs as he reaches out and drifts his fingers across my cheek.

"What do you mean?" I'm breathless, and no guy has left me breathless before. The warm glow in his eyes as he studies me is making my heart beat faster, and I feel like I could practically jump out of my skin as I wait for his answer.

"It sounds so cliché," he admits. Oh, I am living the cliché dream, so I mentally tell him to go for it. "But you're—different."

"Why? Because I don't chase after you? I'm not one of your adoring fans who surrounds you at the bars?" Um, I probably shouldn't have said that.

He chuckles, and his fingers move to my hair, threading in the strands, tucking some of them behind my ear. "That's exactly it. I sound like an asshole, but they all chase after me." He hesitates. "Except you."

"Doesn't the guy prefer to chase?" Yes, yes, I read that in a magazine article too. Men prefer the chase. They don't want to be chased. It's flattering at first, but then the challenge is gone. And that has always been my goal. To be a challenge.

The code he can't crack, remember?

"Most definitely," he murmurs as he leans his head in, his mouth hovering closer. Closer…

Oh God. He's going to kiss me again. I can sense it. Usually I prepare to be spectacularly underwhelmed, but this time, I lock my knees to keep them from wobbling and inhale on a shaky breath, my eyes fluttering closed. Anticipation courses through my veins, making my skin prickle with awareness, and then his mouth is on mine. A gentle press of skin on skin, and like the weakling I never knew I could be, I immediately part my lips, inviting him in.

A jolt courses through him, I can feel it. Like I surprised him in the best possible way. He takes my open invitation, his tongue licking along my lips, a damp tease that makes me gasp. One large hand cups the back of my head while the other one wraps around my waist as he pulls me flush against his hard body, and I go willingly. He completely takes over the kiss, his tongue circling mine, his arm tight around my waist, his fingers stroking my hair. I reach for him, sliding my hands up his broad chest, circling my arms around his neck. He's solid and warm, his mouth hungry on mine as he presses me into the front door.

I rip my mouth from his to stare up at him, and he looks just as shocked as I feel. His damp and swollen lips are parted, his eyes wide as he studies me. Our ragged breaths mingle, the only sound in the otherwise quiet night, and I blink up at him, unsure of what to say or do next.

"Can I come inside?" He phrases it as a question but I see the determination in his gaze. He *wants* to come inside and he really doesn't want me to say no.

Slowly I nod and he loosens his grip on me so I can turn and unlock the door. I do so with shaky hands, getting the key into the lock nearly impossible until I take a steadying breath and tell myself to get a grip.

The door finally opens and then we're both stumbling inside, Rhett kicking the door shut before he spins me around and I'm wrapped up in his arms, my back against the door. His kisses are hungrier, his searching tongue thorough, his hands everywhere. I'm just as greedy, my purse slipping from my fingers and falling onto the floor with a loud thud as I reach for him. He groans when I smooth my hands over his chest, this low, primal sound that makes my insides quiver.

He wants me. I can feel it in the way he touches me, kisses me. He's not just kissing for kissing's sake, he's tasting me. Savoring me. His hands aren't rough and groping like every other boy I've been with. No, he touches me with purpose, like he can't get enough and he wants to make sure I like it too.

We kiss for what feels like hours but is only minutes. My hair is a mess from his hands, my body shaking, and when he slides those big hands of his to my butt and lifts, I go with him, wrapping my legs around his waist, digging my ankles into his backside. He has me braced against the door, our lower bodies pressed together, his hands still gripping my ass. Oh God, the pleasure courses through me as we slowly grind against each other. We're basically dry humping in my living room, our mouths locked, our hands wandering, searching, becoming bolder with every pass. This has never happened to me before. Never, ever, never—and I want more.

More, more, more.

"Damn, you taste good," he mutters after he breaks our kiss, his mouth going for my neck, raining damp, hot kisses everywhere.

I tilt my head back, offering him better access. "Don't stop," I whisper, hating how desperate I sound, but I can't help it.

I want him.

He nuzzles the sensitive skin of my neck just before he nibbles on my ear, his sharp teeth making me suck in a breath. I shiver, my eyes tightly closed, lost in the sensations of what Rhett's doing to me. His hands slide up, up…until he's cupping my breasts and I lean into his touch, eager for more.

His fingers slide over my bra slowly, making me ache. My previous sexual experiences were always a quick fumbling in the dark, bodies in awkward positions in the back of a car or in a bedroom, or in some stranger's bathroom. He'd barely touch me, keeping most of our clothes on except for the important bits, his sole purpose to get his rocks off and that's it. Forget about me. It's like they didn't even know how to make a girl orgasm. Every one of those boys had been self-centered and inexperienced, though they'd tell anyone who'd listen what a great fuck they were.

I just kept quiet. I never complimented anyone, and I never told them they left me unsatisfied either. I used them. They used me. Then we moved on.

Those encounters were completely forgettable.

This experience with Rhett is totally different. He's focused on me. He's not touching me to get something out of it. He's wanting to bring me pleasure, and oh God, he so is. I know it shouldn't feel like this with Rhett. I should be cold and indifferent. Thinking ahead, calculating my next move. Land him in bed, make him fall in love with me, get in good with his family, fuck them all over…and especially destroy my bitch of a mother.

That's what I need to remember. Getting back at my mother is my ultimate goal, the thing that drives me above all else. Rhett is just a small piece of the far more complicated puzzle.

Yet all thoughts of the future and my end goal fly out of my brain when his hands slip under my shirt and connect with my bare skin. His touch sizzles, causing me to squirm, and he pulls away from my neck to watch me, his heated gaze meeting mine.

"We can continue this against the door," he says, his voice a hoarse rasp that sends a chill down my spine. "Or we can find a more comfortable spot."

I'm tempted to keep us right here, to let him take me against the door. But it would end up a frenzied moment, desperate and quick, and I want him to savor me.

Truthfully? I want to savor him too.

"My room," I whisper, inclining my head toward the short hallway, "is over there."

Rhett tightens his hold on me before he turns and carries me to the bedroom, my legs still wound around him, his hands gripping my butt. The room is dark and I direct him over to the right side of the bed, where I lean over and snap the lamp on.

"You do want the lights on, right?" I ask, sending him a cautious look. I want to see every bit of Rhett's body. No way do I only want to imagine it as I stroke him in the dark.

"Oh yeah," he says with a giant grin right before he deposits me on the bed. He drops me so hard, I bounce a little on the mattress, and I glare up at him, shoving my hair away from my face, but he just shakes his head with a chuckle. "You're pretty damn cute when you're mad."

You have no idea, I want to tell him, but my lips remain shut as I watch him with breathless anticipation. He toes off his shoes and kicks them aside, unbuttons and then shrugs out of his shirt, offering me a glimpse of his smooth, well-muscled chest and abs. I stare at him in silence, entranced by his exposed naked skin, and then he's right there in front of me on the bed, slowly guiding me so I fall backward, my head hitting the pillows as he takes my mouth once more.

The doubts creep in immediately, even while he's kissing me. I probably shouldn't move so fast. Allowing him in my bed after only our second date is going to give him the wrong idea. That I'm fast and loose and forgettable. He goes through girls fairly quickly, from what I've observed. I let him get this far this early in the game, and he'll most likely forget about me too.

I brace my hands against his chest, ready to push him away from me, but then he shifts down, his mouth at my neck, his hands on my waist, fingers slipping beneath my shirt. He nudges the fabric up, exposing my stomach, and then he's moved down even farther, his mouth trailing kisses on my bare skin.

I imagine pushing Rhett away from me. Telling him no. But at first contact of his mouth on my flesh, I go weak. Instead, I grab hold of his broad shoulders, just so I can have something to hold on to, and as he draws closer, my hands slide up into his hair. I clutch at the soft, dark strands as his mouth blazes a trail up my stomach to just below my bra.

He tugs on my shirt and I lift up, letting him help me take my shirt off. It's gone in an instant, his mouth returning to my stomach, delivering delicate kisses that make me shiver, make me restless. I shift beneath him, wishing he was kissing even more sensitive places just as he reaches behind me to unhook my bra.

"Let's take this off," he whispers, tugging the straps down until the bra falls away. I drop it over the side of the bed, practically thrusting my chest in his face. Walking around topless for months has made me a lot less shy than I used to be. My butt is kind of flat and my thighs are a little flabby, but there is no shame in my boob game.

Rhett doesn't seem too disgusted by them either. He stares at my chest in utter reverence, gathering both of them in his hands and pulling them close together. His thumbs drift over my nipples, back and forth, back and forth, and I hiss in a sharp breath.

"You like that?" he asks, his gaze lifting to mine.

I nod. "They're—sensitive."

"Hmm." His pleasurable hum vibrates against my skin as he dips down and draws one nipple into his mouth, sucking lightly before he releases it. "What about that? Did you like it?"

Another nod, a little cry accompanying it when he pulls the other nipple into his mouth and sucks harder this time. He caresses my breasts, his fingers light, almost tickling me, his mouth wet and hot as he sucks and sucks. My nipples are tight, pointing at the sky and wet from his mouth as he moves up to take my lips once again, his tongue diving deep. I spread my legs wide to accommodate his big body against mine, and I can feel his erection brush against the very center of me.

There is no doubt that it is very large and very long.

Giving in to my impulses, I reach down and touch him,

my fingers curling around his length, testing him out. Am I too bold? Or is this what he wants? The agonized moan that rips from deep in his chest tells me he likes it, so I continue my exploration. Stroking and caressing, working him into a near fever, and we don't even have his pants off yet.

That's exactly what I don't want. Frenzied fucking with our clothes half-hanging onto our bodies. This needs to be a complete reveal. My clothes and his are coming all the way off, until we're naked and vulnerable in front of each other.

Yes. *Vulnerable.* That's what I need to remember. Most guys like you broken, because then they feel like they can fix you, and so many of them are fixers. They want to be your hero, your savior, but you can't be too broken, though. There's a certain point where they give up, where they consider you beyond fixing. Me? I need to find that fine line and straddle it.

"Wait." I drop my hand from his dick and scoot up the bed and over, as if I'm trying to get away from Rhett. He rolls over and away from me, his features drawn, his mouth turned upside down in a beautiful frown. The man is just too damn good-looking. "Let me catch my breath."

"Am I—" He pants for three heartbeats, like he's desperate to catch his breath. "—moving too fast for you?"

I hesitate. Like I really have to think about it. "A little. Not that I don't want it to happen," I tell him in a rush when I see the wary look on his face, as if he's going to potentially remove himself from the situation. His expression turns shuttered, his body language shifting into flight position. Like he might leap away from my bed and shoot straight out of my house, never to be seen again. "I want you. I just need to, I don't know, slow down for a little bit?" I phrase the last bit like a question, as if I'm unsure.

"Ah. Well, I can do that." He sounds like the perfect, understanding boyfriend. I bet he would be a perfect, understanding boyfriend, if he actually settled down for once.

As he stretches out beside me on the bed, his arm going around my shoulders to pull me in closer to him, I wonder again if Rhett Montgomery is too good to be true. If what he shows me is nothing but smoke and mirrors with a sprinkle of magic, and the minute shit gets tough, he'll reveal his true self. And his true self will be a complete asshole.

I almost wish that would happen. I want to see the cracks in his surface, see him be real and ugly and awful.

Then I'd feel like we have more in common.

"I hope you're not mad at me." I sound contrite, and the slightest bit sad. I need him to believe I'm sincere.

Truly, my body is buzzing with desire. If he reached between my legs right now and gave me one firm stroke of his fingers, I'd probably explode like a shaken-up bottle of champagne. But considering no man has ever made me come before—yes, I know, I've been with some real selfish assholes—I have serious doubts when it comes to his potential skills.

So far, what he's shown me has been impressive. But I'm still not fully convinced.

"I could never be mad at you." I can feel his lips move against my forehead as he speaks, and he presses a kiss there, chaste and sweet. I close my eyes against the onslaught of emotion that threatens to wash over me. He makes me feel good. He's…kind. Yes, I think he's putting on some sort of perfection front, but what if he's not? What if he really is like this?

Then I'm screwed.

THIRTEEN

We lay together on my bed for at least fifteen minutes, our legs entwined, our hands occasionally wandering. We talk about nothing, but we're thinking about everything. I know I am, and I can feel that he is too.

He's probably afraid to make another move, and I can't blame him, since I'm the one who asked to slow down so I can "catch my breath."

That sounds so lame. I wonder if he believed me. All I can think about is when can I feel his hands on me again. My blood runs hot and I'm restless, my legs rubbing against his, my hands aching to reach out and touch him, *really* touch him.

Deciding I'm ready to make my first move, I press my face against his bare chest and breathe deep, inhaling his scent. His skin is so warm and smooth, and incredibly hot. His heart races; I press my palm where it beats, and I purse my lips, kissing him there.

An agonized groan sounds from deep in his chest as I continue to kiss him. His pecs, the center of his chest, his rib cage, his stomach. I kiss him everywhere, the smattering of hair tickling my lips, the salty taste of his skin making my mouth water. I lick around his belly button and he shivers. I curl my fingers around the denim waistband of his jeans, my knuckles brushing against the sensitive skin just beneath, and his hips twitch. Silently begging me to delve under the denim and touch him where he really wants me.

"You don't have to—" he starts when I unbutton his jeans and I lift my head to meet his gaze, sending him a look. Is he for real? Is he actually going to say that? He swallows his words with a simple press of his lips, his gaze never leaving mine.

"I want to," I say firmly, pulling the zipper down slowly to reveal black cotton boxer briefs, his erection straining against the fabric. I drift my index finger down the length of him, noting how his cock jumps beneath my touch.

My entire body goes tight as he lifts his hips, allowing me to pull his jeans off. I swiftly remove them so he's lying in the center of my bed clad in only the black boxer briefs, and I shift away from him, fully taking him in.

He's got a beautiful body. All lean muscle and sinew, he has the start of a six-pack, his legs thick and strong-looking, and I'm tempted to pounce on him.

But I don't. Instead, I move slowly and deliberately. I drift my fingers along his thigh, then back up until I'm at his hips. I tease him with my fingertips, dipping them beneath his underwear, stroking there. He's so hot and so big, and finally, my patience gets the best of me.

I tug his boxer briefs down until they're around his thighs, and his cock springs free. I grab hold of him, wrap my fingers tight around the base as I stroke up. Down. Establishing a rhythm, I'm focused solely on his pleasure, on what he's getting out of it versus what he can do for me.

His pleasured groans, the way he twitches and shifts, his eager hips lifting the faster I get, it's all driving me on. But my mind wanders as it usually does when I'm having sex. I can't help it. It's like I get—bored or something.

A thought flickers in my mind, murky at first, until it grabs hold and doesn't go away. Is it my own guilt that's making me do this? I can give him an orgasm and…what? Does that absolve me from what I plan on doing to him in the future? I study his face, his flushed cheeks, his glazed eyes, and when our gazes suddenly meet, I shift down, brushing my lips across the very tip of him.

Another moan escapes him as I draw him deep into my mouth. The sounds he makes as I continue to lick and suck him electrifies me. Urges me to suck harder, tease the tip of him with my tongue, stroke the base of him with a firm grip of my fingers…

"Hell no," he practically growls, sitting up so fast I startle away from him. "I don't want to come that way."

I stare silently at him, a gasp escaping me when he pushes me backward until I'm sprawled across the bed. He undresses me with ruthless efficiency, until I'm clad in a wispy pair of black-lace panties and nothing else. His hands and mouth move all over my body, his fingers sliding beneath my panties, and I part my legs, letting him test me.

"So damn wet," he whispers right before he tugs my underwear down, and then his face is between my thighs, his tongue licking, searching, and eventually finding my clit. His skillful precision is intense, making me feel like I'm about to come out of my skin and I strain against him, my eyes tightly closed, my muscles clenched. He knows exactly where to touch me, but I want more.

"Higher," I whisper and he does as I ask, shifting higher. "Faster," I gasp, a cry leaving me when his tongue picks up speed.

And just like that, I come quickly, my orgasm slamming into me out of nowhere. My entire body shakes, a harsh cry escaping past my lips as wave after wave of pleasure washes over me, electrified jolts wracking my body. When I'm finally spent, my limbs are shaking so hard, it's like I just ran a marathon in record time.

Again with the clichés, but seriously. No man has ever made me come like that. No man has ever made me come, period. I breathe deeply, trying to regulate my racing heart, and when I finally crack my eyes open, I see the satisfied gleam in Rhett's eyes as he watches me. That look tells me he's proud of what he just did to me, and I'm half-tempted to tell him to get that smug look off his face. But I'm too weak to even speak.

He slowly shakes his head, his gaze drifting over me, making me warm. "Damn woman, you came hard."

I say nothing, the sound of my harsh pants filling the room. I watch as he climbs off the bed and grabs his jeans from the floor, pulling a condom out of his wallet. Unwrapping it, he goes to stand next to the side of the bed closest to me and slowly rolls the condom on. My gaze drops to his erection, and even though I just climaxed, my body clenches, already eager for more.

Without saying a word, he comes to me, climbing onto the bed so he can kiss me deep before he positions himself above me and thrusts his cock inside with one swift movement. I'm wet and loose after that massive orgasm, so he enters me easily, filling me right up. I go completely still, savoring the sensation of him buried deep, how his cock throbs in time like a heartbeat.

Reaching up, I tentatively brush my hands down his back, searching the muscles there. His eyes close as I touch him, and he braces his palms on the mattress before he starts to move. Slowly at first, his hips flexing, pushing, deeper and deeper. I grab hold of his shoulders and cling to him, wrapping my legs around his waist, sending him deeper, making us both groan in unison.

With every thrust, he drives me deeper into the mattress, all the while telling me how good I feel, how I'm so wet and tight, his constant stream of words conjuring dirtier and dirtier images in my brain. I wish I had a mirror so I could see how good we look together right now. So I could watch his butt and leg muscles flex with every push inside my body. He fucks better than any guy I've ever been with before, and I can feel it coming again. That subtle tingle in my belly, that hopeful rise within my body, taking me closer and closer to the edge...

Until I'm coming again, the orgasm like a giant wave of relief as it moves through me. He's coming too—I can tell by the way he goes still, his body tightening and then releasing. He shudders as he moans my name, his movements becoming wild, totally out of control.

No one has ever moaned my name before. Not Jennifer or Jensen or even Jen. I close my eyes against the onslaught of emotions that grabs hold of me and refuses to let go. The guilt and the shame and the pleasure and the tiny glimmer of happiness I'm experiencing all at once. What just happened felt so good, so right.

But it isn't right. It shouldn't feel right. What we just did, is wrong. He's really my stepbrother.

My mother turned me into this. I'm a slut, a whore, a user, a manipulator, a woman bent on revenge. All because of her.

Rhett collapses on top of me, his heavy weight keeping me pinned in place, but it's not an unpleasant feeling. No, in fact it's the total opposite. I like how he feels, our sweaty, sticky bodies entwined, the scent of sex and sweat lingering in the air. His mouth is on my collarbone, damp and warm as he murmurs against my skin, and I can tell his cock has already softened inside of me. I turn my head, my mouth on his temple as I breathe him in deep, and he flexes his hips. That one subtle movement makes my entire body tingle, and I can tell his cock is getting hard again too.

"Hmm, fuck, Jensen, I want you again," he whispers just before he cups my cheek and kisses me, his tongue doing a thorough exploration of my mouth.

And I let him. I let him lead round two completely. I do nothing but take it, let him use me and fuck me until I can't think straight. He doesn't notice how passive I've become. It's either he doesn't realize or he really doesn't care, because I'm putting zero effort into this now. It's like I can't function.

More like I don't want to function. I'd rather feel him completely take over my body. I want him to derive as much pleasure from it as I can give. He sucks my nipples and licks my belly and eats my pussy and strokes me deep with one, two, three fingers at a time. He's feasting on me, making me come again and again, and I am mindless. Helpless.

Vulnerable in the worst possible way.

FOURTEEN

"What the hell is wrong with you? It's like you've never walked in high heels before," Savannah cracks, a dirty laugh escaping her when she witnesses me twisting my ankle yet again as I make my way toward the bar. Is that the fourth time I've twisted it tonight, or the fifth? I can't keep track.

All I know is that I'm a walking, talking disaster at the club, and I think Don is seriously considering firing me. He's yelled at me countless times, threatening that he's going to send me home early, but I just ignore him, trying my best to focus. But it's like I can't. I'm wobbly in my heels, I keep messing up drink orders and pissing off customers. Oh, and my entire body aches in the most delicious way.

I guess this is what it feels like to be so thoroughly fucked, you believe you'll never be the same again.

"I didn't get much sleep last night," I finally admit to my friend. We're both standing at the bar watching Chuck pour drinks for our customers. It's a Saturday night and the club is full—there's literally a line to get in outside, and I've been running and gunning since I started my shift. I'm grateful Savannah and I are working together, but I don't appreciate her teasing either, especially since I don't want to reveal what happened last night.

Her finely arched brows shoot straight up. "Why didn't you get much sleep last night, huh? Whatcha been up to?"

"Nothing," I mumble, trying not to meet her gaze for fear she'll see my truth. I keep my eyes on Chuck, but I can feel my cheeks go pink and I want to smack myself. Savannah will catch on quick. She never misses a beat. And just as I suspected, the knowing look she sends my way within a matter of seconds tells me she's on to my lies.

I just can't ever let her figure out *all* of my lies or I'm done for.

"Uh-huh. Whatever you say, but I can tell. You, my dear, have the look of a woman who's found herself a man who knows how to satisfy her," Savannah drawls as she nudges me with her shoulder. I vehemently shake my head as she asks, "Is it true? Did you have S-E-X last night?"

I'm still shaking my head, my cheeks so hot I feel like I'm burning up from the inside out. "Of course not," I snap.

Savannah laughs. "Liar. You're all shaky and glassy-eyed.

Hmm." She leans in, her face so close to mine I can smell the minty gum she's chewing. "Or maybe you found some high-quality coke and forgot to share."

"Savannah!" Drugs scare me, just like liquor scares me. I'm terrified I'll lose control and do something stupid.

Huh. Though now I've discovered that sex with Rhett makes me lose control too. I would've done anything he asked last night. Anal sex? Yes, please. Introduce a few other people into the mix? Sure, why not? Put clamps on your nipples and tie you to the bed? Of course! Let's do it.

Yeah. That's not good. I've never been into those sorts of things at all. So why would I think it's something Rhett and I could do?

Clearly, it's because he's fucking with my mind and making me have out-of-control thoughts.

"I'm kidding." She pats me on the shoulder. "Though the occasional coke hit will give you the biggest feeling of euphoria. Mmm." Savannah shakes her head, a dreamy expression on her face. "Fucking on coke is like an out-of-body experience."

"I think I had enough out-of-body experiences last night, and I wasn't even on coke," I tell her, making her laugh harder.

"Wow. This guy must be something then. Did you meet him here? Did he take one look at your fabulous ta-tas and throw himself at your feet?"

"Hell no." I wrinkle my nose. "You know we can't fraternize with guests."

"Like anyone sticks to that rule." Savannah tilts her head to the side, her long ponytail sliding over her shoulder. "Does he know you work here?"

Dread consumes me, making me clutch the edge of the bar so tightly my fingers ache. "No. He can never know I work here."

"You want to keep him in your life?" she asks, but I don't answer. "If you do, then you better be honest. He finds out you work here, walking around with no top on all night while men leer at your chest, and he's gonna shit a ton of bricks."

"Trust me, I know," I say with a slight shake of my head. I don't want to talk about this right now, with Savannah, in the middle of the club with the music blaring so loud I can hardly hear myself think. Rhett isn't a part of my life here at City Lights. I compartmentalize everything. When I'm with Rhett, I focus on him and nothing else. When I'm at work, I usually don't think of Rhett at all.

But tonight, my mind is consumed with thoughts of him. Every guy in this place with hair the same color as his has me looking twice, my heart leaping to my throat. What happened between us last night is running on a continuous loop in my brain. How he looked at me, the way he kissed me, the way he made me feel. It was...mind-blowing, when that's the last thing I need.

He's taking up way too much of my brain space. I don't know what I'd do if he showed up here.

"When do you see him again?" Savannah asks just as Chuck adds fresh drinks to her tray.

"I don't know," I answer with a little shrug. He left my house in the middle of the night, around three in the morning. I woke up to him pressing a kiss to my cheek and telling me he'd text me later.

I haven't heard from him since.

"Maybe it's just a one-time thing?" She grabs the tray, her gaze meeting mine. "Sometimes those are the best, you know? One delicious night with a hot man who makes your toes curl, only to never see him again. Your expectations can never be let down, you know?"

I watch Savannah walk away, her skirt swishing, her head held high as she commands the attention of every man she passes. I admire her confidence, wish even the tiniest bit could rub off on me.

"Here you go." Chuck's gruff voice makes me turn around, and I take the tray from him and head out into the crowd. I try to adopt some of Savannah's swagger as I deliver drinks to my customers, ignoring how they stare at me, adopting that *I don't give a shit* mask I've become decent at wearing.

The entire night is like this. I finally find a rhythm and there's no more screwing up drink orders or nearly falling on my face. Don isn't yelling at me anymore, and at one point I do a little twirl for my guests at one of the corner tables that has the best view of the stage. Four men in their late forties to early fifties, all dressed well, their eyes lit with interest as I spin around when one of them asks, my skirt flaring out so far, I almost flash them my ass.

I don't know what possesses me to do it, but I do, and when I go backstage to take my break about an hour later, Don approaches me with an appreciative gleam in his eye. "You turned it around tonight, doll."

I try not to roll my eyes. I really don't like it when he calls me that. "Thanks. I started off bad, but I think I'm okay now."

"You're more than okay." He glances over his shoulder, like he's making sure no one's paying attention to us, before he returns his gaze to mine. "I have a proposition for you."

My stomach bottoms out. Don has only mentioned a proposition to me twice before. Once, a guest requested to, and I quote, titty-fuck me. Another time, a couple wanted me to watch them have sex in the storage room. Both requests would've earned me extra money, but I was uncomfortable, so I turned them down.

"What is it?" I ask, my voice, my head, my entire body weary. My money situation isn't the best. Tuition is due soon, and I can't apply for financial aid since my grades were so bad that first semester I was at the community college in my hometown. The semester when my dad died. I didn't bother going back to my classes and I failed all of them.

I'm on my own. I can't even qualify for a student loan because of that one semester. Yet another regret in the long list of them that makes up my life.

"There's a gentleman you've been serving all evening. He's very interested in you." Don blatantly stares at my boobs. "He wants to get to know you better. Says you're giving off a very friendly, sexy vibe."

Ick. "I don't kn—"

Don holds up his hand, silencing me. "Hear me out. This guy, he's fucking loaded, Jen. He flashed me a fat stack of hundreds and said he had ten thousand *cash* for us if you'd spend a little alone time with him."

I blink at my boss, trying to comprehend what he just said. "What do you mean, ten thousand cash for us?"

"He just wants to spend time with you. Said it would take no longer than an hour." Don hesitates, his gaze skittering away from mine. "I'll split the money with you fifty-fifty."

What an insult.

"No way." I start to walk out, but Don grabs me by the arm, stopping me.

"Fine, you get six, I get four," he offers. So generous. Doesn't he realize I'm the one who has to "spend time" with this guy? I don't even know what he wants from me.

But I can take a guess.

"I get eight, you get two, and we've got a deal." I can't believe I said that. My greed just completely took over me, but this is the perfect opportunity for me to earn some major cash. I always tell Savannah I would never do something like this, but…

How can I let this opportunity get away from me?

Don grins, a chuckle escaping him. Like my negotiating skills are so hilarious. "I can't give you that much, Jen. Come on."

"I'm the one who's going to have to grind on this guy's dick or whatever," I mutter, wrenching my arm out of his grip. I can't think beyond dick-grinding right now. I know it could be much worse, but I don't want to imagine it. "I should make the majority of the money for what I have to do. You're doing nothing."

"I'm the one who's brokering the deal and letting you off early from your shift, so I deserve something too." Don licks his lips, reminding me of a slimy lizard. "Six and four. That's my final offer."

"What exactly does this guy want from me?"

"I don't know. He didn't say. Only mentioned that you looked real good and he wants to get to know you. I bet if you treat him real nice, touch him, kiss him, maybe jerk him off, he'll be happy. Just say yes. Come on." Don sends me a pleading look.

I shouldn't do it. But I'm living paycheck to paycheck, even with the great tips I make here. My shitty house isn't cheap, and school takes up a lot of my money. Once I get in good with the Montgomerys, I know I'll walk away with a huge payoff, but until then I'm fighting for every dollar I get.

"Seven and three or I'm out." I cross my arms in front of

my chest, plumping up my boobs on purpose. Don's eyes drop to them and I let him stare, trying not to feel too creeped out. He's laser-focused on my erect nipples, which is just weird, but I tell myself I'm doing this for seven grand.

Seven. Grand.

"Fine." He sighs, as if I just put him out. "Seven and three it is."

Relief floods me. I may be acting like a whore, but at least I'll be seven thousand dollars richer by the end of the evening.

Ignoring the shame that threatens, I drop my arms to my sides and shake my hair back. "Tell your guest I'll do it."

Don grins and rubs his hands together. "Stay right here. Got a little bit of arrangin' to do."

I watch him walk away, then tell myself that no matter what, I can't run.

Even though I really want to.

FIFTEEN

Three years ago

"Are you serious? What the hell are we going to do now?" Dad follows me as I walk through the trailer toward my bedroom. "How could you lose that job?"

I whirl on him, furious. Like it's always my fault when I bring home bad news. It's so frustrating. I feel for him, I do, but he needs to stop blaming me for everything that happens to us. "My boss tried to cop a feel, Dad. When he grabbed my ass, I told him no and slapped his hand away. He fired me."

My father stares at me, his expression horrified. "What are you talking about, he tried to cop a feel? Jim is my friend! He would never do that!"

"Well, he's your friend who tried to feel me up." I rest my hands on my hips, glaring at him. He looks terrible, pale and weak. His hair is thin and his eyes are bloodshot. He doesn't eat much anymore, and it shows. I bet a strong gust of wind would knock him right over.

Closing my eyes briefly, I take a deep breath, reminding myself that he's not well. He's sick, but I'm so frustrated over what happened, it's hard to focus on being careful when all I wanna do is blow up at him. "When was the last time you went outside?"

"It doesn't matter." He waves a hand. "You need to find another job, Jenny. You know we can't go too long without your income."

The problem is, I can't find fulltime work around here, and that's what I need in order to afford the rent at this stupid trailer park. No one wants to hire an under-experienced eighteen-year-old, but I can't get any experience if no one is going to hire me. It's such bullshit.

God knows my father isn't able to hold down a job, and he's still fighting to get on permanent disability. His depression makes it hard for him to get out of bed. He's lost most of his jobs just because he didn't show up.

It's unbelievable, how my mother still controls him to this day. It's also pitiful.

And sad.

"I'll go look for a job tomorrow." I throw the covers back and climb into bed, desperate to curl up into a ball and forget about all my troubles. I'm so tired, and still weirded out by my boss Jim grabbing my butt. He acted like it was no big deal, like I shouldn't have a problem with him touching my ass, but come on. This guy is old enough to be my father. It's creepy.

I don't regret slapping his hand away. I don't regret telling him no either. I do sort of regret losing the job, because it's never fun to go out and find a new one, but if I let that guy get away with it, what would he try next?

No way did I want to find out.

"You need to get back out there right now." Dad grabs my covers and yanks them away from my body. "Get up and go find another job. We can't afford to lose any more money."

"What did you do with the money I gave you last week?" That check had been almost six hundred dollars, a pretty substantial sum for us.

"It's gone." He snaps his fingers, as if the cash disappeared into thin air. "We need more."

I sit up, smoothing my hair away from my face. "It's all gone? Like, you spent every last dollar?"

"Yep." My father nods, and there's something in the way he's not looking at me that makes me suspicious.

"What did you do with it all?" I leap from the bed so I can stand in front of him, noticing how he won't look me in the eye. He's hiding something. But what? "Dad. What happened to all the money?" I know he didn't spend it on rent. That's not due for another ten days.

"I let Norah borrow it," he admits, his head still bent.

"What?" He jerks his head up at my roar and I throw my

hands up into the air. "You barely know that woman!"

"I know she's good for it! She said she'll pay me back. She's just a little short, is all!"

"*We're* always a little short. We don't have that kind of money to loan out." I can't even wrap my head around what he's saying. He'll support his friend, but not support us? Me? I don't understand. Since when did I become such a low priority in his life? "You need to tell her she has to pay us back ASAP."

"Just go find another job. We'll be fine." He waves his hand, dismissing me, my words, my concern. I hate it when he does that.

Hate. It.

"I don't want to find another job. And no, we won't be fine. You've become the Bank of fucking America, lending out our money to neighbors we don't even know. What the hell is wrong with you?"

He slaps my face so hard, I swear my head snaps back. A gasp escapes me as I rest my hand on my cheek, staring at him. It stings where he hit me. Tears immediately spring to my eyes, and I realize I'm shaking.

"Don't you ever speak like that to me again." He points his index finger in my face, his bloodshot eyes wide, his body vibrating with anger. "I'm the one in charge here, not you. If I want to loan out our money, then that's my right. And if I want you to go out and find another job, then you better damn well do it before I kick your skinny little ass out in the street."

I'm full-blown crying now. His words hurt, hit me in my most painful spots. I'm terrified of being on my own, yet life with my father isn't that great either. As he gets older and more depressed, he becomes meaner. It's hard to deal with. I love him, but his constant anger confuses me.

Maybe life would be better out in the street. Then I wouldn't have to deal with my father all the time.

"You're just like her, you know."

Oh, here it comes. The words are familiar. He started the comparisons about six months ago, when he caught me sneaking back into the trailer way past my curfew. His disappointment had killed me. Made me cry.

Now I've become numb to it. I blame her. *She* broke him. *She* made him this way.

"Lazy. Always said men wanted her, how they would touch her and say suggestive things. You know what I realized?" He sends me a questioning look.

Yes, dear old Dad, please tell me what you realized.

"That your mother was nothing but a worthless whore. And if you don't watch out, you're going to turn out the same exact way," he announces. He wants me to hear what he's saying.

And I do. Loud and clear.

"Thanks for your faith in me, Dad," I mutter as I push past him. I escape out of the trailer, never once looking back, even though he's calling my name. I hop into the shitty old car we share and start it up, pulling out of our space just as Dad exits the trailer. He waves a fist at me, but I ignore him. Instead, I hit the gas, the tires spinning in the dirt until they catch traction and the car lurches forward.

I drive aimlessly with the windows rolled down, the wind in my hair, my tears dried on my cheeks. It still hurts where he slapped me, and the anger fills me.

Fuels me.

SIXTEEN

After I freshen up a little in the bathroom—take a pee, brush my hair, clean up the mascara smudges from beneath my eyes so I don't look like a raccoon, and slick on a new coat of shiny pink lip-gloss—I decide I look pretty good. There's a sparkle in my eyes that wasn't there before, which I blame on last night with Rhett.

There's also a glow in my cheeks that I attribute to my night with Rhett too. It's so weird, how he did this to me. How much my evening with Rhett affected me. I didn't know sex could be like this.

And now here I go, cheapening everything I did with Rhett by letting some perv customer from City Lights feel me up for seven thousand dollars. I'm prostituting myself. There's nothing else to call it, right? I made Don promise he wouldn't tell anyone about this deal, not even Savannah or Chuck. I feel bad enough for my choices—I don't need their judgement too.

What else am I supposed to do? I'm broke, I need money, and this is the easiest way for me to make it. I know I said I don't want to become a stripper, and what I'm about to do tonight is even worse, but I know for a fact that Savannah has done this sort of thing before. She's confessed as much to me, though she doesn't like to talk about it. But when a girl is in a predicament and needs cash fast, you have to take your opportunities where you can.

I can't let my choices make me feel bad. Sometimes we have to do things we're not proud of. It doesn't mean that we're bad people.

At least, that's what I tell myself.

After exiting the bathroom, I sneak into the private room Don instructed me to wait in and glance around, wrinkling my nose. It's a little musty in here, meaning that the room isn't used much, and I'm glad to see Don lit a candle before he left. I clean the room up even further, fluffing the cushions on the sleek black couch and turning on a few more lamps so it's a little brighter, though the light bulbs are faded and dim at best. But if it's too dark, the guy might try and do something extra sketchy. Better to be bright and put this asshole on display as much as possible.

Once I'm finished, I examine the room one more time, unable to fight the frown that takes over. This room is dingy, reminding me of a crappy motel room, but I only have so much to work with. I'm thankful I brought a bottle of water with me just in case I get thirsty. I would've brought my phone too, but I have nowhere to stash it and I didn't want to leave it out so the guy can see it. Besides, not like anyone's texting me right now. Not even Rhett.

Asshole.

There's a knock on the door and before I can do anything, it swings open, and in walks one of the guys from the corner table I was working earlier, the one with the best view in the house. It's the most attractive guy from the table, if I'm being honest. He's probably hovering around fifty, with attractive smile wrinkles fanning from the corners of his hazel eyes and a thick head of hair sprinkled with salt and pepper. He's clutching a full glass of amber-colored liquor, and I can tell he's fit, his black button-down shirt and expensive-looking jeans showcasing a body that he takes care of.

Not necessarily my first choice, but at least he's not some creepy, gross guy with bad breath and a pot belly.

"Hello." He smiles as he approaches me and I smile back, mentally batting away the nerves that threaten to take over.

"Hi." I discreetly check his left hand. Ring finger is empty and there's no telltale white tan line there either, so hopefully that means he's not married. I mean, there's no guarantee, but I'm going to pretend he's single.

Just like me.

"I'm Greg." He holds out his hand and I take it, surprised

by his firm shake. My fingers actually ache when he lets them go, and I'm tempted to shake them out.

"I'm Jen."

He raises a brow. "Just Jen?"

"Just Jen," I say with a nod. He doesn't need to know any more about me than that. I hope he doesn't think I'm going to share my life story, because this is about as much information he's going to get out of me.

"I appreciated your excellent service tonight at our table, Jen." He steps closer, so he's standing directly in front of me. I can smell him. His cologne is expensive—no cheap Axe on this guy. And can you actually smell money on a person? Because this man reeks of it. "I couldn't help but think what a pretty girl you are."

I refuse to let his words bother me, but...he's sort of creeping me out. This man could be my father. He's definitely old enough. "Thank you," I manage to say, stepping away from him and pointing toward the couch. "Would you like to have a seat? Get more comfortable?"

Greg takes a sip of his drink, contemplating me over the rim of the glass. "Did your boss tell you what I want from you?"

Guess he's getting right down to business. Taking a deep breath, I say, "He mentioned you wanted to spend time with me this evening."

"That's true." He contemplates me, his gaze roving over my body, lingering on my chest. Of course. Everyone stares at my tits—it's part of the job. "But I asked for something very specific from you."

A tremble moves through me at the tone of his voice. Damn Don for not telling me what's really going on. "I'm sure I can accommodate your request."

"I'm sure you can." He's standing in front of me again, reaching out and trailing his fingers down my upper arm. "I definitely want to see you naked."

I swallow hard. Yes, I knew this was coming. Who's going to pay ten grand and not get some pussy action? "Okay." I reach for the waistband of my skirt, ready to shed it, but he places his hand over mine, stopping me.

"Not yet." He smiles, a flash of blinding white in the dull yellow light of the room. "I want you to dance for me first."

I slowly back away from him, my nervous laughter ringing in the tiny room. "Um, I don't think so."

"Oh, I definitely think so," he says softly. "I'm sure you know how to move."

What's that supposed to mean? "True confession, I'm a terrible dancer."

"You don't strip?" He appears surprised.

"No." I shake my head. "I don't have any rhythm."

"Oh, come on. I'm sure you can dance just fine. Plus, with breasts like these…" He reaches out and actually cups them, as if he's weighing them in the palms of his hands. He doesn't even look me in the eyes. He's too entranced with the rest of my body, and I find that insulting. "…and that fucking spectacular body of yours, I'm surprised."

I'm frozen, trying to calm my shaky breaths while his hands are still wrapped around my breasts. It's weird, having a stranger touch me like this. An older man who's actually paid a lot of money to touch me. It's one thing to let a teenager paw at me, or to let Rhett have me last night. That I was willing to do.

But this moment…is strange.

"You have perfect nipples," he murmurs, rubbing his thumbs over them. They harden from his touch and I want to close my eyes in mortification, but I don't. "Such a pretty pink."

"T-thank you?" I don't know how to respond. This is incredibly awkward.

He leans in close, his mouth near my ear as he murmurs, "I bet that pretty little pussy of yours is just as pink. Am I right?"

Greg steps away before I can say anything, setting his drink on the end table next to the couch and pulling his iPhone out of his jeans pocket. "I have a song I want you to dance to. Let me find it."

I'm still shell-shocked by what he said to me. I can run right now if I wanted to. Just—throw open that door and bolt out of here. Fuck the ten grand. I know Don would want to murder me and I'd probably lose my job, but do I really want to go through with this?

"Take off the skirt," Greg commands, his soft voice holding the slightest edge. His gaze is still locked on the phone as he speaks. "I want to see you dance in your panties and shoes and nothing else."

Looks like I'm going through with it.

I take off my skirt and fold it with shaky hands, setting it on the counter just behind me. Glancing over my shoulder, I catch Greg scrolling through his phone and making his song selection. He turns up the volume as the music starts, some kind of jazz instrumental tune that's heavy on the piano and saxophone. I swear my knees are knocking together and I grab the water bottle that sits nearby, taking a giant swig from it. Really, I thought the water would help calm my buzzing nerves, but now I feel like my stomach is sloshing around.

"You ready?" Greg asks.

I turn to face him, watching quietly as he sits on the couch, the phone still in his hand, his finger pressing against the side so that the volume turns up. I swallow hard, crossing one foot over the other to stabilize myself. The expectant expression on his face tells me I need to get to it. I need to start dancing.

After all, seven thousand dollars is on the line.

Clearing my throat, I rest my hands on my hips and then slowly start to move. I run my hands over my body and twirl around on my heels, surprised I don't go tottering over. The music kind of sucks, but I'm getting into it. My muscles are loosening, I'm shedding my inhibitions and I tell myself I might actually be enjoying this little dance.

Then again, maybe I'm not.

I finally look at Greg, surprised to see him sitting there so impassively, the phone still in his hand, and I wonder if he's recording me. He's observing me like he might watch a janitor mop the floor. One arm is stretched out across the back of the couch, the other one clutching the phone, his expression impossible to read. He's sprawled out on the couch like he's never seen anything so boring in all his life.

The music is still going but I stop dancing, my arms hanging at my sides as I glare at him. He sits up straighter, his shrewd gaze meeting mine. "Why'd you stop?"

"Why aren't you enjoying it?"

Those brows lift again. For some odd reason, the gesture reminds me of Rhett—the very last person I should be thinking of right now. "Who says I'm not enjoying it?"

"I can tell." I wave a hand at him. "You look bored."

"Well, I'm not." He sets the phone on the couch beside him and leans back, crossing his arms in front of his massive chest. For an older guy, he's actually very big. Muscular.

Intimidating.

"Okay." I drawl the word out, like I'm full of doubt, which I so am.

"And who said you could stop?" He's still glaring at me. "Keep dancing."

I'm annoyed. Not embarrassed or nervous, but full-blown, I-see-red annoyed. It was the way he said that, like he's in total command of me. "You're not my boss," I mutter as I try to reestablish my rhythm.

Greg hears me. He's up and in my personal space within seconds, his fingers going underneath my chin so he can tip my face up, forcing me to meet his gaze. "What did you just say?"

Anger blazes in his eyes, but I don't care. I'm angry too. My voice is clear and firm when I say, "I said, you're not my boss."

His fingers tighten on my chin almost painfully. "I just paid a hell of a lot of money to have you for the night." The smile he gives me isn't friendly. No, more like menacing. "That means I can do pretty much whatever I want to you."

We stare at each other for a tension-filled moment, and he squeezes my chin again, pinching my skin before he releases me. He wraps his arm around my waist, his hand palming my butt before giving it a slap, and I jolt away from him, startled.

My anger dissipates, replaced by a heavy dose of fear. I don't like how Greg is talking to me. Or looking at me. I should've never agreed to this.

It's now or never.

Slowly, I turn and make my way toward the door. The music immediately shuts off and then Greg is chasing after me; I can hear his hurried footsteps. I'm at the door, my fingers curling around the handle, but he stops it from opening with a firm hand pressed against the wood.

"What do you think you're doing?" he whispers by my ear,

his face so close to mine I can feel his lips move against my skin.

The disgusted shiver that runs through me can't be disguised. "I'm leaving."

When I try to turn the handle again, he just presses against the door harder. Trapping me. "You're not going anywhere."

I keep my gaze fixed straight ahead. I don't want to look at him. I'm too scared at what I might see. "I don't want to do this."

"I don't really give a shit." His free arm circles around my waist and he spreads his hand across my bare stomach, fingers reaching, just brushing the underside of my breasts. "I already paid for you, remember."

"And you'll get your money back, I promise." Air is shuddering in and out of my lungs and my head is spinning. I swear if he doesn't let go of me soon, I'm going to black out.

"I don't want my money back." He squeezes his arm around my middle and then picks me up, hauling me away from the door. I kick my legs out and back, trying to somehow nail him in the knees, but I miscalculate my aim.

I nail him with the pointy heel of my shoe right in the balls instead.

"Fuck!" Greg's arms fall away from me, and I practically drop to the ground. Scrambling to my feet, I glance over my shoulder to see Greg hunched over on his knees, his hands covering his crotch. He lifts his head, his murderous gaze meeting mine. "You fucking bitch!"

I grasp for the door handle and turn it, crying out in relief when the door swings open so easily. Without looking back, I run out of the room, and make my way toward Don's office.

SEVENTEEN

Don gives me a thousand dollars for "my trouble" as he called it. I wish he would've given me more. I tried to make him feel guilty over what happened with Greg, because let me tell you, I let him know exactly what happened—in full, explicit detail—when I ran into his office. He flinches with every detail I reveal, shaking his head as the words pour out of me.

I've never seen Don move so fast when he leaps out of his chair and heads for the room where Greg still was. I follow after him, secure in knowing Don is there to defend me, but when we get to the room, Greg isn't anywhere to be found.

He simply vanished. And without asking for his money back either.

"Guess you lucked out, doll," Don murmurs when we're back in his office.

"Lucked out?" I ask incredulously. "Are you serious?" I can't believe he just said that.

"Trust me, it could've be worse."

"That creep tried to *rape* me," I remind him.

"Yeah, and I'm giving you a thousand dollars, right?" Don sends me a look, one that says I shouldn't argue with him.

Fine. I won't argue. Not when so much money is on the line.

I say nothing as Don quietly opens up his desk drawer, draws out a fat stack of hundreds, and starts counting them out, one by one, until he hit one thousand.

"Sorry about that," he says as he keeps his gaze fixed on his desk. Like he can't look at me. "Don't worry about that asshole. I'll take care of him if he comes back. You can take the next few days off if you want."

Without a word I grab the money, shove it into my purse, and walk out, never once looking back. There's no way I want to hang out at this rat hole for fear I'd see Greg again—if that's even his real name.

Over the next few days while I wallow in my misery, Savannah texts me a few times, asking why I'm not around and if I'm okay, but I ignore her. Rhett texts me as well, wanting to know if I want to get together sometime this week, but I ignore him too. Seeing Rhett is the last thing I want after what I went through with Greg. Not that Rhett's to blame or anything, but I can guarantee he's going to want to have sex with me, and there is no way that's happening. Not right now.

I feel too battered and bruised. Too raw and…ugly. Yes, ugly. Greg called me terrible names. He wanted to hurt me.

And comparing what Greg tried to do to me versus my experience with Rhett the night before? How sweet yet aggressive Rhett had been, and how much I wanted him? My brain can't compute all the conflicting thoughts.

I skip school, something I can't afford to do, considering I'm already behind. But I know I won't be able to concentrate on the lectures, so why waste my time? I stay in bed for three days straight, until my hair is stringy and greasy and I've been in the same clothes for so long I'm starting to smell funky. The entire time I do nothing but watch new movies on this illegal download site I find, and when that gets boring I watch a bunch of crime shows on YouTube.

All the tales of murder, double-crossing and serial rapists get to me. Make me think my life was turning into a made-for-TV movie—or at least excellent fodder for one of these crime shows. They always say "based on a true story"—and my true story is so messed up. It just keeps getting worse.

I cry too. I mentally ask myself a lot of questions. Like what the hell am I doing? Do I really want to be this person? I almost let some old guy rape me for thousands. Hell, I *still* got some of the money and I bet that pissed Greg off so bad.

So what does that make me? A whore?

Yes. In my eyes, definitely yes.

I had sex with Rhett just so I can get closer to his stepmother, aka my mother. How messed up is that? Is what happened with Greg karma trying to get back at me for what I'm doing to Rhett? I'm using Rhett, so Greg used me?

I'm starting to think that's it. That's why this happened. My decisions have led me down this path, and now it's become so awful, so fraught with too many scary unknowns, I don't think I can handle it any longer.

When I can't take myself anymore, I finally get out of bed and take the longest shower of my life, almost as long as the one I took Saturday night, when I tried my best to scrub Greg off my skin. I threw away the skirt and panties because they smelled like him and his expensive cologne, and the scent made me want to vomit.

Just the mere thought of Greg makes me want to vomit.

After my shower, I lotion myself up good, blow-dry my hair, apply some light makeup, and then start packing. Like, anything I can shove into my one old suitcase that once belonged to my dad, it goes in there. I don't have a lot of furniture or personal items, so anything left behind I don't care about.

I need to get the hell out of here.

After grabbing the biggest tote bag I own from my closet, I throw my old purse inside as well. I sit on the saggy pleather couch and go on the Internet, searching for a bus ticket back to my hometown, finding one that would leave in about ninety minutes. I could take city transit to the bus depot and leave. Forget school and Rhett and my mother. Forget City Lights and Savannah and Don and Chuck. It's best if I leave everything behind and pretend Jensen never existed.

Despite all the planning and time and energy I put into this, I need to abandon my revenge plan. It's getting me into a lot of trouble. Trouble I don't need.

Deciding I'd rather purchase the bus ticket with cash, I give up my ticket search and go into the kitchen, where I throw away everything that's old or close to expiring. Once I have that clean, I go through the tiny cupboard I call my pantry, tossing out bags of stale chips and boxes of old crackers. I find a few snacks I can take with me on the bus, stuff I can eat later, plus a couple of bottles of water, and I shove it all in my tote bag.

The cash Don gave me plus the little bit I'd saved over the months is bound with a rubber band and stashed inside a flower-printed cosmetics bag my dad gave me when I turned thirteen. It's faded now, and kind of hideous, but I've never been able to part with it.

My one sentimental piece beyond the earrings that belong to my mother.

After eating a giant bowl of cereal with the last of the milk from the fridge, I toss the plastic bowl in the trash along with the milk carton and then move through my tiny house to turn out all the lights. I lock the back door, make sure all the blinds and curtains are closed, and I finally grab my stuff and start to head out the front door. I've paid rent through this month, and there's only a few more days left before a new month starts. When I don't make my next regular payment, I know my landlord will come here looking for me. I should probably leave a note, but screw it. They'll be able to figure out I'm gone.

Not that they'll really care.

With an irritated huff, I throw open the door and stop short at what I find waiting for me on the front porch.

A bouquet of flowers in a glass vase, though they're nothing standard like a dozen roses or anything like that. No, this arrangement is a variety of colorful, vibrant wildflowers, and they are absolutely gorgeous.

No one has ever given me flowers before.

I drop my tote to the ground and leave my suitcase standing upright as I bend down to pick up the vase. I bury my face in the flowers, their velvety petals caressing my cheeks, their delicious scent filling my head. There's no card, and for the briefest, scariest moment, I wonder if they could be from Greg.

That means he knows where I live.

"I've been waiting for you out here for almost an hour."

Whirling around, I watch in disbelief as Rhett walks across my weed-filled yard, a bashful smile on his face. I glance down at the flowers, then back up at him. I'm shocked that he's here. After the ugliness of the last few days, his presence lights me up. *Lightens* me up. Makes me feel…

Hopeful.

"These are from you?" I hold the vase out.

He nods. "You like them?"

Ignoring his question, I ask, "What do you mean you've been waiting out here for almost an hour? Why didn't you knock?"

"I did knock. A couple of times," he answers, stopping just at the edge of my porch. "I guess you didn't hear me."

I must not have. I've been too busy packing and trying to figure out what I'm going to do with my life.

"Looks like you're going somewhere." He nods toward the suitcase next to me.

"Oh." I shrug, trying to be nonchalant. Inside, though, I'm a bundle of nerves.

Rhett is *here*. He came to see *me*. And he left me *flowers*.

What does this mean?

"Oh? That's all you're going to say?" Now he's standing directly in front of me, the only barrier the vase of flowers between us. "I've tried texting you for days, but you haven't responded."

I've ignored all of his texts. I eventually blocked his number a couple of days ago so I wouldn't see them anymore and be tempted to answer him.

So why does he stick around? No one else does in my life.

What makes Rhett the exception to the rule?

"I even tried calling you."

A weak laugh escapes me. "I never answer phone calls."

"I figured that." Rhett chuckles, but he sounds nervous. And this makes my heart want to crack wide open. "I haven't been able to think about anything else since we were together Friday night."

His admission makes my heart crack open even more. Why is he saying this? Why is he doing this to me?

"But I'm starting to think I'm the only one who feels this way, since clearly you're doing all right without me." He waves in the direction of my suitcase, like he's upset. And maybe he is. Maybe he's hurt because I ignored him, and now he's giving me flowers and I look like I'm running away, which I am. I so am. I don't deserve him. "I'll let you get back to whatever you were doing."

He turns and starts walking toward the sidewalk, and I watch his retreating back.

Let him go.

Let him walk out of your life.

You don't owe him an explanation.

It's better that he thinks of you as a fond memory versus that evil bitch who used him.

Let.

Him.

Go.

"Rhett. Wait."

I chase after him, the vase still clutched in my hands, the flowers bouncing in my face. I grab hold of his arm and he stops, turning to face me. There's high color in his cheeks, and his eyes are blazing with frustration and anger and...

Want. Lots and lots of want.

My body responds automatically. I want him too. Despite everything I just went through, I lean into him, wishing he would touch me.

But he doesn't. He's too angry to give in. I can see it in the determined set of his jaw, the wary way he's watching me. He's put himself on the line and I've done nothing but make him feel worse.

"I swear, Rhett, I didn't hear you knock. And I—" Hesitating, I scuff my feet on the sidewalk, feeling stupid. "I blocked your number so I wouldn't text you back," I admit, my voice low.

He's frowning, like he can't comprehend what I just told him. "Why didn't you want to text me back?"

"I was, uh, I was going to leave. My—my grandma is not in the best of health, and no one else in the family wants to take care of her, so it's up to me." There. That's a nice lie that won't hurt his feelings. "I need to leave tonight, and I didn't want to tell you."

"Why didn't you want to tell me?"

"More like I didn't know *how* to tell you." I'm messing this up, but are we really surprised? I don't know how to have a normal relationship with a person. Don't know how to start or maintain one either. "I really—liked you, and I didn't even want to admit it to myself, because it couldn't last. I'm not a permanent fixture here, Rhett. And that means I can't be a permanent fixture in your life."

He's watching me, his gaze locked on my face, his expression so sincere, so earnest, it almost makes me want to cry. I prepare myself for what he's about to say. I can tell it's going to be something sweet and wonderful and his words are going to make me want to cave in and stay.

The last thing I should do is stay.

"Jensen." He says my name like an endearment, and I can feel the tears stinging the corners of my eyes. "You should've told me all of this sooner." He takes the vase from my hands and sets it on top of his car. In my despair to chase after him, I didn't even notice we ended up standing right next to it. "I can help. Whatever you need, I'm here for you."

"You barely know me." His hands feel so good when they gently clamp around my shoulders. Like he could pull me into him and offer up all his strength, all his warmth and I could absorb it. Feed off it. It's so weird, but I instinctively know he'd take care of me, no matter what, and I don't deserve so much faith. "Why do you even care?"

"I told you I want to get to know you better." He hesitates, like he's afraid to reveal more. But he takes a deep breath and forges on. "From the moment we first met, there was something about you. You intrigued me. You still do."

I'm at a complete loss for words.

"Didn't you feel the connection between us the other night? God." He hauls me to him, holding me close, my face buried against the solid wall of his chest, and I breathe in his clean, fresh scent. It's nothing like the cloying cologne Greg used. But Rhett still smells expensive, deliciously expensive, and thoughtful and caring and—

"Let me help you." He slips his fingers beneath my chin, tilting my face up so I have no choice but to meet his earnest, hopeful gaze. His fingers are gentle, a complete contrast to the way Greg touched me. "Do you need a ride? I can take you to your grandma's house. Whatever you need."

"What? Oh." I'd already forgotten my lie to him. Not smart. I need to keep better track. "Maybe someone else can take care of her after all. I don't know." My excuses sound weak, and I clamp my lips shut.

"Okay then." His fingers fall away from my chin. His voice is slow, and he's frowning at me. I'm sure I've confused him. No surprise, since I'm feeling pretty confused myself. "You want to come back to my place?"

"Huh?" He wants to take me back to his *palace?* Well, I don't know if he lives in an actual palace while he's in college, but I know he does when he's home with the parentals. He used to belong to a frat and lived in the house, but he moved out the spring of his junior year.

How do I know this? Googling him—he mentioned those interesting facts on an Instagram post.

God, I'm awful.

"Jensen. Hey." He pulls away from me, still holding onto my shoulders, and I'm thankful he's keeping me in place. My knees are so shaky I'm afraid I could fall. "Are you all right?" He touches my cheek, tucks my hair behind my ear, his fingers so gentle. "You're acting kinda weird."

I am. I always am. Can't he see it? I'm fake. Fake as my pleather couch, fake as the CZ earrings in my ears. Fake as the name that he calls me.

There's nothing about me that's real.

My stomach churns as I blink up at him, and I swear I'm seeing two Rhetts. Like he's a twin egg that split in two. Does that even make sense? No, of course not.

"I, uh, I feel kinda…dizzy." Fuzzy black dots fill my vision and I shake my head, but that only seems to make it worse.

"Damn, your lips are so white. Jensen, what's wrong? Are you okay? Jensen? Jensen!"

EIGHTEEN

wake up to discover I'm sitting in the reclined passenger seat of Rhett's car, a soft, gray fuzzy blanket draped over my lower half. I move my fingers, realizing my arms are under the blanket, and I wonder where it came from.

I also wonder why I care so much about the stupid blanket.

Closing my eyes, I slowly open them again, trying to bring everything back into focus, but it's so dark. Last I remember, the sky was still light, though the sun was fading fast. How much time has passed? What happened to me? How did I get into Rhett's car?

Maybe I should ask him and find out.

"What's going on?" I ask, my voice hoarse. I clear my throat and rise up on my elbows, glancing around. His car is so nice, so expensive. The seats are real leather and butter-soft, while I'm a cheap imitation of a person.

"Oh, hey. You're awake." He smiles over at me, then flicks his chin toward the center console. "There's a bottle of water in there. Hope you don't mind that I took it out of your bag. And if you want to lift the seat up, there's a button you can hit on the base of the seat on the right side."

I do as he suggests, raising the seat so I'm sitting upright like a normal person. My throat is dry—it's like I can't stop trying to clear it—so I reach for the bottle of water and crack it open, taking a long swallow. My head feels so heavy, it hurts. And I still can't figure out how I got into this car.

A weird thought enters my brain and lingers. What if Rhett—*did* something to me while I was out?

No. He would never do that. Ever.

"Thank you for the water. And for rescuing me," I finally say, hating how my voice cracks.

He shoots me a quick look, his gaze full of concern. "How are you feeling?"

"I'm okay." I shrug, then wince. "My head hurts."

"You almost cracked it on the sidewalk."

"Really?"

"Yeah, you fainted, but I caught you before you hit the ground."

"I don't remember doing that," I whisper.

"That's because you were out before I caught you."

"Oh." I don't know what to say or how to explain myself. Instead, I take another sip of water and stare out the passenger-side window.

"Have you been sick? Maybe that's why you fainted?" Rhett asks. I hear the concern in his voice, and I want to tell him I don't deserve it.

"I've fainted before." My father told me my mother used to faint sometimes too. Maybe it runs in the family. "Usually I faint because I'm tired or hungry. Or stressed." Yeah definitely stressed.

"Maybe you fainted because you're worried about your grandma."

I close my eyes and press my forehead against the window, the cold glass relieving my heated embarrassment. I'm so tired of the lies. Tired of pretending. "My grandma's fine," I croak.

"What?" He sounds incredulous.

Sitting up, I turn to look at him. "I don't even think I have a grandma. Not one that I know, at least."

"Wait a minute." He shakes his head. "Are you telling me you made that all up?"

"Yeah." I turn my head so I don't have to look at him when I say, "I did."

He swings the car to the right so suddenly, my shoulder rams into the door, and I yelp in pain. We're in an empty parking lot and he pulls the car into a slot, throwing it into park before he turns and faces me. "What the hell are you talking about?"

"I made it up. My grandma being sick. There's no grandma

in my life." There's no one in my life. Period.

"You lied to me, then." The disgust in his voice is obvious. Of course he's disgusted. I'm not who I say I am. I'm using him. I'm a whore who fucked him on Friday night and almost let another man fuck me again on Saturday. I don't deserve his kindness, or his help.

Lifting my chin, I keep my gaze on his. "I did."

Rhett blows out a harsh breath and looks away, drumming his fingers on the steering wheel. "Where were you planning on going anyway?"

"Back home."

"Where's home?"

I keep my gaze averted. "I don't want to tell you."

He punches the steering wheel, making me flinch and cower away from him, and the pure misery that crosses his face as he studies me almost makes me feel bad for reacting that way.

But not really. His violent outburst is a good reminder that they're all the same. Even the so-called good ones.

"I should go," I say after a few minutes tick by and no one's talking. I grab my tote and sling it over my shoulder. "Where's my suitcase?"

"In the trunk," Rhett mutters as he leans over and hits the button to open it.

Without a word, I climb out of the car and go to the back, opening the trunk and pulling my ratty old suitcase out. Rhett's suddenly there too, trying to take the suitcase away from me, but I jerk the handle out of his hold.

"There's no way I'm going to leave you here," he starts, but I hold up my hand, silencing him.

"Yes, you are. I don't need a ride from you."

"Jens. You're being ridiculous." He thrusts his fingers through his dark hair, messing it up. God, he's so good-looking. I can admit it now. He's gorgeous. And I like him. Though I shouldn't. He'd only disappoint me in the end.

Looks like I already disappointed him.

"Let me take you wherever you need to go." He hesitates, then seems to go for it. "I wanted to bring you back to my house. You can stay there for as long as you want. I have a guest bed—"

I cut him off. "No." I shake my head. Press my lips together.

Another ragged sigh leaves him, and this time he does get hold of my suitcase, jerking the handle away from me and then tossing it back into the trunk. "Get in the car," he says quietly.

"Rhett—"

"Get in the goddamn car." He slams the trunk shut and stalks around the side of the car, climbing back into the driver's seat. I follow his lead, slipping into the passenger side and closing the door behind me.

"Take me to the bus station," I tell him quietly.

"Jensen…" He sighs my name, the frustration and longing so obvious in his voice. I'm making him crazy. And I would continue to make him crazy if I stuck around.

Not in a good way either.

"Please, Rhett." I pause, swallowing past the lump in my throat. "I can't stay here. I just…I can't."

Without another word, he puts the car in reverse and backs out of the parking spot. We're silent for the entire drive, and I can't even look at him. He hates me. I can feel the anger emanating from him in palpable waves, and I wrap my arms around myself, trying to ward off the sudden chill in the air. His stony silence is agonizing. I'd rather deal with him angry and ranting, calling me names and getting physical with me.

But his total withdrawal, the stiff way he holds himself, how it's like he's become so disinterested in me…it's painful.

Rhett pulls into the bus depot and I'm exiting the car the second he puts it into park. He helps me get my suitcase and hands the heavy tote bag over to me, which I grab and sling over my shoulder.

"Unblock my number and let me know you made it home okay," he demands.

"Sure." I shrug. Like I'm really going to text him.

"You're lying again," he says flatly.

I sigh and shake my head. "I think it's probably best if we cut off all communication. Don't you?"

He shoves his hands into the pockets of his jeans, glaring at me. It's almost like he's in shock, and he doesn't know how to feel about me, or how to react. I've confused the hell out of him with my lies and confessions, and I bet he's wondering why he was interested in me in the first place. Worse, he's probably full of regret over us having sex, and him bringing me those flowers…

The flowers. Where are they? Not that I can take them with me on the bus, but what did he do with them? Are they still in his car? I wish he would've given them to me a few days ago. I wish I could've enjoyed them longer. At the very least, I wish I took a photo of them so I could keep it on my phone forever.

But wishes are for fools, and while yes, I can admit I've been a giant fool lately, I don't have time for wishes or hopes or dreams. That's all a bunch of bullshit. I need to move on.

I need to leave this town—and Rhett—and never come back.

"I should go." I hitch the tote bag's strap up higher on my shoulder. "I need to go buy my bus ticket."

"Yeah. Good luck." He turns and walks toward his car, and this time, I let him go. I watch his retreating back, my gaze fixed on him as he climbs into the car, starts it, and pulls away from the curb.

My vision gets blurry, sending me into panic mode, and I realize quick it's because I'm crying.

Blinking rapidly, I grab my suitcase and enter the bus station. It's quiet, only a few people are sitting on the benches in the lobby, and I go to the desk, ready to purchase my ticket back home.

The lady is nice as she tries to help me find the cheapest route, and all I can do is smile and tell her thank you through the tears. I think she feels bad for me.

I feel bad for me, too.

"Will that be cash or charge, hon?"

"Cash." I dig through my tote, searching for the ugly flowered cosmetics bag, but I can't seem to find it. Frowning, I pull everything out of the tote, item by item. My snacks, the bottles of water, my crappy wallet that has maybe twenty bucks inside yet no credit cards, my phone, my actual cosmetics bag full of makeup, and all the other crap that's rolling around in there.

But there's no bag of money.

It's fucking gone.

"Shit," I mutter as I prop my elbows on the counter and rest my head in my hands. Where did it go? Did it fall out of my bag and in Rhett's car? Or did it fall out when I fainted in Rhett's arms? For all I know it could be lying in the gutter right in front of my crappy rental, ripe for the picking.

A wave of nausea washes over me, and I swallow hard. That was *so* much money, at least to me. How could I have lost it?

"Everything okay?" the ticket clerk asks.

I shake my head as I start shoving all my stuff back into my tote bag. "I don't have enough money to pay for the ticket." My voice is shaking and I'm going to start full on balling soon,

I swear.

"Aw, honey. Are you sure?" Her kindness is going to break me.

"Yeah. It's okay, though. I'll be fine." I sniff. "I'm gonna call my friend, see if I can get some help." Feeling numb, I head outside, dragging my suitcase behind me, and I settle on the bench right in front of the station. I cry for a little bit, letting my sadness consume me.

What the hell am I going to do now?

Wiping at my eyes, I glance up to find Rhett's car sitting in front of the bus station. I blink a couple of times, like maybe I'm dreaming this, but nope. His car is still there.

I can't believe it.

He rolls down the passenger side window, his expression contrite when his gaze meets mine. My jaw drops open as we stare at each other. I can't believe he came back for me. *Me.* Everyone leaves. They don't care about me. They never did.

Rhett cares. I don't understand why, but he does.

We keep watching each other for what feels like forever, and then he's climbing out of the car and I'm running toward him, abandoning my suitcase like an idiot. We meet each other on the sidewalk and he pulls me into his arms, his mouth at my ear as he squeezes me tight.

"Come home with me, Jens," he whispers and I nod, too choked up to actually answer him.

NINETEEN

My cosmetics bag full of money isn't in Rhett's car. At least, it's nowhere I can see, and I tried my best to be discreet as I scanned the floorboard where I last had my tote bag. Rhett doesn't say much as we drive back to his place and neither do I, because what can I say?

Tell him I'm sorry for being a lying jerk? It feels pointless to apologize.

When we get to Rhett's house it's dark and quiet, like no one's inside.

"My roommate isn't here," he says as he pulls the car into the garage and puts it in park. He turns to look at me. "Are you okay?"

"Yeah. I'm good." I nod, relieved that his roommate is gone. I'm glad we're alone with no one to bother us. I don't think I can face another person tonight.

I follow Rhett to the back of his car to grab my suitcase and when he opens the trunk, I see my faded cosmetics bag lying there, just beneath my suitcase. My heart racing, I snag it up without him noticing, shoving the beat up old bag into my tote as Rhett grabs my suitcase to bring it inside. The relief that floods me at finding my money is downright overwhelming. As we walk into the house with me trailing behind him, I suddenly feel so tired, so broken down over everything that's happened to me these last few days, I'm afraid I might collapse.

"You should take a shower and go to bed," he tells me as we enter his kitchen, his tone casual, almost indifferent. Like he's merely a friend letting me crash at his place for the night. But maybe that's all he wants us to be now. "You look exhausted."

"I am," I admit as he leads me down the hall, showing me first a giant bathroom and then the guest bedroom, where he leaves my suitcase by the door. I enter the bedroom behind him, dropping my tote bag in the middle of the double bed.

"Well, the bathroom should have everything you need, so…" Rhett's voice drifts and I turn to find him standing there, looking lost. A little uncomfortable.

It hurts, to realize I'm the one making him uncomfortable. I royally fucked this up, and there's no way I can fix it.

"Thank you, Rhett," I say softly. "For rescuing me. Again."

He nods, stuffing his hands in his front pockets. "I know you probably don't want to talk about it."

Yeah. I so don't.

"But I just want you to know that whatever's—going wrong in your life right now, it can be fixed. I know it can." The sincerity written all over his face is sweet.

It's also pointless. What's gone wrong in my life can't be fixed. If he ever finds out what I intended to do to him and his family, he'll hate me forever.

"That's all I'm going to say," he continues when I don't respond. "So…good night, Jensen."

He turns and walks out of the guest bedroom, and I let him go.

Heaving a big sigh, I throw my suitcase on the bed and open it, picking out some clothes to change into before I head to the bathroom. I find the shower fully stocked with soap and shampoo but no conditioner, yet I can't complain. I hop into the giant shower and wash the bus station filth off of me, hoping the shame and sadness I feel slides down the drain too. The water is super-hot and the pressure is perfect, so I stand under that shower head for an extra ten minutes and savor it.

I'm out of the shower and slathering lotion all over my still damp skin when I realize this is the second shower I've taken tonight. This has felt like the longest day of my life, I swear. I need to go to sleep and start over tomorrow. Maybe Rhett and I can talk more then. Maybe I can confess more too, but never the whole truth.

I can't risk it.

When I open the bathroom door and see no lights on at

all except for the guest bedroom lamp, I realize Rhett's gone to bed without saying good night to me.

That hurts too.

Everything he seems to do to me tonight hurts, even though I know he's not trying to hurt me on purpose. More than anything, I crave his approval. I want him to like me. He came back for me, so that's got to mean something, right?

I dump my stuff back in my suitcase and then crawl into bed, shutting off the lamp with a loud click in the otherwise silent house. I lay there for what feels like hours, staring up at the ceiling, thinking bad thoughts, wondering if Rhett's blissfully asleep without a care in the world.

I hope like crazy he's tossing and turning just like me.

When I can't stand it any longer, I slip out of bed and make my way toward the closed door at the end of the hall.

Slowly opening the door, I spy Rhett lying flat on his back in the middle of his giant bed. He must've heard me enter the room because he sits straight up, the sheet falling to his waist and I can see he's shirtless, his hair disheveled.

My entire body goes on high alert at seeing his broad shoulders, his defined chest. I want to touch him, feel his skin on mine, his mouth and tongue…

"Can't sleep?" His voice is scratchy. Sexy.

I stop at the foot of his bed, feeling exposed since I'm wearing an old, oversized T-shirt that barely covers my butt and nothing else. Not even a pair of panties.

Honestly? I 'forgot' to wear panties on purpose. I knew I was going to do this.

With Rhett, when it comes to us, I have no shame.

"Yeah," I finally say.

"Want to join me?" He flips the covers back and I don't even bother answering. I just climb into his bed and snuggle up to him with my head resting on his chest, sighing with happiness when he tugs the covers over us before wrapping his arm around my shoulders and pulling me even closer.

We remain silent and I let my hand wander across his chest, fingers skimming down his stomach. He's touching me too, one hand sliding up and down my back, the other hand toying with the hem of my shirt. His muscles quiver beneath my fingertips and feeling emboldened, I move further south.

To discover he's completely naked.

"Rhett," I whisper, trying to sound outraged, even though I'm not. Of course I'm not. This is exactly what I want. "You don't have any clothes on."

"Yeah, well you're not wearing panties." To prove his point, he reaches beneath my shirt, his fingers grazing my pubic hair.

My legs automatically part for him and then he's touching me, stroking me. I was already wet in anticipation of this and his fingers find my clit, his thumb circling it at the exact moment his mouth finds mine. The kiss is sloppy, all open mouths and searching tongues and mingled gasps and moans. His long fingers feel so fucking good and I strain toward his touch, another gasp escaping me when he strokes my clit just right.

"I want to be inside you," he whispers against my mouth and I moan in agony when his fingers disappear. He grabs hold of my waist and next thing I know I'm on top of him, my legs spread across his hips, his hard cock between my legs. I grab the base of him and guide him into position, sinking on top of his cock slowly, the both of us moaning in pleasure as he enters me.

"Looks like you got what you wanted," I tell him, smiling when he arches beneath me, sending his cock even deeper.

Rhett impatiently grabs at my T-shirt and I take it off, yanking it over my head and tossing it onto the floor. His hands go for my breasts, assured fingers stroking my nipples as I start to ride him. He's so deep, seemingly hitting every pleasurable nerve ending within me and I toss my head back, my hair trailing behind me as I bob and sway.

"Jesus, you're beautiful," he murmurs, his hands going to my hips, guiding my movements. "I could fuck you like this all night."

A thrill moves down my spine at his words. Sweet, respectful Rhett knows just what to say when he's inside me, I'll give him that.

"Go faster, baby," he urges and I increase my pace, crying out when he nudges one particular spot. It feels so good. So, so good. I move faster, faster, faster…

"Oh God," I gasp when the orgasm washes over me, making me shiver. I'm a trembling, moaning mess and he flips me over so I'm on my back and he's fucking me hard, driving me into the mattress, my entire body still shaking from my orgasm as he pounds into me.

And then he's coming too. He moans my name, his mouth on my neck, his hips still working as he spills himself inside me. I swear another, smaller orgasm hits me, and I clutch him close, savoring the feeling of the two of us coming.

Together.

"Goddamn," he whispers against my neck when he seems to find himself again. "That was amazing."

I start to laugh. I can't help it. The utter relief of him still wanting me has left me spent.

Happy.

He lifts up on his elbows so he can look at me, an arrogant yet adorable smirk curving his mouth. "You wanna do that again?"

I shift beneath him, enjoying how we're still connected. He didn't wear a condom, but I'm on the pill. Probably stupid and reckless and I hope to hell he doesn't have a STD, but right now, in this moment, I don't care.

"Jens?"

"Yes," I say when I realize I haven't answered him. I drop a kiss on his damp with sweat chest before I say, "Let's do that again."

So we do. We do it again and again. We fuck all night, and Rhett's right. It's amazing. I let him use me, and he lets me use him. He takes me from behind, his hands gripping my hips as he pushes deep inside me, making me come so hard I see stars. I get on my knees while he sits on the edge of the bed and I give him a blow job. He spreads me wide and licks me until I'm pulling on his hair and screaming his name.

And finally, when it's around three in the morning and Rhett is fast asleep, I slip out of his bed and stand next to it, watching him for a while. He's lying on his stomach, the sheet draped across the back of his calves, exposing his perfect butt and smooth, muscular back. His eyes are tightly closed, his dark hair a complete mess and his cheeks are covered with dark stubble.

He's gorgeous. And for one more night, he belonged to me.

I make my way back to the guest bedroom and change into a pair of jeans and a sweatshirt. I sent out a text to Savannah right before I took that shower, letting her know Rhett's address and begging her to come pick me up when she's done with work.

She sent me a text a few minutes ago saying she was waiting outside for me.

Quietly I make my way out of his house, hoping Rhett will forgive me for not locking the door. I head for Savannah's car and she gets out, opening the trunk for me so I can put my things inside.

"You sure you want to do this?" she asks after she carefully shuts the trunk.

I frown at her. "What do you mean?" I'm tired. I'm sore. And I'm really not in the mood for conversation right now.

"You really want to sneak out and leave whoever it is inside that house?" She waves a hand toward Rhett's house and I glance over my shoulder, hating the longing that seems to spread through me.

"It's the right thing to do," I tell her once I'm facing her. "In the end, I'll just bring him down, and he'll hate me."

That's the absolute truth.

She sends me a pointed look but says nothing. Neither do I. We get in her car and she drives me away from Rhett.

I cry silent tears all the way to her place.

TWENTY

"You're going to be okay to work tonight, right?" Savannah asks as we walk into the club.

Nodding, I head straight for the time clock and punch in, Savannah right behind me. "Yeah. I need everything to get back to normal, you know?"

I can't sit around and feel sorry for myself any longer. I need to forget what happened with Greg the creep, and I definitely need to forget about Rhett and my plans to ruin him and his family.

Yeah, I was selfish taking that one last night with him, but I thought it might get Rhett out of my system.

Instead, I think it made everything worse. He's all I can think about. I'm fucking obsessed.

It sucks.

I also couldn't stand the thought of going back to my

house in the crappy neighborhood and staying there alone. Rhett could find me there, too, and that's the last thing I want. Savannah's letting me stay at her place, thank goodness. She said I could stay as long as I wanted, which was a huge mistake. At the rate I'm going, I'll never leave, but I'm grateful for her friendship.

I went back to school, trying my best to catch up on my assignments, and begging my professors to let me retake a couple of tests I missed. I thought I would give up on the college dream, but what else am I going to do? I already spent all my money on my education, so I need to see this semester through. What I'll do after the semester ends, though, I'm not sure.

I'll worry about that later.

Don is glad to see me back at work, I can tell just by the look on his face, and I let him embrace me for a brief moment before I extract myself from his beefy arms.

"You're looking good, doll," he murmurs, his expression sincere. "I was worried you wouldn't come back."

"She shouldn't come back," Savannah says, coming to stand right beside me. "Not after what happened."

At least Don looks contrite. "Never again. I promise we won't let something like that happen," he says firmly. "We're planning on establishing more strict rules at the club. There will be a meeting about it soon."

The moment he walks away, Savannah rolls her eyes.

"Right. He's too greedy to not take money from customers for 'extra' services. He's just saying that because he feels guilty."

I don't respond. Honestly, I don't want to talk about what happened to me. I'd rather forget it ever happened in the first place. Scrub it from my brain forever.

"Seriously, Jen, what are you going to do if that guy shows back up here?" Savannah asks as we walk over to our lockers. "He could, you know." She's referring to Greg.

"He won't," I say firmly, just as I swing my locker door open. Maybe if I believe what I'm saying, it won't happen.

Yet I can't help but have those thoughts. He could totally show up here whenever he wants, and what would I do? Scream and run? Kick him in the nuts and call him an asshole? Call the cops?

I can't do any of that. So I have to keep believing Greg is never going to come back to City Lights again.

"He might," Savannah says, ever the positive thinker. "I swear I've seen that guy around here before."

Curiosity gets the best of me and I have to ask, despite my wish to never talk about him again. "Do you think he's a regular?"

"Maybe? I'm not sure." Savannah takes off her T-shirt and tosses it into the locker. "After a while, they all start to look the same, I swear."

"I didn't recognize him." Though there was something about him that was oddly familiar. So maybe Greg is a regular?

A semi-regular? "I didn't realize you saw him that night."

"Yeah. I did." Savannah shuts her locker door, her gaze locking on mine. "I saw you taking care of his table. He was originally at one of my tables, but when I came to take their drink orders, he asked for you specifically."

Unease slips down my spine, leaving me cold. "What do you mean? Did he request me by name?"

"Yeah." Savannah tilts her head to the side, frowning. "Or maybe not. Now I can't remember."

"Try your best to remember." How would he know who I was? And why would he request me? It makes no sense. Unless he's some sort of crazed stalker.

"I'm not sure." Savannah offers a helpless shrug. "Maybe he didn't ask for you by name. Maybe he just thought you were cute. Did Don say anything?"

"No, not really." I shake my head. Though I do remember being confused when Don told me I needed to serve that table, since that section wasn't one I usually worked.

"So weird." Savannah smiles weakly. "Guess that Greg guy knew he wanted you from the start."

Her words fill me with dread. "I suppose so."

"Girls, quit your chatting and head on out. It's gonna be extra busy tonight. We've got a big group of guys celebrating a bachelor party coming in," Don says, clapping his hands at us like we're a pack of dogs he's trying to get rid of. "Hurry up! Get out there!"

We head out without protest, Savannah and I going our separate ways the moment we hit the floor. I paste on my best fake smile as I push through the crowd, moving toward the bar. I grab one of the empty trays from the counter, ignoring Chuck's sympathetic gaze. I don't need anyone to feel bad for me tonight, even if they have good intentions.

I've got this.

But the thought of Greg specifically requesting me to work his table that night hangs heavy like a dark, thunderous cloud over my head as I go through the motions with my customers. I'm jumpy, nervous. Constantly glancing over my shoulder. I tell myself everything's going to be okay, but it's hard to focus.

Thankfully, Don was right. The club is extra busy, and the guests are incredibly loud, especially the bachelor party, which is made up of at least thirty men, maybe more. Catcalling their appreciation for every dancer on the stage, shouting their approval when they purchase the groom-to-be a lap dance. The guys aren't very old—they actually look close to my age—and as I watch the future groom laugh while the stripper grinds on his crotch, I wonder what it's like to know you've found the love of your life by the time you're in your mid-twenties.

I can't even wrap my head around that concept.

Thinking of love leads me to think of Rhett, which is the biggest waste of my time. I never did unblock his number so he could contact me, and I bet he's so mad at me. Though really, why would he care? I'm just a bump in the road of his life, a girl he messed around with for a brief moment in time. He'll never know what I intended, or how I wanted to ruin him and his family.

And that's okay. Giving up on my revenge plot was the right thing to do. I don't have the energy to go after my mother any longer. I feel defeated. Alone.

Adrift.

The bachelor party grows even bigger, and Don asks me to help the servers who've been working it the entire night, including Savannah. I find her at the bar filling another order, her hair falling out of her ponytail and her cheeks pink. She's totally frazzled.

"Tell me how you want me to help," I say.

She blows the wayward strands of hair out of her face, a grateful smile curling her lips. "A new group of dudes just showed up and they ordered a round of tequila shots. They're at table nine. If you could take the shots to them while I handle the bachelor and all his buddies at their table, I'd really appreciate it."

"No problem." I turn to Chuck to let him know that I'm the one taking over the shots order. He loads up my tray with eight shot glasses of the most expensive tequila we've got, plus a small bowl of limes and a shaker of salt.

I lift the tray above my head as I wind my way between the crowded tables. The music is extra loud since there's a girl up on the stage performing, and the lights are flashing in time to the beat. I can feel men's eyes lingering on my bare chest as I walk past them, and my arms suddenly feel wobbly, like I might drop the entire tray at any moment. My heart starts to race and my breathing gets short.

Relax, I remind myself as I take a deep breath. *You've done this five nights a week for months. Don't let the bullshit get in your head and cause you to mess up.*

Thankfully, the panic attack leaves me as swiftly as it arrived, and I end up at table nine, my fake smile extra big as I greet the guys waiting enthusiastically for their drinks. I can barely make out their features thanks to the flashing lights, and I mentally pray they aren't a bunch of rude assholes.

"Who ordered tequila shots?" I ask, smiling when they all start hooting and hollering, shouting *me* over and over again.

With a nervous laugh, I start handing out the shot glasses, leaning over a little bit to let them get a look at my tits. I realize quick they're young, and they're respectful, and I can tell this might be the first visit to a strip club for some of these guys, the ones who seem nervous and can barely look at me. There's no leering, rude older men contemplating how they might touch me sitting at this particular table tonight. I almost feel…

Comfortable.

I offer them the bowl of limes and the saltshaker and they thank me profusely, most of their gazes still locked on my chest, but they don't bother me. For some reason, I can tell these guys are harmless.

The stripper on stage finally ends her performance to much applause, meaning it's the end of the constant flashing lights, and I go to grab my empty tray, turning back toward the bar when I spot a familiar face in the crowd.

My heart drops into my stomach.

He sees me too. There's confusion etched all over his handsome face, his big brown eyes going wide when they land on me. I immediately hold the tray in front of my naked torso like some sort of shield, and I swear I see him mouth my name.

Jensen?

No.

It can't be.

It's Rhett Montgomery. Rhett Montgomery is at City Lights.

And he's headed in my direction.

HIS
WASTED
HEART

ONE

She's topless. In a strip club.

Jensen. The girl who haunts my dreams is topless in a strip club.

What the is my future girlfriend doing topless in a strip club?

I come to a complete stop when I spot her. My friend and roommate Chad, who brought me here tonight, keeps talking, rambling on about strippers.

"These girls take it off," Chad says, his voice extra loud. "And I mean of it. Fully naked. You see everything. Tits and ass and a pretty little kitty cat." He starts laughing at his crude joke.

I stop listening. Instead, I grab Chad, giving him a look that makes him shut up. Maybe I even stop fucking breathing. Because there she is. Like out of a wet dream. And I was lucky enough to have under me. In my bed. Wrapped all around me.

Every man is staring at her as she walks through the room, like a partially naked sex nymph with a come-hither look in her eyes. She's like every sexual fantasy come to life. Gorgeous and confident and half-naked, coming right for you.

That's Jensen.   Jensen.

Turns out, it's not so hot in real life, when there are a ton of guys wanting pussy looking at the same thing you are.

And the more I study Jensen, the more I realize she doesn't have a come-hither look on her face. She's so distracted, she hasn't even seen me yet.

But I see her. Hell, I see only her, all of her. Her gorgeous tits—tits I've kissed and sucked. Her bare shoulders. Her slender, toned arms.

My blood boils in my veins. No, with lust. Wait. No. This feeling is too damn primitive for that. My fists clench at my sides. I want to punch something, but I don't know who to punch, or what. Even if I knew, I'm not sure I could do it.

It's like one of those moments in a movie, when you're frozen in place yet life continues on around you. You can't move, even though someone is calling your name and strangers are bumping into you as they pass by.

That moment is happening to me. Right now. I've just walked into a crowded strip club on a Saturday night and the first person I see is the girl I fucked not even a week ago.

The same girl who slipped out of my bed in the middle of

the night, never to be seen again.

The same girl I thought was mine.

A toxic mixture of anger and shock swirls within me and I whisper, "Jensen," in a low growl of disbelief, though I know she can't hear me. But now she definitely sees me. I can tell from the surprised expression on her beautiful face that I'm the last person she expected to be here tonight.

Well, the feeling's mutual, babe.

The black skirt she has on is extra-short and skintight, and the heels she's wearing are sky-high. She's carrying an empty tray—really holding it in front of her as if I won't notice the fact that she's not wearing a shirt—like she works here.

I slowly shake my head, the realization sinking in. I'm fairly certain she   work at this club. Hell, I sound like a dumbass in my own head, but that's how slow I'm processing everything.

"Bro, what's your problem? Let's go. They're waiting for us." Chad—who's older brother is the guy having the bachelor party we're here for tonight—nudges me in the ribs with his elbow. "Our table is over there." He points in the table's direction, and I see a bunch of guys with flushed faces sitting around a giant table covered with empty glasses.

It takes everything within me to tear my gaze away from Jensen's, but I somehow manage it. I can still sense her watching me as I follow Chad over to the table, and anger fills me with every step. Seriously, what the hell is she doing here? What made her think it was a smart choice to work at a freaking strip club? And why didn't she tell me?

I almost snort out loud. That girl didn't tell me shit. And when she did talk to me, it feels like everything that came out of her mouth was most likely a lie. She's a liar.

Fake.

It's embarrassing to realize that the sexy girl I've been chasing after for the last month has constantly lied and tricked me. That she works at a strip club as a topless cocktail waitress. If my fraternity brothers found out about this, they'd all be high-fiving me and asking if I get free lap dances. Then they'd probably ask how   could get free lap dances.

Bastards.

I quickly glance over my shoulder as we make our way to the table and find Jensen still watching me. I immediately look away. Anger and curiosity go to war within me, and I wonder which one will win. My guess?

Anger.

In general, I'm a pretty easygoing person. I get along with everyone. I was popular in high school, and I know why—I'm not a judgmental asshole. Yeah, my circumstances could've made me a total snob, but I didn't let that happen. So my dad is worth a lot of money. So what? I've never let that define me. I never tried to get anywhere because I'm Parker Montgomery's son. My older brother—our father's namesake—uses that shit whenever and wherever to get what he wants. My little sister is too sweet to do that sort of thing.

And then there's me. The typical middle child who wants everyone to like him.

Right now, though? I don't give a shit. I'm freaking If I'm being totally honest with myself, I'm also hurt. But thinking like that makes me feel like a total baby, so I shove all my hurt little feelings aside and focus on my anger instead.

When we reach our table, they all greet us with drunken shouts and Chad's older brother Emmett jumps up to pull him into a bear hug. Chad immediately pushes him away, but they're both laughing and slapping each other on the back. When the bro fest is over, we head for the last remaining empty chairs to settle in.

I'm thrown by seeing Jensen, but determined to have a good time tonight. We're celebrating Emmett's last days as a free man, and though I don't know him that well, it's a big deal.

I refuse to let that girl ruin my good time.

"You guys want drinks?" Emmett asks as we sit.

Chad nods enthusiastically. "Hell yeah."

"We just placed another order with the waitress, but she's moving pretty fast, so it should only be a few minutes." Emmett grins and leans in closer, his voice lowering. "You should see the tits on this chick. They're pretty amazing."

My blood boils, but I smile in response. I'm guessing he's talking about Jensen. I don't want to think about anyone else looking at her naked breasts, but I guess that's not up to me anymore, is it?

"You ever been here before?" Chad asks me as he looks around the crowded room.

"Nope." I shake my head. This sort of place isn't my typical scene. I sound like an asshole, but I don't need to go to a strip club to see naked girls. Hell, go to a sorority party on a Friday night and you'll see all sorts of topless girls by the end of the evening. You won't even have to pay a cover charge.

"Me either," Chad says with a grin, flicking his head toward the stage. "But so far, I like what I see."

The music is blaring, bright lights flashing in time with the beat, and there's some hot mostly-naked girl writhing around on the stage. She's clad in a red G-string and nothing else, her enormous boobs swinging as she sways to the music. She tosses her head, her long black hair sweeping across her shoulders, and when she draws closer to the guys sitting by the stage, one of them leaps to his feet to stuff a twenty in her G-string. He snaps the waistband, his fingers lingering on her bare hip, and she flashes him a look, wagging her finger at him as she gracefully backs away from him to resume her dance.

"Hope you brought lots of extra dollar bills," Chad says as he starts to laugh. I like my roommate, but he's rarely as funny as he thinks he is. "I know I have plans on stuffing them in more than a few G-strings tonight."

"Go ahead and get started then," I say, waving my hand toward the stage. The stripper's fingers are curled around the thin waistband of her nonexistent panties, like she's ready to shed them at any moment. "Looks like she's still working for them."

With a dirty smile stretching his lips, Chad takes off toward the stage, waving a fiver at the stripper, though she's not even looking at him. Rolling my eyes, I turn back toward the table just in time to watch Jensen make her approach with a full tray of drinks.

"Here you go, boys," she calls, her voice ringing hollow despite the forced cheer. She starts dispensing drinks, every single guy at the table staring at her chest, with the exception of me.

Been there, done that.

"Hey, we have some new guys who just showed up," Emmett tells Jensen, his eyes going from her face to her tits in rapid-fire motion. "You want a drink, right, Chad?"

He's not even paying enough attention to us to realize Chad isn't at the table. "Chad will be right back," I tell Emmett, who grimaces when he looks my way. "And yeah, I definitely want a drink." My gaze lands on Jensen, and she guiltily averts her head.

The anger simmers in my blood as I watch her, and I think of all the shitty things I could say to her. She'd deserve it too, for all the lies she told me. Did she tell me anything that was true? Or was it all a bunch of crap?

I don't even know anymore.

Chad miraculously reappears, sweat beading his forehead

and a glazed look in his eyes. He collapses in the chair next to mine. "I want a beer and a tequila shot," he tells Jensen's chest.

"Hold on little brother," Emmett says, amusement in voice. "Let her give everyone else their drinks first."

Jensen seems to move extra slow as she hands out the rest of the drinks, and I remain stiff, trying my best to look indifferent as she draws closer. Her nearness is unsettling. I can smell her familiar sweet scent, and it both arouses me and pisses me off.

The last time I was with her, I was balls-deep inside her tight little body, savoring the way she touched me, how she called my name when I made her come. That night had been amazing. Unbelievable. I think I came three times, maybe four. And I'm pretty certain I made her come at least five times…

"What would you like?" Jensen's voice interrupts my dirty thoughts, and I glance up at her, my gaze narrowed. I can't think about what she looks like when she comes, or how beautiful she was that night. Her naked skin flushed, her lips swollen, her nipples hard and damp from my mouth.

Yeah. Can't think about any of that.

"What beer do you have on tap?" I lift my brows, silently daring her to say something more. Is she really not going to acknowledge that we know each other?

Am I also going to sit here and pretend I don't know her?

Looks like it.

She rattles off a few different beers, her voice shaky, and I choose one of the local IPAs, the bot of us looking past each other. Like strangers. She takes down my order and Chad's, and I watch her as she walks away, heading toward the bar.

"She's hot," Chad says.

"Uh huh."

"She was giving you the look."

I turn my head, glaring at Chad. "What do you mean?" What is he talking about? We barely made eye contact.

"She kept…I don't know,   at you. Like she was interested." He shrugs. "Maybe you should go for it. She's got a great body."

"I don't go for skanks who work at strip clubs," I sneer. The moment the words leave me, I feel like shit. Because I actually go for skanks who work at strip clubs.

I just didn't realize it until tonight.

TWO

An hour later I'm exiting the bathroom to find Jensen waiting for me in the darkened hall, biting her lower lip.

A week ago, I would've found that gesture sexy as hell. Right now, I wonder if she's putting on an act. Ready to play me yet again.

"Rhett—" she starts, but I cut her off by raising my hand and practically putting it in her face.

"Not interested," I say gruffly as I try to walk past her.

She puts herself right in my path, and the hall is narrow, so I would have to physically move her out of my way to get past her. Meaning I'm stuck. "Listen, I just want to explain a few things."

I can hardly look at her I'm so annoyed, but I do. And then I tell myself to stare at her real hard. She's got a lot of makeup on, especially around her eyes. Thick black eyeliner and lots of mascara, and her lips are painted a deep blood-red. Her skin shines and sparkles, like she sprayed herself with some kind of glitter lotion, and all at once, I'm disgusted. Disappointed. In her myself.

I don't know how to deal with her. I don't want to deal with her right now. I'd rather lose myself in alcohol for the rest of the night and forget my troubles.

Instead I'm stuck in a dark hallway with a girl I still care about, even though I know I shouldn't.

"What do you want to explain, huh? How you lied to me? How you told me a bunch of bullshit stories about your life and what you do?" I step closer but she never backs down. Instead, she tilts her head back, her gaze locked on mine, appearing fully prepared to take what I have to say. "I tried to help you, Jens. I brought you to my house that night and I was perfectly willing to do whatever it took to be there for you."

Like a fucking sucker. What was her real plan on getting to know me? Was she using me because I'm rich?

She still hasn't said anything. She's just watching me with those big blue eyes, now shiny with— —tears.

"And you still ran out on me," I finish, my voice bitter. I hate hearing that bitterness. Makes me think I actually cared.

Damn it, I did care, I just don't want her to know it. Not anymore.

"I know," she whispers, blinking up at me. "I messed up,

okay? I didn't mean to hurt you. Well…"

Her voice drifts and I'm confused. What does she mean by that 'well'? I've had a few drinks, a couple of shots, so I'm full on buzzin'. And confused.

Jensen licks the corner of her lips, sexy as hell even though I'm so freaking mad at her. "I just…Rhett, I'm—sorry." She practically chokes that last word out.

"You're only apologizing because you got caught," I mutter, grabbing her by her naked shoulders and gently pushing her out of my way so I can walk past her.

"Rhett, please!" she calls after me.

"I don't want to hear it!" I yell over my shoulder, picking up my stride as I head back toward the table. I fall into the seat next to Chad and he claps me on the back, a goofy grin on his face.

"You're just in time for the next act," he says, his gaze hazy and unfocused. He is so fucking drunk.

But then again, so am I.

"Ladies and gentlemen, please welcome…"

The lights go dark and the stage is lit with a single spotlight. A woman in a black slinky dress is on stage, sitting on a chair. The entire crowd is quiet, rapt with attention as the music starts, and the woman slowly rises from the chair and begins to move.

Minutes pass as I watch her, already bored, my mind filled with thoughts of Jensen. How sad she looked only a few minutes ago, her eyes filling with tears, that bullshit apology falling from her pouty lips. I don't know what to believe. I don't know what to think. I want to hate her, but sitting here just thinking about her, I can feel it taking over me.

The wanting.

Damn it. I scrub a hand across my face, annoyed. I still want her. I'm still attracted to her. It's ridiculous, but it's there, staring me right in the face.

And I don't know what to do about it.

Glancing up, I find her leaning against the wall not too far from our table. She's watching me. And there's a hunger in her eyes that matches mine. Her chest rises and falls rapidly, and my gaze drops to her chest. Her breasts. I swear her nipples harden just from me staring at them. And when my gaze lifts to meet hers once more, I can see her hunger has intensified.

So has mine.

Without thought I rise from my chair, my gaze still never leaving hers.

"Where you going?" Chad asks, his words slurred from too much alcohol.

"I'll be right back," I answer, not even looking at him.

I'm too busy looking at Jensen.

I walk toward her slowly, the sensual beat of the music driving me on. I send her a knowing look, a quick flick of my head to indicate where I want her to go. Chancing a glance over my shoulder, I see she follows me, until we're both back in that darkened hallway we just vacated, tucked away in the deepest, darkest corner.

Where no one can find us.

"Did you want to talk to me?" she asks breathlessly as she turns to face me.

Without a word I grab hold of her slender waist and press her back against the wall. A gasp escapes her, her mouth curling into a small, satisfied smile just before she opens it to say something.

I rest the palm of my hand over her blood-red lips, shutting her up. "Don't talk," I whisper. "I don't want to hear your excuses."

Her eyes are wide as my hand continues to cover half of her face. She slowly nods, a little whimper escaping her when I lean in and nuzzle the side of her neck.

Christ, she smells so good. I run my lips across her skin, lightly, just a tease, and a jolt moves through her, as if I electrified her. I keep my hand in place, and I can feel her lips moving, her damp breaths against my fingers. I nudge my hips against hers, letting her feel what she does to me, and she moans, an agonized sound contained by my hand.

That sound goes straight to my dick.

"I shouldn't do this," I murmur close to her ear. She shivers and I kiss her there, just below her lobe, my mouth lingering as I breathe her in.

I know I shouldn't do this. Touch her. Kiss her. I said it out loud in the hopes I'd convince myself this is wrong. I fucking it's wrong.

But right now, at this moment, I don't care. I'm too caught up.

Caught up in her.

My hand drops from her mouth and she takes a deep breath, her lips parting, mine crashing down on hers to shut her up before she says something to ruin the moment. I kiss her fiercely, thrusting my tongue in her mouth, my hands wandering along her waist, her hips. She returns the kiss with equal, hungry force, a whimper escaping her when I cup her left tit, my thumb strumming the already hard tip. My mouth waters, and I tear my lips from hers to bend over her chest and suck and lick her nipple.

She thrusts her hands in my hair, holding me there, keeping me there, like she never wants me to leave. I cup her ass and break away from tasting her skin to lift her up. She automatically wraps her legs around me, her skirt riding up her thighs as she presses her heels into my ass. Wincing from the pain, I hold her against the wall, my erection nudging her right between her legs, and I swear I can feel her panties and her hot pussy beneath.

I'm losing control. Right here in the hallway by the bathrooms in a seedy strip club. I want to fuck Jensen against the wall, thrust deep inside her welcoming body, and damn the consequences.

"Rhett," she whispers, her hands greedy as they reach for me. She grabs hold of my face and brings my head down so our mouths are mere inches away from each other. "Please. Kiss me."

I do as she asks, drowning in her taste, in the swirl of our tongues, our bodies straining against each other. I'm drunk as hell and messed up in the head over this woman.

This has to stop.

I break the kiss and she clutches my hair tighter. "No," she whispers against my lips, her tongue darting out for a lick. "Don't stop. Please."

It takes everything I've got to lower her back to her feet. Tug her skirt back into place. Release my hold on her and step away.

I'm shaking. She's quivering. Our panting breaths fill the tiny space. Her nipple is still wet from my mouth and my cock presses against the fly of my jeans, horny and ready to slip inside her.

But I can't. Not like this. Not here.

Maybe never again.

"You still want me," she says, sounding surprised.

Her statement pisses me off. What does she think, that I'm inhuman? I can't turn my feelings on and off like a light switch. I   about her. I   her that.

Yet she's still surprised I want her.

"Of course I do. I mean, look at you." I wave a careless hand in her direction, trying to play this off. Trying my damnedest to be as callous and unfeeling as she seems. "Who wouldn't want you? You're walking around with hardly any clothes on, with your tits hanging out. They   want you." I run a hand through my hair, trying to fix the mess she made with her fingers, trying to play this entire thing off.

Though deep down, I know what I just said was my way to try and hurt her.

The look Jensen gives me is full of so much pain, that I immediately feel like an asshole.

But by the time I can find my voice to correct my wrongs, she's already gone.

♥   ♥   ♥

"You missed   performance of the night," Chad tells me when I return to the table.

I say nothing, reaching for the first semi-full glass I see. I down the liquid in one long swallow, grimacing when I feel the burn of alcohol slide down my throat like fire. That tasted like absolute shit. "She was that good, huh?" I ask, wiping my mouth with the back of my hand.

My thoughts immediately go to Jensen, and how good she felt in my arms.

But then I remember what I said to her, and I banish her from my brain.

"You just finished my drink, asshole," Chad says incredulously.

I shrug. "I'll buy you another one."

"Yeah, you will," Chad mutters just before he raises his hand. "Hey, sweetheart, get your fine ass over here. I need a drink, stat."

I want to growl in irritation at the way Chad just commanded Jensen. Calling her sweetheart and talking about her fine ass isn't sitting well with me, but what the hell can I say? I can't expose our so-called relationship to him.

Jensen approaches us, her expression unreadable. She's mad. At me. I don't look at her as she asks in the fakest, sweetest voice I've ever heard, "Sir, what would you like?"

"Another scotch. Neat," he tells Jensen with a cocky smile. Then he reaches out and actually palms her ass, like he owns her. "What time you off the clock, babe? Wanna come dance for us?"

"Leave her alone," I mutter, hating how he's treating her, how he's talked about all the women in this club since we got here. I clench my hands into fists and watch with satisfaction as Chad does what I asked, his hand dropping from Jensen as if she'd suddenly turned into a dead body. Now is my time to say something, but how can I? He has no idea I dated this girl, since he's never seen me with her before. And maybe that's for the best.

So I say nothing else. I'm mad at myself. I'm still mad at

her too. And I feel like shit for talking to her like I just did, for mauling her in the hallway like a crazed pervert.

"Rhett." Her voice saying my name startles me, and I glance up to find both Chad and Jensen watching me closely. "You're really going to let your   talk to me like this?"

Didn't she hear me tell him to leave her alone? Or is she trying to call me out in front of Chad?

Chad's eyes practically bug out of his head. "How does she know you, bro? You been keeping secrets or what?"

"I don't know—" I start, but Jensen cuts me off.

"We've fucked a couple of times." She shrugs those pretty bare shoulders, the light catching on the flecks of glitter on her skin, making her sparkle. Like an angel. "No big deal."

I glower at her. This girl is the complete opposite of an angel, I swear.

Chad starts to laugh, so hard that everyone else sitting at the table focuses their attention on us. "Are you serious right now? You've actually fucked this chick, Montgomery? And you never told us? You've been holding out."

"Guess he wanted to keep the good pussy all to himself." Her smile is brittle as she tosses her dark blonde hair over her shoulder and walks away. I can't believe she just said that. And if she was trying to humiliate me or make me feel like a fool, then...

Mission accomplished.

THREE

This is the longest damn night of my life. The guys won't stop giving me shit about Jensen. After the truth bomb she dropped, she sent over another cocktail waitress to serve our table drinks, and they start harassing her, jeering and commenting on her curvaceous body, Chad trying to grab this one's ass too.

But she's not having it. The tall, platinum blonde gives us all a death stare and literally slaps Chad's hand away from her butt when he tries to cup it.

"Touch me again and I'll break your fingers," she says, punctuating her vicious statement with a sweet smile.

The look Chad sends her when she walks away tells me he might still be a little in lust. I guess he likes them mean.

Jensen never comes back to our table, and I'm thankful. It's bad enough, all the questions I'm fielding about her the moment she left. Doesn't help that Chad blabbed to everyone that, His big mouth needs to shut the hell up.

We shut the club down and I wander out into the parking lot with everyone else, the icy cold night air like a harsh slap in the face. But not hard enough to sober me up. I'm drunk and I know it. And I drove my ass here too. Chad's going home to his brother's house and everyone else seems to have come in groups with a designated driver at the wheel.

"You want to come back to my place?" Emmett asks, but I can tell that's the last thing he wants.

"Sabrina's gonna kill you," Chad mutters. He sends me a look. "That's my future sister-in-law."

"It's good, guys." I hold up my hands, like it's no big deal that they're all going to abandon me. They aren't my friends. The majority of these guys I don't know at all, with the exception of Chad and his brother. I don't expect them to help me. Hell, most of them are gone already. "I'll take an Uber."

"You sure?" Chad asks, looking guilty. He glances over his shoulder at his brother before he steps closer to me. His voice lowers as he says, "It's just that, his fiancée wasn't too thrilled about him coming to a strip club tonight. She already bitched about me coming back to their apartment. If we bring you too? She'll probably freak the hell out."

No way do I want to deal with another upset female.

"Yeah, no, I'm good. I'll call Uber right now." I reach into my front pocket to find it empty. My keys are in my other front pocket, but that's it. I pat my butt down and realize both of my back pockets are empty too. " "

"What's wrong?" Chad frowns.

"I think I forgot my phone inside." The last thing I want to do is go back into the club and possibly face Jensen. "I gotta get in there before they close down for the night. I'll see you guys later, okay? Thanks for inviting me Emmett, and I'll see you tomorrow, Chad," I call to them before I start jogging toward the front doors of City Lights.

The place is locked, and I tug on the handles, making the glass in the doors rattle. A big, burly guy with a shiny bald head barely cracks open one of the doors, glaring at me through narrowed eyes. "We're closed for the night, asshole."

Nice customer service. "I left my phone inside."

He studies me for a moment. "You were with the bachelor party."

"Yeah." I nod.

"What kind of phone?"

"An iPhone X."

"Uh huh. One of the girls said a fancy new phone got left behind. Come in." He pushes the door open farther and I slip inside, surprised at how different the club looks with all the lights on. It's nothing special, with the harsh fluorescent light making everything look dark and dingy. Rundown. There's a guy about my age mopping the floor, and the bartender is behind the counter washing up.

"Come over here," the bald guy tells me with a wave of his hand.

I follow after him, going through the very hallway where I made out with Jensen, pushing through a black door into a very dark, small room. There's a bunch of chairs stacked in one of the corners, and a giant round table covered in all sorts of miscellaneous items. Discarded jackets, a small purse, a couple of wallets.

And my phone.

"This is our unofficial lost and found," the bald guy tells me. "You're lucky someone turned in your fancy-ass phone. Not everyone is that nice around here."

I snatch up my iPhone and shove it in my pocket. "Thanks for letting me back in so I could get it."

"No problem. Take better care of your phone." He slaps me on the back so hard, I take a couple of faltering steps forward. "Now get the hell out of here. I wanna go home."

I exit the room and make my way toward the doors, checking my phone as I walk. I have a text from some hot girl named Micki I met at a party a few weeks ago, before I was having serious thoughts about Jensen. I don't bother answering her. Last thing I need is another woman in my life.

There's a few other notifications, but nothing important, so I swipe out of everything and open up my Uber app.

"Hey, watch where you're going," a familiar voice says right when I collide with a very soft, curvy female. I grab hold of her waist to stop her, clutching fistfuls of a soft black sweater, and I realize quick it's freaking Jensen.

The look she sends me is full of disgust. "Why are you still here?"

"Forgot my phone." I hold it up to show her, then shove it into my front pocket. "Now if you'll excuse me…"

I start to walk past her, but she stops me with her words. "You know, you were a real asshole earlier."

"At least I don't have to lie to make friends." I turn to face her.

She crosses her arms. Thank God she has that sweater on. I couldn't take another moment of staring at her perfect breasts on such obvious display. "You're also a   asshole."

"Hey, I've got nothing to be ashamed of," I remind her. I'm offended she called me judgmental, though I guess I was judging her earlier.

That hurt look crosses her face again, and I immediately feel awful for what I just said. What I've said and done the entire night.

"You ready to go, Jen?" The ferocious blonde who took over our table magically appears by Jensen's side. She eyes me up and down, a frown on her pretty face. "This guy bugging you?"

"No." Jensen hesitates, a sudden gleam in her eye. "Not really."

The blonde sneers. "You need to get going, jackass. We're

closed."

Remaining silent, I walk out of there, sick of all the bullshit. Sick, period. I swear I'm getting the spins. And my head is starting to pound. Too much alcohol will do that to a person, and it doesn't help that I mixed my liquors either.

My ass is going to be hurtin' tomorrow.

Opening my phone, I go back into the Uber app and start looking for a car to come pick me up. But after a little searching, I realize there isn't one available.

As in…

I'm screwed.

"Fuck me," I mutter as I open up a browser and start searching for a taxi service.

"Already did that," Jensen says from behind me, making me whirl around. "Remember? You wanted to keep all the good pussy to yourself."

She's smiling. Meaning she's joking. Though, of course, she lies too, so I don't know if I can trust that she won't turn on me in a quick second.

Her constant mood shifts leave me on edge.

"Why did you even say that?" I ask.

"I don't know, I wanted to watch you squirm." She shrugs. I swear that's the most honest she's been with me all night. Minus when I had her in my arms in the hallway. "Why are you still here?"

"Can't find an Uber."

"What? And all of your friends left you here alone?"

"They weren't my friends. I came tonight because my roommate invited me. His brother is the future groom." Why am I telling her all this? She doesn't fucking care.

More like, she doesn't deserve to know.

"They still abandoned you, Rhett." Her voice is soft. So are her eyes. She has the most beautiful eyes. Big and blue and full of secrets.

It's like I know nothing about her.

I glance down at my phone again and misstep on the edge of the sidewalk, nearly toppling over before I right myself.

"You're drunk." She states the obvious.

"Only a little bit." I hold my thumb and index finger up, with barely any space between them. "I'll be fine. I'll get a taxi."

"Isn't that your car out in the parking lot?" She points.

I look where she's pointing. "Yeah, that's mine."

"You're going to leave it here overnight and take a taxi home?"

"I can't drive home, Jens. I'm drunk, remember?"

She blows out an exaggerated breath and turns to the ferocious blonde, who just exited the club. "I need to take him home," Jensen tells her.

"Oh, hell no," I start, but she sends me a look. I lower my voice. "I don't want you driving me home, Jensen."

"You leave your car here and someone is going to break into it," she tells me.

"At the very least," the blonde adds. "More like they'll flat out steal it."

"Savannah's right. You'll come back here tomorrow and your car will most likely be gone," Jensen says. "I'll drive you home."

I stare at my car with longing. I love that fucking car. I don't make a big deal about my financial situation, but I do appreciate driving a truly excellent vehicle.

"Are you sure you want to do that?" Savannah asks Jensen.

I turn to look at them, wondering at the meaningful looks they're giving each other. Does Savannah know about me? Does she know Jensen is a liar?

Probably not.

"I'm sure," Jensen says firmly before she walks over to me and holds her hand out, palm up. "Your keys."

Reluctantly I hand them over. I don't trust her, yet I'm going to let her drive my car. Let her drive me home. But I'm too drunk to protest, and she knows it.

"You want me to follow you back to his place?" Savannah asks as we start walking out into the parking lot.

"Go ahead and go home. I'll text you later," Jensen answers.

"Jen." The warning tone in Savannah's voice is obvious. "Be careful."

"I've got this handled." She smiles at me, and all the hairs on the back of my neck stand on end. "Don't worry."

She hits the button on the keyless remote to unlock the

car, and then we're both climbing in, me on the passenger side for once in my life. It feels strange, to be in your own car but not driving it. I never realized what a control freak I am.

"Don't wreck it, okay?" I tell her gently as she hits the button to start the car.

"I won't wreck your precious car, Rhett," she promises, just before she thrusts the gear into drive and pulls out of the parking spot, the tires squealing and the back end of the car swaying.

"Jesus, Jensen!" I sober up real quick as she drives like a maniac out of the parking lot, laughing the entire time. But once we're on the road, she drives at a normal speed, her gaze focused on the road in front of her.

"Did I scare you?"

"Yeah," I admit, feeling like an idiot.

"Sorry. I couldn't resist. You were looking at your car just like you look at me when we're…" Her voice drifts and she clamps her lips shut.

"When we're what?" I ask, curious.

Her gaze meets mine briefly before she returns her focus to the road. "When we're—fucking."

"Well, don't forget. You do have the good pussy," I remind her, going for humor. We can't fight if we're trying to be funny, right?

She laughs, her sparkling gaze landing on me briefly. "You really think so?"

"You really expect me to answer that?" There's something different about her. She seems more confident, not as closed off.

It also feels like she's teasing me. Toying with me. I don't know if that's a good thing.

Probably not.

"Be honest, Rhett." Her voice is low. Sultry. Sexy. "You could've had my pussy earlier. In the club."

I say nothing, just shift in my seat, trying to ignore my growing erection. The word pussy drops so easily from her lips, and it's kind of a turn on.

"You can have it right now, if you want it." She comes to a stop at a red light, causally stretching her legs out in front of her, causing her tight skirt to ride up and expose her slender thighs.

"Jens." My voice is a warning, but my resolve is weak. So fucking weak.

She squirms in her seat and reaches for her skirt, tugging it up so it's bunched around her waist, exposing her panties. They're black lace and barely cover her.

Damn.

"You left me high and dry in that hallway, Rhett," she murmurs, hitting the gas when the light turns green. "I wanted you so bad. For the rest of the night, all I could think about was you touching me, and it made me ache in the worst way."

Her words are messing with my head again. She knows

exactly what to say to seduce me. And my guard is down. I'm drunk and horny and dying to reach over and slip my fingers in her panties. See if she's wet.

I'd bet a million bucks she's soaked.

"You're a fucking tease," I tell her gruffly as I settle my hand on her thigh. Her skin is warm and smooth, and I run my fingers up, closer and closer to her panties.

"I'm not teasing you. I'm letting you have me. Take what you want." She spreads her legs a little and I brush my fingers against her very center.

Yep. The fabric's wet.

"I touch you like this, you'll wreck my car," I warn her.

"You don't touch me like this, and I guarantee I'll wreck your car out of pure frustration." She sends me an evil smile. "What will it be, Rhett?"

FOUR

She's driving me out of my mind. I can't do this, not while she's driving my car. We get a little too into it, and next thing I know we're wrecked. Literally.

I'm not in the mood to die tonight.

"Pull over," I demand.

She frowns at me. "What?"

"I said, pull over." I wave a finger at an upcoming parking lot to the right. "Now."

Jensen turns on the blinker and pulls into the parking lot of an old church. She cruises to the very back, behind the building, and guides the car into a spot in the deepest corner of the lot so we're facing a rickety old fence. She puts the car in park, shuts off the engine and unbuckles her seat belt before she turns and faces me. "Tell me what to do now, Rhett."

My blood heats at her soft words. I slowly undo my

seatbelt, anticipation thrumming in my veins. We're playing some sort of game tonight, and I am a willing participant. I blame the alcohol.

And the woman.

"Take off your sweater."

She does as I ask, whipping the thin black sweater up and over her head, tossing it behind her so it lands in the back seat. She had no bra on, so all I see are her perfect breasts, her tiny pink nipples hard and begging for my mouth.

But I decide to show a little restraint first.

"Your skirt." I flick my chin at her. "Get rid of it."

It's gone in a matter of seconds, a crumpled ball on the floor.

"Now your panties."

Jensen arches a brow, then slowly removes her underwear. There is something so goddamn sexy about watching a woman slip out of a delicate piece of lacy panties, sliding them down her long, slim legs. They get tangled around her ankles and heels, and when she finally kicks them off, her knowing gaze meets mine. "Do you want them?"

"Yeah," I croak, clearing my throat. I stare at her naked form, sitting in the driver's seat of my car, and I know I will never forget this moment, this night.

This girl.

She hands her panties over and I take them, crumpling the damp fabric against my palm. In the close confines of the car, the musky smell of her fills the space, and I know she's aroused.

Fuck, I'm aroused too.

"Come here," I whisper, and she crawls over the center console, settling her warm, naked body on me. She slings her arms around my neck, her hands clasped loosely at my nape, her knees bent on either side of my hips, with her thighs spread wide. Open and willing and all mine.

A tiny smile still curls her lips as she studies me. "You got me where you want me, Montgomery?"

I rest my hands at her hips, squeezing gently. "You want this? A few hours ago you looked like you wanted to throw a drink in my face."

She leans in close, her lips just above mine. "That's because you were an asshole."

"And last week?" When she frowns, I continue, "When you slipped out of my bed in the middle of the night?"

Her frown deepens, and guilt clouds her eyes as she shifts away, creating distance between us. "I…panicked."

"Why?" I touch her breast, circling her nipple with my finger. "You didn't like it?" If she says she didn't enjoy that night we shared, I'll know she's a pathological liar, unable to help herself. The way she responded to me was too real for me to believe she faked it.

If she did, she's the best actress I've ever witnessed.

"I liked it too much," she whispers, her eyes fluttering

closed when I pinch her nipple with my thumb and index finger. She hisses in a breath when I squeeze tighter, and I drop my hand, leaning forward and bathing her skin with my tongue to ease the pain.

She sinks her hands into my hair, tugging on the strands extra hard, as if she wants to hurt me too. "I shouldn't like you so much," she confesses.

Now I'm confused. I lift my head away from her chest, my hands remaining on her breasts, her hands still in my hair. "Why not?"

"I'm supposed to hate you. Uh, your type, I mean." I don't get what she's saying, but I sort of don't care either. Not while I have her naked and willing in my car in the back of a church parking lot.

It feels…wrong. But in the best way possible. Like we could get caught. Someone could see us. She doesn't have a stitch of clothing on. All I can see is naked skin and light brown pubic hair, and I reach for her there, sinking my fingers inside her wetness, finding and rubbing her clit with my thumb.

"Oh, God," she chokes out as I stroke her. I want her to come.

Immediately.

Leaning in, I suck her nipple into her mouth as I explore her pussy with my fingers, coming back to her clit every few seconds. She trembles. She moans. She lifts her hips and rides my hand, helping me increase the pace. Back and forth she shifts, her breaths coming quicker, her skin becoming flushed. Hotter.

She's the hottest thing I've ever seen.

"Faster," she gasps, and I give her what she wants, watching her the entire time, my gaze locked on her pretty face. She comes apart in my arms, her body quaking with her orgasm. She whimpers, her eyes tightly closed, as if she's solely focused on the way I'm making her feel, and when it's finally over, she opens her eyes, her blissed-out gaze meeting mine.

My hand still cupping her, I lean in and kiss her, whispering against her lips, "You're beautiful when you come."

She pushes at my shoulders so I fall back against the seat. "Don't say that."

I'm frowning again. This girl is damn confusing. "Why not?"

"It's…embarrassing." She shakes her head, and I notice her cheeks are extra pink. Like I actually did embarrass her.

"No one has ever told you that before?" Of course, this makes me think of her having sex with other guys, and I'm immediately annoyed. Jealous. Possessive.

Yeah, all of those stupid caveman feelings are swamping me.

"No. No one has ever told me that before." Her voice is flat and her gaze is distant, and no way in hell am I going to let this go to shit. Not after witnessing the hottest thing I've ever seen in a long-ass time. Maybe ever.

Reaching with my right hand, I search and eventually find the lever and recline the seat, until I'm practically horizontal, Jensen sprawled across the top of me. She puts her face in mine, her breath tickling my lips, and then we're kissing.

I slip my fingers into her hair as I slip my tongue into her mouth, clutching her close. I keep the kiss soft. Romantic. I'm trying to coax her back into it, because what I just saw was her closing herself off, shutting me out.

And I don't want that. Despite everything she's done to me, and all the lies she's told, I'm still into her. Maybe that makes me an idiot, but fuck it.

I'm too turned on to care.

I cradle her head in my hands and drink from her lips. Lick them. Thrust my tongue into her mouth so I can taste her. She moans as if coming back alive, her hands going for my shirt and hurriedly unbuttoning it. I help her help me out of it and she breaks away from my mouth to kiss along my neck, my chest...

"I want you inside me," she murmurs, her fingers undoing the button, then sliding down the zipper of my jeans. She spreads the fly wide open, her fingers skimming over my erection, and a groan escapes me at her teasing touch. "Please, Rhett."

She sounds desperate. I desperate.

We work together to take off my jeans, tug down my boxer briefs until my cock springs free. Before I can do anything she's guiding me inside her, both of us groaning when I slip into her wet heat. She sinks all the way down, until I'm fully engulfed, and I close my eyes. Grit my teeth. I don't want to come too fast.

But she feels so damn good.

Jensen starts to move and I help her, my hands at her hips, lifting her, pulling her back down. She's fucking me hard, so damn hard. Her hands are braced on the roof, her breasts jiggling as she rides me. I stare up at her, captivated by her face, her body, the way she moves, the sounds she makes, how she's so utterly lost to the feeling of the two of us together...

She opens her eyes and comes to a pause, smiling down at me. "You're staring."

"I am." I don't bother denying it.

"You like watching?" She raises her brows.

"I like watching you."

Her smile fades and she shifts, the subtle movement of her hips causing her pussy to squeeze me tighter. "Why do you like me, Rhett?" Her rhythm picks up, distracting me for a second.

"Wait, what? Why do I like you? Is that what you asked?" I say the words between panting breaths. I'm close to the edge, and trying not to lose it.

She nods, lifting her arms to push her hair away from her face, thrusting her chest out. Christ, she looks sexy as hell doing that. I've never been big on asking for or taking photos of a naked girl I'm with, but right now, I'd like to capture Jensen in this moment.

"I treat you like garbage," she finally says.

"No, you don't," I start to deny, but she rests her fingers across my lips, silencing me.

"Yes," Jensen says quietly, removing her fingers. "I do."

I lift my hips, sending myself deep inside her body, and I must nudge a certain spot because her mouth falls open, a little, " " escaping her lips.

"Maybe I'm just using you," I tell her, right before I nudge that particular spot again.

Her eyes are glazed over, as if she's overcome. "For sex?"

"Yeah. Definitely for sex." I start thrusting faster, hitting that spot again and again. It not only feels amazing for her, but it's pretty damn amazing for me too. Her body goes lax, like she's starting to melt, and she collapses over me, her hands clutching my shoulders, her face in mine.

"Oh God, Rhett," she whispers, her wild eyes unfocused. "Don't stop, don't stop, don't st—"

Her body goes stiff, and then her pussy is clenching and unclenching around my dick, sending me straight into my own orgasm. We come together like some sort of magical movie moment, in the passenger seat of my car with the windows steamed up.

She curls around me when it's over, her racing heart matching my own, and we lie there together, silent, trying to slow our breathing.

I could fall asleep right now, swear to God. A night of drinking topped off with good sex always puts me right to sleep. My eyes drift closed and I run my fingers up and down Jensen's bare back, making her shiver.

"That feels nice," she whispers against my chest.

"You feel nice," I whisper back.

She sniffs, and I swear she might be…crying? No freaking way. She's not a crier. Is she? "I'm really not nice, though. Not even close."

I slip my fingers under her chin and gently force her to lift her head so I can look her in the eye. "What do you even mean? You keep saying stuff, Jens. And I don't like it."

Frustration is written all over her face, and she shakes her head, wayward blonde strands falling across her eyes. "I say stuff. I do stuff. I'm a rotten person, Rhett. I'm not nice. I never have been."

"Come on." I get ready to give her a short speech about self-esteem or whatever—a little too drunk and sleepy to focus right now, but I'm willing to give it a try—when a bright beam of light suddenly flashes in my darkened car and a loud knock sounds on the roof.

"Open up! Now!"

FIVE

I toss Jensen my shirt and she puts it on, trying to do the buttons with shaky fingers. The guy outside is still pounding on my roof and waving his flashlight, nearly blinding me.

"Hit the ignition button," I tell her as I stuff my dick back in my underwear and tug my jeans up over my hips.

"Why?" The fear in her eyes is blatant.

This is not a great way to end the evening.

"It won't start the car, but it'll power some things up, including the windows," I explain.

She does as I ask and I immediately open the passenger side window to reveal a skinny white dude wearing a security uniform that's too big for him. It's like he's a kid wearing a Halloween costume.

He shines the flashlight in my eyes, causing me to throw a hand up. "Can I help you?" I ask him.

He drops the flashlight so I can actually see again. "You're on private property." His deep voice belies his thin frame. I could probably break this kid in half, not that I'm going to.

"Sorry. We'll get out of here," I tell him.

The security guard shines the flashlight on Jensen, who's crawled out of my lap and is settled in the driver's seat. "You okay, miss?"

She nods, offering him a little smile, but says nothing.

He frowns. "You sure? Are you here of your own consent?"

I don't say a word. This guy could call the cops on me and I'd be up shit creek. So I remain still, waiting for her answer.

A thought crosses my mind, one I don't want to confront. But hell, Jensen has sort of screwed me over before. Would she be so bold, so freaking heartless to say I brought her here against her will? No way.

The fact that I doubt her is fucking scary.

"I'm fine," she reassures the security guard, making me nearly sag with relief. "Just…hanging out with my boyfriend." She smiles and points at me.

Another lie.

This guy has to know what we're up to. I'm shirtless. She's wearing my shirt and nothing else, her hair a total mess. She looks freshly fucked, and the car smells like sex.

"Well, you two find somewhere else to fuck around. You're trespassing, and I can have your asses arrested with one call to the cops." The security guard sends me a meaningful look.

"Get the hell out of here."

"Will do, sir," I tell him with a little salute, then hit the button to slide the window closed. "Let's go, Jens."

She starts the car and we're soon back on the road, me giving her directions to my house since she doesn't remember how to get there. When she pulls the car into the garage, she shuts it off, turning to look at me. "I should text Savannah so she can pick me up."

"You could—" I can tell by the look on her face doesn't want to stay.

"No." She shakes her head and reaches for her purse, pulling her phone out. "I need to go, Rhett. I can't stay here."

She didn't say the words, but I know what she means.

We sit in the car in silence as she taps on her phone, sending a text to her mean friend. Frustration rips through me and I climb out of the car, still shirtless, and slam the door with all my might.

Jensen follows after me, wearing only my shirt and her shoes, the buttons done up wrong so I can catch a glimpse of one of her breasts. It's practically falling out. "What, are you seriously mad at me right now?"

"No." I spit the word out. "I'm fucking frustrated."

"Why?"

"We just had sex in my car and now you're bailing on me. " I am not having this fight with her in my garage with the door wide open so we can wake up my neighbors. It's a quiet neighborhood. Nothing ever happens around here. I'm not about to put on a show.

I head for the door that leads into the house and I open it, glancing over my shoulder to see Jensen is still standing in the same place I left her. She's clutching her purse strap in one hand, her phone in the other. Her makeup is a little smudged, her hair is a mess, and those long, slender legs are on full display. She's naked under my shirt and she's sexy as hell.

All I have to do is look at her, and it's like I can't resist her.

"You going to come inside? Or wait out here for your friend?" I ask quietly. I still sound pissed, though.

Because I am.

If she chooses to wait outside for Savannah to come and rescue her, she's ridiculous. And I'm ridiculous for thinking we could work.

Actually, if I'm being honest with myself, I need to face facts. Jensen and I will most likely never work. She lies. She's lied to me constantly, and she's probably lying to me right now. Is she really texting Savannah? Or is she texting someone else? A guy? For all I know, she might have a boyfriend.

Jealousy ripples through me, and I try to contain it.

She sinks her teeth into her lower lip and shifts from foot to foot, checking her phone with a quick glance. "She hasn't responded yet."

Maybe she telling the truth. I let the door shut and cross my arms, impassive. "She's probably asleep."

Jensen nods. Checks her phone again.

"She's probably not going to answer you," I tell her.

Another nod. Yet another phone check, like she can will Savannah to respond.

"You can stay in my guest room," I start, but she shakes her head, a sarcastic laugh escaping her.

"You know that won't happen." When I remain quiet, she sighs. "I'll end up in your bed, Rhett."

"Then stay the night in my bed."

Another sigh leaves her, and then she's walking toward me. I open the door and she slips inside. I shut the garage and lock up, then lead her toward my bedroom.

"This means nothing," she tells me when we're in my bed minutes later.

"I agree," I say, staring up at the ceiling.

We're both naked. I can smell her. Feel her warmth reaching out to me, and I try to resist it. Resist her. We're quiet for so long, I think she might be falling asleep, and I'm envious. I was so tired earlier, but now that's gone. All I can do is think. Think about the girl in my bed, lying next to me. She's bad for me. I know she is. If I continue down this road, she's going to fuck me over. Fuck me up.

Again and again and again.

She slides closer, her naked body nestled to my side, her breasts pressing against my arm, her hand on my dick. I remain still, thinking I can trick her into believing I'm asleep.

But you can't trick someone like Jensen. My cock stiffens as she strokes it. She kisses my chest, her damp lips making me crazy. I still don't touch her, don't react, and then she slips beneath the covers, slides down the mattress, her mouth right there. Sucking me deep.

Those three words rattle through my brain on repeat. Jensen's right. It means nothing. It   mean nothing.

So why does being with her feel like it has the potential to mean everything?

SIX

"It's your sister's birthday Wednesday. Don't forget to text her," Dad reminds me, like I'm a dumbass who doesn't keep track of a calendar.

I'm at home on a Sunday by myself. Chad still isn't back from his brother's. Jensen left first thing this morning, Savannah showing up to drive her home before I was fully awake.

At least Jensen told me she was leaving. That's progress.

"I know it's her birthday," I tell him. How can I forget Addie's birthday, since it's the same day my mother died?

You don't forget those sort of things. No matter how hard you try.

"We're having a party for her this Saturday." Dad pauses, and I can hear someone talking to him. A woman's voice, one I don't recognize. Probably one of his mistresses. Can't be a secretary since he doesn't work on Sundays. His wife won't let him. "You're expected to attend."

I bristle at his demand. I planned on going anyway, but when my father commands me to do shit, my automatic instinct is to rebel. But I won't do that.

I love Addie too damn much to disappoint her.

"I'll be there. You know that." Now it's my turn to pause, wondering if I should ask the question on the tip of my tongue.

Fuck it. I'm asking.

"Is Park going?" My older brother's automatic reaction to our father's demands is to rebel against them too. Only he actually goes through with it. He has the balls to defy our father on a constant basis. He just doesn't give a fuck.

"He says he is. We'll see." The disappointment in Dad's voice is obvious. They argue all the time. Funny thing is, they don't realize they're exactly alike. Exactly the same. That's why they butt heads.

"I'll text Addie and ask her what she wants for her birthday."

"She wants a car."

I laugh. Of course she does. They didn't get her one last year, even though she was so hopeful. She cried that night, after everyone left her party and the two of us were alone. I held her in my arms as she bitterly complained that our stepmom hated her, and that's why she didn't get a car. Two weeks before that, our father bought his wife a brand-new Ferrari. Just because, he said.

Sometimes my father does really stupid things.

"Are you getting her one this year?"

"Already purchased," he snaps. "It'll be in the driveway the morning of her actual birthday, with a giant pink bow on top."

"What kind of car?"

"A white Jeep Wrangler."

Her dream car. "She'll like that."

"Diane's not pleased. Says they're not safe."

"What the fuck ever, Dad. You could buy Addie the safest car on the planet and Diane would still find a way to bitch about it," I say.

"Watch your mouth," he warns me. I can tell he's walking, moving to another room so he won't talk about the wife in front of the other woman, I assume. "You can't speak to me like that about your mother."

"Jesus, Dad, really? That woman isn't my mother." He constantly tries to convince us otherwise, and I don't know why he wastes his breath.

"She's raised you since you were six."

Five and a half, but who's counting? Diane moved in so fast on my dad. The dirt was still fresh on our mother's grave and she magically appeared by his side one night, the balm to heal Dad's wounds after losing his wife in such a tragic way.

She moved in when Addie was six months old. She immediately hired a team of nannies to "take care of the baby's every need". Right before Addie's first birthday, Dad and Diane went on a tour of Europe. Diane had never been before, Dad told me and Park right before they left. He wanted to treat her right and show her the world.

They missed Addie's first birthday. The nannies held a small party for her, and Park and I were there to watch her smash the chocolate cake with pink frosting and chocolate crumbs coating her tiny fingers. I will never forget that day. How Park and I cried for our dad, our mom, who we still had a hard time believing was dead.

I think that was the last time I ever saw my older brother cry.

"I don't want to talk about her," I tell Dad, and from the tone of my voice, I know he understands I mean it. Nothing good ever comes out of talking about Diane. No matter how much he tries to convince us we're one big happy family.

We're not.

"Will you go to dinner with us on Addie's birthday?" he asks, deftly changing the subject.

"Who's going?"

"Addie insists on bringing her boyfriend." Dad hates that kid, but I like Trent. He's good to my sister, and that's all that matters. "Diane and I will be there, of course. And hopefully you."

"I'd like to bring someone." Shit. I have no idea if I can convince Jensen to go to an awkward family dinner for my little sister's birthday, but I'd like to try.

I'm a sucker for punishment, I guess.

"Of course. Who is it? Someone we know?" He's hoping it's a daughter of one of his associates, or neighbor, or golf buddy.

"I met her on campus."

"What's her name?"

"Jensen."

"Jensen what?"

That I don't know. And I don't really want to admit that fact either. "You don't know her."

"You'd be surprised. I know a lot of women." He chuckles, the bastard.

"She's too young for you."

"They're never too young, son. Trust me on that." His laughter grows.

Sometimes my dad is a sexist asshole. I wonder why Diane tolerates his cheating and constant bullshit. He hasn't been faithful to her in years.

Wait, I know why. Because he has more money than God and she likes to spend it.

"I'm bringing her," I say, my voice determined. "Where are we going?"

Now he sounds truly annoyed. "Your sister insists on going to the Cheesecake Factory."

It's my turn to laugh. That is so beneath Dad and Diane it's fucking hilarious. "When was the last time you went there?"

"When your mother was still alive. She loved that place."

His voice is wistful, and despite all the crap my father has done over the last twenty-plus years, I know without a doubt, he still misses our mother.

"Then it makes sense that Addie loves it too," I say firmly. "Give her what she wants."

"I am. I always do." I start to say something and he cuts me off. "I try to, at least."

I want to tell him to try harder, but I keep my mouth shut.

We end the call, and within minutes Chad is strolling through the front door and collapsing on the couch, a weary look on his face.

"Where have you been?" I ask.

"We went out to breakfast. Bridezilla wanted to talk wedding plans." Chad covers his face with both hands and groans.

"With you? Why?"

He drops his hands. "I'm the best man, so she has certain expectations of what I'm supposed to do. I told her I already met those expectations by hosting the bachelor party, and she got pissed at me."

"What else does she expect from you?"

"The list is too long to go into, bro. Pray your brother doesn't get married to a total bitch, Rhett. Bitches suck." Chad shakes his head, a gleam suddenly shining in his eyes. "Hey, whatever happened to that hot waitress?"

I tense up. I do not want to talk about Jensen, especially

with Chad. "What do you mean?"

"You went back into the strip club looking for your phone." Chad grins. "You sure that wasn't some ploy to chat up our waitress?"

"No, I legitimately left my phone in the club."

"To talk to the hottie?" Chad peers at me. "Is it true you really fucked her?"

I don't have to answer him. It's none of his business.

Chad's eyes go wide when I remain silent. "You did. Holy hell, I can't believe it! That chick is hot. But you've always been able to pull hos."

"Don't call her a ho," I bite out. "Don't insult her."

"Relax, relax." Chad shakes his head, chuckling. "So were you lying when you told me you've never been to the strip club before?"

"I wasn't lying."

"So where did you meet her?"

"On campus. Actually, no. At a bar. And then I kept seeing her on campus, and I finally convinced her to go on a couple of dates with me," I explain.

"And you had sex with her."

I nod.

"So is it serious?"

"No," I immediately say. "It's definitely not serious."

"Is she good in bed?"

"I'm not going to answer you."

"Which means she's fucking unbelievable in bed. Any girl who can walk around so casually with her tits out has to be pretty open to anything."

She's definitely open to lots of things. Last night in the car was…interesting. And mind-blowing, no denying that. I felt like she was pushing me. And I was pushing her. It was a turn-on. She's a turn-on.

I want to see her again.

"I'm jealous, man. Not going to lie." Chad stands, stretches his arms above his head. "I'm gonna go take a shower and then crash out. I'm finished with this weekend. Swear to God I'm still hungover."

The moment he walks out of the living room I'm on my phone, sending a text to Jensen.

 she immediately answers.

She doesn't reply for a few minutes, making me anxious. My heart sinks. That's something a guy would say to get in a girl's pants. Hell,   said that before to some poor, innocent girl. Yeah, I'm not proud of some of the things I've done, but I'm trying to change my ways.

She's right. I am a liar. The more this girl resists, the more I want her.

I tell her.

 I don't want Chad to see her. I don't want to hear his big mouth.

It takes her a while to respond again. I'm pretty sure I've

blown it. When five minutes tick by, I'm certain I've blown it.

But long minutes later, Jensen finally responds. If I admit that she is, does that make me an asshole?

She sends another text. All right. So we're on the same page.

I tell her.

SEVEN

I roll over on my back, my breathing heavy, my heart racing. Closing my eyes, I swallow hard, trying to calm my overstimulated body. I hear the rustle of sheets, the comforter falling onto the floor softly. Turning my head, I crack open my eyes to see Jensen lying beside me, her golden body glowing with a faint sheen of sweat, her feet moving, kicking everything off the bed.

Reaching over, I slide my hand over her smooth ass, my fingers lingering. "Hot?"

She says nothing, just shifts closer to press her ultra-warm body against mine. I kiss her, my overused dick stirring to attention despite my bone-deep exhaustion, but I break away from her swollen mouth before it turns into something else.

With Jensen, it's guaranteed to turn into something else.

"You're insatiable," she murmurs against my lips, her

fingers slipping down, down until they're curled around my cock.

"So are you," I tell her.

We've been fucking around for hours. I don't even know what time it is since I haven't check my phone since Jensen walked in the door. All I know is that it's dark outside, and the house is quiet. It feels like there's no one else in the world right now. Just me and Jensen, doing the most primal, basic thing a man and woman can do.

Her stomach growls. Loudly. She coughs, maybe trying to cover up the sound, who knows, and then she's moving away, rolling over on her side so her back is to me. "I should probably go," she tells the wall.

I grab her shoulder and gently flip her over so she's facing me again. "I can feed you if you're hungry."

"I'm not hungry." Her stomach growls again.

"Really." My voice is flat, because—yet again—she's lying. About the stupidest thing possible.

She sighs. "I hate it when you look at me like that."

"Like what?"

"Like…" She hesitates, pressing her lips together. "I don't know, like you're disappointed in me."

I say nothing, since that's exactly how I feel.

"Yeah, like that." She crawls out of bed and is on the floor, no doubt searching for her clothes. "I don't want you to act like you're my dad, Rhett."

"What the hell do you mean?" I spring to my feet, annoyed. She does this a lot. Gets defensive, purposely starts arguing with me.

Maybe this girl is too much trouble. Maybe she won't be worth the heartache.

"If you're sticking around because you think you can fix me, you're wrong." She pulls on the black leggings she'd been wearing earlier, forgetting all about her panties. "I'm unfixable."

"I don't want to fix you." I touch her arm, and she pauses, her gaze meeting mine. "I told you, I have no expectations."

Her brows wrinkle. "Is that supposed to make me feel better?"

I throw my arms up in the air, frustrated as shit. "What do you want me to say? You want me to tell you I'm just using you for sex? That seems to piss you off. Or should I say that I care about you and think I could fall in love with you? I'm guessing that would probably piss you off even more."

I'm not sure if I mean either scenario. Sex with Jensen is amazing. But I also like talking with her. Even arguing with her. It all feels like foreplay. But could I fall in love with her? I don't know. Considering I don't trust her, that's a huge barrier.

She grabs her sweatshirt off the floor and puts it on, leaving her bra on the floor. "Do we really have to define this? Whatever's happening between us?"

"I don't know. Do we?"

A sigh escapes her and she looks away, wrapping her arms

around herself like she's suddenly cold. It's warm and stuffy in my room, and I'm tempted to open the window despite the fact I'm standing here buck ass naked.

"One minute all I want is to feel your skin pressed against mine and the next I want to punch you in your perfect face," she murmurs, her gaze lifting to mine. "You frustrate me."

"You frustrate me too."

"I don't want to like you."

"I don't understand why."

"You are everything I should hate."

I flinch, shocked at the passion behind the word hate. "What did I ever do to you?"

"Not the literal you, the figurative you. The kind of guy you are," she explains.

"You're making zero sense," I tell her, and now it's her turn to throw her arms up in the air.

"Because you confuse the hell out of me!" She comes at me, and shoves at my shoulders with both hands, making me take a step back. "I didn't mean for this to happen. Well, I did, but I didn't think I'd like you so damn much."

"So you...what? Wanted a hookup and can't believe that I'm actually decent human being?" She talks in circles. Acts like she had some sort of plan with me yet I'm the one who messed it all up.

"Yes! That. Exactly that." She grips my shoulders, her fingers sliding down my skin. "You're actually nice, Rhett. I didn't expect that."

"Then why would you even be interested in me, if you thought I was an asshole?"

"I've always been attracted to assholes." She settles on the edge of the mattress, her entire body seeming to sag under the weight of her emotions. "The first guy I ever had sex with could burp the entire alphabet."

I start to laugh, but when I spot the serious expression on her face, I stop. "What a talented dude."

"He was a douche. The minute we started having actual intercourse, I was full of regret. But it was done. Couldn't take it back." She offers me a small smile. "The story of my life. I can't take it back, no matter how much I want to."

"Do you regret all of your sexual encounters?"

"The ones from when I was a kid, yeah. They were meaningless." Her gaze locks with mine, her blue eyes stormy. "I'm not good with my feelings. Expressing them."

I'm no expert either. Growing up essentially motherless will do that to a person. Diane claimed she wanted to be a mom to us, but she just said that to appease our father. When Park and I got older, she neglected us big time, especially me. None of us mattered. She only cared about the money.

Still does.

Jensen is so bottled up, so tense and jumpy, I can tell she's not comfortable with expressing kind of emotion.

"Why not?" I kneel in front of her, resting my hands on

her knees. "I know your mom is gone. Your father passed away. You have no brothers or sisters. Was it really that bad, just living with your father?"

She nods. Presses her lips together. "We were broke. He never worked, not really. And things got worse and worse as he got older. And sicker. He wasn't well. Mentally, he could never handle my mother's abandonment. He wasn't strong enough to be there for me. He tried at first, but near the end, he gave up. He was too angry at the world."

"He should've been there for you," I say firmly. My dad isn't the best, but when things gets tough, he's there for us as much as he can be. Diane is a major roadblock, but I know if shit got serious, he would put us above her.

At least, I think he would.

"I don't want to talk about this." She rests her hands on top of mine and then shoves them off her knees. "I should go."

I rise up so my face is directly in hers. "I don't want you to leave."

"You can't fix me, Rhett. No matter how much you think you can, it's impossible," she says softly.

Reaching for her, I cup the back of her head, pulling her in for a kiss. "I don't want to fix you. I like you just as you are." I press my lips to hers, our mouths parting, the lingering kiss soft and perfect, and just like that, my dick stirs to attention.

"Then you're crazy, because I'm a nightmare," she says, but I kiss her again to shut her up. The kiss turns deeper, our tongues lazy, my other hand slipping beneath her sweatshirt to touch her soft, smooth skin. I slowly push her so she's lying flat on the bed, her legs dangling over the side of the mattress, and then I'm reaching for the waistband of her leggings, tugging them off until they're a crumpled ball on the floor.

"Just let things happen," I tell her, kissing her stomach, darting my tongue in her belly button. "It's like you want to control every aspect of what's happening between us, and that's not how this sort of thing works."

"That's the problem." I watch her as she stares up at the ceiling, her expression woeful, like she's so utterly confused she doesn't know which way to turn, or how to think. "I don't have any experience with…relationships."

"I don't either."

She lifts her head, glaring at me. "Really?"

I shrug, not comfortable reviewing my relationships over the years when I'm about to go down on this girl. "I've had a few girlfriends. Nothing too terribly serious."

"Uh huh," she drawls, lying back down so she can look at the ceiling once more. I grab her thighs, spreading them slowly so she's on full display, pretty and pink and glistening. I drape first one leg, then the other over my shoulders, pressing my mouth against her inner thigh.

"Take off your sweatshirt, Jens," I whisper against her skin, my breath, my closeness making goose bumps rise. "You're gonna be here for a while."

Jensen does as I tell her without hesitation, whipping that sweatshirt off so she's once again naked. She truly has the most beautiful body I've ever seen. All long limbs and perfect proportions, breasts that are a generous handful and topped with rosy nipples. A round ass and assured hands. I could feast on her for hours.

Days.

I dip my head and nuzzle her pussy just before I start licking. She moans, scooting down so her pussy is even closer to my face and I give her all I've got, licking and sucking and teasing with my tongue. Sliding first one, then two fingers deep inside her, my lips attach to her clit. She bucks against my face, her fingers going into my hair like she never wants to let go, and I slip a third finger inside of her, stretching her wide. Filling her up.

This is all about her, this moment, right now. I just want her to come. I'm here to make her feel good. That's it. No expectations, no selfishness either. I'm here, at her service.

Going down on her like this is making me hard too. I grip my cock with my free hand and stroke. Once, twice, establishing a rhythm, the same one as my fingers inside her. She grinds her pussy against my mouth. I'm buried in her, and when I flick her clit in a particular way, her entire body goes tense before that orgasm washes over her, making her cry out.

I open my eyes, watching her fall apart against my lips. She's so fucking sexy when she does that, completely uninhibited, offering me a glimpse of the real her. The raw, vulnerable version of Jensen. This is what I want, what I crave. The girl, the sweet one who's giving in bed, who wants me, who responds so beautifully to everything I do to her.

She's not even finished with her climax and I'm crawling on top of her, slipping inside of her. I pound her hard, fuck her with everything I've got, grunting with every thrust, my vision hazy, my brain blank. I'm going on pure, primal instinct, and I feel like some sort of caveman, taking what's mine.

That's the weird thing about me and Jensen. Since the moment I first saw her, I felt like she belonged to me. There's some sort of undefined connection to this girl that I want to explore further.

But first, I need to find out why she lies.

And what she's hiding from me.

EIGHT

'm leaving the gym when I first spot her, covered from head to toe in black as she waits under the building's overhang and out of the rain. It's stormed all day, and now it's lightened to a faint drizzle, darkness fully settled in since it's six o'clock on a mid-November evening.

Smiling, I approach Jensen, pleased that she waited for me. I told her I had basketball practice earlier, when we were texting. I even told her where I practiced, though pretty much everyone on campus knows what gym we use. I didn't outright ask her, but I'd hoped she would've sought me out tonight. I still haven't mentioned the family dinner in celebration of Addie's birthday tomorrow at the Cheesecake Factory, and I wanted to ask her in person from the start, though I never really got around to it.

"What are you doing here? Waiting for me?" I ask when I

get closer. She's wearing black leggings and a giant oversized black sweatshirt with the hood pulled over her head, reminding me of some   overlord.

Jensen rolls her eyes, a tiny smile teasing the corners of her mouth. "No, I'm waiting for someone else. Of course, I'm waiting for you, Rhett."

I pull her into a quick hug and she shoves her way out of it. Public displays of affection are definitely not her thing, but I'm trying. "I'm fucking starving."

"How was practice?" She falls into step beside me and I tug the hood of my sweatshirt over my head as we walk together toward the parking lot.

"Good. Exhausting. Coach ran us extra hard." We have a game on Thursday, though it doesn't count. The season officially starts next week, and the team feels ready, though our coaches disagree, as usual.

"Oh. Maybe you're too tired to hang out?" She glances up at me with those sad blue eyes, and I wonder if something happened today.

And would she even tell me about it.

"Nah, let's go get something to eat. I wanted to talk to you anyway."

We get to my car and I drive to a nearby shopping center, where my favorite California poke bowl place is. The restaurant is packed, like it always is, and Jensen and I get in line, her nervous energy tipping me off that something's up.

"You don't like this place?" I ask her.

"I don't know. I've never been here." She studies the menu, frowning. "I don't know what half this stuff is."

For some reason, I'm happy she actually admitted that. I remember when I took her to the Italian restaurant, how lost she looked while staring at the menu. She didn't know what to get, didn't know how to pronounce the words, and I felt like an asshole, taking her there, making her feel uncomfortable when that was the last thing I wanted to do.

"I'll help you, promise. This place is like Subway, but for poke bowls, since you pick all of your ingredients as you go down the line. And a poke bowl is like sushi, but all mixed together in a bowl. Do you like sushi?" I ask her.

"Never had it."

This girl hasn't experienced much but hardship and bullshit, I swear. "Well, the base is white or brown rice and wontons if you want, or a vegetable mixture. Then you add a protein, like shrimp or chicken, or ahi tuna, which is raw tuna." She makes a face, but I keep talking. "And then you mix the protein with a sauce. They have all kinds—sweet, spicy, a miso sauce."

"What's miso?"

"It's a spice, I think. Ever had miso soup?" When she shrugs, I continue. "Well, after the sauce, then you can add vegetables, add even more sauce if you want, crunchy toppings, and you're done."

She examines the bowls currently being made, her eyes lighting up with interest. "They look kind of good."

"They're fucking delicious." She turns to look at me, a smile on her pretty face. "I'm a hardcore fan. Come here at least once a week, maybe twice."

"Really," she drawls, nudging her shoulder against my arm. "They're that good, huh."

"Trust me, they are. I wouldn't steer you wrong," I promise.

Her eyes take on a serious light. "I know you wouldn't. That's what I like about you."

That admission felt real, like a damn gift, and unable to help myself, I sling my arm around her shoulders and pull her in close, pressing my lips against her forehead in a quick kiss. "I'm glad you waited for me after practice. It was a nice surprise."

She gently pulls away, but not so far that my arm drops from her shoulders. I'm still holding her, an obvious public display of affection. This is progress. "I wanted to see you," she admits.

"I'm glad." So fucking glad, not that I can make a big deal about it. She's sketchy, like a wild animal that's close to being tamed. One wrong move and she might run away.

Or scratch your eyes out.

We get our bowls, me helping her out with her order as we move down the line, making recommendations based on her likes and dislikes. I pay for our bowls, Jensen getting us cups of water and our silverware, and when we finally meet at the table she's settled on, I'm eager to see her reaction to her poke bowl.

"Try it," I say, setting her bowl in front of her.

She picks up a forkful and tastes it, chewing slowly, her expression completely blank. I'm fidgeting in my chair, afraid she hates it, which is so stupid. Why should I care whether she likes poke bowls or not?

"What do you think?" I ask when she still hasn't said anything.

She swallows, takes a sip of her water, and then shoves another bite into her mouth. "It's okay," she mumbles, her mouth full.

I watch her eat, smiling as she keeps going. "You love it," I tell her after about her sixth bite.

"I do," she laughs, smiling. "Now stop staring at me and start eating."

We eat, making idle conversation about the last few days. I haven't seen her since late Sunday night, when her friend Savannah took her home after she got off work at the club. I wanted Jensen to stay the entire night, but she wouldn't have it, saying she needed to get some actual sleep, versus endless bouts of sex.

Not that I'm complaining about all the sex we're having, but I get what she's saying.

We're almost finished with our food when I finally decide

to ask her about going with me to dinner tomorrow. "So it's my sister's birthday," I start.

Jensen lifts her gaze from the bowl, her expression neutral. "How old will she be?"

"Seventeen. My family's getting together for dinner tomorrow to celebrate." I pause, letting my words sink in before I go on. "I'd like you to come with me."

" " Her expression is nothing short of horrified, like I just suggested she should have sex with my dad or something equally twisted and weird. Definitely didn't expect that strong of a reaction.

"It's not a big deal," I quickly reassure her. "Just a typical family dinner at the Cheesecake Factory. It'll be loud, my dad might tell bad jokes, my sister will be embarrassed because her boyfriend is there with us, and my stepmom will bitch about the bad service and how much she hates that place."

"I don't know…" Jensen starts, slowly shaking her head. At least that horrified expression is gone. Somewhat. "I don't do well with family dinners."

"Have you ever been to a family dinner with someone else?"

"No," she admits quietly.

That's what I thought. "Then how do you know you don't do well with them?"

Jensen pushes her bowl away from her, like she's lost her appetite. "This feels—serious, Rhett."

"What, going to Cheesecake Factory? Trust me, it's not." Actually, it is, but I'm trying to play this off. I don't bring girls around my family. It gives them expectations that I can't meet. Like we're serious when we're not.

But there's something about this girl that makes me want to push her into being in a serious relationship.

With me.

Am I crazy? Probably. One minute I can't trust her, the next I want her to be my official girlfriend. I'm making no sense. But this girl does something to me. The more she pushes me away, the more I want to reel her back in.

Maybe I'm just a glutton for punishment. I don't know.

"You want to introduce me to your family?" Now she appears shocked.

"Well…yeah. You can be my buffer, so I won't have to suffer with my family alone." I smile and reach across the table to grab her hand, trying to charm her. "Come on, Jens. Say yes. It'll be fun."

She absently rubs her fingers against mine, her gaze seemingly far away, like she really has to think about this before she can answer. "Are you sure you want me there?"

"I asked you, didn't I?" I give her fingers a squeeze, and she looks at me. "I want you to be there."

A sigh escapes her and she rolls her eyes. "Can I get a piece of cheesecake?"

I take a deep breath, not realizing I'd been holding it.

This girl leaves me on edge, I swear. "You can have an entire cheesecake if that's what you want."

"I might take you up on that offer." She smiles.

"Done." I bring her hand to my mouth and press my lips to the back of it. "Want to get out of here?"

A knowing smile curls her lips as her answer.

♥ ♥ ♥

It's much later in the night, when we're both naked and exhausted, our hands idly searching each other's bodies as we drift off to sleep, when she makes a revelation.

"I lied to you about working at City Lights because I didn't want you to think less of me," she admits, her voice soft in the quiet, dark night.

Her words wake me up completely and I blink up at the ceiling. "Yeah?"

"I was afraid you wouldn't like me if you knew I was a topless waitress. Or that you'd think I was nothing but a big joke. A slut. A whore." She lifts her head, propping her arm across my chest so she can look at me. I can barely make out her features in the darkness, but I see the whites of her eyes, and can tell just how serious she is. "I hate that I lied to you."

"It's okay." I rest my hand on top of her head, stroking her hair. "I understand why you did it."

"I don't like hiding pieces of me from you. But it's

something I've always done, with everyone." She ducks her head, her face in my chest, and my hand falls away from her. "There's a lot of stuff I've done that I'm ashamed of."

"Can I be real with you right now, like you're being with me?" I ask her.

She lifts her head once more, nodding.

"I don't like your job. I don't like the idea of guys staring at your naked chest while you serve them drinks." It makes me feel possessive in the worst possible way. Like I want to kick ass and destroy people. "But I respect your choices. You did what you had to do to make money and survive. Who am I to judge you for that?"

"You're too good to be true," she whispers, her voice shaky, her eyes glassy. "I don't deserve you."

"Don't say that." I touch her cheek, stroke my fingers along her velvety-soft skin. "I hate it when you put yourself down."

"It's true, Rhett. I've made terrible choices. I've done things that could…hurt you. I want to tell you everything, but I can't. Not yet."

Unease slips down my spine, but I fight against it. I can't judge her. She's being honest with me, which is exactly what I want. Getting mad won't solve anything. It will only make the situation worse. "Take your time. Tell me whenever you're ready, and I'll be here."

"You are here for me, aren't you? You really are." She slides up, until we're hip-to-hip, chest-to-chest, face-to-face. Eye-to-eye. "You're the first person to ever do that for me."

I frown. "Do what?"

"Be there for me. No one ever has been before."

I cup the back of her head once more, threading my fingers through her thick, silky hair. "I really doubt that—"

"No, it's true." She rests her fingers against my lips, silencing me. "I kept pushing you away, yet you always came back. I didn't understand why. I still don't." She traces my upper lip with her index finger, her gaze thoughtful.

I kiss her fingertips and they fall away from my mouth. "Maybe it's because I don't want to give up on you."

"Everyone else does."

She seems so sad, so down, and I hate it. Why does she act like her life is always such a disappointment? I don't know enough about her past to understand, not completely, and I don't think it's safe to ask yet. "Not me."

"I know, and I've grown to appreciate you." Jensen takes a deep breath, like she's working up the nerve to say something. "I'm broken, I know I am. I've told you before that I'm…not nice. You make me want to be a better person, Rhett, but I don't know if that's possible. And I just wanted to warn you that I might hurt you. No matter what you eventually find out, no matter what you see or hear or read, you need to know that right now, tonight, I don't want to hurt you anymore. I haven't wanted to for a while."

I kiss her. She's talking nonsense. I don't get why she's

trying to tell me all this shit. It's kind of freaking me out, when the logical part of my brain is telling me she's just being dramatic. "You can't hurt me," I whisper against her lips. "I won't allow it."

"You can't control everything either, Rhett," she reminds me, her lips on my cheek, my neck. I really fucking love it when she kisses my neck, and she knows it.

Our conversation gives way to kissing, which gives way to actually having sex, which is a typical night for us.

But I can't help but think much later, long after Jensen's fallen asleep in my arms and I'm wide awake at two in the morning, remembering everything she said…

And wondering if maybe I should actually take her advice.

NINE

Our local Cheesecake Factory is huge, located right by the biggest mall in town. It's always crowded, even on a Wednesday night, and we're late to dinner, which I know will piss my dad and Diane off.

But when I picked Jensen up at her friend's apartment, I took one look at her standing in the doorway in her black sweater dress that hugs every curve and shows off her long legs, and I knew I had to have her. I pushed my way inside the apartment, lifted up her skirt, tore off her panties and fucked her right there against the door.

"Um, Savannah is at work," she told me after we both came, my jeans around my ankles, her dress bunched up under her breasts, making both of us crack up. I didn't even think of Savannah seeing us like that. Apparently neither did Jensen.

It took a few minutes for us to put ourselves back together.

Jensen fixed her hair and even had to reapply some of her makeup, though I told her she was beautiful enough and didn't need it. She seemed nervous, even a little shaky, though usually sex relaxes her, which is why I went for it.

Well, and I couldn't resist her in that dress.

Now we're entering the Cheesecake Factory fifteen minutes late—not as bad as I thought it would be, but my dad is a stickler for timeliness and that's usually Park's job, to show up late. But there he is standing with Addie and her boyfriend Trent, Dad and Diane sitting nearby. Diane's on her phone, her index finger sliding on the screen, scrolling, scrolling, scrolling, not paying attention to anyone.

Dad's glowering at me, his arms crossed, still wearing his suit, like he just came from the office. "You're late," he tells me in greeting when we stop in front of him. "You know they won't seat us until the entire party is here."

No, I didn't know. "Sorry." I grab hold of Jensen's hand to find that she's trembling, staring at Diane like she sees a ghost. "Dad, this is Jensen."

"Nice to meet you," he says gruffly, standing and holding out his hand to shake. I drop Jensen's hand so she can shake his. "This is my wife, Diane."

Diane stands as well, sending Jensen a withering stare before she heads for the hostess stand. "I'll let them know we're all here so we can get our table. " she calls over her shoulder as she walks away.

I ignore her jab at me, angry that she so blatantly dissed Jensen. "Don't mind her," I whisper close to Jensen's ear. "She's a total bitch."

Her answer is a shaky exhale.

"Rhett!" Addie tackle-hugs me and I squeeze her close, kissing her cheek. "I'm so glad you came."

"Happy birthday, Ads." I steer her so we're facing Jensen. "Addie, this is my friend, Jensen. Jensen, this is Addison, my little sister."

Friend. Jensen is so much more than a friend to me, but I can't call her my girlfriend yet. We're not at that point in our relationship and I know she would freak out if I use that word, especially to my family.

Hell, I might freak out if someone used that word.

"His seventeen-year-old sister, as of today." Addie grins and wraps Jensen up in a friendly hug. "It's so good to meet you! Rhett never brings girls around. Neither does Park."

Jensen hugs her back, looking awkward. Uncomfortable. But there's a smile on her face and her cheeks are flushed. "It's nice to meet you. Happy birthday."

"Thank you! You remember Trent," Addie tells me, and Trent and I shake hands. "Jensen, this is my boyfriend."

"Good to meet you," Trent says, staring at Jensen like he's checking her out. Considering he's seventeen years old and a walking horn dog, I can't blame him for blatantly staring at my girl.

But he better keep his hands to himself.

Everyone's shaking hands and making nice, and then there's Park, pushing himself into Jensen's personal space, introducing himself, gripping her hand tight and taking a long time to let it go. Jensen smiles at him and steps back when he releases his hold on her, her gaze skittering around as if she's looking for someone else. When Diane reappears, Jensen's eyes go wide and she scoots closer to me.

For some reason, she's intimidated most by Diane. But I guess I can't blame her. We're all used to Diane and her typical snobby bitch ways. Like tonight, I can hear her snapping at my dad like usual, because I swear she's always mad at him, the sneer on her face seemingly permanent. She looks put together though. She always does. With her blonde hair perfectly curled and freshly colored. Her Botoxed face and enhanced lips make her look plastic, and she's wearing every designer label she can find, like she's some sort of walking billboard for the finer things in life.

I hate her.

"Parker, you should have a word with that hostess," Diane tells my dad, her disgust blatant. "They won't seat us even though everyone's here."

"Diane, give them a minute," he starts, but she cuts him off, shaking her head.

"I don't want to be here all night," she whispers harshly. "This place is so incredibly "

Dad's eyes flash with anger, and Addie's flash with hurt. Trent wraps his arm around her shoulders, tugging her to his side.

"Hey, be cool," I tell Diane, stepping forward so I'm closer to her. "This is Addie's night. Don't mess it up."

"Are you warning me?" Diane asks, her voice shrill.

"Diane, settle down," Dad says, grabbing her elbow and pulling her away from our group. From their expressions and the tone of their voices, I can tell their conversation is turning heated.

"Nothing like dear old Dad getting into it with the missus," Park drawls, smiling at me. "Talk about tacky."

Addie laughs and disengages herself from Trent so she can wrap herself around our big brother, giving him a smacking kiss on the cheek. "I love you."

I slip my arm around Jensen's shoulders and bend my head so it's close to hers. "You okay?"

"Your family is very—overwhelming," she admits, her voice shaky. "I don't know what to think."

"Don't think at all. That's what I always do when I hang out with the fam," I answer just before I nuzzle her cheek. She smells fucking amazing. I can't believe we were having sex a little over thirty minutes ago and now we're here, making nice with the family.

I wish we were still at her apartment, her bare ass pressed against the door as I pushed inside her. That was a lot more fun than this shit.

"Rhett," she warns, right when Park decides to open his big mouth.

"You two are cozy." The smug look on his face tells me he thinks I'm an idiot. But my big brother has never been big on commitment. People may say I'm a player, but the real player in this family is Park. Or Dad. "Is this serious or what, Rhett?"

"Like I'm going to answer that question right now." I squeeze Jensen's shoulders reassuringly. "But don't be surprised if I bring her around you guys some more. As long as you all behave."

Park laughs, highly amused. "Guess she won't be coming around then, since none of us know how to behave."

"Hey, speak for yourself," Addie adds, smiling. "I'm so excited Jensen's here, Rhett. Someone for me to talk to instead of a bunch of rude guys all the time."

"Hey," Trent protests and she gives him a quick kiss on the lips, shutting him up.

"What about Diane?" I ask innocently.

"The Wicked Witch of the West doesn't count." Addie reaches over and swats my chest. "And you know it."

Jensen laughs, the first time I've seen her look relaxed since we've arrived, and I'm thinking she's going to be all right.

And the evening goes pretty smooth, despite our arriving late and throwing off our seating chances. They finally take us to our table, and I make sure and sit as far away from Dad and

Diane as possible. Trent and Addie sit directly across from me and Jensen, and Park sits on the other side of her. Conversation is flowing, Addie telling us how Dad surprised her with her car that morning.

"Sadie was there." Sadie is Addie's best friend. "And she's got her phone out, taking a video as we walk out the front door. I'm so completely clueless, I had no idea what she was doing, but when we went outside, there it was, sitting in the driveway. My beautiful white Jeep with a giant pink bow on top. It was so awesome, I started crying and screaming, and she got it all so we could post it on my Snapchat story. I hugged Dad so hard he said I was choking him. Huh, Daddy?" Addie leans forward, smiling at our Dad.

"You got a little excited," Dad says dryly, making us laugh.

"Anyway, it was the best present ever." Addie smiles, sending Trent a look. "Trent and I went to the cemetery after school. We left flowers on Mama's grave."

I'm usually the one who does that with Addie. I'll call or text her the week before, and we'll arrange a time to meet on Addie's birthday to take flowers and…talk to her. Addie likes to call her Mama, because that's what Park and I always called her when we were little, and when we told her that, she seemed to latch onto it.

I hate that she never got to know her. That Addie has no memories of our mother at all. Only what we share with her, photographs and videos, a lingering reminder of our mother's vibrancy and pure joy.

"Ads, I'm so sorry." I reach across the table and rest my hand over hers, giving it a brief squeeze. "I've been kinda busy." Completely distracted by Jensen.

My excuse sounds lame, but I can tell Addie isn't angry with me.

"It's okay. Trent took me to the cemetery and it was nice. I didn't even cry. I told her all about my new car, and about Trent, and school. It was good. I like talking to her now, though it used to make me sad." Addie smiles, and in that moment, she resembles our mother so much, it almost takes my breath away.

I wonder if Dad sees it. He has to. I wonder if it bothers him, to look at his daughter and see his dead wife.

"Did Rhett tell you that our mom died giving birth to me?" Addie asks Jensen.

"Addie," Park chastises, scowling at her. "Should we really talk about this right now? It's your birthday."

Park isn't comfortable talking about Mom. Ever. That's more for me and Addie.

"It's also the day our mother died," Addie points out.

"Right, but let's focus on the positive stuff, okay?" Park's voice is gruff, his gaze distant. Sometimes I wonder if he's going to explode someday, since he rarely expresses his feelings about…anything. He keeps everything bottled up inside, and that can't be good.

"I was just curious," Addie says, looking hurt. "I think she should know, because I sound like a crazy person right now and I wanted to explain my birthday ritual to her."

"He did tell me about your mother," Jensen says, her voice soft, her eyes lit with understanding. "And I'm so sorry."

"It's okay. I didn't know her, so it's not like I miss her, though actually, I do." Addie squints her eyes and twists her mouth, like she's thinking real hard. Our baby sister is animated and silly and she'll talk a mile a minute. She drives Diane batshit crazy. Sometimes she drives Park and our dad crazy too.

But I love her. She's the closest reminder of our mother, and I like spending time with her.

"I lost my dad last year." At Addie's blank look, Jensen continues, "He died."

"Oh, I'm sorry. I thought you meant he was literally lost. Like, you know, people go missing, right? Oh my gosh, you must think I'm a complete idiot! I'm just nervous. I don't know why." Addie smiles brightly, reaching across the table to grab Jensen's hand. "I'm sorry. That must've been hard."

"It was."

"Do you ever go visit his grave?"

Jensen shakes her head. "It's too...new, his death. I'm not ready to face it yet. Going out to the cemetery, seeing his gravestone. I don't know if I could handle it."

I listen to her explanations, appreciating Addie's questions. Jensen's opening up to her, and it's nice. They share something.

We all have the dead parent thing in common, and while that's not a great thing to share, it's there.

"I go visit our mom's grave every year on my birthday. Rhett and I have been going together for years," Addie tells her.

Jensen turns to look at me. "And this year you forgot?"

I nod, feeling guilty.

"It's not a big deal! We'll go another time. We don't just visit her on my birthday, but we go during the holidays too. Thanksgiving is coming up. You can talk to her then, Rhett." Addie beams. "I'll drive you in my Jeep."

Our meals are served and Dad takes over the conversation, talking about work, the holidays, how he expects all of us for Thanksgiving and Christmas. Diane complains that she wants to go to Hawaii for the holidays and Dad tells her, "Absolutely not," in the rudest voice he's got. "Addie is still at home. We can't leave her during Christmas."

"Do you have plans for Thanksgiving, Jensen?" he asks.

Jensen blinks, her eyes extra wide, like she can't believe Dad spoke directly to her. "Um, not really."

"You should come to the house with Rhett," he suggests, surprising me. He sends me a look. "It would be nice to have her for dinner, son."

"Yeah, I bet it would be," Park murmurs under his breath, making Trent almost snort his drink out his nose.

Dad sends Park an irritated scowl while Diane appears ready to spit nails, she's so annoyed. "You know what I meant.

I don't mean actually Jensen for Thanksgiving dinner. I meant we could have her   for dinner."

"We know what you meant, Dad," I tell him, hoping like hell he'll stop this particular conversation.

Jensen remains quiet, picking at her dinner. Park sends me a look over her bent head, his expression smug.

I look away, focusing on my food. I want out of here. I want to go back to my house, lock ourselves away in my bedroom, and get naked with Jensen. At least the night would end positively.

After we're done eating, Addie pushes away from the table and stands. "I'm going to the restroom. Jensen, you want to go with me?"

Jensen looks over at me and then at Addie. "Um, sure."

The moment they're gone, Park's in Jensen's chair, his voice extra low as he starts to talk. "I know your girl."

"What are you talking about?" Unease washes over me. I don't like where this is going.

"Jensen. I recognize her from somewhere, and it's been driving me crazy all damn night," Park says with a growl. "Where does she work?"

Fucking great. Does Park go to City Lights? No way am I telling him Jensen works there. "We go to school together. And she cleans offices at night, so I don't think you'd have a chance to run into her."

"Weird." Park frowns and stares off into the distance. "I

swear I've met her before."

"She seems like a nice young woman," Dad tells me. "Is she coming to Addie's party Saturday night?"

"I'm sure Addie will convince her to go." Not that I've mentioned it yet. One step at a time with this one.

"I meant what I said about having her over for Thanksgiving dinner. I'd rather encourage your relationships with nice girls." Nice girls, ha. Dad would shit if he knew Jensen is a topless waitress. "Though I wish Park was the one getting serious." He sends Park a pointed look, who's moving back into his own chair.

"It's not serious, Dad. We've really only just met," I tell him, but I'm kind of full of shit. I don't want to think of anyone else. I don't want to see anyone else. I've ditched all my friends, my frat brothers. I haven't gone to a party since I've met Jensen. Only the bachelor party for Emmett, and thank Christ I went to that, or else I might've never seen Jensen again.

Yeah, this will get serious. As long as she's straight with me, I can see this working between Jensen and me.

"She looks at you with adoring eyes," Dad says, chuckling.

"No, she doesn't," I start to protest, but Park interrupts me.

"Yeah, she does. It's kind of disgusting."

Trent laughs, but otherwise doesn't say anything. He's nice enough, but not much of a conversationalist.

"Don't laugh, dude, Addie looks at you in the same way," Park tells him, pointing a finger at Trent.

"I look at Trent in what way?" Addie asks as she and Jensen returns to the table. She slips into her chair and so does Jensen, who flashes me a soft smile when our eyes meet.

"Like you think he's the fuckin' shit," Park says, purely for shock value.

Addie laughs. Trent grins. Dad is scowling.

"You shouldn't speak so rudely to your sister," Diane says.

Diane defending Addie, that's a laugh.

"Well, shouldn't treat Addie so rudely either," Park returns with an arrogant smile. "If you'd had your way, we wouldn't be at this crap restaurant celebrating your stepdaughter's birthday in the first place. Am I right?"

I can't believe he went there, yet I can. But he usually saves those insults for when we're at home versus in a restaurant.

Diane doesn't say a thing. She just rises to her feet, throws her napkin onto her chair, and storms off.

"You should go apologize to Diane," Dad tells Park the second she's gone.

"What? Right now?" Park shakes his head. "Hell no."

"Hell " Dad points at him. "Go find her and apologize. That insult was uncalled for."

"But so scarily accurate, don't you think?" Park drawls.

We're all quiet, even Trent. Especially Jensen. I swear she's trembling once more, and I'd bet big money she never wants to come to a family outing with the Montgomerys ever again.

"Park." Dad says his name as a warning, though he doesn't

disagree with Park's statement.

Telling.

"Fine. I'll go find her." Park stands, shaking his longish dark hair back. We look a lot alike, my brother and me. But he's shorter, with broader shoulders, and an almost-but-not-quite unkempt appearance to him. Like he just doesn't give a damn.

Which describes Park's personality perfectly.

We make small talk while Park and Diane are gone, and our server appears, asking if we want dessert. Addie and Trent both do, but my appetite is long gone. And when Jensen declines the cheesecake offer, I lean in close to tell her, "Order a slice to go."

"Are you sure?"

"Yeah, you mentioned you might want an entire cheesecake, right?" I smile, trying to lighten the moment.

"I was joking." She rolls her eyes, but at least she's smiling. "And you're the one who suggested I order an entire cheesecake."

"True. You're right, so go ahead and pick out a slice. Whatever you want." I crack open the menu. "I'll order one to go too."

Park and Diane are gone so long, Dad starts calling both of their cell phones, but there's no answer. "I refuse to referee their arguments," he proclaims with a grunt. "I've been doing it for too long, and they both know it. I've told them before they have to learn how to work out their differences."

"I'll go look for them," Addie volunteers, rising to her feet.

"No, sit down, birthday girl. I'll go find them." I leave the table and wander the restaurant, but they're nowhere to be seen. I go back by the bathrooms, even go into the men's room, but nothing.

Weird.

I send Park a simple "where are you?" text and head outside, checking out the small groups of people standing around, waiting to get in or chatting before they go their separate ways for the night. Diane and Park aren't there either, and I'm starting to get worried.

What the hell is going on?

Heading around the side of the building, I find a small alcove, created for smokers, maybe. And that's where I spot them. Park.

And Diane.

In each other's arms.

Their mouths fused together.

I stand there completely frozen for I don't know how long. It feels like hours, but was probably only a few seconds, and Diane is the first one to open her eyes.

Diane is the first one to actually see me.

"Rhett!" she shrieks, causing Park to spring away from her. "What are you doing here?"

I can't find my voice. I'm in too much shock.

"Hey." Park whirls around, wiping his mouth with the back of his hand, a rueful smile on his face. The fucker got caught, and he knows it. So how's he going to get out of this? What's his excuse, his explanation? I think he can tell by the expression on my face that I've seen a lot more than they ever wanted me to witness. "This isn't what you think."

"What is it then?" My voice is so calm, I surprise myself. Inside, I'm a jumble of nerves. Shock. Disbelief.

Park freaking Diane. Like, hates her with all he's got. And Diane has been our so-called mother since Park was nine and I was five.

So what they're doing right now is totally fucking crazy.

And an absolute betrayal.

Deciding I'm not going to wait any longer to hear his bullshit answer, I turn around and head back for the restaurant.

TEN

I nstead of going straight to our table, I return to the men's room, where I can wash my hands and splash water on my face, like that will help me unsee my big brother kissing our stepmother.

Like, what the actual fuck is happening right now? Is this for real? Because it's just too crazy to comprehend.

Park enters the bathroom minutes later, slamming open the door with a loud bang when he strides inside. "Let me explain," he starts, stopping directly in front of me.

I dry my hands, crumple the paper towel into a ball and toss it into the wastebasket. "How the hell are you going to explain what I saw, Park?"

"It was a one shot deal."

"My ass. You two were gone for a long time. You were her. God knows what else you were doing while you were gone."

I step closer to him, my gaze never leaving his. His eyes are a dark brown, just like mine. And they are deceptive, I'm realizing. He's a liar.

I'm surrounded by liars.

"It's nothing."

"It's definitely something, Park, considering how stressed out you look right now. You're sweating," I emphasize, pointing at his forehead. "Here." I hit the lever and crank out a sheet of paper towel, ripping it off and handing it to him.

He goes to the mirror and dabs at his face, his gaze meeting mine in the reflection. "You can't tell Dad."

"Yeah, don't worry about that. That's the last thing I want to do." I'm not going to be the one who breaks the news to Dad.

But what am I supposed to do now that I know?

"You've put me in a real shitty position, you know," I tell Park.

He turns to face me. "You didn't have to chase after us. We were on our way back to the table."

"When? After your make-out session? Jesus, Park!" I roar. "You were gone for fifteen minutes. Dad called you both. He was mad, said he was done refereeing your fights. Looks like he needs to keep doing it, since clearly you two need a chaperone."

"Fuck off. You don't know what you're talking about." Park starts to exit the bathroom, but I grab hold of his arm, stopping him.

"Are you fucking her?"

He's breathing heavily, his nostrils flaring, his mouth thin, but it's his eyes that give him away. They're swirling with guilt.

"You are, aren't you." It's not a question, though. I realize without a doubt they are totally fucking each other. "Goddamn, Park! "

He shrugs. "Why the fuck not? I'm proving she's a total whore. She's been begging for my dick for years."

The last thing I wanted to hear. "That doesn't make it right. Dad is going to lose his shit when he finds out."

"He's not going to find out. You won't tell him, and Diane and I certainly won't tell him either. So don't worry about it."

"Fuck you," I spit out, leaving the bathroom before he can. I return to the table to find Diane already there, snuggled up against my dad's side, batting her eyelashes at him as she talks in that annoying baby voice she sometimes uses. I can see from where I'm sitting she's reapplied a fresh coat of lipstick.

Right, because my fucking brother just kissed it all off.

"Are you okay?" Jensen asks when I still haven't said anything.

Turning my head, I find that she's watching me, her brow wrinkled. "I'm fine. It's just…my brother," I tell her, purposely vague. "He, uh, pisses me off sometimes."

She touches my thigh, her fingers way too close to my dick. "I'm sorry. He's kind of—volatile, isn't he?"

"That's one way to describe him." I reach for my water glass and down it. I wish I had alcohol. Something to make me forget what I saw.

"Are you all right, Rhett?" I glance up to find Diane watching me, her eyes a warning but her face schooled into a pleasant expression, like she doesn't have a care in the world. Not a trace of guilt in sight.

"I'm fine," I bite out.

Her smile is extra pleased, which leaves me extra pissed. "Good. So very glad to hear it."

No one is paying attention. No one else caught that subtle statement but Jensen. She's looking from Diane to me and back to Diane again so many times, she looks like she's at a tennis match.

Park returns to the table, all flustered and out of breath, like he just ran a fucking marathon. "Sorry, got a phone call that stressed me out."

"What about?" Dad asks.

"The Latham deal." Mergers and acquisitions is my father's business, and Park works for him as well.

Me? I have no interest in that. Though I don't know exactly what I'm going to do with my life once I graduate.

They start talking business, and Park is so damn smooth, you'd never know he was just tonguing his dad's wife in public only minutes ago.

"Addie invited me to her party on Saturday night," Jensen

says, knocking me from my disturbing thoughts. "But I don't think I can make it."

"Why not?" She has to be there. No way do I want to be alone at the birthday party so I'll have to listen to Park's excuses, or Diane will try to corner me and explain her way out of what I witnessed.

"I have to work. I work every Saturday night," Jensen answers.

"Call in sick. Or trade shifts with someone," I suggest.

Jensen smiles. "Addie said the same thing, calling in sick. She told me she wanted me there."

"I do, so give the birthday girl what she wants," Addie says with a nod. "Please say you'll come."

"Yeah, Jens. Please." I settle my hand over hers, which is still resting on my thigh. I drag her hand up, so it's settled over my cock, and I get even harder at her innocent touch.

Yeah, I'm pissed as hell, and for some reason I want to work it out sexually. As in, get Jensen back to my place and fuck her brains out.

She gives me a squeeze, her sparkling eyes full of mischief. "I'll try my best."

"Yeah, well, try harder," I tell her, and she squeezes me harder, just like I requested.

I look over at Park sitting on the other side of Jensen, blatantly staring at us, watching Jensen stroke me through my jeans. And I'm so disgusted with myself, I push her hand off me, so suddenly that she cries out, but not loud enough for anyone else to hear.

Except for Park. The asshole.

"Looks like you've got yourself a little firecracker," he tells me later, after Dad's paid the dinner bill and we're all exiting the restaurant. He falls into step beside me, Addie talking to Jensen a mile a minute as they walk ahead of us. "Giving you a handjob while at dinner with your family—nice."

"Shut the fuck up, Park. She wasn't giving me a handjob," I say irritably.

Park raises his brows. "Looked like it to me."

"Listen, you're not allowed to talk about her. She's off limits," I practically snarl.

He's fuming. He doesn't like that I told him what to do, but he can't say a goddamn word. I now know his deepest, darkest secret. I wish I didn't. I wish I never saw what happened today, but I did. And now I can't unsee it, no matter how hard I try. That image is burned in my brain, just like his confession is too.

"You don't understand," he tells me, his tone casual, like we're discussing the weather. "My relationship with Diane is… complicated."

"I'll say. Far more complicated than I want to think about."

"Look." Park stops me with a touch of his hand on my arm, while the rest of them file out of the restaurant. "I need you to keep quiet about this."

"I already told you I'm not telling Dad."

"Yeah, but I don't want you telling your little girlfriend either. We don't know her. What if she has a big mouth? What if she talks?" Park shakes his head. "I can't risk it, Rhett. If this gets out, I'm fucked forever."

"You sure as hell are."

He sends me an irritated look. "And I can't have that. He's going to retire soon, and he's going to leave me in charge. I can't mess this up."

"You should've thought of that before you stuck your dick in our stepmom's vag." With that statement, I hurry out of the restaurant, catching up with Jensen, Addie and Trent with ease. "Where's Diane and Dad?"

"They already left." Addie wrinkles her nose. "They were all lovey-dovey and acting like they're going back home to hook up or whatever. It was gross."

"You can't hook up if you're married," Trent tells her.

"Whatever, it was awful to witness. Like I need brain bleach," Addie says with a little laugh.

If Addie had witnessed Park and Diane together, she'd probably need something even stronger than bleach. I turn to my date. "You ready to go, Jensen?"

She nods and hooks her arm through mine as we make our goodbyes. And then we're finally in my car, driving away from the Cheesecake Factory and one of the worst nights on record. Like this is top five shit.

"Did you guys have an argument?" When I send her a confused look, she says, "You and Park."

"Oh. Yeah. I guess." I know I'm being kind of a dick, but I can't help it. I can't wrap my head around Park and Diane's relationship. What sort of ratifications will this have if they're exposed? What will Park do? What will Dad do?

And what about Diane?

"What happened between you two? You seemed so angry earlier. You still do." She hesitates, twisting her hands together in her lap. "This has nothing to do with me, does it? You weren't disappointed in how I acted tonight, right? Your dad was really nice to me, though Di—Diane wasn't very friendly toward me. At all."

Statement of the century. "She's not nice to anyone." Well, except my brother, probably.

Disgusting.

"She was totally rude to me. I mean, what did I ever do to her?" Okay, there's some of Jensen's attitude back. And I'm glad to see it. Being with my family tonight made her meek and quiet, and I'm not used to Jensen acting like that.

"Nothing. She's an equal opportunity rude bitch," I say, my voice bitter.

"And she never did explain where she was when she up and disappeared earlier," Jensen continues.

I need to divert the conversation. "She likes to pout. Play games. Diane is the ultimate drama queen."

"And your dad actually puts up with it?"

I have no explanation for this, since I don't understand it myself. "I think he likes Diane's flare for drama. As long as he's not dragged into it too much, he's happy." This is why I can't tell anyone about what I saw. Park will have my fucking head, and I know it.

So I'm not messing with that.

"Are you going to Addie's party Saturday night?" I try to change the subject.

"I'm going to try." Jensen smiles. "I really like your sister. She was so sweet to me tonight, when she didn't have to be."

"She's the sweetest girl I know, I swear. Wouldn't harm a hair on your head…if she likes you."

"What does she do if she doesn't like you? Make your life a living hell?"

"Probably." We both laugh, but I immediately sober. "I hope she's not mean to the people she doesn't like. Like…the kids at school. I have no idea what she does there beyond go to class, but I hope she isn't some shitty mean girl who treats people like they're worthless."

For all I know, she could. Addie does live with Diane, after all.

"Oh, I doubt that. She's too sweet-natured to do such terrible things," Jensen reassures me.

"Yeah." I'm distracted. I don't want to have this conversation, not anymore. I don't want to talk at all, but Jensen seems like she wants to give everyone at dinner a personal analysis, so I let her.

But I don't really comment and I think she senses something is wrong, because she eventually goes quiet, until she finally says, so low I almost don't hear her, "Park saw me touch you like that, huh."

I exhale loudly. "Yeah. He did."

"You think he'll tell your dad and...Diane?" She's chewing on her lower lip. "God, I hope not."

"Don't sweat it. He won't tell anyone."

"Are you sure? Can you trust him? I just, I don't want to make the wrong impression on your parents."

I don't know why she cares so much. My family is a wreck. My parents...they're not normal. What they're doing to each other isn't right, not by a long shot, and they don't deserve Jensen's fearful concern.

"You didn't. You made a great impression," I say, trying to sound as final as possible. I really don't want to talk about this anymore. It's a pointless conversation. "Dad invited you over for Thanksgiving. That's huge."

"I guess." She stares out the window. "I just don't want Park to think I'm some easy whore who feels up his brother at the dinner table."

"You're not a whore, Jens," I say firmly. "And he has no room to talk. Trust me."

And I leave it at that.

ELEVEN

"Rhett." She's breathless, her hands gripping my shoulders, her body squirming beneath mine, and that's all because of what I'm doing to her. I can't keep my hands or mouth off her. She's all I can focus on, all I to focus on.

The second we arrived at my place, I took Jensen by the hand and pulled her into the house, leading her back toward the bedroom. Chad was sitting on the couch watching TV, his mouth dropping open in disbelief as we passed by him, but I didn't say a word. Just glared at him, as if daring him to open his mouth and say something stupid.

He didn't, thank God.

Now I've got her in my room, the door locked. Her dress gone. She's on the bed clad in a black bra and a skimpy pair of black panties, and I'm kissing her, caressing her, desperate for her.

I want to lose myself in her. Forget all the shit that went down tonight and concentrate on Jensen. She's the only thing that feels right in my life, which is messed up since for all I know, she's still lying to me about everything.

I'm an idiot, but I don't care. My need for her outweighs the lingering doubt.

"Rhett." Her voice is firmer. Louder. I lift my head from her neck, one hand cupped around her breast, the other toying with the waistband of her panties. She's frowning at me, her blue eyes turbulent, her lips thin. "You're not even listening to what I'm saying."

"What are you saying?" I slowly pull her panties down, exposing her completely, and she kicks them the rest of the way off, then presses her hand against my forehead to stop me from going down on her.

"You're still not listening to me." She actually sounds mad. Great. I shift away from her so I'm sitting on the edge of the bed. "Is something bothering you?"

"No." I practically spit the word out. I really don't want to have a big meaningful talk. More like I just want to have meaningful sex and that's it.

She lifts a brow. "Are you always this grouchy after having dinner with your family?"

"No, but I'm grouchy because you won't let me do what I want."

Sighing, she shakes her head, reaching behind her back to unhook her bra. "Is this all you want from me tonight?" She whips her bra off, tossing it on the floor so she's completely naked, while I'm still completely clothed. "You just want to use me for sex?"

I don't say the word out loud, though. Instead, I look away, staring at the wall, feeling like an asshole.

The mattress shifts and I can feel her crawling toward me. And then she's touching me, her hand on my shoulder, her scent driving me wild. I don't turn around, though. If I do, I'll probably attack her and she'll get mad at me all over again.

"I know you're upset about something, and that it has to do with your brother." Her voice is soft. So is her hand that still rests on my shoulder, and I'm tempted to spill everything.

But I can't. I promised Park I would keep my mouth shut, though he doesn't deserve my loyalty. He's the jerk who's banging his stepmom while she's still married to our dad.

Like, who fucking does that? When did it start between them? Was it years ago or recent? And why hasn't it ended?

My family is completely messed up. No, we're beyond messed up. I can't tell Jensen about my recent discovery. She'd probably run screaming once she heard Park and Diane's dirty little secret.

"I've said some things lately that makes it seem like I don't care about you." She clears her throat, like she's having trouble getting the words out. My chest grows tight in preparation for what she might say next. "I told you straight up that what we're doing means nothing to me."

She did.

"And you said it meant nothing to you too."

Guess I'm the liar now.

"You taking me to dinner with your family tonight makes me feel like there's more here. Between us." Jensen pauses, and all of this unspoken tension seems to grow and expand in the room the longer she remains quiet.

I still won't look at her, not until she's finished with what she's saying.

"Do you want more, Rhett?" She rests both hands on my shoulders now, and slowly starts massaging them. "You're so tense," she murmurs.

"Do want more?" I ask the wall, ducking my head and closing my eyes as she continues to rub my shoulders. I can already feel the muscles loosening up, and while that has something to do with her massaging me, it has more to do with the woman who's touching me.

I just...I can't explain it. I have a thing for Jensen. She comes around, and I automatically react.

"I want to," she whispers near my ear, making me shiver. "But I know I'll probably mess it up."

"How?" I turn to face her, her hands falling away from my shoulders. "How will you mess this up? You always say things like that, but you never explain yourself."

She shrugs. Like she doesn't want to answer me.

Or maybe she doesn't know how.

"I think that's complete bullshit, Jens," I tell her vehemently. "You'll either make it work, or you won't."

"It's not that simple…" Her voice drifts, and I grab hold of her waist, hauling her into my lap.

"It that simple." I kiss her, a soft, lingering kiss that makes me practically vibrate with wanting her. "I like you, you like me."

She smiles, but her eyes are sad. "Uh huh."

"And I don't want to see anyone else."

"I don't want to see anyone else either." She wraps her legs around my hips, slings her arms around my neck.

"Okay then, it's official. We're committed." I kiss her again to seal the deal, and she starts to giggle against my mouth, as if I just told her a joke. "Hey, I'm serious."

The giggles stop. "I know you are, and I like this idea. I do. I just don't know if it's—realistic."

"Why the hell not?" I am so over game-playing and lying and bullshit. "Are you still feeding me a bunch of lies?"

She looks me straight in the eyes. "No."

Notice how she doesn't deny that she's fed me a bunch of lies before.

"Are there things I should know about you?" I lean in close, our noses touching. "Are you still keeping secrets from me?"

Her eyes slide closed as she kisses me, rendering me

stupid with her lips and tongue. I let it happen, and I know deep in my soul that this is a distraction. This kiss, the way she's touching me, trying to help me shed my shirt, stroking the front of my jeans. I don't protest—why would I protest? This is exactly what I wanted from the start.

We kiss like this for minutes, until she finally breaks away and runs her mouth along my jawline. I take a deep breath, holding on to her tight, afraid if I let go she'll slip right out of arms and disappear.

Irrational, but fears are rarely rational, am I right?

"All this serious talk freaks me out," she murmurs against my neck, just before she kisses the sensitive skin below my ear. "Can't we just have fun?"

"That's what I was trying to tell you earlier."

She lifts her head, her smoldering gaze meeting mine. "No, you were trying to get all aggressive with me because you were pissed at your brother."

"I'm still pissed at my brother. I'm pissed at all of them, except for Addie." And she is the last person I want to talk about right now.

"You never told me what was bothering you."

"You never tell me what's bothering you either," I return.

We stare at each other for a tension-filled moment, and then I'm pushing her back onto the bed, kicking off my shoes and jeans and underwear, shrugging out of my shirt. She watches me while I strip, her expression almost…void, and I freeze. But then her eyes grow warm when they meet mine, as if she appreciates what she sees, and I stand at the foot of the bed for a moment, studying her.

With Jensen, I'm completely uninhibited. Not that I was a prude or anything like that, but I usually followed the girl's lead. What she wanted, I wanted, and as we grew more comfortable, we'd get a little more adventurous.

Jensen and I have been adventurous from the first moment we had sex, and she's led me down some pretty interesting paths. Ones I still want to explore.

I think of us in my car. I think of us in the hallway at the strip club. I think of the many ways I've had her, the many times I've tasted her, and the fact that I've only known her for a short while.

Touching her hip, I give her a gentle nudge. "Roll over."

Without a word she does as I say, rolling over so she's lying on her stomach, her pretty ass on display. I grab her hips and tug, pulling her into position so she's on her hands and knees. She looks at me over her shoulder, a tiny smile curling her lips as she wags her butt at me.

I break out into a sweat just looking at her.

"We've never done it like this before," she says.

"I know." I crawl onto the bed on my knees and position myself behind her. "Spread your legs a little bit."

She repositions herself, her legs spread, and I can see she's wet. And I'm hard as a damn rock. There's no foreplay tonight.

I don't have it in me.

All I want to do is fuck.

I hold on to her left hip and grab my cock with my other hand, rubbing the tip back and forth, teasing her pussy. She bucks against me, a low moan sounding in her throat, and I easily slide in, pushing until I'm balls-deep.

My name falls from her lips as she lowers herself to her elbows, grabbing hold of one of my pillows to clutch it in her arms. I don't bother taking it slow, and I'm definitely not gentle.

Instead, I immediately start thrusting, my hips hitting her ass with every stroke, her hot, tight pussy clutching me deep. She moves with me, taking what I give her, her face buried in the pillow, muffling her loud moans.

I'm quiet, concentrating on the friction, the in-and-out rhythm, how she clenches around my cock like her body is trying to keep us forever connected.

And still I pound into her, not even close to coming yet.

She cries out, her hips jerking, her pussy milking my dick, and I grit my teeth, powering through her first orgasm. It would've been so easy to let go, to let my own orgasm wash over me, but I'm not ready. Not yet. There's something so satisfactory about taking what's yours without any restraint. That's what I'm doing. I'm taking Jensen because she's mine.

She belongs to me.

"Rhett," she pants, and I open my eyes, watching as my dick slides in and out of her body. Christ, that'll send me over the edge for sure. Her body shines with sweat, my fingers slipping around her hips as I try to get a grip on her. I'm sweating too. My chest is tight, my heart is racing, my breathing's ragged, and I shake my head, running a hand through my hair to push it off my forehead.

And still she keeps moving, sliding up and down on my cock, driving me out of my mind.

I reach for her, my hands on her waist, pulling her up so she's on her knees bowed up against me, my cock still inside her. She presses her back to my front, her breathing just as loud as mine, her entire body shaking, and I put my hand to her cheek, turning her head so I can take her mouth.

"You're going to kill me," she whispers against my mouth, and I growl, nipping at her lower lip.

"What do you mean?"

"I've already come two times." She shivers when I stroke her neck, her chest, and I wonder how I missed the second orgasm. "How much longer are you going to last?"

"Until you come a third time," I whisper, releasing my hold on her head. She faces away from me, throwing her head back so she's leaning on my shoulder. I can see the rise and fall of her breasts, those rosy pink nipples tempting me. Slowly I start to move once more, though it's harder to establish a rhythm in this position.

But I like the closeness we're sharing. I wrap my arms around her and she bends forward a little, sending me deeper, making both of us groan. I increase my speed, hammering into her, until she's crying out my name and I'm coming so hard I swear I could black out.

I'm exhausted, ready to fall into the deepest sleep once we're done, and I'm pulling the blankets over our still-covered-with-sweat bodies. She doesn't bother saying she's going to leave, and I'm glad.

I want her to stay.

Right before I drift off, she tucks her body close to mine, and I'm spooning her. My mind wanders as I breathe in the sweet scent of her shampoo, enjoying the way she lightly scratches my arm with her sharp nails.

I fall asleep quickly and dream of being at my dad's house, wandering the halls and calling Jensen's name, unable to find her. The house is three times as big in my dream, with an endless hall and so many doors, and for some reason, I have to open every single one.

I finally try the last door, swinging it open to find a giant bed dominating the room. Jensen is there, lying in the center of the mattress, naked and beautiful, her eyes closed in ecstasy, her full lips parted as she moans. She's getting fucked, but I can't see who he is. His hair is dark.

Like mine.

His shoulders are broad, his butt pumping up and down, and all I can do is watch.

She's getting fucked all right.

By Park.

I jerk awake with a gasp, sitting straight up, the comforter puddling in my lap. My heart is racing triple time and I run my hands through my hair, tugging on the ends so hard it hurts, my eyes squeezed tightly shut.

It takes me a while to calm my wild thoughts and heart, and I finally get out of bed to take a piss. When I return I find Jensen awake, sitting up with the sheet clutched to her chest, her hair a mess, her eyes big in the dimly lit room.

"I had a bad dream," she admits when I crawl back into bed.

"What about?" I pull her into me, her head on my chest, her hair in my face, my arm around her shoulders. I can't tell her about my dream. It's too weird.

Too freaking scary to think about.

"I was back at my old house, where we lived before my dad died." Her lips tease my skin as she speaks. "And you were there too, but I was so ashamed."

"Of me?"

"No, of you being there and seeing everything. Our place was kind of a dump." She hesitates before she says, "We lived in a trailer park."

"Oh." What do I say to that?

"Anyway, my dad was yelling at me. Calling me a slut, saying I was a whore, just like my mom."

A mom reference. She doesn't make those very often.

"He kept saying it and looking at you, like he was trying to convince you to say it too. Eventually you did, you both started yelling at me, calling me a slut and a whore, and I finally slammed my hands over my ears and screamed. I wouldn't stop screaming. Then I woke up." A shuddering breath leaves her, and I hug her close.

"You had that dream because you're worried about what my family thinks of you. You basically said that to me in the car," I explain.

"I know. You're right." She presses her face against my chest. "It was awful. It felt so real."

"You're not a whore—you do realize that, right?" I press a kiss to the top of her head. "It's not like you get paid to have sex with guys."

She goes completely still, to the point that I worry she's passed out or something.

"Jens?"

Nothing.

I shake her shoulders. "Jensen."

"Yeah?" Her voice is small. So small. She doesn't sound right.

What's wrong with her? It's like I ask that particular question, and she's having a quiet freak out.

"Are you okay?" I ask.

"Um…" She rubs her cheek against my chest, and I wonder if she's stalling for time. "Yeah. I'm just…really tired."

I kiss her forehead, trying to be understanding. I don't want to talk about all of this either. It feels too heavy, too difficult. Our bad dreams are revealing our fears, and I don't feel like analyzing them any longer. "Go to sleep," I tell her.

"Okay."

Her weird reaction stays with me for the rest of the night. Even in my dreams.

TWELVE

C had is grinning at me when I enter the kitchen the next morning. Like full-on beaming so hard, it's like I can see every single tooth in his head.

"Mornin'," I mumble as I shuffle my way over to the coffeemaker. I'm exhausted. My head is pounding from lack of sleep and I'm desperate for a shot of caffeine straight to the bloodstream.

"Good morning, you lucky motherfucker." He chuckles, and it's too early to deal with his shit, so I ignore him and pour myself a cup of coffee instead. I sit next to him at the kitchen counter and start scrolling through my phone, hoping he won't talk to me.

"Where's your waitress?" he asks nonchalantly.

My hopes evaporate just like that.

"Why do you care?" She's currently still asleep in my bed,

looking like a goddess. Seeing her naked body when I first crack open my eyes in the morning is how I want to wake up all the time, if I had my choice. I wanted to wake her up with my morning erection, but she was out, completely unresponsive to my insistent whispers. But at least she was breathing, so that's a positive.

"Maybe I want to give you two shit for keeping me awake with your constant moaning and groaning and your headboard banging against the wall." Chad starts laughing and holds out his hand like he wants me to high-five him.

I scowl at him instead, and he drops his hand, his laughter dying. "Come on, bro. I'm just giving you a hard time."

"It's not funny," I mutter as I sip from my cup. I stare straight ahead, silently willing him to remain quiet.

But he can't. Chad's biggest problem is that he never knows when to shut up.

"How did you two hook up again anyway? Have you been sneaking her into the house when I'm not around?"

"I kept hearing her moan your name," he continues. "She must really like your dick."

I ignore his crude remarks. "Are you spying on us, Chad?"

"I can't help but hear everything when the house is quiet and our walls are thin. You two really went at it." Chad shakes his head, that goofy smile still on his face. "Props to you, brother. She must have a magic pussy."

"Don't talk about her like that," I snap.

"Aw, why? You actually like the topless waitress?"

I smack the back of his head, making him yelp. "Don't disrespect her."

Chad sends me an incredulous look. "Come on, are you serious? Don't tell me you actually care about the waitress."

"She has a name," I say through clenched teeth.

He raises his brows. "What is it then?"

"Jensen."

"Huh. Fancy rich name for a girl who works at a strip club. Bet you twenty bucks it's made up." Chad slides off his stool before I get a chance to grab him by the collar and sock him in the mouth. "I gotta go. Class starts in less than fifteen minutes and I'm gonna be late. Catch ya later."

I say nothing as he exits the kitchen and heads outside. My mind is too busy contemplating the idea that maybe…

No. Her name is not made up. Why would she do that?

Strippers make up names all the time. So do prostitutes. They don't want anyone to know their true identity.

Jensen has told me enough to clue me in on her identity. She's made some admissions.

Casual ones.

Ones that, if I'm being honest with myself, don't amount to much.

My phone buzzes with a notification. A text from Park. I do not want to see my brother today.

Growling in frustration, I send him a reply. Yeah. Don't

want to go there either. It's full of good memories from when we were little, when Mom still wanted to hang out on campus and pretend she was young and carefree. She actually told us that once, right before she gave birth to Addie. It was the last time we went there as a family, minus our dad. But a lot of my memories from early childhood don't involve our dad. He was too busy working.

I've gone to the café a couple of times since I starting going to college, but mostly for takeout during lunch. I took a girl there once on a date, but we didn't last long beyond that.

My phone buzzes again. I answer before dropping my phone onto the granite counter with a loud clatter. I don't want to talk to Park, I don't want to make nice or listen to him go on about him and Diane and his twisted reasons for having an affair with Dad's wife. He can't rationalize his actions to me, no matter how hard he might try.

"Hey."

I turn to find Jensen padding into the kitchen, wearing an old black hoodie sweatshirt of mine and nothing else. Her feet are bare on the cold tile floor, and her legs look endless. Her hair is a mess and there's black smudges under her sleepy eyes, and I'm tempted to grab hold of her and drag her back to my bedroom so I can keep her naked and in my bed all day.

But I have classes to go to and my brother to meet, so there's no time for any of that.

"Good morning," I tell her, rising to my feet. "You want coffee?"

"Please," she says with a nod, and I go to pour her a cup. She follows after me, grabbing the creamer and dumping a bunch of it in her coffee before she grabs the nearby spoon and gives it a quick stir.

"Is that even coffee?" I ask her as she walks over to the counter and settles her cute butt on the stool Chad just vacated. "With all the creamer you just poured in it?"

She shrugs and takes a sip. "This is the way I like it."

Noted.

"You have any classes today?" I ask.

"Yeah, just one. You have a couple, right?"

"How do you know?" We've not really shared our school schedules with each other. At least, I don't think I have. And after what Chad said about her name, I'm feeling suspicious. Just when I think things are cool between us, someone has to go and say something to freak me out and screw it all up.

"You've, uh, mentioned it to me before. How Thursdays are busy for you, with class and practice." She smiles.

I don't remember ever telling her that. But maybe the constant sex is literally burning brain cells. I don't know. Though I do remember some things. Like, "I have a game tonight. You should come watch me."

Her face falls in disappointment. "I wish I could, but I have to work."

The reminder that she has to work at the strip club sucks. It both depresses me and makes me angry. "You're going to try and switch shifts so you can go to Addie's party on Saturday night, right?"

"I'm going to try."

So tempted to tell her trying isn't good enough, but that sounds like something my father would say and I'm not going down that road. "Addie will be really disappointed if you can't go."

Irritation fills her eyes. "Are you purposely trying to make me feel guilty?"

"No." "Well, you are. I need this job, Rhett. I know you don't approve, but I have to make money to live."

"Can't you find another job?"

"I don't want to," she stresses, her eyes flashing. "I make a lot of money at the club. The tips make the long hours on my feet worth it."

Of course her tips are good. She's flashing her fucking tits at everyone all damn night. "But don't you find it—degrading, walking around the club for hours, serving drinks with no shirt on?"

"No, not really. And I'm not ashamed of my body, if that's what you're asking," she retorts.

"You shouldn't be ashamed of your body. You have an amazing body. I just don't like the idea of a bunch of perverts getting to see it. It's the job itself that's…shameful. The location. You know what I mean?" I can tell Jensen's getting pissed. I'm making a mess of this, and that's the last thing I want to do.

"So what you're telling me is that   the one with the problem, not me." She stands, and starts pacing the kitchen. "You're ashamed of where I work, aren't you?"

"It's not something I want to tell my family," I admit, feeling like a douche.

But come on. What guy wants to admit the girl he's seeing works at a strip club? She doesn't strip, but she might as well…

"Why not?"

"You know why not. It sounds bad, you working at a strip club. You don't wear any clothes while you're working," I remind her.

"I'm topless. Big deal." She shrugs, looking extra small wearing my hoodie. Extra vulnerable, though there's fire in her eyes as she glares at me. "There are lots of topless beaches, you know. Being topless is the most natural thing in the world."

"Yeah, well, not to me. Did you know Park kept telling me last night he thought you were awfully familiar? He swore he'd seen you somewhere before."

Her eyes go wide and she drops her hands to her sides. "Do you think he's seen me at City Lights?"

"Maybe." Probably. "I told him you cleaned offices at night when he asked me if you worked anywhere."

"So you lied for me."

"I didn't want to tell him you worked at City Lights. I would've never heard the end of it," I explain, but she's already halfway out of the kitchen by the time I finish speaking. I chase after her. "What's wrong?"

"You're just proving my point," she calls as she heads for my bedroom. "You're totally ashamed of me."

"Not you, Jensen." I grab her hand, stopping her in the hallway. "Your   I'm not telling my family you work there."

She jerks her arm out of my grip and enters my room, shedding the hoodie as she walks, leaving her completely naked. "If you don't have the balls to tell them, Rhett, then that's on you."

I lean against the doorjamb and watch as she yanks on her panties and then pulls her sweater dress back on. She doesn't even bother with the bra, and I can see her hard nipples through the fabric of her dress. Fuck me, she looks sexy as hell, her eyes blazing with anger, her cheeks flushed.

But if I try to touch her right now, she'd probably do something crazy, like try to hurt me. She looks that angry.

"Where are you going?" I ask as she shoves her bra in her purse.

"I'm leaving. I can't be with you if you're too ashamed of me and what I do."

My mouth drops open in surprise and I enter the room, stopping directly in front of her. "Are you serious?"

She grabs an elastic out of her bag and gathers her hair in one hand, pulling it into a messy topknot. "I'm dead serious. Clearly this is an issue for you. And this is me. This is what I do, this is who I am."

"Your job doesn't define you," I start, but she cuts me off with a look.

"Right now it does. Savannah is my best friend. My friend. And she works there too. She's not ashamed of what she does, and neither am I. I don't want to—to spend time with you, Rhett, and always worry that you're judging me over my job. I'll always feel like a disappointment to you, and I've put up with enough of that in my life. I refuse to ever let it happen again," she explains as she slips on her shoes. She grabs her purse, slings it over her shoulder and proceeds to walk straight out of my bedroom.

I step out of the way to let her pass by. "So you're really leaving."

"Yes," she says over her shoulder as she marches toward the front door.

"How are you getting home?"

"Don't worry about me. I'll be fine."

I follow after her. "I don't judge you, Jens. You're not a disappointment to me."

She whirls around, thrusting her index finger in my face. "Don't lie, Rhett. It's not a good look for you."

And with that, she turns, opens the door, and leaves.

THIRTEEN

I show up early to the café, and of course my brother is nowhere to be seen. The waitress seats me at a booth in the very back of the restaurant, and she asks how my day is going and if I'd like something to drink.

I can't tell her truth, that so far my day has been total shit. First, my somewhat girlfriend walks out on me after a stupid fight, and now I have to meet my douchebag older brother for lunch so he can fill me in on all the lurid details about his affair with our bitchy stepmom.

Yeah. It's a bullshit day. But I smile at her and tell her that so far, my day is going great, and could I get a glass of iced tea, please?

She leaves me with a menu and I check my phone, almost hoping Park won't show up. But I couldn't be that lucky, because yep, there he is. I watch him as he enters the café, smiling broadly at our waitress, examining her up and down as he follows her to the table.

"How's it going?" Park asks once he's seated and the server has left.

I keep my gaze focused on the menu, unsure of what to say to him yet.

"You going to be pissed at me forever?"

I glance up to find Park watching me, his eyes filled with amusement. The asshole. There's nothing about this situation that I find even remotely funny. He flips open his menu, though he's not looking at it. "I should be," I tell him. "What you're doing is fucked up."

Sighing, he closes the menu and rests his clasped hands on top of it. "He cheats on her too, you know."

"So that makes it okay?" I shake my head in disbelief. "That's some fucked up logic you've got there."

"You're right. But let me explain everything first before you're so quick to judge," Park throws back at me.

Second time I've been called out for being too judgmental today. I never thought I was, but maybe I am. Maybe I'm a complete asshole, and worse? I don't even realize it.

"Okay. Explain," I tell him, leaning back against the booth seat.

The server arrives with our drinks and we both order sandwiches, sending her on her way quickly. I'm impatient and it's like he is too. I know I shouldn't want to hear how this whole mess started, but, I'm curious. I want to understand how he could do something so messed up.

"It started about five years ago—"

I interrupt him. "Five years? You've been having sex with Diane for ?"

"Shhh." He glances around to make sure no one is paying attention. "Off and on, yeah. I have."

"Holy shit." I rub my hand over my face, my mind having a difficult time wrapping itself around this revelation. "That's insane."

"If you'd stop interrupting me, I could tell you more," he says irritably.

"Fine, sorry," I mutter.

"She's been pretty flirtatious with us ever since we graduated high school. Did you ever notice that?"

The summer after my senior year I was swimming in the pool alone at night, and when I came out she touched my shoulder and told me I'd grown up extra big and strong, her tone appreciative, her eyes full of interest.

It totally skeeved me out, and I did my best to banish that memory from my brain.

"Yeah, I noticed."

"Right, well, I started to play along with it after a while. She flirted, I flirted back. She'd touch me, I would touch her back. One night we stay up late, just the two of us in the family room, watching a movie. By then I was almost done with college, and I was home for spring break, wanting to spend time with you guys. But you went out with your friends, and Addie was in bed because it was a school night, and Dad was on a business trip." He pauses, takes a sip of his beer, and all I can do is watch him.

"And next thing I know, she's touching my dick. She reaches inside my shorts, pulls it out, goes to her knees and gives me a blowjob, right there in the family room."

I'd shove that bitch off me so fast if she tried something like that. I know I would.

"Nothing happened for a long time after that. At least another year, maybe almost two. Until the time I stayed in the guesthouse when we were in Maui for Thanksgiving that one year. Remember that?"

Barely. I spent most of the trip in a sunburned, drunken haze.

"You were in the main house with the rest of the family. She offered up the guesthouse to me so I could have privacy, which didn't make sense. You were the one who brought, like, four friends. You guys needed your space, but I wasn't going to complain." He takes a deep breath and exhales slowly. "She'd come to the guesthouse every night and toy with me. Flirt, touch me, test me, kiss me, then leave me just when shit got good. Drove me insane." Park drains half his beer and I watch him in silence.

The way he's talking, it's like he actually enjoys his sexual relationship with Diane, which is blowing my freaking mind.

"Spare me the details," I finally say. I don't need to hear about blowjobs and her teasing him. In fact, that's the last thing I want to hear. "Are you two currently—seeing each other? Or was that kiss I witnessed just a one-off?"

"We've kept up the affair pretty steadily for the last year," Park says, his voice nonchalant, like his crazy story is no big deal. "It's not like she's the only woman I'm seeing, though. There are others. There have always been others."

"Why are you doing this anyway? Are you trying to get back at Dad for something? Trying to take everything that belongs to him? His wife, his business?" I ask.

Park messes with the edge of his napkin, his gaze locked on the table. "I don't know. It was just…something to do, I guess."

"Something to do." My voice is flat, my thoughts going haywire. "So there's no reason at all? You're just messing around with dad's wife because it was   What the actual fuck, Park?"

"I can't explain why I did it. I'm messed up, okay? After Mom died, I felt lost—"

I interrupt him. "So did I."

"Yeah, but you were allowed to cry out for your mommy at night. I wasn't. Dad told me I had to be strong, because I was the oldest. I couldn't cry." Park's gaze grows distant as he stares out the window. "And then Diane came into our lives, Dad treating her like she belonged with us, that she was a part of our family, and I was so confused. I didn't want her there. She wasn't our mom. She was a stranger. He just…replaced Mom with Diane."

I remember feeling the same exact way too. One minute our mother was there, the next she was gone, and then a few minutes later, Diane moved in.

"I've always resented him," Park continues. "Everything he tells me to do, I want to do the opposite. I've only been towing the line the last couple of years because I want the company. I want to take over, and he wants to retire early so he can get a few years of travel in with Diane before he kicks the bucket."

"So you take his wife, his company, his life. Is that your plan?" When Park doesn't say anything, I keep talking. "Because that's a messed up plan, Park. It's not going to work. He finds out you're banging Diane, he'll take the company away from you. For good."

"That's why he'll never find out." Park smiles, then finishes off his beer. "You can't tell him, Rhett."

"I won't," I say, though honestly, he doesn't deserve my silence. But he's my brother. I'm loyal to him, I've always been loyal to him. He's taken care of me since I can remember. Helped me with homework, sometimes even helped me cheat. Gave me girl advice, beat up that kid who tried to bully me in the seventh grade, and he let me crawl into bed and sleep with him for the first three months after Mom died.

So yeah. Park has been there for me as long as I can remember.

But so has Dad.

Our server appears with our sandwiches and we remain quiet as she sets the plates in front of us. Once she's gone, I start talking again. "What about Diane?"

Park has already started eating. "What about her?" he asks, his mouth full.

"Do you trust her? Do you believe she'll keep her mouth shut?"

Park sends me an   look before wiping his mouth with a napkin. "Absolutely. That bitch has it made. She gets to spend all of Dad's money, travel the world and bang me on the side. She's not about to ruin that by confessing her love for me or whatever to Dad."

"Does she love you?" I can't imagine real emotions playing a part in this weird scheme, but they have been doing this for a while. Could they actually care for each other? "Do you love her?"

"No. Yes. I don't know."

He's not going to give me a straight answer. Maybe that's because there is no straight answer. The line has blurred between those two, and now that line is so blurry, they don't know what's right or wrong anymore.

Am I making excuses for them? Probably.

"Listen, I don't want to be a part of this—situation," I tell him. "Don't ask me to lie for you or hide something for you. I can't be involved any further than I already am. And I don't want Diane to know you met me for lunch today. I don't even want you to mention my name to her, okay?"

"Too late." The easy smile on Park's face annoys me so damn bad I want to slap it off him. "I told her last night."

Exhaling loudly, I rest my elbow on the table and run my hand through my hair. "What the hell, Park? I don't want to talk to her about any of this."

"Fine, you won't talk to her about it. Whatever." Park digs into the second half of his sandwich.

"You know what you're doing is messed up, right?" I'm thinking he doesn't.

Park shrugs, then takes a sip from his beer. "Fucked up things happen every single day, Rhett. You think the world is normal? You're wrong. It's not. We're all out there fucking around, doing forbidden things, excited that we might get caught. Even more excited when we don't. The thrill of doing something you're not supposed to is intoxicating stuff, brother."

His words stick with me after I leave the café and head to my two o'clock class. I hate to admit he's right, but…he is. It's exciting to be with someone you shouldn't be.

Like Jensen.

I think of our earlier fight, and how stupid it was. Though I guess she did have the right to be angry with me. She thought I was trying to tear her down, when really I was hoping she would say, "You're right! Let me go find another job ASAP."

That didn't happen. Her confession that she actually likes her job surprised me. When I first saw her there, before she noticed me, she looked weary. Almost…

Sad.

I hate that she shows her tits to everyone who walks into that place, but do I also like it because I can claim those tits as mine? What kind of asshole does that make me?

The worst kind?

FOURTEEN

'm sitting on the hood of my car wearing my thickest jacket and a beanie, my ass staying warm thanks to my car's engine. It's past two in the morning and I'm exhausted. I took a nap after our game—which we won, but it doesn't count yet so who cares—and now I'm here, in the parking lot of City Lights on an early Friday morning.

Waiting for Jensen.

I thought about texting her, but she probably would've ignored me, and I didn't want that. Apologizing to her in person for our earlier argument is the right thing to do.

So here I sit, waiting for her to walk out the back doors of the club so I can talk to her.

And finally those doors do swing open, and she and Savannah exit, their heels clicking loudly in the otherwise quiet night. I can hear the low murmur of their conversation as they draw closer, though I can't make out any particular words.

Is she talking about me? Did she complain to Savannah about our argument from this morning? Or does she keep that kind of thing to herself? She did call me her dirtiest little secret, but Savannah knows what's up. She's been drawn into the middle of our drama more than I'd like.

"What are you doing here?"

Jensen's voice rings out and I glance up to find her standing two cars away from me, clad in a pair of black leggings that she pulled on under her skirt, and she's wearing a thick, dark gray sweater. Her hair is swept up into a ponytail, the ends curled, and her eyes are lined with the heavy black eyeliner she wore the last time I saw her here.

Every time I see her, I swear she gets more beautiful. With all the makeup or without, Jensen is the most gorgeous woman ever.

"I wanted to talk to you, if you'll let me." I rest my arms on my bent knees, linking my hands together.

"You want to talk now? Here in the parking lot?" She sends Savannah a look, one I can't decipher.

"You can come back to my place, and then I can drive you home," I suggest. My heart is thumping wildly and I'm nervous. This girl sets me on edge. I never know what she's feeling or thinking. We've grown closer, but she's still a mystery.

One I'm dying to figure out.

Jensen studies me for a moment, her gaze closed. "You want to take me home after we talk?"

"Or you can stay the night with me," I offer. "Whatever you want, Jens. No pressure." I hold my hands up like the police have me at gunpoint.

"You know I'm mad at you," she murmurs as she starts walking toward me. Savannah lingers behind, but she's still listening. I really didn't want an audience for this, but looks like I don't have a choice.

I slide off the hood of my car so I'm standing directly in front of Jensen. "I'm sorry for what I said this morning. I was out of line."

She tilts her head back, her gaze meeting mine. "Are you really sorry, Rhett? Or are you sorry I didn't agree with you?"

Fucking really hate it when she calls me out like that. "I'm sorry for what I said, and how I made you feel. I don't ever want you to think you're a disappointment to me, or to anyone." I take her hands and clutch them in mine. "I can't help it if I'm a jealous dick."

She bursts out laughing, shaking her head. "You're not a dick. You've never really been a dick. You're too nice."

"I'm not that nice." I pull her into my arms, holding her close. Damn, she feels good. Smells good. I've missed her even though I saw her earlier this morning. "You've called me an asshole more than once."

"I never really meant it." She turns her head so her mouth

is at my neck, her lips brushing my skin when she speaks. "You're the nicest guy I know."

Curling my fingers around the base of her ponytail, I give her hair a little tug. I don't doubt for an instant that I'm the nicest guy she knows. She's met up with some major losers. "I'm sorry."

"You already apologized."

"Just wanted to say it again." I press a kiss to her forehead and she leans in closer, a tiny smile on her face.

"Hey Jen, do you need a ride from me or not?" Savannah asks.

Jensen pulls away from me to look at her friend. "I'm going home with Rhett."

My heart soars, I swear to God. Sounds corny as hell, but it's true. I hustle her into my car before she changes her mind, and we drive back to my house. We waste no time making our way to my bedroom, both of us shedding our clothes until we're just in our underwear, Jensen's teeth chattering when she dives under the covers. I climb into bed and haul her to me, my arms going around her waist, her head resting on my chest.

"How is it I always wind up in your bed?" she asks, her voice laced with amusement.

I run my fingers through the ends of her ponytail, my eyes closed, my thoughts drifting. This worked out way easier than I thought. I figured she'd put up a major fight, and even told myself I shouldn't be disappointed if she didn't come home with me.

Looks like I got what I wished for.

"I'm very persuasive when I want to be," I murmur.

She lifts her head and I can feel her watching me, but my eyes remain closed. "Are you tired?" she asks.

"Yeah. I played that basketball game earlier."

"Oh, right. Did your team win?"

"We did, but it was a scrimmage, so it doesn't count toward our season. That starts next week."

"I'm sure you'll be very busy."

"You should come to one of my games. They're fun."

"I don't want to go alone."

"Bring Savannah."

"I'd love to watch you play," she admits.

I smile. "I'd love to have you there. You'd need to make me a sign, though."

"A sign?"

"Yeah, something with my last name on it or my number—which is twenty-one, by the way—that's how you can show your support." I sound like I'm joking, but I'm actually serious.

"My being there isn't enough?"

I crack open my eyes to find her looking totally perplexed. Like she can't imagine making a sign for me. "Your being there would be more than enough."

She rests her head back on my chest with a sigh. "Good. I'm artistically challenged, so my sign would look like total crap."

"I doubt that."

"No, it's true. I can't draw. I'm terrible at arts and crafts." She's quiet for a moment and I continue playing with her hair, fighting off sleep. She's only wearing panties and I'm sporting a halfhearted erection, but I don't think we're going to have sex tonight. I'm too tired, and she doesn't seem into it either.

Which is fine. This relationship doesn't have to be all about sex. I don't want it to be, even though I can't deny my attraction to her. But I have to show some restraint every once in a while, right?

"Were you able to get Saturday off?" I ask.

"I talked to one of the girls I work with and we're going to trade shifts," she answers. "So yes, I'll be there."

"Addie will be happy." And so will I.

"I like her a lot," Jensen says.

"She likes you too. She texted me earlier, telling me how great she thought you were," I say.

"Really? That's so sweet."

"Yeah." My eyes are closed. My breathing slowly deepens. I could fall asleep like this so easily...

"I should apologize to you for this morning too," she finally says, her voice quiet. "I said some shitty things."

"Don't worry about it. We were both on edge," I reassure her.

"No, I was super defensive. I just." She hesitates and I wait, all the air lodged in my throat. This moment feels big right now. Like she's going to reveal something. "I was feeling really low. I get that way sometimes."

"I think we all do."

"I couldn't stop worrying about your brother seeing me touch you like I did at the dinner table. I don't want him to think I grab your dick all day long." I chuckle and she lightly slaps my chest. "I'm serious. I don't want him to have the wrong impression of me."

"Don't worry about Park. He's an asshole. My dad likes you, and that's all you should care about."

"Your stepmom didn't like me at all."

"Why do you care what she thinks? No one else does."

"For some weird reason, I want all the Montgomerys to like me." She sighs, nuzzling her cheek against my pec. "Do you remember what you said to me last night, when I told you about my bad dream?"

I scrunch my eyebrows, trying to think. The quick change of subject is throwing me off. "Not really."

"You said I'm not a whore because I don't get paid to have sex with guys."

"Okay," I say, drawing the word out.

"I have something to tell you." She takes a deep breath. "I tried it once."

My eyelids snap open and I stare up at the ceiling, my gaze zeroing in on the ceiling fan. "What do you mean?"

"Having sex for money. I tried it once." She ducks her head

into my chest and I glance down to see nothing but her blonde ponytail. I gently yank on her hair and she lifts her head, her expression full of shame and embarrassment.

"So what you're telling me is, you had sex with a guy and he paid you for it after it was over." I can't wrap my head around this. I can't, I can't, I can't. I've dealt with enough bullshit today from Park. "What the hell, Jensen?"

"No, wait." She scrambles so she's sitting cross-legged on my bed. I scoot up so my back is against the headboard and I can see her better. Plus, there's distance between us now, and I kind of need it. "Let me explain."

Instead of explaining herself, she's silent, pressing her lips together, her eyes extra wide, until I can't stand the suspense any longer. "I'm waiting."

"Hold on! I'm trying to figure out how to tell you this." She rubs her forehead before lifting her gaze to mine. "Okay. I'm broke, right? I mean, I make good money there, but it all goes to my college expenses, or to rent and bills and stuff."

Rent. Her house. "Whatever happened to your little house?"

"I never went back," she whispers. "I just—it doesn't matter. Let me tell you what happened, okay?"

"Okay, okay. Go ahead." I both want to know more and hope she doesn't say anything else. As in, I'm quietly freaking out over here, but keeping a straight face because I want her to confess. I want her to be honest and open with me.

"One night, my boss tells me a customer likes me, and asks if I would be interested in providing—extra services to him. At first, I tell him no. Absolutely not. But then Don says how much the guy wants to pay, and it's so much money, I have to say…yes."

"Jesus," I mutter, cradling my head in my hands. "When did this happen?"

"It doesn't matter."

I lift my head. "Yeah, it kind of does."

"Please, Rhett. I'm not even done with my story. Let me get it out." She clears her throat before she continues. "I met the guy in one of the private rooms we have, and at first, everything was…okay. He was a little older, a good-looking guy, though, in good shape, wearing nice clothes, and I'm pretty sure he was very wealthy. But, he would give me backhanded compliments, and he never seemed that in to me."

"You wanted him   to you?" I can't even wrap my head around this.

"When he's paying ten thousand dollars to be with a girl for a few hours, you'd think he would be interested, right?" she asks sarcastically.

"   "

She nods. "I know. That's a lot of money, and I was going to get a huge piece of it. More money than I'd ever had in my lifetime. That's why I said yes."

Money is a huge motivator when you don't have it.

Something I've never had to experience before. Does that make me privileged?

Yes. Yes, it does.

"Anyway, it started to downward spiral quick, and I got irritated with him, and he got mad at me. Then he started getting rough with me, and I had to fight him off. Luckily, I got away from him. And he never came back either. He left his ten thousand dollar payment with Don, and disappeared."

We're both quiet and I try to process what she said. She's so matter-of-fact while telling her story. Hardly showing any emotion when it sounds like it was a terrible experience. And the same thing keeps running through my brain: He got with her.

"What do you mean, he got rough with you? Are you saying he tried to— you?"

Jensen nods again, lifting her chin, trying to look tough. But she doesn't. She looks vulnerable and scared and a little shaky. I have no idea what it's like to be in her situation, to live her life. From everything she tells me, she had it far from easy growing up, and I wish I could change that.

I can't, though. There are reasons she makes certain choices, ones I can't begin to comprehend, and when she's ready to share more with me, I'll be there for her.

I want to be there.

I'm here for her now.

"Come here," I whisper as I open my arms wide.

She dives into me, slinging her arms around my neck, burying her face against my shoulder. She's trembling, and I hold her close, smoothing my hands up and down her back. "It was so scary. I thought he was going to rape me," she whispers. "I've never run so fast in my life."

"You haven't seen him again?" My voice is tight, my anger barely contained. If I knew who the asshole was, I'd beat his face in.

It's probably best I don't know who he is.

"No. He told me his name was Greg. Savannah said he specifically asked about me that night, because he was sitting at one of her tables. But he wanted me to be his server instead of her." She sighs, her cheek on my shoulder. "I've done a lot of stupid things. I let my emotions drive me. But that was the scariest thing that's ever happened to me, and I told myself never again."

"That's why you shouldn't work there, Jensen. You need to quit that place." The words fall out of me before I can stop them, and I clamp my lips shut, hoping she doesn't think I'm trying to start another fight.

She lifts her head, her gaze meeting mine. "You're right," she whispers. "I should leave City Lights."

Relief floods me, making me hold her cheeks with my hands and lean in to kiss her. "It's not safe there," I whisper against her lips. "What if he comes back?"

"I'll call Don and tell him I quit. I swear." She kisses me

again, her soft, sweet lips lingering. "Thank you for listening to me."

"Thank you for telling me." I lean away and tilt her head up so our gazes lock. "You can tell me anything, you know. You can trust me."

She stares up at me, her lips parting, like she wants to say something else.

But she kisses me instead.

FIFTEEN

A ddie's party is in full swing by the time we arrive
on Saturday night. I wanted to get there sooner, but
Jensen took forever getting ready. Her hair had to
look a certain way, and so did her makeup. She bought three
dresses and borrowed a bunch more from Savannah, giving
her endless options to choose from. She pretty much changed
into every single one of those dresses too, sometimes twice,
until she finally made her decision.

And what a decision she made. She's wearing one of the
three dresses she bought. It's black and the material is thin,
with a deep V-neck in the front and back, showing off plenty
of cleavage. She looks so fucking sexy, I want to tear the tiny
dress off of her. I tried, in fact, right before we left my house to
come over here, but she slapped my hands away and told me,
and I quote, "Keep it in your pants."

I laughed. Then I tried to take it off of her again, making her laugh. Making her kiss me. Making her shove me away when I got too handsy.

I tried my best, but she wasn't having it.

Now she's a chattering, nervous mess by the time we walk into the backyard of Dad and Diane's house. There are teenagers everywhere, the music is loud, and I see Addie dancing on a makeshift stage close to the DJ's setup. She's got her arms raised above her head, surrounded by a group of friends, including Trent.

She looks like she's having the best time ever, and I'm happy. My baby sister means the world to me.

We wander back into the house hand in hand, Jensen holding the gift bag for Addie in her other hand. "I see a gift table," Jensen tells me. "I'll be right back."

Before I can say a word she slips away, and I watch her go, my gaze glued to her swaying hips, those long, bare legs. The dress is short and has a huge cutout in the back, making it impossible for her to wear a bra. I'm not even sure if she's wearing panties. She wouldn't let me look either.

Jensen also insisted on buying a present for Addie, even though I told her it wasn't necessary. I had already purchased my sister a gift card to one of her favorite stores, but Jens told me that was a thoughtless present. Then she went to Target, bought a gift bag and filled it with all sorts of girly things. Nail polish, hair ties, makeup, candy. She had so much fun putting it together that I figured Addie would love it just as much.

"You came alone?"

I turn to find Park standing before me, a glass of amber liquid clutched in one hand, his expression one of pure boredom. "Did   come alone?"

Park smiles, flashing straight, white teeth. "Hell no. I brought a date just to aggravate you-know-who." He leans in closer, as if we're sharing a secret, which I suppose we are. "And it's working."

"Where's your date? And who is she?"

"She went to the bathroom." He takes a sip from his drink. "Her name is Veronica. I met her on Tinder."

"Nice." I start to laugh, and so does he. "Are you two serious?"

"We've gone on a couple of dates. Messed around a few times." Park shrugs.

"What about…" I let my voice drift. He knows exactly who I'm referring to.

"What about her? She's got someone else, and so do I." Another smile from Park before he drains his glass.

I decide not to mention that the someone else he's referring to is our father.

God, I really don't want to deal with that bullshit tonight. In fact, as soon as we make our appearance, talk with Addie and wish her a happy birthday, I want to get the hell out of here. I know Addie wants us at her party, but does she really care that much? She's got all her friends with her. She doesn't need us tonight.

"I didn't come alone either," I tell him when I catch a glimpse of Jensen headed our way. "Jensen's here with me."

"Really?" Park spots her and whistles low, his eyebrows shooting straight up. "Damn, that girl of yours is sexy as fuck."

I like Park calling Jensen my girl, but I don't appreciate his rude comment. "Watch your mouth," I mutter.

His eyebrows lift even higher, if that's possible. "What, you don't like me making comments about your new piece?"

Irritation fills me. "Don't call her that either."

He chuckles and sets his empty glass on a nearby table. "So sensitive. You must really like her."

"I do." The admission comes easily, which surprises me. Though I guess it shouldn't. I've always liked her.

"Still bothers me, that I think I know her. I swear I've met her before, but where?" Park tilts his head contemplating her.

"She probably just reminds you of someone," I suggest, starting to sweat. I do not want him to figure out that he's seen her at City Lights. Hell no.

"Maybe. I don't know. It's weird."

"Hey." Jensen appears by my side, curling her arm through mine. She looks up at me before shifting her attention to Park. "Hi, Park."

"Hello, Jensen." He aims his I'm-going-to-charm-your-panties-off smile right at her, but she appears unfazed. Thank

God. "Looking extra delicious this evening."

"Seriously?" I ask him, my voice—hell, everything about me—tense.

His innocent expression is immediate. "What? She looks good! Your girlfriend is gorgeous, little brother. Take pride in it."

Jensen doesn't say a word. Just watches the two of us battle it out.

A tall, dark-haired woman approaches us, snuggling up close to Park. "Did you miss me?" she simpers, tipping her face up like she expects a kiss.

Park gives her a quick peck, his lips brushing against her glossy red ones. "Always do," he says easily. They both turn to look at us. "Veronica, this is my baby brother, Rhett, and his girlfriend, Jensen."

"Nice to meet you." Veronica barely looks at us, she's too enthralled with Park. For some reason, I'd peg her as older than Park, maybe in her early thirties. There's something in the eyes, and her face is…weary. Her black hair is long, almost to her waist, and she's wearing a purple sequined dress that's a little too flashy for the party. "Let's go outside and hang out by the pool," she suggests to my brother.

"You should join us," Park tells me, his gaze zeroed in on Jensen and her low-cut dress.

"In a little bit," I answer with a brotherly smile. "We're going to go find Dad first."

"He's in the dining room, chatting up his friends," Park tells us as we start to walk away.

"Jesus," I mutter as I steer Jensen into a nearby alcove. "My brother is annoying as hell tonight."

"I didn't think he was so bad," Jensen offers. She leans against the wall and I stand in front of her, propping my hand on the wall above her head. "He was perfectly nice."

"Sure he was, and he stared at your tits the whole time just now too," I say irritably.

"Rhett." She lightly slaps my chest. "That was rude."

"He's the rude one. He thinks you're hot." Her mouth drops open, but I keep talking. "He told me that when he saw you in that dress. That is the last thing he should've said to me."

"You should've said it to him about Veronica," Jensen suggests, an evil smile curling her lips.

"Right, and that would make me a liar, because she is definitely not hot." I slip my other arm around her waist, pulling our lower bodies close together. "But you are so hot. I shouldn't have let you out of the house in that dress."

"You like it?" She arches a delicate brow.

"I love it." I lean like I'm about to kiss her, my mouth hovering just above hers. "I know you're not wearing a bra."

"How?"

I press a brief kiss to her lips, pulling away when she tries to kiss me back. "I can see your nipples."

"Rude." She gives my chest a tiny shove with her fingertips.

"Are you wearing panties?"

"Maybe." Her lips curve. "You'll have to check and see."

I glance around. There are people milling about everywhere. "I can't check right now. Too many people."

"Guess you'll have to wait then." She laughs and I kiss her again, squeezing my fingers around her waist, pulling her a little closer. If I don't watch it, I could pop a boner right here in the middle of this party…

"Ah, the two lovebirds have arrived."

At first sound of my dad's voice and I'm springing away from Jensen, all thoughts of an erection evaporating just like that. "Hey, Dad," I say weakly. Jensen is tugging on the hem of her dress, like she can magically make it look longer.

"Hello, son." He claps my back with his hand, nodding toward Jensen. "Good evening, Jensen."

"Hi, Mr. Montgomery." She smiles, and I can tell she's nervous. Probably not too thrilled my father found us in semi-compromising position/situation either. "Thank you for inviting me to Addie's party."

"Ah, you should thank Addie. This is all for her tonight. I'm glad you could make it." He's smiling at her, his expression friendly and open. Very unlike my dad. Though he did say at dinner a few nights ago he wanted to encourage me dating a nice girl.

I'm not one-hundred percent sure Jensen is actually a nice girl, though…

"You two just get here?" Dad asks me.

"Yes, a few minutes ago."

"Talk to Addie yet?"

"No, we saw her outside dancing with her friends and Trent when we first got here. Didn't get a chance to say hi to her, though," I explain. "We just saw Park."

Dad's face goes stern. "With his date?" he asks through tight lips.

"Yeah. She seems all right." I shrug.

"She's a thirty-five year old tramp with three children born to three different fathers, and not a one of them she married either," Dad says disgustedly.

What the hell? Guess I was right about the age thing. "How do you know all that? Park tell you?"

"Sort of." He lifts his head, a smile appearing on his face. "Ah, there's Diane. Come here, sweetheart. Come say hi to the kids."

Diane spots Dad and plasters a fake, closed-lipped smile on her face as she makes her way toward us. Jensen is immediately standing extra close to me, reaching for my hand. I interlock our fingers, noticing how cold hers are. Diane sets her on edge every single time she comes around, and I don't get it.

"Darling, please. I don't have time for this. I need to go speak with the caterers," Diane says, leaning away from Dad when he tries to kiss her cheek. His irritated expression tells me he knows he just got dissed. Funny, I figured my old man was used to it. "There seems to be a problem in the kitchen, and I need to go check on them."

"I'm sure they can handle whatever—" Dad starts, but she cuts him off.

"No, they can't handle it. I need to supervise. No matter how much you spend or how often you work with them, the hired help are   incompetent." With an irritated huff, Diane walks away, not once acknowledging me or Jensen.

"I'm sorry she was so—short just now," Dad says once Diane is gone. He's speaking directly to Jensen, since I already know Diane's rude almost all the damn time. "Parties seem to stress her out."

"There's a lot that goes into planning them, I'm sure," Jensen says sympathetically.

I squeeze her hand. "Yeah, Diane must be planning parties all the time, since she always acts that way."

"Rhett," Dad chastises, and with a shake of his head, he's gone too.

"You think I offended him?" I ask Jensen after he leaves.

She releases her death grip on my hand. "You were a little rude just now."

" was rude?" I rest my hand on my chest. "You know I'm not wrong."

"You probably shouldn't have said it to your dad, though. He knew she was being awful. He didn't need the reminder."

Jensen winces.

"Yeah, but he's always making excuses for her. It sucks. And it's so unnecessary. We all know she's rude. Why can't he see how terrible she is?" I rub the back of my neck, thoroughly irritated, and we've only been here for fifteen minutes tops.

"Sometimes it's hard to see what's right in front of your face," Jensen murmurs, her gaze meeting mine.

"Well, I'm seeing what's in front of my face right now, and I like it." I slip my arm around her waist and pull her in close. "I like it a lot."

She rests her hand on my chest, smiling up at me. "You're going to get us in trouble again."

"No way. We can sneak off somewhere, and no one will find us," I say, an idea forming.

"I don't know. We should probably go try and talk to Addie…"

"Nah, we'll find her later. Come on." I take Jensen's hand and start leading her toward the stairway up to the second floor, where all the bedrooms are. "I want to show you something."

"I'm sure you do," she says with a little laugh.

SIXTEEN

I crack open the door and pull Jensen into the room with me, shutting and locking the door behind her. The room is completely shrouded in darkness and I reach out, feel along the bed as I make my way, switching on the lamp when I get to the bedside table. "Well, what do you think?"

She looks around the room, at the old sports posters on the wall, the bookshelf with the trophies covering the top shelf, a giant framed photo of me and the rest of the varsity basketball team dominating one wall.

"Is this your old bedroom?" she asks.

"Yeah." I come up behind her and slip my arms around her waist, resting my chin on her shoulder. "Do you like it?"

She leans into me, still checking everything out. "It looks like a typical teenage boy's room."

I try to take it in like I've never seen this room before,

but it's hard. I pretty much grew up here. We moved in to this house when I was in middle school, after Diane told Dad she was tired of living in a "dead woman's house".

She's so nice, isn't she?

Besides, the old house wasn't big enough for Diane. She wanted a monster mansion and my dad gave it to her.

"Yeah, it does look like a typical teenage boy's room," I finally say.

"Your parents didn't try to turn this room into something else once you left home?" Jensen asks.

"They've got so many guest bedrooms in this house, they don't need another one," I say, chuckling.

"Must be nice." Her voice is the slightest bit sarcastic, yet also tinged with envy.

"It is. I'm lucky." I pull away from her slightly so I can turn her around to face me. "I know I take advantage of my luck."

She frowns. "How so?"

"I just…do what I want, spend what I want, and I don't have to worry about it. I've been taken care of my whole life." I smile and shake my head. "In other words, I'm spoiled rotten. I honestly don't know what you see in me."

"You're not all bad, Montgomery," she teases, her voice light.

"You think?" I'm being serious, and I think she senses it.

She nods, her expression solemn. "Trust me, I know."

I glance over at my queen-size bed before I return my gaze

to her. "Want to try out my childhood bed?"

She makes a face, wrinkling her nose. "When you put it like that, it sounds kind of gross."

"I technically didn't get this bed until I was fourteen, so…" I grab her hand and lead her over to the bed, sitting down on the edge of the mattress and spreading my legs so she's standing in between them. "I wish we could leave."

"We just barely got here."

"Yeah, and I realized quick that I don't want to be here. Thank God you're with me." I roll my eyes. "My brother is an asshole."

"Don't worry about him." She touches my cheek, her fingers feather-light on my skin. "Let him have fun with that old tramp Veronica."

I burst out laughing. "Wasn't that crazy? And where did my dad get those particular details anyway? I bet he has a file on his desk right now with all of Veronica's personal information in it."

"I don't know. When you think about it, that's kind of scary. He could check up on anybody." Her smile is tremulous. "Even me."

"He would never do that," I say immediately, trying to make her feel better. But I wouldn't put it past him. Not that I can tell Jensen that. She's nervous enough, trying to make a good impression on everyone, even if they don't deserve her kindness. Like Diane. "You like my father?"

She nods. "He likes me, so that's a good thing."

"And what about Diane?"

Jensen rests her hands on my shoulders. "What about her?"

"Do you like her?"

"I don't think she likes me."

"I don't even think she's looked at you." I shake my head. "It's like you don't exist to her."

"Guess she's too good for me," she says with a sigh, her eyes flashing with…

Hurt?

I don't know. But her reaction to Diane is surprising.

"Don't let her bother you. I'm serious." I grip her waist, then drop my hands so I'm toying with the extremely short hem of her dress. I decide to change the subject. There are much better things for us to focus on right now. "I think I'm going to check to see if you're wearing panties or not."

"Rhett, we probably shouldn't do this here," she says, trying to slap my hand away, but I'm too persistent.

"No one's looking for us. And besides, the door is locked. It's room." I lift her skirt from behind, my hands touching her bare thighs, then shifting up, lightly cupping her ass checks. "So far, my guess is no panties."

"Keep searching," she teases, and so I do. She spreads her legs a little, giving me easier access, and when I try to touch her between her thighs, I discover she's…covered. With the thinnest fabric I think I've ever felt.

"Damn, you're wearing panties."

She laughs, shaking her head. "You sound so disappointed."

"That's because I am." I'm really not, though. Anytime I have my hands up Jensen's dress, I'm happy as hell.

"Maybe you should take them off of me so you won't be disappointed anymore," she whispers.

Okay. I can get on board with that.

I smooth my hands up, over her outer thighs, her hips, my fingers tripping over the string-thin waistband of her panties. I tug them down her thighs, past her knees, her calves, until they're a lacy tangled mess around her stiletto heels.

Just looking at her crumpled panties wound around her ankles gets me hard. What the hell? I must have some kind of weird fetish.

She kicks them off as I slowly lift up the dress to reveal her to me. Seeing her naked flesh makes me even harder, and I lean in. "Spread your legs," I murmur, and she does as I ask, revealing herself even more.

Reaching out, I touch her there, sliding between her lips, encountering creamy, hot flesh. A shuddery breath leaves her as I continue to stroke her folds, gently circling her clit with my fingertip.

"Take your dress off," I demand, and she glances down at me, her brows wrinkled.

"Wh-what?" Her cheeks are flushed and her voice is shaky.

I think she likes it when I get commanding.

"It's getting in the way. Take it off, Jens."

She whips her dress off over her head, and it lands on the floor just behind her. I grasp her ass and pull her to me, my mouth on her pussy as I begin to devour her. I lick her everywhere, slip my finger deep inside her, and she bucks against me, a tiny cry falling from her lips. Her hands fall to my head, her fingers sliding in my hair as I continue to lick and suck.

She tastes amazing. I fuck her with two fingers, my tongue flicking her clit, teasing her. She twists against my face, seeming at war within herself.

Get closer because it feels so damn good? Or move away because it's too intense?

Closer wins. I can't stop licking her, and she starts to tremble. She's close. I've done this enough, made her come enough times, to know her tells. She's moaning, her voice low, like she's trying not to be too loud for fear we could get caught, and I'm reminded of the time in my car. How exciting that had been, knowing someone could come upon us at any moment. Or in the hall at City Lights. Anyone could've walked in on us, and we still went at it, like we had no control.

That's my problem. When I'm with Jensen like this, I have no control. None. She seems to feel the same way.

I grip her ass tighter, increasing my speed, licking and sucking her clit, drawing it between my lips. She grinds against my mouth, her entire body going tense, inhaling sharply, her teeth sinking into her lower lip.

"Oh God," she says in anguish as she shudders and shakes, her orgasm completely taking over her body. I hold on to her, slowing my movements, watching as she completely falls apart. Her hips buck hard against my face, once. Twice. Until the orgasm finally seems to stop.

Jensen pulls away from me and falls onto the bed, sagging into the mattress. I watch her, enthralled with her naked body, those long, long legs and her pretty breasts. Her body is gorgeous. Everything about her is gorgeous.

And she's mine. All mine.

"You're trying to kill me," she murmurs, making me laugh.

"No, you're trying to kill ." I rise to my feet, pointing at the tent in my pants.

She sits up, her breasts gently swaying. "I can take care of that for you."

"I'm sure you can." I wipe at my face with the back of my hand and realize I need to wash my face and hands, stat. I head for the adjoining bathroom. "But we don't have time for that. We need to go back to the party."

I switch on the light and go to the sink, turning the water on. After I wash my hands, I splash water on my face, staring at my reflection. I look happy, despite the downright painful erection and the bullshit going on with my brother and Diane. I happy. Life is good.

Jensen makes my life better.

Drying my face and hands, I reenter my old bedroom to find Jensen has slipped her dress back on, all traces of the woman who came all over my face gone. Only the flush in her cheeks is a tiny remnant of what just happened between us.

"You had your own bathroom too?" she says when she sees me. "Talk about spoiled."

I laugh, pulling her into my arms and giving her a quick kiss. "Let's go find Addie and wish her a happy birthday."

"And then we can go back to your place?" she asks hopefully.

Nodding, I kiss her again. "Definitely."

SEVENTEEN

We find Addie as she's walking into the house, summoned by Diane, who wants her to come inside and get ready to cut the cake. Soon everyone crowds around the dining room table, where Addie's triple-tier cake covered in bright pink frosting sits in the middle, and we all sing "Happy Birthday" to her. Jensen remains in my arms the entire time, seemingly content, singing loudly and cheering when Addie blows out all the candles in one breath.

After the cake cutting and sharing a too-sweet piece of cake, we wander the house, chatting with the few people I recognize, but otherwise, everyone here is either a work associate of my father's or a friend of Addie's.

As in, Jensen and I are bored out of our minds, and we want to leave.

"I need to use the bathroom, and then we'll go?" she

suggests.

Nodding, I rub her lower back before patting her butt. "Sounds perfect. I'm ready to get out of here."

She smiles. "Me too."

I watch her walk away, a view I never seem to grow tired of. I can't wait to get her home and get her naked in my bed. That's all I want to do for the rest of the night…

"I figured it out."

Turning, I find Park standing there with a smirk on his face. "You figured what out?"

"Where I recognize her from." His smirk transforms into a shit-eating grin. "You will   believe it, bro."

I'm literally starting to sweat. "I won't believe what?"

His smile falls, a knowing gleam in his eyes. "Maybe you already know. Yeah, I think you do know."

"You're talking in fucking riddles," I mutter just before I turn and walk away. I push my way through the clusters of people talking, ignoring my brother, who can't stop calling my name.

He knows. He knows Jensen works at City Lights. I need to get her out of here before she freaks out. Before Park blabs her secret to my dad and Diane and the shit really starts hitting the fan.

I lose him when he gets stopped by one of Dad's friends, and I rush to the guest bathroom on the other side of the kitchen, knocking repeatedly on the door. "Jensen, you in there?"

"Hold on, I'll be out in a sec!" I hear the toilet flush, and then the sound of water running.

Glancing over my shoulder, I see Park is still chatting with Dad's friend, and he's annoyed, looking around the room. He spots me, his entire face lighting up, and he tells the older gentleman something before he nods and starts heading my way.

"Hurry up, Jens," I tell her, pounding on the door. "We gotta go. Now."

"Calm down, Rhett. I'm almost done." I'm annoying her, but fuck it. We need to leave before Park corners me.

"Lingering around bathrooms now, hmm?"

I turn to find Diane standing before me, a glass of champagne clutched in one hand. Fucking great. The silver sequined dress she's wearing is nearly blinding, it's so flashy, and her too blonde hair is piled high on top of her head. The better to show off the very expensive, very large diamond earrings dangling from her ears.

"Just waiting for Jensen," I tell her, wishing she'd leave.

Diane purses her lips. "What? Do you not trust her to be at a party alone? You have to follow her everywhere?"

Irritation fills me. "No, but Dad shouldn't trust   at a party alone, that's for damn sure."

Park chooses this exact moment to show up, his gaze landing on Diane. "We shouldn't be seen together."

"Why not? Rhett's here with us. We're not doing anything

but having a simple conversation during your sister's birthday party," Diane says, her tone innocent, her expression anything but.

Park appears extremely uncomfortable. I'm hoping he'll forget all about our earlier conversation. "We can talk later," he tells Diane.

She mock-pouts. "I haven't seen you all night. You're too busy with your— "

"Veronica is not my girlfriend," Park says.

"Where Veronica?" I want him to get the hell out of here and go find her. I wonder if Jensen realizes we're all on the other side of the door, and that's why she hasn't come out of the bathroom yet.

"Outside dancing with the teenagers," Park mumbles.

"Figures," Diane says with a little snort. "Maybe she likes them extra young."

"Same goes for you," Park accuses.

I say nothing. This is getting juicy, but I don't want to be in the middle of it.

"Let's meet in, say, thirty minutes. In your old bedroom," Diane suggests.

This makes me taking Jensen up to my former bedroom feel sleazy. "Are you two really going to plan a tryst in front of me?"

"What does it matter? You already saw us together," Park says, sending Diane a quick too-intimate smile.

"You two disgust me." I wish Jensen would just come out of the bathroom already.

"What's your girlfriend doing in the bathroom, anyway?" Diane asks me. "She's taking forever."

"Oh, that reminds me." Park's eyes light up as he turns to Diane. "Did I tell you what I found out?"

"No, what is it?" She sends me a quick look, like she knows what Park is about to reveal will blow my mind.

"Rhett's new girlfriend isn't what she seems." Park literally rubs his hands together. I hate how much he's enjoying revealing this surprise. "She has a secret career."

"Do tell," Diane says encouragingly.

"Shut up, Park," I tell my brother menacingly, but he barely acknowledges me. "Want me to let Dad in on what I know about you two?"

"You wouldn't dare," Diane says, her voice friendly, but her eyes are dark and full of hatred.

"See, you do know about your precious Jensen," Park says, pointing at me. "I knew it. I bet that's how you two met."

"Where does she work?" Diane asks Park.

"It kept bothering me, how her face was so familiar. I knew I'd seen her somewhere before, I just couldn't figure out where." Park chuckles. "Until it all came together, when I saw her walking in that sexy dress she's wearing tonight."

"Park," Diane says, her tone a warning.

He waves a dismissive hand, dismissing her. "Anyway, I

realized that I've seen her at a strip club. She actually works at that one place on the outskirts of town, City Lights."

Diane rests her hand on her chest, as if she's scandalized. "Are you telling me Rhett's new little girlfriend is a "

I'm about to go off on these two when the bathroom door swings open and out walks Jensen. "I'm not a stripper," she says, walking right up to Park so she can poke him in the chest with her index finger. "I'm a cocktail waitress."

"Yeah, a cocktail waitress," Park adds, his gaze meeting Diane's.

"Is there any difference?" Diane drawls, sending Jensen a withering glare.

Jensen sucks in a sharp breath, shaking her head and sniffing loudly. She glances over at me, her expression pained, her eyes glassy with unshed tears, before she turns to face Diane. "I you," she spits out before she runs away.

"Aw, I guess I hurt your girlfriend's feelings," Diane coos, making Park laugh.

"You're such a bitch, Diane," I tell her as I start to follow after Jensen.

"Hey, wait a minute." Park grabs my arm, and I jerk out of his hold. "You can't call her names."

"Fuck off, Park. Jesus." I leave the two idiots and search the crowded house for Jensen, but I don't spot her anywhere. Her reaction toward Diane was strong. She's been worried about Diane since she first met my family, and I don't quite get her fixation with my stepmother. Though Diane has been totally awful to her, so I get why Jensen is so hurt.

Fucking Park and his big mouth. I'm tempted to tell Dad about Diane and Park's affair, but what good will that do? And it's like Park knows I'll keep my mouth shut, while he can say whatever the hell he wants.

It's so goddamn unfair.

I head for the front door, which suddenly swings open to reveal my uncle Craig making his grand late entrance, as usual. He's my father's younger half-brother, the life of every party, the rich womanizer, the guy Park and I looked up to when we were kids. He'

Now everything he does just seems kind of sleazy.

"Rhett! What's up, buddy?" He approaches me with a wide smile, a pretty blonde trailing after him. He wraps me up in a bear hug and I disengage as fast as possible, unable to breathe after inhaling his strong cologne.

"Just about to leave, Uncle Craig," I tell him, sending him a regretful look, my gaze searching everywhere for Jensen.

"No way. You should stay for a little while longer. We can catch up. It's been a while." He pats me on the shoulder. "You're looking good. Heard you got a new girl."

"Yeah." I say the word slowly, wondering if my father told him about Jensen. If so, that was fast. They only just met a few days ago. "Speaking of my new girl, I need to go find her. Maybe we can talk another time."

"Sounds good. And she's right outside, I think," Craig says easily, patting me on the shoulder before he starts to walk away. "I'll see you at Thanksgiving."

"See ya," I say weakly, my mind turning over everything he just said.

How does he know what Jensen looks like?

I rush outside to find her standing by my car, her arms wrapped around her middle and she's uncontrollably shivering. I go to her and grab her by the shoulders, giving her a gentle shake so she looks up at me. "Are you okay?"

She shakes her head, her teeth chattering. "C-can w-we g-get in the c-car, pl-please?"

I hit the keyless remote and then we're both entering the car, me hitting the button to start the engine. I mess with the buttons and temperature knobs, cranking up the heat and turning on her seat warmer. "You should feel better in a few minutes."

"Th-thank you." She leans back against the seat and closes her eyes, sighing loudly. "I'm sorry I ran off. It's just, this entire evening has me on edge, and Diane and Park were so cruel just now. And then..." She shakes her head, sniffing again. A single tear slides down her face, then another.

Then another one.

She's full-blown crying, her shoulders shaking from her sobs, and I pull her into my arms, holding her close. I touch her hair, my lips at her forehead, hating that she's falling apart in my car. I want to hold her, but it's awkward with the center console between us. "Diane isn't worth your tears, babe. Trust me."

"I know, I know. This isn't about Diane." She hiccups. "I don't know how to tell you this. It's just so—freaking weird, and you're probably not going to believe me."

"I will believe you, no matter what. Do you understand?" I slip my fingers beneath her chin to tilt her face up and her gaze meets mine. "You can tell me anything, I swear."

Her face is blotchy and her eyes are red. She rubs her tears away and then closes her eyes, like she can't look at me. "It is the craziest thing ever."

Unease slips down my spine and my heart is racing. "Just spit it out, Jens. What's going on?"

"A man just walked into your father's house, right when I was walking out. He looked right at me and winked, and I know he recognized me. He had to." She opens her eyes, shuddering. "I him, Rhett."

She's talking about my uncle. There's no one else who walked into the house only a few minutes ago. "Who is he to you?" I ask.

"You're never going to believe me."

"I already said I would. Tell me, Jensen." The words come out sharper than I meant, but that's because I can take the suspense for only so long.

"He's the one—the one who attacked me that night at City

Lights." Her eyes are wide as she stares up at me, and my head starts to spin. "He's Greg, Rhett. The man who tried to rape me just walked into your father's house."

DAMAGED
HEARTS

ONE

Jensen

'm crying. I don't know how to tell Rhett what I just saw— I just saw. Greg, the man who tried to assault me at the club. Walking right into the Montgomery house like he belongs there, like he freaking the place.

Rhett's trying to hold me. Comfort me. But it's incredibly awkward sitting in his car with the center console in between us. "Diane isn't worth your tears, babe," he murmurs. "Trust me."

He's so sweet. Too sweet. I don't deserve him. And every time he calls me babe in that dreamy voice of his, I want to melt. I've given up all pretense of trying to resist him. It's pointless.

Despite my original plan, I like him too damn much. Something I didn't think was even possible.

"I know, I know. This isn't about Diane." I hiccup, but I

am beyond caring how I look or what I sound like. I just need to get this out. "I don't know how to tell you this. It's just so— freaking weird, and you're probably not going to believe me."

"I will believe you, no matter what," Rhett says fiercely. "Do you understand?" He slips his fingers beneath my chin, tilting my face up so our gazes meet. "You can tell me anything, I swear."

I rub the tears away with my fingers, then close my eyes. I don't want to look at him, see all that earnest sincerity shining in his gaze. It's too much, what I'm going to say. "It is the craziest thing ever."

"Just spit it out, Jens. What's going on?"

His growly voice spurs me on, and I do exactly what he demands—I spit it out.

"A man just walked into your father's house, right when I was walking out. He looked right at me and winked, and I know he recognized me. He had to." I open my eyes, a shudder moving through me. "I him, Rhett."

A shadow passes over his face, and I wonder if he knows who I'm talking about. Did he see him? Did he speak to him? God, does he know him too?

"Who is he to you?" he asks.

"You're never going to believe me." I keep repeating myself, but I can't help it. I'm having a hard time coping with this.

"I already said I would. Tell me, Jensen." The words come out sharp. I'm testing his patience. I can't blame him for snapping at me.

"He's the one—the one who attacked me that night at City Lights." I blink up at him, trying to keep the fear out of my voice, but it's no use. I'm terrified, and shaking. "He's Greg, Rhett. The man who tried to rape me just walked into your father's house."

Rhett's arms fall away from me, his mouth open in shock. He's quiet, as if he needs to absorb what I just said, and I wait anxiously for him to say something. Anything.

Within seconds, he's speaking, but it's felt like minutes. Hours. "What did you just say?"

"The man who entered your father's house a few minutes ago. He's the same one who paid for extra services from me at the club. Remember how I told you that story?" I'm about to explain further, but he cuts me off.

"Of course I remember," he practically growls. "Are you— that's the same man?"

"I'm positive. I will never forget his face," I say solemnly. Or his voice or his hands, or the way he looked at me, or the things he said…

I take a deep breath, shivering as I watch Rhett. How he winces and slowly shakes his head. "Do you know who I'm talking about?" I ask.

He says nothing. Just rubs his jaw, his fingers brushing against the stubble and making a rasping noise in the otherwise quiet confines of the car.

"Rhett." When I say his name, his tortured gaze meets mine. "Please. Do you know who he is?"

His lips go thin and he offers a curt shake of his head before averting his gaze from mine. "No. I didn't see him."

He's lying.

The thought runs through my mind, unbidden. No. I can't believe Rhett would lie to me.

Now I'm the one averting my gaze, staring out the passenger side window. The Montgomery mansion looms ahead of us, every window lit, magnificently impressive in the darkness.

Intimidating. Just like the entire family is.

Well, with the exception of Addie. I adore her. I shouldn't. She's the enemy too, but how can I blame a sweet seventeen-year-old for my mother's sins?

"Hey." I turn to look at Rhett when he finally speaks again. "I'm going inside, see if I can find him."

"No," I say vehemently. "I don't want you to confront him. He's not worth it."

I don't understand the panic rising within me. What do I care if Rhett does this? He's a big boy. He can take care of himself.

But what if Greg is—dangerous? What if he tries to hurt Rhett? Or me?

"I'm going in." He reaches for the door handle, then turns to study me. "Lock the door when I leave. The car key is right there." He points at the center console. "If something happens, leave. Just…you know how to drive my car. Get out of here."

I'm shocked silent, blown away by his offer. He's rushing to my defense. He's going to find and confront Greg. And he's giving me an out too.

I push the ugly thought out of my head.

"Be careful," I whisper, reaching out to touch his forearm. "Don't do anything stupid."

The look he gives me is grim, his dark eyes unreadable. We stare at each other in silence, the only sound our breathing, and then we're reaching for each other, our mouths meeting, hands grasping, tongues twisting. We kiss like this for seconds. Minutes. Until finally he breaks the kiss, and without a word, exits the vehicle, slamming the door so hard I jump in my seat when the car rattles.

A shuddery breath escapes me as I hit the button and lock the car doors. I watch Rhett's tall frame as he makes his way toward the house, pushes open the door, and walks inside.

Now all I can do is wait.

TWO

Rhett

I feel like an asshole as I push my way through the crowded house, my gaze scanning the room as I try to find my uncle. I still can't wrap my head around it. He's the one who attacked Jensen at the club that one night—or so she claims.

That I doubt her because she's accusing someone I know, someone I'm   to, makes me feel even worse.

"Hey, I thought you already left." Park grabs hold of me, stopping my progress, and I whirl on him, jerking my arm out of his grip. He raises his hands like he's defending himself, that fucking smirk on his face making me want to punch him. "Hold up, bro. No need to get violent."

I ignore his comment. He's just trying to provoke me. What else is new? "Say one more thing and I'll fucking take you out."

"I'd like to see you try." Park laughs, but the humor is gone.

I've just pissed him off. He hates it when I threaten him with physical violence, especially considering the last couple of times we've gone at it, I've won.

"I don't want to get into it with you, Park," I tell him, ignoring the anger in his gaze. "You have no right to be angry with me, considering you're the one who said those shitty things about Jensen."

"You should've done your due diligence before you brought a stripper into the house, Rhett," Park returns. "I'm not taking the blame on this one, little brother. Pick better next time, okay?"

I don't bother correcting him about Jensen's job. What's the point? He's going to think what he wants. And like he has any right to judge me. He's the one who's fucking our stepmother behind Dad's back.

Talk about a twisted mess.

I decide to change the subject before this argument gets any worse. "Have you seen Uncle Craig?"

Park appears momentarily taken aback by my question, but at least he answers me. "Talked to him a few minutes ago, right when he first got here. I think he went outside. Said something about wanting to check out the young tail." Park laughs again, and I leave before he can say anything else, heading for the kitchen and the back door that leads outside.

Right before I open the kitchen's French door, I check my phone to make sure Jensen hasn't sent me a text or tried to call me.

But there are no notifications, no missed calls. I'm tempted to text her, reassure her I'm all right, but she could start asking questions. Questions I don't want to answer.

So instead I shove my phone back into the front pocket of my jeans and head outside.

The backyard is even more crowded than it was before we left, and I look around, still in search of Uncle Craig or even Addie. The music is loud. I see a group of teenagers nearby passing a bottle of Fireball between them, and I wonder if Addie is drinking.

Christ, I hope not.

"Rhett! You decided to come back after all, huh?"

I turn to find my uncle standing in front of me, a friendly smile on his face, his arm slung around the shoulders of the blonde he brought as his date. She stares up at him with adoring eyes, her large breasts nestled against his chest.

"Yeah, thought I'd come back after all," I repeat to him with a smile, but it's difficult to maintain, so I let it fade. Did he really lay his hands on Jensen? And why? Or is this just some random coincidence? "Figured it's too early to leave the party."

"That's my boy." Craig grins, pulling the blonde closer to him and squeezing her shoulders. "Lara, this is my nephew, Rhett. He got all his good looks from me."

"Pleased to meet you," Lara simpers, reaching out to shake my hand, her long, pale pink fingernails reminding me of weapons. As in, she could probably scratch my eyes out.

"Same," I tell her, shaking her hand quickly before taking a step back. This chick barely looks older than me. Where does my uncle find girls like this?

I banish the thought.

"Did you get chance to talk to Addie and wish her a happy birthday?" I ask Craig.

"Oh yeah, we chatted for a few minutes. Just before her boyfriend whisked her away so they can go grind on each other on the dance floor," Craig says, shaking his head. "How did she grow up so fast?"

"I don't know," I say with a shrug, hating the small talk, but shit. How am I supposed to approach this with him? I can't just ask him if he's ever attacked my girlfriend at City Lights.

Yeah. No. That wouldn't be smart. I gotta play this just right.

"I haven't seen your dad yet," Uncle Craig says, disengaging himself from Lara so he can step closer to me. "Is he all right?"

Unease washes over me, making me tilt my head. "Why wouldn't he be all right?"

"I don't know," he says slowly. "Shit hasn't been right between him and Diane for a while."

"Why do you say that?" It hasn't been any worse than normal.

"She calls me sometimes and complains." Craig smiles. "I'm the little brother, always there for my sister-in-law. You'll find out what that's like someday, when you've got Park's future wife whining at you about how awful her husband is."

I say nothing. I hope to hell I never deal with something like that.

"You and me, we're a lot alike, you know," Craig continues. "We're both the younger brothers in the family. The ones born with all the money but hardly any responsibility. We can do whatever the hell we want, and no one is trying to hold us down."

"I'm not like that," I immediately say, sounding like a bratty little kid.

"Really? Then tell me what you're going to do once you graduate college." When I don't respond right away, he's pointing both index fingers at me, laughing like he just told the best joke. "See, you don't know. And what's so great is that you don't to know. You can travel the world, you can fuck a thousand women, you can backpack through the woods in the middle of fucking nowhere and no one is going to give a shit. You can do whatever the hell you want, no questions asked."

"You make me sound like an irresponsible fuck," I mutter, annoyed with his assessment. Annoyed further by him saying we're alike.

We're not. We can't be.

Craig raises his brows. "You said it, not me."

My phone buzzes, and I check it to see a text from Jensen.

"Already pussy-whipped by the girlfriend, I take it?" He laughs again, then takes a sip from his drink. "Don't ever let them trap you, Rhett. No pussy is worth millions, I don't care what they tell you."

"Hey." Lara slaps Craig's arm with her sparkly little purse. "Don't be rude."

"Oh, you're different, baby." Craig grabs hold of his date, his hands settling on her curvy ass and giving it a squeeze. "Your pussy rocks my world."

"Don't you ever forget it," she says, tilting her head back in preparation for his kiss.

Craig leans down, his gaze meeting mine. He winks at me just before he devours his girlfriend right in the middle of this party.

He's worse than the teenagers surrounding us.

Disgusted, I turn away, tapping out a quick response to Jensen before I start walking. I make my way through the yard on the side of the house, my mind full of conflicting thoughts, all of them about my uncle Craig.

He's a jackass. There's no other way around it. But is he an attempted rapist?

According to Jensen, that's a yes.

But is she lying? She's done it before.

And she might be doing it again.

THREE

Jensen

R elief floods me when I see Rhett striding toward the car, his expression determined, his mouth thin. I hit the button and unlock the car, dipping my head when he opens the door, fear making me shake. Why I'm scared, I don't know. Is it because of Greg? Or is it Rhett that scares me?

I'm not sure.

The men in my life have never really cared. Oh, Daddy told me he loved him, and I know he did, in his way. But he didn't show it very well. He was too selfish, too wrapped up in his pain over what my bitch of a mother did to him. She ruined him, and with that, she ruined me. I'm rotten. Like a bad piece of fruit. Still shiny on the outside but totally disgusting within.

I study him out of the corner of my eye as he slides into the driver's seat. He slams the door, his hands gripping the steering wheel so tight his knuckles turn white. I hate how furious he looks. The worry comes back at me tenfold, making me weak.

"Did you find him?" I finally ask when he still hasn't said anything. "Where is he? Did you talk to him? Please tell me you didn't talk to him."

"I didn't talk to him," he mutters as he hits the button and starts the engine. Putting the car in reverse, he glances over his shoulder and backs out of the spot. "I didn't find who you were looking for."

"I should've gone in there with you." I bite my lower lip, my mind racing with all the possibilities. "I could've found him." Not that I wanted to, but shouldn't we warn them? Warn his family and their friends?

A realization hits me, making me suck in a sharp breath. What if Greg is a friend? What if he's…

Family.

"And what would you have done when you saw him, Jens? Screamed at him in the middle of my parents' house? Called the cops on this guy?" Rhett shakes his head as he puts the car in drive and peels out of the driveway. "I can't imagine you making a scene during Addie's party," he continues as he pulls onto the street, revving the engine so hard my head knocks against the back of the seat.

He remains quiet as he drives through his parents' neighborhood, and all I can do is think. He's right. I know he's right. But I don't like how he's assuming things. It's almost like he's telling me what to do, or how to feel. He's not very talkative either, and Rhett loves to talk.

I never want to talk. Saying too much means you reveal too much, and I've already given Rhett more than enough information about myself.

It's like I can't help myself, though. I want to know more. No, I   to know more. I don't understand why he's being so damn quiet.

"Did you see Addie?" I finally ask when I can't take it anymore. "Greg wasn't near her, was he?"

"Addie was with Trent. She's fine," he murmurs irritably, his gaze zeroed in on the road ahead of him. Which is a good thing, right? I want him to concentrate on his driving, not on me.

But I can't take the silence, I can't take the not knowing. The unknown is making me crazy and I squirm in my seat, tap my fingers on the center console. He sends me a look when my nails make a loud clicking sound and I snatch my hand away, clutching them together in my lap.

We remain silent, the tension building between us to nearly unbearable, and when I realize he's driving me back to his place, I break.

"I want to go home." Not that I have a home, since I'm referring to Savannah's apartment. I gave my home up, like an idiot. What was I thinking, never going back to my little house, just leaving it abandoned and not telling my landlord? It's almost like I do reckless, stupid things on "Why?"

"I don't know." I shrug. I lie. "I don't think we should spend the night together."

"Why not?"

I flinch at the tone of his voice. I can't even describe it. He just…he doesn't sound like himself. "I don't know. Maybe because you seem mad."

"I'm not." He says nothing else, and I almost want to laugh. He's the liar at this particular moment.

He remains quiet and it's driving me crazy. So crazy and I want to yell and scream and make a scene, just to get a reaction out of him. "Are you sure?" I finally ask when I can't stand the silence any longer.

"I'm sure," he says, he murmurs.

"Right." I hesitate, then decide to go for it. "Then why won't you talk to me?"

"What do you want me to say? How am I supposed to react, when you tell me that the guy who paid ten thousand dollars to spend the night with you, the same guy you claimed tried to rape you, just walked into my dad's house? That this is here to celebrate my baby sister's birthday." We come to a stop at a red light, and he turns to look at me with fire in his eyes. "Are you positive that was him?"

Hasn't he already asked me this before? "I already told you it was. Do you not believe me?"

"I never said that."

"You don't have to. You keep talking about my seeing Greg

walking into your parents' house like maybe I'm mistaken or something." I look away from him, staring out the passenger window once more. What I wouldn't give to just burst out of this car and run away, never to see him again.

No. I don't really mean that. I would miss him. Damn it, I caught feelings for him and I regret it. I so regret it.

"I just want to make sure." His voice is gentle, not so full of anger like it was a minute ago, but I still won't look at him. Too afraid of what I might see in his gaze. Like judgment. "What you're saying is…huge. A life changer."

"Why?" My voice cracks and I clear my throat. "How is it a life changer that we just saw Greg?" I look at him now, and all I see is pain etched into his features. "You know him, don't you?"

He slowly shakes his head. "I told you. I don't know a Greg."

A horn honks behind us, and we both glance up to see the light turned green. Rhett hits the gas, speeding through the intersection. If he doesn't watch it, he's going to get a ticket, and I'm sure that would piss him off even more.

"Just take me home," I say, crossing my arms. I feel like a pouty child, but clearly he's not listening to me.

"No."

"What do you mean, no?" I turn in my seat to glare at him, but he's too focused on driving. "What, are you holding me hostage?"

We come to a stop at another light and his gaze meets mine. "If I take you back to Savannah's, I'm afraid I'll never see you again."

My lips part, but I can't come up with anything to say.

He knows me better than I thought.

"I can't risk it." Rhett looks away, working his jaw. "Just—will you come back to my house? Please? We can talk about this more then. Or we don't have to talk at all. I just—I can't chance letting you go, Jensen. I'm afraid you won't come back to me."

I want to cry. I want to leave. I want to stay. Too many conflicting thoughts run through my brain, though I already know my answer.

I'm staying.

♥ ♥ ♥

We don't speak as we move through the dark, quiet house. I follow him back to his bedroom, turning to watch as Rhett closes and locks the door behind him. He leans against the door, studying me in the near darkness for a moment before he says, "Come here."

Any other guy would've said that to me, and I would've told him to suck my nonexistent dick, but for Rhett, I'll go to him. And when I approach him, he reaches for me, his hands cupping my face so gently, I almost want to cry.

"Do you want to talk?" he asks, his breath wafting across my face. I slowly shake my head and he caresses my cheeks with his thumbs. "Me either."

Instead he kisses me. Sweetly. A mere brushing of lips that sends a scattering of tingles all over my skin. I tip my head back, part my lips, but he still won't take it beyond soft, innocent kisses that make me melt and fill me with frustration all at once.

This is so typical of Rhett. My feelings for him aren't easy. They aren't black and white. They're every color of the rainbow, every temperature you can think of. He makes me run hot and cold, angry and sad, mad and happy. He challenges me, he frustrates me, and he makes me want to love him.

Yet I don't know if I'm capable of that emotion.

He makes me feel like I am, though. His hand drops to my waist and I suck in a breath at first touch of his warm fingers burning through the thin fabric of my dress. I remember earlier in his old bedroom at his dad's house, before I saw Greg and I felt happy and free. When Rhett stripped me naked, laid me out on his bed and put his mouth on me. How he made me come so easily, then wanted nothing in return.

The need to give back to him overwhelms me, and I break the kiss first, resting my fingers on his belt buckle. "I want you," I murmur against his lips as I start to undo his belt.

"Jensen…" he starts to protest, but I drop to my knees in front of him, biting my lower lip as I determinedly undo his belt, then his jeans. He's already hard. I can see his erection straining the front of his boxer briefs, and I glance up to find him watching me.

"You want this." It's not a question, because I know he wants me. I drift my fingers across the front of his underwear, making him groan. "Tell me you want it."

"You know that I want you," he starts, but he stops talking when I yank on his jeans and underwear at the same time, pulling them both down so his cock springs free right in front of my face. I grab hold of the base of him, rising up on my knees a little so my mouth is directly in front of the tip.

"Say it, Rhett. I need to hear you say it." I release my hold on him so I can whip my dress off, tossing it onto the floor so I'm only in my panties. My nipples are so hard they hurt, and I can feel him staring at me. Staring at my body. He seems entranced with it, like I'm the most beautiful, sexiest woman he's ever been with, and his reverence makes me feel powerful.

"I want you," he growls, his hand going to my hair, smoothing it away from the side of my face. "You're so fucking beautiful."

"What do you want me to do?" I almost laugh when he toes off his shoes and shoves his jeans and underwear down to his ankles, kicking them off downright violently. I lean away as he bends over and tears off his socks, his hands going to the front of his shirt so he can undo the buttons as fast as he can. Until he's standing before me naked, proud and erect and gorgeous, and I'd bet he's even a little pissed still. The look on his face tells me that.

I'm worried and upset and mad still too. Seeing Greg threw me. Rhett's reaction to me seeing Greg threw me too.

But I still want Rhett. I want him to want me too.

"You know what I want," Rhett says, his deep voice breaking through my troubled thoughts.

"I want to hear you say it." I'm constantly pushing him, but only because he pushes me, and I don't even think he knows it. He makes me want to be adventurous. He makes me want to experiment. Only with him.

"Suck my cock," he demands, thrusting his hips toward me, the head of his cock almost brushing my lips.

I grab hold of his erection once more and lick it, circling my tongue around the tip, my gaze never leaving his. His eyes are hungry, his lips parted as he watches me flick my tongue back and forth before sucking him deep into my mouth. His eyelids lower, a long exhale escaping him, and then I'm the one closing my eyes, savoring the salty taste of him, how he feels inside my mouth.

Before, I never liked giving blowjobs. They made me feel powerless. Vulnerable. As if I was being forced into doing it, and truthfully? Most of the time, I was. That's all a guy wants—at least, the guys I knew. When they're in the early teens, they want handjobs. Then they graduate to blowjobs. And all those boys I messed around with in high school? They were so damn demanding. Forget the female orgasm. All they cared about was shooting their wad.

Not Rhett. He gives to me so selflessly. He cares about my pleasure. And that makes me care about his.

"Jesus," he murmurs when I take him extra deep, nearly choking myself. He slips a hand into my hair, cradling the side of my head, his fingers tightening, making me wince. But I welcome the pain. It means I can feel, that this man makes me feel all sorts of things, all of them good and positive and wonderful and…

Hopeful.

Who knew Rhett Montgomery, the man I viewed as my mortal enemy, would turn into the person I would depend on the most? The one who would actually make me feel like a normal person for once in my life?

FOUR

Rhett

I can't take it anymore. Seeing Jensen on her knees in nothing but those tiny panties, my dick stuffed in her mouth, my fingers tangled in her thick, silky hair…

She keeps this up, I'm going to come. Fast.

With a moan I pull away from her, grabbing my stiff cock and giving it a short stroke. I could've let this continue. I wanted it to continue. But I have to show some goddamn restraint.

The look she sends me is nothing short of irritated. "I wasn't finished. weren't finished."

"I don't want to finish. Not like this." I scoop her into my arms and carry her to my bed, where I drop her on the mattress and fall down on top of her. Before she can protest, I kiss her, stealing her words, her breath. When I finally break the kiss, I whisper, "I want to come inside you."

Her gaze flares and her lips curve into a tiny smile. She arches beneath me, her breasts brushing against my chest. "Whatever you want."

Smiling at her in return, I dip my head and kiss her again, thrusting my tongue against hers, my hands wandering all over her body, touching all my favorite parts of her, making her gasp. With Jensen, I feel like I can never get enough. She makes me greedy. Possessive. Like I want to beat my chest and tell the world she belongs to me.

Like I want to grab the person who hurt her and bash his face in with my fist.

I banish the distracting thought and focus on the woman lying beneath me. Breaking our kiss, I run my mouth along her jaw, down her neck, across her chest. I kiss her breasts, suck first one nipple, then the other, into my mouth. Press tiny kisses to her stomach, drop one on each hipbone, my fingers sliding between her legs, beneath her panties, to find her drenched.

She lifts her hips and thrusts against my hand, her breaths quickening as I increase my pace. I shift down and push aside her panties, lowering my mouth to her pussy to tease her with my tongue, slipping two fingers deep inside her. Once. Twice. In. Out.

I remember what I said earlier about wanting to be inside her when I come, and I pull away right before I make her climax. She moans in pure frustration, her eyes snapping open to glare at me. With a smile I reach for her, tugging her panties off with impatient, fumbling fingers before she's finally, gloriously naked. Leaning back on my haunches, I study her for a moment. She has the most beautiful body ever. It's like she's not even aware of how fucking sexy she really is.

Grabbing her waist, I pull her in closer, her legs spreading to wrap around me, her body wide open and ready. Without pause I enter her, slowly, easing in to pure heaven, groaning when I'm fully inside. She's tight and hot, her thighs trembling, her body arching, and I watch in fascination as she closes her eyes, her hands going to her breasts, fingers absently playing with her nipples. Her lack of inhibition is such a turn on. She touches herself boldly, demands more from me without hesitation, and all I want to do is give.

Give, give, give to this girl until I've got nothing left inside me.

I begin to move, pulling out. Pushing in, staring intently at where our bodies are connected. Jensen moves with me, her body undulating, her head thrown back in pure abandon, her hair spread out on my pillow. She closes her eyes, her lips parting on a short gasp, her hands moving away from her breasts so she can throw her arms above her head. Craving closeness, I shift so I'm on top of her, our chests pressed close, my cock sinking deeper inside her welcoming body. She winds her legs around my hips, anchoring herself to me, and I increase my pace.

Our relationship might be complicated, but the sex isn't. It never has been. We're sexually compatible in every way. We move together fluidly, Jensen countering my every move, like we choreographed it beforehand. She digs her heels into my ass, pressing me closer, her hands in my hair, her mouth on my neck, her hot breath setting me on fire. I work my hips, driving deeper, my mind drawing a complete blank as my impending orgasm hovers closer. The base of my spine tingles, everything inside of me clutching, drawing up, going tense. When we're like this, I can't think. We don't need to think. We're operating on raw, animal instinct. All thoughts and worries gone.

We only want to fuck. To give each other pleasure.

There's a hitch in her breath, and her body freezes, those tiny Jensen tells that let me know she's so damn close. She murmurs my name, her voice choked, and then she falls over that delicious edge with a breathless gasp, her entire body shivering, her pussy milking my dick and sending me straight into oblivion. I follow right after her, my orgasm draining me, leaving me exhausted. Blissed out.

Beyond satisfied.

She pushes me off her when we're finished, and climbs out of bed, heading for the attached bathroom. I watch her go, admiring the sensual sway of her hips, the perfect curve of her ass cheeks, how they bounce when she walks. Sitting up a little, I curl my arms and rest my hands beneath my head, waiting for her to exit the bathroom.

Mere minutes later she opens the door, the light from the bathroom casting her in a sexy silhouette. I stare at her unabashedly, savoring the rosy flush of her skin, her still hard nipples, how unashamed she seems in her nakedness.

And she knows I'm staring too. Resting a hand on her hip, she watches me, her delicate brows lifted, her mouth formed in a sexy pout. "You look disgustingly pleased with yourself."

"Sounds like you're accusing me of something," I tell her.

"Maybe I am. No one has a right to look that happy." She waves a hand at me, like I'm an annoying fly she wants to shoo away.

I'm immediately offended. And I almost think she's serious. "Maybe you make me that happy."

Why is that so hard to believe for her? I don't get it.

Most of the time, I don't get her.

With a sigh she flicks off the light in the bathroom and approaches the bed, standing at the foot of the mattress, suddenly appearing unsure. "We were fighting only a few minutes ago."

"So?" I shrug. "Having sex tends to make me forget all about fighting."

She says nothing in response. Just watches me with both hands on her hips now, totally confident in her nakedness.

"You want me to be honest?" I ask.

She says nothing. Probably because she's not big on being honest.

Ouch. I roasted her in my own head.

When she still hasn't said anything, I continue. "I don't even know what we were fighting about," I say with a sigh, though I'm a liar.

I remember everything.

"I don't like it when you lie," she murmurs, slowly shaking her head. Like I've disappointed her or some shit.

I sit up straight, glaring at her. "I don't like it when you lie either."

Her mouth drops open, the hurt on her face obvious. I automatically feel like an asshole, even though I shouldn't. I have every right to call her out on her lies. After all, she's lied to me before. Plenty of times. What's going to stop her now?

Deep down, I know what this is really about. Why I'm saying these things, why I'm feeling this way. I can't stand the thought of my uncle being the one who attacked her. I'd almost rather think she was lying to me.

How fucked up is that?

"Are you calling me a liar over the whole Greg thing?"

"No." Maybe. She knows me better than I realize.

Jensen lifts her chin, defiant. "Please. You so are."

"Don't put words in my mouth."

"Don't give me that judgey tone."

"Judgey?" I sound incredulous because I sort of am.

But maybe she's right. Maybe I'm being totally judgmental right now.

"You're so high and mighty. Mister Rich Boy, with all your money and social status and fancy cars and clothes and houses. You don't appreciate shit. Instead, you're the spoiled little wealthy son who's rebelling against his father by going out with the slutty topless cocktail waitress from the wrong side of the tracks. So you can stir the pot and drive your family crazy with your 'rebellious' choices." She adds air quotes around the word .

Now it's my turn to stare at her with my mouth hanging open. "What the hell are you talking about?"

"Let's be real here, Rhett. I'm a passing phase. The naughty girl you can bring home and show off to say, 'See? I don't follow the rules the time.' Because that's who you really are. A rule follower. You're a good boy."

She says that like it's a bad thing.

"Once you dump me—and you will, don't deny it—you'll find some nice, respectable girl to bring home to Daddy. You'll get Mommy's engagement ring and propose, and you'll have a grand wedding followed by a month-long European honeymoon. You'll put a couple of kids in her belly real quick like and you'll have a perfectly lovely, if perfectly boring life. Traveling for work and always out of town, so you'll sleep around on the side with more slutty cocktail waitresses because you find yourself drawn to those types. All while wifey-poo sits at home and minds your babies and wonders if she Botoxed all her worry wrinkles away enough so you don't notice them anymore. Hoping the tummy tuck and the boob lift she got after the babies fucked up her body will make you want her again."

Her words infuriate me. Only because she's probably not far off with her assessment. Describing a life that I don't want but will probably end up having, because that's what happens. You try and try to fight against your destiny and you still end up just like your dad.

"You think you've got me all figured out," I say, my voice cold.

"I know I do. I can see it in your eyes. And you're pissed because you know I'm right. I nailed it. I nailed you." She climbs onto the bed, crawling along the length of my body until she's settled in my lap, her legs wrapped around me, the comforter the only thing between us. She slings her arms around my neck while I remain stiff. Unmoving.

Well. The only thing moving currently is my dick. It tends to do that whenever she gets close.

"You say and do this shit to push me away," I tell her.

"Is it working?" She smiles, but there's no emotion behind it. I spot the tiny flicker of pain in her gaze, but then it's gone. Blinked away, like it was never there in the first place.

"No." I touch her breasts, my thumbs brushing her nipples, and she bites her lip, trying her best to contain her reaction, I can tell. "You're not a rebellious stage, Jens."

"Mmm, lies are much prettier when you tell them, Rhett,"

she murmurs just before she leans in and kisses me. Her lips are plump and soft, her body warm and pliant as she melts into me, and we kiss like this for long, tongues tangled minutes. Until I'm shoving away the comforter and pushing my cock inside her and she's riding me, all her rude words forgotten, both of us chasing after that orgasm until we finally find it.

We're chasing after each other too. And our fucked up emotions.

But we never seem to find those.

FIVE

Jensen

"Let's go out of town for Thanksgiving. Just the two of us."

I chance a quick glance at Savannah, who's sitting next to me on her couch in complete silence, listening in on my conversation with Rhett. He called only a few minutes ago and I immediately put him on speaker, never letting him know that Savannah is in the same room with me.

Why I'm doing this, I'm not sure. To show her what a fake asshole he is? Though he's not. Most of the time, he's so genuine, so sweet he makes my teeth freaking hurt. But I keep thinking maybe I'm getting played. Maybe I'm in a sex-induced haze and all I care about is the next time I can get Rhett naked, when really he might be the one who's set on destroying me.

Yeah, right. I'm totally fooling myself.

"I don't know…" My voice drifts and I stare at my phone,

unsure of how to answer him. I don't want him to whisk me away on a special holiday vacation so he can make me feel special. I'm trying to distance myself from him. I've been trying to do that for a while, ever since I realized I can't go through with my original plan.

Yet that never seems to work. Just last night I said all sorts of horrible things about him right after we had sex, to his face, yet he still wanted to be with me. We had sex   after I totally insulted him. What's wrong with this guy?

The bigger question is: what's wrong with me? Why do I keep trying to sabotage us? Why won't I let this happen?

Oh, maybe because I've told him a pack of lies since the moment we met and I don't want to get caught? Yeah, that's probably it. The longer I stay with him, the more it's going to hurt. The lies will be revealed. I can never doubt that. And once they are, he'll hate me forever. I can't stand the thought.

This is why I should bail. Now.

"Come on. It'll be fun. We'll go somewhere, maybe on the coast. Get a hotel room with a giant bed and never leave it." He chuckles, the sound extra sexy for some reason, and I immediately take the phone off speaker and hold it up to my ear. "I want to be alone with you," I hear him say.

My face flushes hot and I hope Savannah doesn't notice. "You're always alone with me."

"What I really mean is, I don't want to spend Thanksgiving with my family." He lowers his voice. "I want to show my thanks to you."

I laugh. I can't help it. He's flirting with me and being cute, and when he's like this I don't feel like I'm being played. I start imagining he actually cares for me. "Your dad asked you to come over for Thanksgiving dinner. He even invited me."

That still blows my mind, that I have Daddy's approval. I thought Parker Montgomery was a mean asshole, but I guess I was wrong about that too.

"I don't want to go there," Rhett says, his tone final.

"Why not?" I'm genuinely confused by his behavior.

He hesitates, and I almost wonder if he's scrambling for a reason. "I'm pissed at my brother."

"So? I bet you're always pissed at your brother. Plus, Addie will be disappointed if you don't show up." Not that I want to go. I don't want to deal with my—mother. God, it's so difficult to think of Diane as the one who actually gave birth to me. And really, why would I want to be with the very woman who so carelessly left me behind? Who still treats me like absolute shit, not that she knows who I really am.

"She'll live," Rhett reassures me. "I'll make her a deal and we'll spend Christmas with the fam."

He uses "we" so easily. So carelessly. There's no way I want to spend Christmas with his family. I'd be awkward and uncomfortable, and I would probably annoy Rhett. I'd have to buy them gifts, and I don't have much money. In fact, I need to find a job. I can't live off Savannah's generosity forever.

"I can't," I murmur, hoping he doesn't ask any questions.

But this is Rhett and he loves to ask questions. "Why? You have plans? Are you going to see your family?"

"I told you I have no family," I snap.

"I'm sorry. I, uh, I forgot." He does a quick subject change. "Listen, I really think we should go out of town for the weekend. We can leave Thursday afternoon and just drive until we get tired and want to stop. Let's go on an adventure."

I'm tempted. So tempted.

"Maybe." I look over at Savannah, who's gesturing and whispering at me. Frowning, I tilt my head and she mouths, I hold up my hand in a wait movement and concentrate on Rhett.

"Spending Thanksgiving with my family is overrated. Diane doesn't even cook the meal. She has the dinner catered every single time. Park will pick a fight and I bet Addie won't stick around long. She'll probably end up at Trent's house and spend the holiday with his family," he says.

Is it wrong that after hearing him describe the holiday with his family, I kind of want to spend Thanksgiving with the Montgomerys? Because honestly, I have no idea what it's like to have a real holiday with a real family. It was always just my father and me, and no one else around. I don't remember what it was like when my mother was still with us. When we were still a complete family.

As every year passed, our so-called holiday celebrations got worse and worse. To the point where I barely acknowledged a holiday when it came upon us, especially Christmas. We didn't put up a tree or lights or decorations. I didn't give my father any gifts, and he didn't give me any either. The most I got was when my friends and I exchanged a little something at school, and that one year when my math teacher felt sorry for me and gave me a tin of Christmas cookies someone else had brought for her.

Depressing, I know.

But I contradict myself too. It's like the more Rhett tries to convince me, the more resistant I get.

"I feel like you're running away from your problems," I tell him.

He's quiet for a moment, and I know I just offended him. I'm nervous, though this is the right thing to do. Make him mad, get in a fight, force him to end it. Would he really end it that easily? A girl can hope. I can't keep letting him have little pieces of my heart. Soon he'll have the entire thing, and then what will I do?

"You should have plenty of experience with that," he says snottily. "The running away part."

Whoa. "That was mean."

"What you said was mean too. Listen, I gotta go. We'll talk about this later." He ends the call before I can say another word.

I drop the phone on the coffee table in front of me and

sink into the couch with a heavy sigh.

"What happened?" Savannah asks.

"He hung up on me." I can't believe he did that, but then again, I can. "I think I pissed him off."

"I'm guessing you piss him off on a daily basis?" Savannah's brows are up, like she's expecting me to agree with her. But I can't.

"See, that's the weird thing. I've said some pretty awful stuff to him, and he still doesn't seem to mind. Like, he puts up with me and I'm terrible. Last time we were together, I gave him some big story about how he's going to end up married to a boring society wife with too much Botox and they'll have a bunch of brats and he'll cheat on her on the side. And then I climbed into his lap and it was like what I said to him turned him on. The next thing you know, we're having sex again," I explain. I sound like a crazy person.

"Maybe he considers that foreplay?"

I grab a throw pillow and toss it at Savannah, making her laugh. "I don't understand him." The moment the words leave my mouth, I hear how sad and almost desperate I sound. It's embarrassing to admit, but I really do wish I understood Rhett, or what motivates him. He's so confusing sometimes, but I can guarantee I confuse him too.

"You want me to be honest?" Savannah asks, her voice hesitant.

"Go for it," I say warily.

"I don't understand   You have this guy who's totally hot, who's totally rich, and he's also totally nice. He's so into you, Jen. You two fuck like bunnies every chance you get, he introduced you to his family—which is freaking huge, let me tell you—yet you keep pushing him away." Savannah slowly shakes her head. "Don't be dumb and do something you might regret. Keep this guy around, Jen. He could change your life for the better."

Savannah doesn't know my deepest, darkest secret. Once that's revealed, I'll be the one changing Rhett's life. And not in a good way either. And I'm already full of regret. My middle name could be regret, I have so much of it.

"I'm a fucked up mess. Trust me, he doesn't want me in his life."

"No, you don't seem to get it. I don't think any of that matters to him. You've showed him all your ugly scars, he knows you've worked as a topless waitress, that you're broke, that you're not some rich snot who'll please Mommy and Daddy with your pedigree, yet he still seems to want you. That's so amazing.   seems amazing. Or he's a total psychopath who's going to lure you into his trap and then eventually kill you." Savannah starts laughing.

"He's not a psychopath," I reassure her with a frown. Let's be real. I'm probably the one who's a psychopath.

"Okay, then. What's the problem? And don't say you are," she adds when she sees me open my mouth, ready to blast myself. "You're not that bad, Jen. I don't care what you say. You're not a total bitch. You're in college, trying to better yourself. You're just…trying to get by, you know?"

"I've made bad choices," I admit.

"Haven't we all?"

"Not Rhett."

"Oh, come on. No one's that perfect. I'm guessing he hasn't told you about all his bad choices yet."

"No, I really think he's that good of a person. He makes bad choices. He does what's right every single time." Unlike me. I make the worst choices ever every single time, never caring about the consequences. If I hurt someone, so what? That's life.

Rhett makes me want to be a better person. He makes me want to choose right, instead of constantly messing up, acting on impulse. Always reacting versus taking something in and coming up with a plan of action.

But it's too late for us. I've already messed up, betrayed him in the worst way, and he doesn't even know it yet. I'm a terrible person who doesn't deserve Rhett Montgomery in her life. To keep seeing him would be stringing him along, and that's not fair. To Rhett or to me. I need to end it. I keep trying, but he keeps coming back around.

I need to do something to finish it between us once and for all. Clean and easy break so we can both get on with our lives and forget each other.

"Just—think about what you're doing, Jen. If you're smart, you'll stop pushing him away. You keep that up, he'll eventually leave you forever," Savannah says just before she gets off the couch and heads for the kitchen. "You want something to eat?" she calls over her shoulder.

"No thanks." I'm not hungry. My stomach is too twisted up with my overwrought emotions. What the hell does Savannah know anyway? Maybe I want to push Rhett away for good. What's the point in keeping him around? Once he finds out my secret, he'll be so angry, so hurt, he'll never want to see me again.

And that's fine.

Really.

SIX

Rhett

I haven't heard from Jensen since I ended our call without warning her yesterday. It's so typical that she hasn't reached out to me since. She had a lot of nerve, telling me I was running away from my feelings. She's the queen of that shit.

As time goes on, I start to wonder. And worry. Where is she? Is she okay? I tell myself not to care, yet it's all I can do. Like the sadist I am, I give in and try to call her, but she won't call me back, and she won't respond to my texts either. She's avoiding me and I've been busy too, but I'm here.

Right now. Standing on her front porch and pounding my fist on the door. It swings open before I've even finished knocking and there's Savannah, her expression going from friendly to completely closed off the moment she sets eyes on me. "Oh. Hey. Um, you looking for Jen? I'm not sure where she's at ri—"

Jensen magically appears behind her, proving Savannah wrong. "You should leave," she tells me, her gaze unwavering.

What the ever loving… "Nice greeting," I say sarcastically.

Savannah steps out of the way before she gets caught up in our argument. "I'll let you two hash this out," she murmurs before she darts back into the apartment.

"I didn't realize there's anything to hash out," I tell Jensen once Savannah's gone.

"There's not. I just…" She glances over her shoulder before stepping out onto the front porch, closing the door behind her. "I don't think we should see each other anymore, Rhett. This isn't working out."

I'm stunned speechless. My lips part, my brain races with all sorts of things I should say, but I can't come up with anything. I thought we were okay. I know we just had a minor argument, but big deal. Couples have arguments all the time. We've been getting closer. It's getting good, becoming real.

But maybe it was only getting good and becoming real for "It's been fun, and I'll never forget you, but this…isn't a good idea anymore. We're too different." Like she doesn't expect me to protest, she turns, her hand on the door handle, ready to push herself back inside the apartment, but I stop her from fleeing. I brace one hand on the door, the other going to her waist, my body pinning her in place, her back to my front.

"Come on, Jensen, are you serious? Are you really trying to break up with me?" I lean in close, my hand leaving her waist to push her hair away from her neck, exposing the sensitive skin. "Just a few words from you, and I'm supposed to leave?"

"That's how it's usually done." Her voice is shaky, and a trembling exhale leaves her when I dip my head, my mouth right at her ear.

"Why do you keep doing this?" God, her scent drives me wild. She's saying the craziest shit yet I still want her so damn bad. It's like I first set eyes on her and I'm immediately horny, every single time. It's ridiculous.

All-consuming.

"Keep doing what?" she asks breathlessly.

"You always push me away when shit gets bad. One little argument and now you're trying to end it. That's what couples do sometimes—they fight."

"You think we're a couple?" She sounds doubtful. Typical.

"I thought we had a good thing going." I slip my arm around her waist, holding her to me, my mouth still by her ear. "You told me I run away from my problems, but so do you. Every time life throws a curveball your way, your first instinct is to bail."

"Why the baseball reference? You're a basketball player." If she's trying to tease me, her timing is awful. I growl near her ear and she leans into me like she can't help herself, her body molding itself to mine, and damn, she feels good. "I don't bail every single time," she protests weakly.

The little liar. "You do too and you know it." I spread my

hand wide, my palm pressed against her stomach. "Let me inside, Jensen." Those words mean way more than just me asking to come inside the apartment.

"I was about to leave."

I pull away and study her, really taking in her outfit. She's wearing a black floral-print dress that nearly reaches her knees and black flats, her hair curled at the ends, a thin gold necklace wound around her neck. "Where are you going?"

She turns slightly and hip checks me, so I have no choice but to take a step back. "None of your business."

I throw my hands up in the air, frustration rolling through me, pushing me straight to the edge. "Come the fuck on. This is getting old."

Jensen fully faces me, her expression neutral. "I agree. It getting old. I don't know how many times I need to tell you this."

"Tell me what?"

"That we're done! We're through! Quit trying to make what we have into something real. It's not. It never has been. We're too different. It would never work between us." There's frustration in her voice, and she's slinging her words at me like weapons, but something tells me what she's saying is kind of...

Phony?

Maybe not, though. Maybe that's me hoping she's full of shit.

When I'm quiet for a too long moment, she practically

shrieks, "Don't you have anything to "

"You really believe that." My voice is flat while my emotions are kicking into chaos. Does she actually believe what she's saying?

She lifts her chin, looking determined. The tiniest bit scared. "I really believe that," she whispers.

Backing away from her, I slowly shake my head. "You need time, I think," I say just before I turn and make my way toward the parking lot. More like I need time to figure out what's going on.

"Time won't help us, Rhett," she yells after me, but I don't respond.

I'm too busy heading for my car, my mind filled with everything I need to do.

It may take me a while, but I will get to the bottom of this.

I have to.

SEVEN

Jensen

I posted my resume on one of those job search websites at Savannah's urging, and out of nowhere I receive an email this morning requesting an interview for later this afternoon.

"I've had my resume on that site for " Savannah tells me as I'm putting on the last of my makeup in the bathroom we share. "And no one has ever contacted me like that. Not once."

"I guess I'm lucky then." I slick on one more coat of mascara and put the tube away in my cosmetics bag, staring at my reflection in the mirror. Not bad, though I'm wearing the same dress from yesterday when I went out and dropped my resume off at a few businesses around town.

Despite my encounter with Rhett, I didn't let it get me down. Nope, I let our stupid argument fuel me, push me to try my best to find a job despite what he said and how he acted. Savannah's wrong and he's wrong too. I don't need him to change my life for the better. I can do this shit on my own.

I got this.

"I suggest if anything looks strange or if you have a weird feeling about the interview, you should run," Savannah says as she follows me out of the bathroom and into the living room.

"What are you talking about?" I sit on the edge of the couch and slip my shoes on, then run my fingers through my hair. I'm nervous. The business that contacted me has a position listed for an assistant, and I've never assisted someone in my life. I don't even know why they emailed me. I don't have any administrative skills. Everything on my resume is restaurant or fast food work. Oh, and that one time I worked at the grocery store in my hometown, but that job barely counts. I think I worked there two weeks, tops.

"I think it's odd how this place sought you out and asked you for an interview out of the blue." Savannah presses her lips together. "I Googled the business, but there's nothing listed."

Of course she Googled the business. I'm the queen of Google, so why didn't I think of that? I was so impressed and excited that they actually wanted an interview, I guess I forgot. "So?"

"So, it's as if MP Industries doesn't even exist. And that's strange, Jen." Savannah starts pacing the short length of the living room, chewing on a fingernail. "I want to go with you to your interview. Make sure you're okay."

"Savannah, I appreciate your concern, but that is the

lamest thing ever." I rise to my feet and grab my purse, slinging it over my shoulder. "I don't need you to babysit me. I'm a big girl. I can handle this."

"What if it's a setup? What if it's that—" She hesitates, her eyes wide as she stares at me. The fear on her face makes my stomach churn with nerves. "What if it's that Greg guy trying to get back in contact with you?"

My stomach dips. I never did tell her about my run in with Greg at the Montgomery house. She'd probably call the cops if she knew I hadn't done anything, and that could've caused an even bigger problem. One I absolutely don't need.

"That's crazy, Sav. Your imagination is running wild."

I head for the front door, but she's quicker, inserting herself in between me and the door so I have no choice but to stop. I don't bother arguing. What's the point? May as well let her do what she wants. Plus, she might have a point. I'd rather be safe than sorry.

"Fine, you can drive me to the interview."

Her expression turns hopeful. "Are you serious? Let me get my shoes on."

"Hurry up! I don't want to be late," I tell her as she runs toward her bedroom. With a big sigh I check my phone, secretly hoping for a notification from Rhett, but there's nothing. Not that I should be surprised.

Guess I finally pushed him away once and for all.

The ache in my chest is hard to ignore and I rub at it

absently, reminding myself I'm being overdramatic. Like Rhett and I had a fighting chance anyway. My lies are too big to overcome. It's a relief, really, not having him around anymore, not having to pretend that everything is fine when it's so not.

But as I sit in the car while Savannah drives me to MP Industries, I realize that these last few weeks together, I wasn't pretending with Rhett. I care about him. I had fun with him. He's so sweet to me, so thoughtful and caring and smart. I liked that his father approved of me. I liked getting to know Addie—funny since at one point in my life, she was the Montgomery I hated the most, I was so jealous of her and the relationship I thought she had with my dear old mother.

Even his brother Park's okay, though he's kind of an ass. I know I could handle him if I had to. I've dealt with guys like that before.

It's my own mother I don't know how to deal with. I don't understand Diane Montgomery. She's so callous, so rude, so incredibly selfish. Every time I came around her, she couldn't even look my way when all I wanted to do was shout and say, "See? This is me! I'm your daughter! The one you forgot all about!"

I have a feeling that even if I would've shouted all of that at her, she never would've heard me.

When Savannah finally pulls up in front of the mostly abandoned-looking building in the middle of the industrial part of town, we send each other skeptical glances.

"I don't like this place," Savannah says uneasily. "It's creepy."

"It's fine." Taking a deep breath, I grab my bag off the floor, shoving my phone inside.

"It's not fine. There's no one around. Where are all the cars?" She's leaning over the steering wheel and peering out the window, looking up and down the street. She's right. There are no cars around. It's weird.

"I don't know." I grab the handle and open the door, stepping out of the car, Savannah doing the same. I study the drab building looming in front of me, holding my hand to my forehead to shield my eyes. There's no sign on the front, the windows are dark, and the unease that slips cold down my spine gives me major second thoughts.

"Maybe you should walk inside with me," I say to Savannah.

"Absolutely," she agrees with a firm nod.

We enter the building, the doors swinging open with ease and a wall of cool air enveloping me, making me shiver. Why run the air conditioning when it's the end of November and cold out? Weird.

The cavernous lobby is mostly empty, save for the beautiful dark-haired woman sitting behind a large desk on the far side of the room. When she notices us, she stands. "Hello. Is either one of you Jensen?"

"I am," I say with a faint smile as I step toward her.

The woman smiles in return, moving from behind her desk to come stand in front of us. "It's so nice to meet you,

Jensen. I'm Sandra, and I'll take you to your interview. I hope your friend doesn't mind waiting out here for you?"

I turn to look at Savannah. "You okay with waiting?"

Savannah raises her brows and looks around, her gaze lingering on the nearby couches. "You okay with me not going with you?"

"I'll be all right." I take a step closer and lower my voice so only she can hear me. "I'll make a run for it if things get out of hand."

She smiles. "Good idea."

"See you in a bit," I tell her before I turn to Sandra. "Okay, I'm ready."

Sandra leads me down a long, narrow hall, making small talk, asking if I have any Thanksgiving plans, and do I have a job currently? I offer up vague answers. I'm not one for casual conversation, especially when it has to do with me. I'd rather keep my private details private, thank you very much.

There's a door at the end of the hall and she reaches for the handle, opening it slowly. "You can go in now."

"Um. Wait a—" I turn to look at her, but she's shooing me in then closing the door behind me so quickly, I have to leap forward so she doesn't slam the door on me. I look around the room, spotting the desk angled in the farthest corner, and a man sits behind it.

And not just any man.

It's Park. Rhett's big brother.

What. The. Hell?

"Jensen." He stands and makes his way toward me, immaculate in a black suit, his dark hair slicked back, his expression open. Friendly. The total opposite of how he behaved during our last encounter, when he revealed my job status to Diane with such uncontained glee. Like he couldn't want to humiliate me, the jackass. "I'm so glad you could make it."

I take a step back, confused. Annoyed. This feels like a setup. A trick. "What are you doing here?"

"I'm the CEO of MP Industries." He offers me a crooked smile, somehow looking bashful and smug all at once.

I'm having a hard time comprehending what he's telling me. "Are you the one I'm supposed to interview with?"

"Well. Yes. I need an assistant." He slips his hands in his trouser pockets, deceptively casual. I don't know what he's up to, but it definitely doesn't feel legit. "I didn't know how to tell you it was me. Plus I figured if you knew you were interviewing with me, you wouldn't show up."

"You figured correctly," I tell him just before I turn and start heading for the door. He's right behind me, his steps increasing, and before I can reach for the handle, his hand is there, smacking against the door and pressing on the sleek wood to keep me captive.

These Montgomery men are determined, I can give them that.

"Hear me out, Jensen," he says, stepping away from me when I turn to face him. "I want you to come work for me."

"Why?" I ask incredulously, crossing my arms. "I don't understand. How did you even find me?"

He offers a little shrug, still going for nonthreatening. I don't believe him, though. I think he's a bigger threat than he's letting on. "I was scrolling through that career site and stumbled upon your resume. I checked out your qualifications, and realized quick you'd make the perfect assistant." That smile is still pasted on his face, but his eyes have gone a little dim. "Come on, Jensen. Sit down, let's chat for a few minutes."

"No." I shake my head. "I can't work for you."

"Why not? I know you don't have a job right now." When I frown at him, he continues, "I called City Lights. They told me you didn't work there any longer."

Is he stalking me? This makes zero sense. I decide not to acknowledge the lack of job comment. "Why are you doing this?"

"Doing what?" He blinks his big brown eyes and I sort of want to punch him.

"Showing such— in me? What are you doing? Trying to make your brother jealous?"

Park actually scoffs. "Please. My little brother has been jealous of me since the day he was born. I don't need to make him feel that emotion. He experiences it every single day with everything I do."

I doubt that. Rhett's never given me even a hint of jealousy when he speaks of his brother. "Then what's the point? There must be something driving you to do this."

"There's nothing going on, beyond me being in search of a qualified assistant. And you just so happen to top the list," Park says easily, mimicking my position by crossing his arms.

"My topless waitressing skills are what sent me over the top of the qualified list, am I right?" I arch a brow, and he actually has the decency to appear momentarily chastised. "You know I don't have an office or assistant experience."

"Fine. You want to know the truth?" He drops his arms to his sides and comes closer, his mouth curved in a barely-there smile, the scent of his expensive cologne tickling my senses. He reminds me of Rhett, but older looking. No, harder looking. Like he has a lot more distrust for people than his brother does. As if he's been wronged one too many times and he's not going to let his guard down anymore.

"I would love to know the truth," I tell him, lifting my chin a little bit, going for strong, fearless woman. Really, I'm quaking inside, my stomach a jumble of twisted nerves.

"You look like a girl who knows how to keep a secret," he murmurs, reaching out to touch just beneath my chin with his index finger. He strokes me there, a feather-light touch that's there and gone in a matter of seconds, his hand falling away from me. "In fact, I'd bet you keep lots of secrets."

I try my best not to visibly tremble. It's like he knows.

Does he, though?

When I say nothing, he continues, "I need someone by my side who's discreet. Who can keep her mouth shut. Someone who'll work hard for me, who'll help me grow this business since my asshole father won't give me his. Even though I'm the one who's worked more than he has for the last five fucking years."

I'm shocked by the venom in his tone. Blinking up at him, I try to comprehend what he's saying. "So you're starting a business without your father knowing about it?"

Park clamps his lips shut so tightly, they practically disappear. "I won't talk about it with you any further unless you sign a NDA."

I frown. "Sign a what?"

"A nondisclosure agreement. I have to ensure your silence before I can say anything else." He strides toward the desk, glancing over his shoulder so his gaze meets mine. "Come with me."

I follow after him as if I have no control of myself, stopping just in front of his desk. He hands me a piece of paper and I glance at it. There's a lot of writing, a bunch of legalese that I don't really understand, along with two blank lines at the bottom of the page for us both to sign.

"Before this interview can continue, I need you to sign this," Park says solemnly.

I squint at the paper, wishing I could understand it. I

mean, I'm not a total idiot, but I don't like reading when I'm under pressure. I don't like doing anything under pressure. It's not cool. Not at all.

"I can't sign your NDA," I finally say, lifting my gaze to Park's.

The irritation on his face is obvious. "Why not?"

"I don't think I want to continue with this interview." When he tilts his head, I realize he's going to make me say it. "I don't want to work for you, Park. Not like this."

"Not like what? I don't understand what you're trying to say."

"I don't want to sneak around without your dad knowing." I can't believe I'm saying this. "It doesn't feel right."

Park grabs another piece of paper from the desk and hands it to me. "This is what your salary would be if you came to work for me, along with a list of benefits the position at MP Industries would provide."

My eyes nearly bug out of my head when I see the total at the bottom of the piece of paper. He wants to pay me over one hundred grand a year to be his assistant? Is he out of his freaking mind?

"It's a very competitive salary," he adds, like he hasn't just blown my mind.

"Are you for real right now?" I ask, my head spinning at the thought of all the money I could make. It might suck, having to deal with Park on a daily basis, but for over one hundred thousand dollars a year, I could put up with a lot of shit with a big ol' smile on my face. It goes without saying that this is way better money that I could ever make at City Lights. Hell, at any potential job I might consider.

I'm not qualified for the job, though. Claiming he wants me to work for him because of my secret-keeping skills? That's not enough. He has another motive. I just haven't figured it out yet.

"Come on, Jensen. You know you want the position. Just say yes, sign the NDA, and the job is yours." He smiles, a flash of blinding white teeth, his brows lifted expectantly.

I glance around the mostly empty room, tucking my hair behind my ear. I'm apprehensive, yet tempted, and he knows it.

He thinks he's got me.

EIGHT

Rhett

My phone lights up in the darkness from where it sits on my nightstand and I reach for it, checking the text notification from...

Jensen.

It's past eleven and thank Christ we're on break for Thanksgiving week, but I had a basketball game earlier and I'm wiped out. I was trying to go to sleep but my mind was filled of thoughts of Jensen, which is nothing new. I can't shake her no matter how hard I try, though I'm not really trying that hard.

Unplugging my phone from the charger, I start typing.

She answers me immediately.

A mixture of hope and irritation fills me. This better not be a bunch of misleading bullshit.

Biting my lip, I contemplate what I want to say next.

Aw, fuck it.

She takes what feels like forever to answer me, when it was probably only a couple of minutes.

I don't respond yet, because I can see the little gray bubble that she's still typing. She takes so long, I wonder if it's a trick, but then finally another text appears.

Another text.

My heart starts to race. I want to go over there. I do. For once, she's not pushing me away. She needs me.

I push the annoying thought into the far corners of my brain.

Before I say something stupid via text and ruin everything, I decide to call her instead.

"You really want me to come over?" It's the first thing I say when she answers.

"Yes." She lowers her voice. "I can't talk about it over the phone, Rhett. I don't feel comfortable saying it like this."

Damn, what could it be?

Guilt swamps me when I think of my secret I'm keeping. I've called Uncle Craig a couple of times and left him messages, but he still hasn't called me back. I want to tell her that the man she thinks is Greg is really my uncle, but how?

"Give me fifteen minutes and I'll be there," I tell her, ending the call before she can change her mind.

I hop out of bed and slip on some clothes—shorts and a black hoodie—and I'm in the car and headed to Savannah's apartment in under five minutes. I arrive at the apartment in less than fifteen and when Jensen answers the door, she looks surprised to see me.

"That was fast." She opens the door wider to let me in.

"You told me you needed me." I sound like a sap, but damn it, I want her to realize that if she ever needs me, I'm there for her. Always.

She slowly shuts the door and then locks it, leaning against it when she's done. I'm standing in the middle of the tiny living room, both of us staring at each other from across the small space. She's wearing a pair of tiny pale blue shorts and one of my T-shirts she must've snagged. Seeing her in my shirt, looking small and vulnerable and so goddamn beautiful, I want to yank her into my arms and never let her go. Confess my secret, confess my feelings and hope like hell she'll be as real with me as I want to be with her.

"I don't know how to start," she finally says, her gaze meeting mine.

"Just tell me what happened," I say, my tone coaxing. I know without a doubt that   happened to push her to seek me out.

"Let's sit on the couch." She waves her hand toward it and we both settle in, me on one end and her on the other, like we don't want to get too close.

We're being ridiculous right now, but I'll take what I can get.

"I've been looking for a job. Savannah showed me one of those career job sites that you upload your resume on, so I did it, thinking I'll never hear from someone, because Savannah said she never has, but it wouldn't hurt, right?" She's rambling, and I can feel her nervous energy. She's got her foot propped on the coffee table in front of her and she's bouncing her knee, making the table shake.

"Okay." I say the word slowly, frowning at her. I have no idea where she's going with this.

"So a business contacted me the very next day, asking if I'd come in for an interview. A place called MP Industries, and they're looking for an administrative assistant. I have zero qualifications for that sort of job, but I'd love to find a nine to five position, so of course I go for the interview." She pauses, her gaze meeting mine once more. "You'll never believe who was waiting there to interview me."

Apprehension fills me, making me sick to my stomach. God, it could be anyone, but I'm specifically thinking of Uncle Craig. "Who?" I ask weakly.

"Park."

It takes a moment for the word to sink in, but once it does, I'm leaping to my feet, my hands on my hips, my head feeling like it's going to explode. "What the actual fuck? interviewed you? For what business?"

"MP Industries." Never heard of it. "I figured out it stands for Montgomery Parker. He reversed his initials."

"I don't understand." I feel like a complete idiot, but what she's saying doesn't make any sense.

With a sigh she looks away, staring into the far-off distance. "Park said he was starting his own business because he's mad at your father. I think he feels like he's devoted his entire career to your dad and he gets nothing in return."

"Right. He only gets a huge salary and barely has to work. Whatever." I actually snort, I'm so disgusted.

She turns to look at me once more. "I'm just saying what I think your brother might feel, not that it's right." Her gaze is wide and earnest. "I think he wants to somehow screw your dad over with his new business. I don't know his actual plan or anything, but he says he chose me to be his assistant because I know how to keep a secret."

Well. Park's right about that. "And so he hired you as his assistant?"

Jensen sinks her teeth into her lower lip for a moment. "He wanted me to sign a NDA before he'd tell me anything substantial."

"So you can't discuss the details with me, then." This is complete bullshit. Now my brother is trying to get my— girlfriend? whatever the hell Jensen is—to work for him? So they can both somehow sabotage our father? Fuck that. I start heading for the door.

"Where are you going?" she asks, her voice panicked.

"I'm gonna go talk to Park. Find out what the hell he's

trying to do."

"Rhett! Don't leave!" She's right behind me now, tugging on my arm, and I turn to face her. "Please. Let me finish."

I cross my arms, quietly fuming. "Go on then. Tell me," I bite out.

With a sigh she rubs her forehead, then lets her arm fall to her side. "I didn't sign the NDA. I didn't accept the position, even though he wants to pay me over a hundred grand a year."

My jaw hangs open. "Seriously?" What the hell is Park up to?

"Yes, seriously. But I don't want to work for Park. Your father has been nothing but kind to me since I met him. I don't want to risk making him mad, you know?" Her shoulders slump and she looks so defeated, so sad, I give in to impulse and pull her into my arms, holding her close.

"You did the right thing," I murmur against her soft hair, running my hand up and down her back, loving the feel of her so snug in my arms. "I'm glad you turned him down."

"He really tried to guilt me into it too. Well, more like bribe me into it. He kept talking about my salary and perks of the job." Her voice is muffled against my chest and I strain to hear her. "I don't get what he's trying to do, Rhett. I don't know why he wants me involved."

To get back at Dad and me? But why me? What did I ever do to him? I'm keeping his and Diane's secret, and it's a big one. A life changer.

Why would he want to piss me off?

Of course, he already pissed me off at Addie's party when he called out Jensen for her job. That was utter bullshit. He's being so careless, like he just doesn't give a damn.

One day, his carelessness is going to bite him in the ass.

"He hasn't been making the best decisions lately," I say.

That's an understatement. He's been screwing up left and right.

Jensen pulls away so she can look up at me. "After I left the interview, I couldn't stop thinking about you. And how I needed to tell you the truth."

I frown. "The truth about what?"

She seems to hesitate, taking a deep breath and letting it out in a shaky exhale. "The truth about…" Her voice drifts and she closes her eyes. Shakes her head once. "About this. About what your brother asked me to do."

Maybe she was trying to tell me something else. I don't know why I feel this way, but I do. There are more secrets here. I have them, she has them, and I don't know how to confess mine.

Maybe she feels the same exact way.

NINE

Jensen

ecause I'm weak, I let Rhett stay the night. We sleep wrapped around each other on the tiny double bed in Savannah's even tinier second bedroom that I've been using, my head on his chest, his steady heartbeat lulling me to sleep. Nothing happens sexually, which is fine by me. I'm emotionally exhausted and I think he is too. I can't keep up with the lies and the outlandish requests.

Worse, after much discussion with Rhett, neither of us can figure out Park's motive in asking me to be his assistant, beyond his odd "you know how to keep a secret" reasoning. That's not good enough.

There has to be something more.

I wake up in the morning to find my face still pressed against Rhett's now bare chest, his thick arms holding me tight, our legs tangled together. I'm sure I have wicked morning breath and I bet he does too, so I'm trying to disengage myself from his hold so I can go brush my teeth. But my pulling away seems to make him only hold on to me tighter, and when I lift my head to check on him, I find that he's awake, watching me with narrowed eyes, a tiny smile curving his perfectly sculpted lips.

"You can't get away that easily," he murmurs, his sleep-roughened voice extra sexy, making everything within me tingle with awareness.

Of course.

"I wanted to go brush my teeth," I admit, going for honesty. If we're really going to make this work, I need to be open with him.

One step at a time though. One step at a time.

"I probably should too." He doesn't let go of me, though. It's like he's not going anywhere and I squirm against him, trying to slither out of his grip. "Not yet, babe. You're so warm."

Aw. My heart does a flip at him calling me   in that sleepy-sexy voice of his. I push thoughts of bad breath out of my brain and snuggle in close, enjoying his warmth, the smooth skin of his chest, the reassuring sound of his heartbeat. I could go back to sleep if I wanted to. Escaping the pressures of reality for a few more hours sounds awfully pleasant…

But then I feel Rhett's large hand on my butt, caressing me there, his fingers tickling, making me wiggle. It feels like his hand is actually on my skin, burning me, lighting me up inside, and when he slides his hand to the front of my shorts and dips inside, I suck in a sharp breath at first touch.

"No panties?" He doesn't sound surprised as he slides his fingers between my thighs.

"No." I shift, spreading my legs a little bit, giving him better access.

"How'd I know you'd be so wet?" he murmurs against my forehead, his fingers gliding back and forth, searching me, penetrating me easily. He groans, his thumb pressing against my clit.

We turn into a fumbling mass of bodies, him pulling away from me, me rolling onto my back and kicking my shorts off. He rids himself of his underwear as I reach out and touch him, smooth and hard and wet at the tip, all for me. I stroke him and he strokes me, our breathing accelerating in tandem, that familiar rush already looming. I pull Rhett on top of me, his hips nestling in between my legs, and he enters me with ease.

Every time. Every damn time it's so good, it almost pisses me off. He touches my clit as he pumps inside of me, making sure I get off. Always thoughtful, always sweet Rhett, just as concerned about my pleasure as his own.

He's too good for me. I keep thinking this, reminding myself, but I can't help it when he proves to me again and again just how great he is.

It's downright annoying.

We forget all about morning breath as he kisses me deep,

his tongue everywhere, circling around mine. I'm too caught up in the tingly sensation of my impending orgasm to worry about anything else. He slides, deep, deeper, deeper still, and then I'm clinging to him, overcome as every bone in my body feels like it's going to melt into a puddle, I'm quivering and shaking and whispering his name. He follows soon after me, his hips pressed close to mine like he's trying to burrow inside of me, his mouth against my neck as he groans.

When it's all over and he's rolling away from me, I murmur, "You do realize we've never used a condom."

He's lying on his back next to me, breathing hard and staring up at the ceiling. The moment the word   falls from my lips, he whips his head to the side, his gaze meeting mine. "Fuck," he says with a gulp.

"Yeah, we've been doing lots of that." I roll on my side to face him, reaching out to touch his hair. It's thick and soft, the strands clinging to my fingers, and he closes his eyes as I continue to play with his hair. We should've had this conversation eons ago. "I'm on the pill, though, so we should be good. Unless…"

His eyes fall closed. I know he likes it when I touch his hair. "Unless what?"

"Unless you're full of STDs."

"I'm not." His eyes open and he stares at me, fierce sincerity in his gaze. "I get tested every year when I get my athletic physical."

"I don't have an STD either." At least six months ago I didn't, when I got my free physical and birth control prescription from the college clinic.

"Then we're good." He winces. "I'm an idiot."

"No, you're not," I tell him, but he shakes his head, silencing me.

"I am. I've told myself before to grab a condom, but every single time we're together, it's like I can't even—think. And that's the lamest excuse ever, right?"

No, not really. I pretty much feel the same exact way.

"You probably think I'm a selfish asshole because I've never talked about any of this with you before."

I heave a big sigh. "Rhett, you are the least selfish person I know, I swear. I guess we're always just…too caught up in the moment."

"Yeah. That's not a good enough excuse, though, right?"

"You're going to beat yourself up over it?"

"No, I guess not. Unless you want to beat me up for it."

"I don't." I can't help but smile at him.

His smile in return is boyishly sweet. "Let's take a nap. Sex makes me sleepy."

I laugh but don't protest when he pulls me back into his arms.

Rhett takes me to lunch at a small sandwich shop that's in

a shopping center with a major supermarket. The parking lot is full—everyone in the store buying all of their Thanksgiving needs before the holiday, so we have to park in the farthest corner of the lot.

"This place is insane," he mutters as he takes my hand and leads me toward the sandwich shop.

The easy way he clasps my hand in his makes me giddy, and I tell myself to chill. This is no big deal. Being with Rhett like this could actually happen if I let it. But I need to come clean.

Maybe I should now, at lunch? Before Thanksgiving, so he at least knows what Diane means to me? What he means to me? That, in all actuality, he's my stepbrother?

Yeah. So weird. I'm attempting a relationship with my stepbrother. I sound like some girl straight out of a romance novel, right?

"Everyone's shopping for turkeys and mashed potatoes," I tell him, trying to keep my voice light, all while my head is swimming with potential conversation starters.

Yeah, no.

Talk about shocking.

There is no easy way for me to tell him this. Easing into it seems the best tactic, while blurting out the facts over lunch might be the easiest. Like pulling a Band-Aid off, you know? Quick and easy and relatively painless.

Well, somewhat painless.

Fine, it's going to hurt no matter what.

"You okay?" Rhett asks me as we enter the sandwich shop. There's a line at the counter, and we stop almost just as soon as we walk in. When I shoot him a questioning look, he continues. "You seem distracted."

"I am, a little." But I can't admit why while we wait in line to order. This is the last place I can drop my truth bomb. "Still thinking about what Park did yesterday."

That's also true. I still don't understand what Park is up to. I usually have guys like that figured out. But he's like a big question mark in my head. I don't know what he wants from me. Or what he wants from any of us.

Rhett's entire face goes tight. "I'm going to talk to him later."

"What? No." I cling to his arm, gazing up at him. He's the tallest, handsomest guy in the restaurant, and I'm aware enough to know I'm so damn lucky to have him in my life. But I can't have him going to his big brother and confronting him. It'll make the entire situation an even bigger mess. "Let it go. Pretend I never told you."

"I want to, but I can't, Jens. He's up to something and I want him to know I'm on to his game," Rhett explains through thin lips.

"So what is his game then?"

He takes a deep breath and glances around the place. It's packed—the tables are full and there are people milling about everywhere. Definitely not the right time to talk about this.

"I'll tell you what I know later."

Curiosity makes me stand a little straighter. Hmm, so he knows more than he's let on? Interesting. I always thought I was the secret keeper, but maybe Rhett is too.

Maybe he has more secrets that I haven't found out yet.

We order our lunch, and Rhett pays because he's a gentleman and I'm broke. I take both our soda cups and fill them while he waits at the counter for our sandwiches, and when I'm done, I go in search of a table. I'm about to sit at a small one near the front door when I hear an unfamiliar voice say, "Jenny Fanelli, is that you?"

I whip my head around in horror to find a blast from my past standing directly in front of me, a wide smile on his face.

Yes, face. Some forgettable boy I went out with for a while, during our senior year. He was cute and drove a truck, and he happened to fuck me in the back of his truck whenever he got the chance. I let him, because he offered up a taste of freedom, you know? He'd tell me he had big dreams, playing baseball for the pros and a bunch of nonsense like that. I nodded along with his stories, wanting to believe him, but the practical, jaded side of me said no way was that ever going to happen.

And clearly it didn't. Mike Storm—yes, his name is perfect for a pro athlete, right?—is staring at me with bug eyes, like he can't believe he found me.

"Hey, Mike. Funny running into you here," I say weakly.

"Damn girl, you look great." He yanks me into his arms

and holds me close, his fingers almost but not quite resting on my butt. The jerk.

I carefully pull myself out of his embrace, trying to keep my distance. "You look good too. What brings you here?"

"Ah, my girlfriend's family lives nearby. We're here visiting for Thanksgiving, and I volunteered to grab sandwiches for lunch." His gaze roves over me, lingering on my chest. "I almost forgot about you."

My smile feels more like a baring of teeth. The asshole always did have a way with words. "I'm that forgettable, huh?"

"Nah, it's just been so long. Once school was done, you disappeared completely, when I thought we had a good thing going."

Good thing for him. I found out near the end of senior year he suddenly had a girlfriend—and I'd been regulated to his side piece. I told him I didn't want to see him anymore and that was the end of it.

"I broke up with you," I tell him. "Remember?"

"Sure. But we made some good memories, Jenny." His gaze becomes thoughtful, like he's in full-on reminiscing mode. "Remember that time I stole my dad's bottle of Grey Goose and we got drunk off our asses?"

I do. And at the time, it had felt fun. An escape, which was what Mike always provided me. "Yeah."

"And then you got scared when we parked on Old Man Larson's property and you ran out of my truck buck naked?"

He starts to laugh. "I had to chase you down."

He chased me down all right. Caught me in his arms, pressed me into the grass, and we had sex right there. I hadn't protested, though. No, I pretty much begged for it, because that last year of high school, I'd turned into a full-blown nympho. Always looking for someone to make me feel good about myself. Always wanting that escape from my bleak reality, even if it only lasted for a few minutes.

Now when I think back on it, all I feel is shame.

"Right. Listen—" I start, but Rhett magically appears with our tray of sandwiches, his expression thunderous when he catches sight of Mike.

"Who's your friend?" he asks tightly.

Mike smiles at Rhett, completely oblivious. "Hey, nice to meet you. I'm Mike. Jenny's ex."

Rhett sends me a look, one that's wondering at the nickname, I'm sure, before he resumes his attention on Mike. "Rhett. Jensen's current."

Mike frowns, confusion written all over his face when his gaze meets mine. "Jensen? What the hell? You go and change your name or what?"

"It was nice seeing you," I tell Mike, my voice final, my eyes full of meaning. But is Mike getting it?

I don't think so.

"Nice seeing you too," he says confusedly, rubbing his forehead as if I hurt his brain. Maybe I did. He was never what

I'd consider especially bright. "Best go get in line before it's out the door."

Rhett doesn't say a word after Mike leaves. Just plops the tray onto the table, hands me my sandwich, sets his in front of him, and starts eating.

The silence lasts no longer than two minutes, but it feels like two hours. I stare at my sandwich, my appetite evaporating with every second that ticks by, and finally, I can't freaking take it. I have to say something.

"I went out with Mike in high school," I tell Rhett, lifting my head to meet his gaze, but he's not really looking at me.

"That's nice," he says, his mouth full, his expression...void. Oh man, he looks pissed. Wait. Worse, he looks—indifferent. Like he doesn't care about what just happened.

And I want him to care. I want him to care a lot. I may have had a lot of sex with Mike back in the day, but none of it was near as meaningful as what Rhett and I share.

How can I tell him that, though, without sounding like some sort of sex-crazed maniac?

"We were never serious."

"What you've done in your past means nothing to me," Rhett says, still eating his sandwich.

And now I want to throw my sandwich at him. "Seriously? You don't care that Mike and I were together?"

Rhett shrugs, damn him. "You have a past, I have a past. It shouldn't matter because we're together now, right?"

"Right," I say weakly, dropping my gaze to my turkey sandwich on sourdough. Just the thought of trying to put that sandwich in my mouth makes me want to gag.

"Or are we?" When I scrunch my brows in confusion, he explains, "Together."

My heart feels like it's lodged in my throat. "I think we are," I admit softly.

"Good."

We're silent for a moment, me absorbing what he said, about us being together, but then he says something else.

"I didn't like the way he was looking at you, though," Rhett adds.

A glimmer of hope shoots through me and I glance up once more to find Rhett staring at me. "How was he looking at me?"

"Like he remembered the way you look naked."

Okay. He's not as indifferent as I thought he was. "He did try to reminisce with me about old times."

"I bet he did," Rhett muttered, shaking his head. "Look, you want to know what really bothers me? Not that you have old boyfriends, or that one of those old boyfriends just ran into you and acted like he wished he had X-ray vision. No, what   bothers me is that you have a past, you have a life, and you barely let me in it. You rarely talk about yourself, if ever."

I lean back in my chair, surprised at the emotion I hear in Rhett's voice. "I've told you some stuff—" I start, but he cuts me off with a firm shake of his head.

"You've barely told me anything, Jens. And why did he seem so surprised by your name anyway, huh? He called you Jenny. I don't get it."

My stomach sinks as we stare at each other.

How am I going to explain this?

Standing up straighter, I look him square in the eye. I know what I have to do.

He deserves to know who I really am.

TEN

Rhett

I watch her closely, remembering what my roommate Chad said about her name, and how he thought it might be phony. That strippers have fake names all the time. Not that Jensen is a stripper, but…she worked at a strip club, so close enough.

With a sigh she pushes away her still-uneaten sandwich, her gaze dropping to the table. "I changed my name."

I'm surprised, yet not, by her revelation. "Why?"

"After my dad died, I wanted to escape. To, I don't know, renew myself? I didn't want to live with that old name, which I never really liked anyway."

"What's your actual name?" I ask.

"Jennifer," she admits, her voice soft. A little laugh escapes her, but it doesn't hold an ounce of humor. "I say the name and it means nothing to me. Weird, right?"

"I guess." I hesitate, not sure what to say next, or how to

approach this. I decide to just go for it. "You know, you've never even told me your last name."

Her eyes go wide. "I haven't?"

"No." I shake my head. "You're just Jensen. Or Jens."

"Oh. Well. My last name is—Fanelli." She's staring at the table again. "Though I'm considering changing that too."

"Why?" That single word holds so much emotion, even I'm aware of it. I see the way she recoils from me, her eyes wide and full of mistrust. I need to correct myself before she thinks I'm being—her words—too judgey. "It's just your name is your—identity, right? That's who you are. That you can want to change it blows my mind."

"It wasn't an easy decision," she admits through tight lips. "I've been thinking about this for a long time. My last name brings me nothing but awful memories. I just want to—move on from the past, you know?"

No. I don't know. Why would she want to move on? I know her life wasn't the best, but to change her name seems so drastic…

Does she want to forget her father? I know from what little she's told me that their relationship wasn't the best, but he was her father. And now he's gone. She needs to hold onto something, right? It's like she's…

Heartless.

"But your father died. Don't you want some sort of connection to him, especially now that he's gone?" I ask incredulously.

She rises to her feet so quickly, she knocks her chair into the woman sitting behind her, who turns and glares at the both of us. We ignore her, though. I'm too focused on a now very angry Jensen, her hands clinched at her sides, her eyes full of fire.

"Why are you making such a big deal about this?" she asks, her voice shrill. "I thought of all people and what you've gone through, you'd understand."

Guilt swamps me, but I push it aside. "I'm trying to understand," I say calmly.

Jensen stares at me for a long moment before grabbing her purse and heading straight out of the sandwich shop.

Guess that was the wrong thing to say.

"Jesus," I mutter, annoyed that I can't finish my lunch. Annoyed that everything seems to blow up into a dramatic argument between us.

I've been thinking all along that I want to help her, that I want to fix whatever's wrong with her. But maybe I'm wrong. Maybe she's not worth the trouble.

It's hard for me to believe I'm thinking like this. But I'm frustrated. And tired. So very tired of all the game-playing. My family doesn't make it easy either. They're just as bad— hell, they're worse—than Jensen is. And it doesn't help that I'm keeping secrets too. It's fucking exhausting.

I find her standing just outside the restaurant, her arms

wrapped around her middle, her face pale. She almost looks green, like she's going to throw up at any second. "I don't want to fight with you," I start out, but she cuts me off.

"I'm sorry." She chokes the words out before she throws herself at me, her arms wrapped tight around my neck as she clings to me. "I'm so, so sorry, Rhett. Please forget what I just said. Forget how I acted. I was wrong."

I have no choice but to wrap my arms around her in return, holding her tight as she cries—actually —against my chest. I run my hand over her hair, down her back, trying to soothe her, curious as to why she's reacting so strongly. There's something she's not telling me, and I don't know what it is, but if I had to bet on it, I'd guess it has to do with her past.

I wish for once she'd open up and let whatever's bothering her pour out.

"I know I've said this to you before, but you can tell me anything," I say against her hair, tightening my hold on her when she shudders. "Whatever it is you're holding on to, we can share the burden together."

Damn, I sound corny, but I want her to know I mean it. I'll help her with whatever's bothering her. I wish I knew exactly what it was. Does it have to do with my uncle? I don't know what to do about him either. That entire situation bothers me, and I hate the tiny bit of doubt that still lingers. I wish she would just come out and tell me, once and for all. I'd guess it would be a relief for all of us.

But she hides those secrets of hers tightly. Throws up that steel wall whenever I try to get too close. It's frustrating.

The entire situation is frustrating the hell out of me.

"I want to tell you," she whispers, so soft I almost can't hear her. "But I'm scared if I do, you'll hate me forever."

"I would never hate you," I say firmly when she lifts her head to study me.

"Don't say that too quickly. After you hear what I have to say, your entire opinion of me will change. I can guarantee it."

Her words are freaking me out. And I'm tired of her almost— me like this, only to reveal something that isn't a huge deal.

My phone rings from my jeans' pocket, but I ignore it. "Let's get out of here. We can talk when we get back to my place."

I'm not going to let her keep dodging my questions. She's going to come clean, and that means I'll need to as well.

My phone rings again just as I'm about to climb into my car, and I pull it out of my pocket to check who it is. My heart trips over itself when I see the name flashing across my screen.

His timing is impeccable.

Jensen is already in my car, so I decide to answer. "Hey, how are you?" I ask warily.

"I'm good. Wondering about you. Looks like you've been looking for me, what with all the texts and voicemails you left," he says jovially.

"Yeah, you're a hard guy to get a hold of."

"Always on the move." He chuckles. "What's up, buddy?"

He's always so chummy, always there for us. The uncle we could always count on if Dad couldn't help us. It's still hard for me to grasp the concept that he was the one who tried to rape Jensen.

My problem? I don't to believe it.

"I was wondering if we could…talk soon," I tell him. "Maybe before Thanksgiving?"

"Rhett, tomorrow is Thanksgiving."

"Right." There is no way I can bring Jensen to my dad's house if Craig is there. One look at him sitting at the family dinner table, and she'll feel like I set her up. "Maybe we could talk tomorrow then. At Dad's house."

Terrible idea. I don't want to go there. But I to talk to him. I need to find out the truth.

"Ah, son. Turns out I can't make it to your dad's house. Got other plans."

Relief floods me at his words and it takes everything I have to sound disappointed. "Seriously? With who?"

"Something else came up at the last minute. Opportunity to get out of town and do something fun for once during the holiday," he says.

"Does this have to do with the woman that you brought to Addie's party?"

"Oh, another woman. One who owns a vacation house in

Lake Tahoe." He sounds terribly pleased with himself.

We make idle conversation for another minute and then I end the call, frustrated that I can't figure out a way to talk to him. I slip inside the car to find Jensen scrolling through her phone, her head whipping up when I slam the door shut. "Everything okay?" she asks.

"Yeah," I tell her, my gaze straight ahead. "Everything's going to be just fine."

ELEVEN

Jensen

I don't know who Rhett talked to on the phone before he got back into the car, but whoever it must've been convinced him to give up on the "let's plan a magical escape for Thanksgiving" idea. Instead, he reconfirmed that we're going to his parents' house for sure. I didn't protest, though I probably should've. But I'm starting to realize that when I suggest to him that we should break up, or that I don't want to see him anymore, he flat out doesn't listen.

Well. That's not quite true. He's definitely listening, but he doesn't like what he hears. What's closer to the truth is that he doesn't believe me. And why should he? I say that sort of stuff, and then reach out to him whenever I need help, which is more often than not. Plus, he knows I'm a liar.

When it comes to my feelings for Rhett, it's not that I'm lying. More like I'm in denial. I don't want to admit to him or myself how much I care about him. Because I care for him.

I glance over at him to watch him drive. He's gripping the steering wheel loosely, his dark eyes narrowed in concentration, his lips slightly pursed. His window is cracked, the cool air ruffling his thick hair, and I sigh at how handsome he is.

God. My feelings for Rhett are so overwhelming and confusing, sometimes they're...

Terrifying.

"Do we need to bring anything for tomorrow?" I ask just to make conversation. Sitting quietly and dreaming what my future could be like with Rhett in it is pointless, right? Let's focus on the here and now.

"No, Diane has everything covered. She caters the entire meal, remember? It'll probably be the fanciest Thanksgiving meal you've ever had," he says with a chuckle.

He has no idea how accurate his words are. Dad brought home a Thanksgiving meal once from Boston Market. That had felt pretty fancy to eleven-year-old me. Crap, even the slices of dry turkey and mashed potatoes with runny gravy meals the school cafeteria would dole out the day before Thanksgiving when I was in elementary school impressed me.

When I was younger, I was easily impressed, especially because I had nothing. Material items were a luxury, not the norm. I still am easily impressed, if I'm being truthful. Rhett's world is dazzling. Even overwhelming. His family wants for nothing. They have no idea how lucky they are.

No. Idea.

"What time do we have to be there?" My voice is tight. My thoughts focused solely on Diane. How is she going to behave tomorrow? Will she ignore me yet again? Will I lose my temper and finally confront her? Admit who I really am? Wouldn't that shock everyone around the celebratory dinner table?

Satisfaction hums through my blood at the image, and I'm so tempted…

"We usually eat around three, which means we should aim for showing up at two-fifty-nine." He flashes me a grin and I can't help but smile in response. It's automatic. "The less time we have to spend with them, the better."

"Why are you so down on them?" I am truly baffled.

"What do you mean?"

"I thought you liked your family. You've always spoken so highly of them."

He's quiet for a moment, his expression thoughtful. Like he really has to consider what he might say. "I love my sister. I usually get along with Park too. But I don't know what he's doing right now. I don't understand him."

"Are you talking about his seeking me out to be his assistant?"

"Yeah. There's that." He hesitates. "There's other stuff too."

My curiosity level spikes. "What other stuff?"

He says nothing. Just shifts in his seat, obviously

uncomfortable.

"I get it if you don't want to tell me." Though I'm dying to know. I'm just trying to be the understanding girlfriend.

Kind of.

"Can I trust you not to say anything?" He shoots me a wary glance.

The old me would answer immediately with a firm yes, even though I would be lying through my teeth. But he shouldn't trust me. Not at all. He could give me information I have no choice but to share. Or possibly use against someone.

"Who am I going to tell?" I ask, shrugging one shoulder, going for total nonchalance. I try to ignore the guilt inside me, the temptation to store whatever Rhett is going to tell me and use it for later.

This makes me a very bad, terrible person. I know I shouldn't do this. My plan fell apart weeks ago when I fell for Rhett, but there's still one last chance here. I can still pull it off. Expose my mother for the horrible bitch she is, destroy her life and everyone around her, and then walk away with a satisfied smile on my face.

But would that be enough? Would I be able to live with my choice? I could end up hurting a lot of people. People I like.

Addie.

Rhett.

Especially Rhett.

His deep voice knocks me from my crappy thoughts. "I

don't know who you could tell. Anyone." He pulls into his driveway and shuts the engine off, turning to look at me once more. "Can I trust you, Jensen?"

He's not just asking if he can trust me with this bit of information. No, he's asking if he can trust me, Can he? I will say yes no matter what, but I also want to mean it.

I to mean it.

"You can trust me," I murmur, my gaze locked on his.

Sucking in a sharp breath, he exhales loudly. "That night we went to the restaurant for Addie's birthday?"

I nod to encourage him to keep talking.

"Remember when I went to look for Park and Diane?"

More nodding.

"Well, I found them. Together." He taps the steering wheel. " together."

My mouth slowly drops open as I comprehend exactly what he's saying. And he's saying what I think he's saying... right? Or maybe he's not.

Yeah. No way is he talking about that.

"What were they doing exactly?" I ask for clarification. I can't assume anything. I don't want to assume anything.

He makes a face, clearly uncomfortable. "They were, uh, in each other's arms. Kissing."

" " Yikes. I clamp my lips shut, embarrassed. That came out louder than I meant it to.

"I know, I know. It's crazy, right?" He stares out the

windshield at his house. "I couldn't believe what I was seeing when I found them. It felt like a dream—or more like a nightmare. Diane saw me first, and she literally screamed my name, so I know I shocked her as much as they shocked me."

This is unbelievable news. Like type news. "Did you confront them?"

"Not really. I took off and Park chased after me, full of excuses."

"So how did he explain their—affair?"

"He tried to make excuses, but it felt so fake. I sincerely believe they never thought they'd get caught." Rhett shakes his head, his expression pained. "I met Park for lunch a couple days later and he gave me all the dirty details, trying to convince me that what they're doing isn't that bad, I suppose, but I don't understand. I don't think I'll understand. She's our stepmom—she's been in our lives since we were little kids. It's all so fucking weird and twisted, and I don't think they realize what the consequences will be when they get caught by my father or someone who will rat them out. It's going to blow up in their faces."

I keep silent. What I should confess to Rhett is fucking weird and twisted, let's be real, so I have no room to talk or judge.

"You really think it's the right thing to do, though? To keep it a secret from your father?" I ask, knowing I need to tread lightly. I can't tell Rhett what to do or how to think, but I do want to point out that maybe it would be to his advantage, telling his dad that the missus and his oldest son are involved with each other in a scandalous affair. Parker Montgomery could be the one who boots Diane from the family and strips her of her money and status. Meaning I wouldn't need to do or say a damn thing about my connection to her.

The more I think about it, the better that sounds.

"I don't know if he'd believe me. He'd probably call me a liar," Rhett admits, sounding sad. "I don't want him angry with me. Then Park and Diane will be mad at me too, and it turns into a total shit show. That's the last thing I want."

"You really think your father would be angry with you? You're not the son who's sleeping with his wife," I point out.

"Yeah, but Dad is getting ready to hand Park the reins to his business so he can eventually retire."

I raise a brow. "The same business Park wants to sabotage by starting his own competing business. Remember?"

Rhett scrubs a hand over his face, suddenly looking exhausted. "This is so freaking messed up."

I want to comfort him, but I also want to stick with the idea that he should tell his father about Park and Diane. It would be so much easier for it all to go down this way. I wouldn't get my hands dirty.

Diane and Park would've done it all to themselves.

"Park made me swear I wouldn't tell you about their relationship either. He said we don't really know you well enough yet, so how can we trust you?" Rhett exhales slowly, like he feels bad admitting that. He probably does, too. He has a heart of gold. He rarely wants to hurt my feelings, though he has no problem being brutally honest with me. He's been almost too brutally honest with me lately. He confuses me.

Which means we're most likely on equal footing, since I'm pretty sure I confuse him too.

When I still haven't said anything, he keeps talking. "Despite everything, I want to trust you, Jens. I want to be able to share these secrets with you and know that you're going to keep them safe," Rhett says, his voice earnest. "My brother tells me not to trust you, then he tries to get you to work for him because he claims you can keep a secret. He makes no sense. Besides, he's not the one in your life. I am."

My heart sinks. At one point, Park was right. I shouldn't be trusted, especially with this information. I could use it to destroy the entire Montgomery family if I wanted to.

Do I want to? I like Addie and I like their father. I can't blame him for marrying a total bitch who just so happens to be my mother.

"You should do what you think is right," I tell him gently.

"What do you think is right?" His gaze finds mine once more, like he's seeking all the answers from me.

We both know I am the last person he should ask. "I think your father deserves to know the truth. But I'm not you. I don't know him as well as you do. So it's up to you."

"Yeah. Great," he mutters. "This sucks. I have no clue what I'm supposed to do. There's so much more…" His voice drifts and he clamps his lips shut, looking away. His jaw is tight, his lips firm, and he's practically vibrating with tension. I want to reassure him, tell him everything's going to be all right. It'll all work out in the end.

I don't know if that's true.

"I'm here for you. Just know that, okay? And I'm not going to say anything," I murmur, reaching out to touch Rhett's knee and give it a squeeze. "I promise."

TWELVE

Rhett

"Why'd you ring the doorbell? You know you can just walk in." My father's happy smile at seeing Jensen and me standing on the doorstep immediately makes me feel guilty.

But then I remember I'm not the one cheating with his wife, and I focus on the good stuff, what little there is at the moment. That's how overwhelmed I'm feeling right now.

It's Thanksgiving, though, so I need to remember that I'm here with my family and my girl by my side. A girl my father actually approves of, which is saying a lot, especially when you consider what she used to do for a living.

Did Dad ever find out about Jensen working at City Lights? Did Park or Diane tell him? I have no clue. Don't really want to ask him about it either.

Jensen sends me a look before she tells my dad, "Oh, I was

the one who insisted on ringing the doorbell. I didn't feel right just barging into your house."

Dad pulls her in for a brief embrace. "You can barge in any time. You're more than welcome in my household."

She appears momentarily rattled, and I can't blame her. He's so open and warm toward her, it's almost strange. "Oh. Well, thank you. I appreciate that."

"Any girl who can keep my boy happy has my approval." Dad's face turns serious. "Wish Park could find someone who'd take good care of him like your Jensen, Rhett. He needs to find a woman he can trust. Not those same old bar whores he picks up at random."

Ah, there's the dear old dad I know and love. Jesus, I thought he was getting soft in his old age. Apparently not.

Jensen's eyes flash with shock at what he said but her expression smooths out quick. "Is Park here?" she asks politely.

"Everyone's here, even Addie and Trent. Come in." Dad opens the door wider and we walk inside.

The house smells amazing. There are fresh fall flowers everywhere, and candles burning on pretty much every available table service. The house is warm, downright homey-looking, and I grab hold of Jensen's hand, pulling her close to me.

Her fingers are ice cold and she seems jittery, like she drank too much caffeine. Every time she gets around my family, she becomes nervous. I don't know why. Dad does everything he can to make her feel welcome, and Addie adores her. Though it might be weird with Park, what with him asking her to work for him on the sly only a couple of days ago. And Diane? It's always weird with that woman, so who gives a shit?

"Hey!" Addie runs up to us, pulling Jensen into a bear hug, squeezing her extra tight before she releases her and hugs me. "I'm so glad you're here. Park is making everyone insane," she murmurs close to my ear.

"Fun family times, huh?" I tease, trying to blow off the unease I'm feeling over Addie's comment about Park. "What's he doing?"

Addie wrinkles her nose. "He's being rude. Very short with everyone. Practically bit Trent's head off earlier when he asked him a basic question. We almost left, but Daddy convinced us to stay."

"That bad, huh?" I rub my jaw, glancing around the giant room. Park is nowhere in sight, and Diane's not around either.

Uh oh.

"He's being awful," Addie says.

"Where is he?"

"Outside. Said he was going for a smoke." Addie makes a little face. "Since when does he smoke?"

"Off and on since college." When her expression turns incredulous, I shrug. "We've always been protecting you from the bad stuff, little sister. But now that you're seventeen, the gloves are off."

"Whatever." She laughs, socking me in the arm with her fist before she turns to Jensen. "Are you hungry? There are appetizers in the kitchen, and they're yummy."

"Go," I tell Jensen when she turns to look at me with a question in her eyes. "I'm going to go find my brother. I'll meet up with you in the kitchen later."

The worry that fills her gaze is surprising. "Be careful, okay?"

I squeeze her hand. "I'll be fine. Promise."

Dad escorts Addie and Jensen to the kitchen while I go in search of Park. I find him in the backyard all alone, standing by the pool and flicking the ash end of his cigarette into the water like an asshole.

"Dad would kill you if he caught you doing that," I call out to him.

Park lifts his head, his gaze meeting mine from across the pool. When he sees it's me, he shrugs. "Like I give a shit. There are lots of reasons Dad wants to kill me right about now."

I can name three off the top of my head, but I decide to keep quiet. "How are you?" I ask after I circle around the pool and eventually stop to stand right next to him.

Park takes a drag off his cigarette, blowing out hazy smoke. "I've had better days."

When he says nothing else, I ask, "Things been going kind of rough or what?"

"Yeah." Another drag off the cigarette. "I'm sure Jensen

told you about our interview and what a disaster that was. Right?"

Guess we're going straight to the problem. "She did."

"Such a good little girlfriend, telling you about your asshole big brother."

"I don't even understand why you asked her to work for you," I say, hoping he'll give me a real answer. "It's like you tried to trick her into the interview."

"I did trick her into the interview, and it was so damn easy, you know?" I send him a dirty look, but he ignores me. "There's something I see in Jensen that makes me feel like we're—kindred spirits, or whatever. I'm probably talking out my ass."

"You definitely are." It feels like he wants everything he shouldn't. Dad's wife. Dad's business. My girlfriend…

Park drops the cigarette butt in the pool and shoves his hands into his jeans pockets, staring out at the water. "I'm surprised you didn't call me and chew my ass out after she told you."

"Didn't think it was worth my time."

"Ouch." Park actually grins when he glances over at me. "Are you saying   not worth your time?"

Irritation fills me and I tamp it down. "No, I'm saying arguing with   is not worth my time. I'm over it." I stare out at the water too. "She didn't want to work with you, she turned you down. End of story. The problem is solved."

"There's still a problem, though," Park admits, his gaze growing distant. "There are all sorts of problems."

"Like what?"

"Like Diane," Park practically spits out, his tone venomous. "The woman won't get off my case."

"About what?"

"About me trying to start my own business so I can leave Dad. Can you believe she's actually pissed at me about it?" Park shakes his head. "She keeps trying to discourage me, telling me I'm making a huge mistake, that I'll ruin everything."

Why the hell is my brother so damn clueless? "I get why she's telling you that. You're trying to pull away from Dad and somehow sabotage his business, and that's her , Park. She him." Sounds crazy, but yes, she loves Dad in her own special way.

"She loves me too. I don't know why she can't take my side for once." He sounds like a petulant baby.

"You're being ridiculous."

"Why? Because I want something of my own for once?" He turns to face me, his eyes full of anger. "I've been under his control for years. I'm sick of it."

"Do you really think you can do it on your own then? I'm sure you have plenty of contacts, but is there enough confidence in you from the clients you've handled over the years? Are they willing to jump ship for you and leave him?"

I'm sure he's already thought all this stuff out. Right?

"Sort of." More shrugging. "I don't know. So many of them are Dad's old cronies. They'll want to stick with him. They're all loyal to a fault. So I figured I could find new clientele. Do some advertising, ramp up the social media, pull in new business."

I want to slap some sense into him. "Before you make such a radical change, you need to make sure you can do this on your own. One wrong move and Dad's cutting you out of his life forever."

"Like I'm going to take advice from you, little brother. You're still in college—what the hell do you know?"

Feels like I know more than he does.

"And besides, you really believe he'll cut me off forever? Come on. That's pretty extreme." Park barks out a laugh. "He needs me too damn much. I threaten to leave and he'll be begging me to stay."

More like Park's convinced himself that's true. He's too confident, too cocky. "What exactly is going on with you and Diane?"

"Nothing. Why, what is she telling you?" His skeptical gaze lands on me.

"What is she telling " I take a step back, resting a hand on my chest. "Come on, Park. We don't talk. She doesn't divulge her secrets to me."

He inhales deep, looking like he could breathe fire. "She's not telling me much either, beyond nagging my ass and trying to get me to drop my plan."

"For once, I'm going to have to agree with her." When he turns to glare at me, I continue. "Be real with yourself and admit it's not a good idea, Park. Dad's going to retire soon and leave you the business. Why can't you be patient and wait him out?"

"I want it now, that's why. He's holding me back. He's always held me back." He turns his back to me, his shoulders drooping almost in seeming defeat. "You don't understand what it's like, to be his namesake. To be constantly compared to him and feeling like you don't measure up."

He's right. I don't know what that's like. I'm sure it's a lot of pressure. "Just—reconsider what you're doing, okay? You're making a mistake. I don't want you to regret it."

Park actually scoffs. "What, is that some sort of threat?"

I'm taken aback by the hostility in his voice, and what he actually said. "A threat? No, why the hell would I threaten you?"

My brother doesn't have an answer for me.

Instead, he storms back into the house, slamming the door behind him.

THIRTEEN

Jensen

I t is so awkward, hanging out in the Montgomerys' grand kitchen, watching my very own mother buzz around the room, tasting this, checking that, bugging the catering staff with her incessant hovering, all while swigging away from her very generously sized wineglass. She barely bothered to greet me when Parker brought me and Addie into the kitchen, and the more I watch her, the more queasy I get.

She literally makes me sick to my stomach.

"Stuffed mushroom?" Addie practically thrusts the tray of mushrooms in my face and I'm tempted to violently shove them away.

But I don't. "Um, no thank you. I'm not very hungry," I tell her with a wan smile.

"Oh, that's too bad. They're delicious." Addie pops one in her mouth and sets the tray on the counter.

"Where's your boyfriend?" I want to make small talk, anything to avoid Diane. I can't help but look over at where she's standing, near the oven, Parker in front of her and both of them talking in low murmurs. They don't look upset with each other, but I can't help but let my hackles rise. Their vibe isn't positive.

"He's in the movie room playing video games." Addie rolls her eyes. "He was so mad at Park earlier when they got into that argument, I figured he can do whatever he wants. I just want him calm and happy."

"What were they arguing about?" I ask carefully.

"I was complaining about Diane trying to keep us from eating the appetizers. I was starving, you know? And so was Trent. So we start grumbling about it, and Park overheard Trent say something about Diane being stingy with the food, and Park lost it. Called my boyfriend an asshole, told him he was going to kick his ass—it was ridiculous. I'm so glad you weren't there to witness it," Addie finishes with a little shudder.

I sort of wish I witnessed it. "Sounds like maybe Park has other problems on his mind," I say with a little shrug.

"Yeah, I guess, but he shouldn't take it out on Trent, you know? It's not fair. He blew up over nothing." Addie checks her phone, biting on her lower lip. "Trent's texting me. He wants me to come to the screening room. I'll be right back, okay?"

Before I can reply, she's gone.

"Care for something to drink?"

I whirl around at the sound of Diane's voice, my gaze meeting hers, her eyes the same color as mine. That same shade of blue—does she see it? Does she? I do. I see the familiarity even in her overly Botoxed features, the arch of her brows, the angle of her nose. I look like her. I   her, just the younger version.

But she's blind to it. Too self-absorbed, too caught up in her own bullshit.

God, I really cannot stand this woman, yet I want to know more. The conflicting emotions that war within me make me nauseous.

"Jensen? That's your name, isn't it?" The pleasant smile on her face is fake. I see the strain around her eyes, the lack of emotion in their depths. I glance just beyond her shoulder to see Parker standing a few feet away, carefully observing us with a hopeful smile on his face, as if he wishes we could be friends.

She's doing this, talking to me, for him. For her husband. Not because she's kind and wants to reach out. More like she just wants to please Parker.

I swallow hard, hating how dry my mouth has suddenly become. "Yes, my name is Jensen."

"Glass of wine?" She raises a thin, elegantly arched brow. Her cool politeness is a complete contrast to the wickedly mean woman I encountered at Addie's party. The one who laughed with Park and made fun of me.

"Yes, that sounds perfect," I respond, lifting my chin. Going for strong. Probably looking stubborn more than anything else.

Diane moves about the kitchen, plucking a wineglass from the cabinet, uncorking the already half empty bottle of wine near the sink. She pours me a glass of rosé, then offers it to me with a slight smile. "Enjoy."

I take the glass from her with shaky fingers, bringing it to my mouth and gulping down almost half of it in one long swallow. The wine is cold and crisp, and I pray the buzz hits me quick. I'm not sure how much of this I'll be able to take, pretending to get along with this woman who is really my mother.

"So tell us, Jensen," Diane says with a devious little smile as she moves to stand next to Parker. He wraps his arm around her waist, pulling her even closer to his side. The perfect united front. "How did you and Rhett meet?"

I'm sure the bitch is fully expecting me to scramble while coming up with a lie. She most likely thinks we met at City Lights. She's probably already convinced I gave Rhett a lap dance, rubbed my crotch against his junk, and poof—it was true love.

"On campus, at the library," I tell her.

"Really?" The doubt in her tone is obvious.

"Actually, Jens, that's not true," Rhett says from behind me as he strolls into the kitchen like he doesn't have a care in the world.

I catch sight of the triumphant gleam in Diane's eyes, and I try my best to keep my expression neutral. I'm sure she thinks I've been caught in a horrible lie.

And I sort of did lie just now, though it wasn't on purpose.

"Oh, that's right. It was at that bar…" My voice drifts when Rhett comes to stand beside me, slinging his arm around my shoulders so we're the perfect united front too. He's solid and warm, firmly planted by my side and for once in my life, I don't feel so alone.

It's a heady experience.

"A bar?" Diane asks, dragging the word out as if she's scandalized. "How…quaint."

"Yeah, it was at that one bar just off campus where everyone hangs out." Rhett smiles down at me. "She was sitting all alone."

Spying on him.

I send him an adoring look. Not like I'm ever going to admit that.

"She was so beautiful and looked so damn sad, I had to approach her." His smile grows as our gazes lock. I don't like him mentioning the sad part, but too late now. "Turns out she got stood up by her date, meaning his loss was totally my gain."

My cheeks go hot. I love it when he's so sweet, but it's still a little weird when he's so sweet to me in front of other people.

"So that's all it took?" Diane asks incredulously. "You locked eyes at a bar and you fell madly in love?"

"Oh no," I say with a slight shake of my head. "He started talking to me—"

"Laying on the Montgomery charm, as usual," he adds, making his father laugh.

"—and when he wouldn't stop flirting with me, I bailed on him," I finish with a sweet smile.

"What?" Parker looks from Rhett to me, then back to Rhett again. "You left him?"

"I ran out of the bar." I lower my voice, like I'm sharing a secret. "I thought he was too pushy."

"I bumped into her again at the library a few days later." He squeezes my shoulders, drops a kiss on my forehead. "My lucky day, right?"

"Right." I lean my forehead against his jaw, closing my eyes for the briefest moment, savoring the intoxicating feeling of being a part of something, of belonging somewhere, of belonging to someone.

When I open my eyes, I catch the open hostility in Diane's gaze and I don't look away. I return her measured stare, secure with Rhett by my side, his arm around me, my hand on his chest.

After all, she's the one with the messy secret.

💟　💟　💟

I sneak off to the bathroom after dinner. Yes, I have to pee, but really I wanted to escape the tension still lingering in the dining room. It feels like a hostile environment, and for once in my life, I'm not one of the key players. Park's shooting visual daggers at his dad, or at Diane. Trent's shooting daggers at Park. Addie's shooting daggers at Diane. Rhett's shooting daggers at Park.

Parker? He's oblivious. I pretend to be, but I know what was going on. And I want out, at least for a little while.

The moment I exit the bathroom, I find Park waiting there for me, that rotten smirk on his face, his arms crossed in front of his barrel chest as he leans against the wall. He eyes me up and down, making me vaguely uncomfortable and thankful I wore jeans and a sweater versus a dress.

"Déjà vu," he tells me, like we're sharing a private joke. "Remember the last time we met at this bathroom?"

"Not one of your finer moments," I practically snarl, ready to push past him and make my way back to the dining room, but he stops me, his fingers curling loosely around my upper arm. I glance down at his fingers clinging to my sleeve. "You should let me go."

"Talk to me for a moment." He releases his hold on me. "Please?"

I doubt he tosses that word around easily.

"Come on, Jensen. Just give me two minutes." The pleasantness is gone, replaced by total exasperation.

Taking a step back from him, I lean against the closed bathroom door and wait for what he has to say.

"You told Rhett. About our interview."

"Of course I did. I couldn't keep that a secret from him."
I've already kept enough.

"Yet he didn't run off and tell my father."

"No, he didn't."

"Is that because of you? Did you tell him to keep his mouth shut?"

I slowly shake my head. "Your brother is loyal to a fault."

"And I'm—thankful for that." Park runs a hand through his thick hair, messing it up. He reminds me so much of Rhett in so many little ways, but the way he acts, the things he says, are nothing like Rhett whatsoever. They have similar features, but not exact. Similar builds, but not quite. And they definitely don't have similar personalities. Park is a snake.

Rhett is thankfully not.

"I didn't ask him to keep quiet, if that's what you're trying to find out," I say. "But if you really think I could go to that interview, find out it was you, and not mention it to Rhett afterward? Then you don't know me very well."

"You're right. I definitely don't know you very well. I took a major chance, contacting you like that, trying to get you to work for me." He flashes me a rueful smile. "Too bad it didn't work out."

"Park, it would've never worked out. I can't cross your father like that. I like him too much," I say, my voice soft.

His face turns red and I realize he's angry. "He's nice to you just to get under Diane's skin. You do realize that, right? It's his way of flirting, of showing his wife he can be with whoever he wants and there's nothing she can do about it."

I'm surprised by his words and the passionate anger behind them. Parker has been nothing but nice to me. He doesn't flirt. He's just friendly. He seems genuinely pleased to see Rhett and me together.

"You don't know what you're talking about." I start to walk away, but he stops me again, his fingers gripping my elbow tight.

"I've seen him do this shit before. He's done it to me and one of my ex-girlfriends. I was serious about that girl. I was in love with her." Park's grip goes so tight, it starts to hurt. "Until I found her naked and in bed with my father. That was the end of that relationship."

"Park, let go of me." I jerk out of his hold, rubbing my elbow.

He doesn't even acknowledge what I say. His brown eyes have grown so dark, they appear almost black. "Just watch out, Jensen. My father can be very persuasive when he wants to be. He likes them young and pretty, so I'm sure he's already got you in his sights."

His words disgust me. Why does everyone's accusations and warnings have to do with sex? Why can't Parker Montgomery like me for who I am to his son? Surely he can look at me as a possible future daughter versus a future conquest.

I'm so angry at Park, I say the first thing that comes to

mind. "Is that why you started the affair with Diane? So you can get back at your dad for having sex with your old girlfriend?"

Park goes terribly still, his gaze locked on mine, his lips slightly parted. He clears his throat, tilts his head to the side. "What did you just say?"

I retreat another step, feeling backed into a corner. I should've never said that. Should've never revealed I know his dirtiest little secret. Turning, I'm about to flee, but yet again he grabs me, this time hooking his arm around my waist and pulling me toward him, my back to his front, shifting his arm so it's around my neck, so tight I'm afraid he'll cut off my breathing.

"He told you, huh? I knew Rhett couldn't keep his fucking mouth shut." Park's lips are right by my ear, his breath hot, his closeness making me shake with fear. His body is rigid, his breathing coming faster and faster as he keeps his grip on me. "You rat me out, I'll make your life fucking miserable. I'm not messing around either. I mean it. You're nothing but a little whore my brother found at a strip club."

Tears automatically spring to my eyes and I blink hard, trying to get rid of them. I hate that his words hurt so much.

Park gives me a little shake. "Are you listening? Don't fuck with me."

"I-I won't say anything." That was a definite threat. One I don't want to mess around with.

"You better not." He releases me so quickly I almost

collapse on the ground. "Better hope you don't have any major secrets either. You betray me or Diane, and I'm putting you on blast for all the world to see. Mark my fucking words."

He leaves me in a rush and I stumble my way back into the bathroom, shutting and locking the door behind me. I stare at my reflection in the mirror, my face pale, my eyes hollow, my stomach churning.

I make it to the toilet just in time, losing my entire Thanksgiving dinner with a couple of painful gags. My hands braced on the toilet, I close my eyes against the stinging tears, swallowing with a grimace past the terrible taste in my mouth. God, if Rhett finds out my secrets from Park…

I'm screwed.

FOURTEEN

Rhett

"I'm sorry Jensen got so ill," Dad says, clapping me on the back as we stand on the front porch. "I hope she feels better soon."

"Maybe she drank too much wine," Diane suggests in her simpering voice. She's standing beside Dad, ever the dutiful wife. Maybe Jensen saw too much of that bullshit and it made her feel sick. I know I can barely stomach it. "She needs to learn how to handle her liquor, Rhett. You don't want some foolish drunk girl in your life. They're too—risky."

Leave it to her to drop insults even after Jensen puked her guts out.

"She had two glasses, tops," I mutter, annoyed at Diane's suggestion. What the hell does she know? "I need to go. Jensen's waiting for me in the car."

Trent and Addie already escorted her out there. They were

the ones who discovered her stumbling out of the bathroom, her face pale, her hands clutching her stomach. I feel terrible that she got so sick so fast and I wasn't there to help her.

What kind of boyfriend am I?

The moment I climb into the car, I cup Jensen's cheek. Her skin is cool, her eyes closed, and when I touch her, the faintest smile curves her lips.

"Thank God you're here," she croaks. "Take me home, Rhett."

"You want to go back to Savannah's?" I fire up the car and burn rubber as I pull out of the driveway. I can already hear my father complaining that I left a mark, but right now, I don't give a shit.

I need to take care of Jensen.

"No, take me back to your place." She reaches out to touch my knee, her fingers warm even through the denim. "Please."

I do as she asks, secretly happy that she chose to come back with me. I'm breaking down those walls, one by one. Persistence is key.

The moment we get back to my house, I escort her in, taking her straight to my bathroom so she can clean up. She brushes her teeth with the toothbrush she left at my place, but she seems tired, a little out of it, and I turn on the shower for her, making sure it's nice and hot.

"I'm not a baby," she says, slapping my hands away when I attempt taking off her sweater. "I can undress myself."

I try not to stare as she strips her clothes off, considering her sick state, but damn, her body is perfection. She slides past me and enters the shower, shutting the glass door behind her. There's not enough steam from the hot water yet, so I can see every inch of her as the water cascades all over her body, and I can't help but watch her. Admire her. Wish like hell she didn't feel so awful.

"You're a pervert, Rhett Montgomery," she calls over the steady sound of the water hitting the tile wall.

"I am." Yeah, I can't hide it.

"I'm sorry I made you leave early." She sounds contrite.

"Don't worry about it. I wasn't having much fun. Don't think you were either." I start to laugh. "This is way more enjoyable."

"I'm glad someone is enjoying it," she teases.

"You still feel sick?"

"No, not really. I actually feel a lot better. Thank God Addie gave me some mouthwash to swish around after she found me. There's nothing grosser, if you know what I mean," she explains.

I make a face. "I hate throwing up."

"Yeah. Same."

"Why do you think you got so sick?"

"I don't know." She shrugs, the sudsy, soapy water sliding down her back. "I must've—ate something that didn't agree with me."

"Diane says you can't handle your liquor."

Jensen turns so she's facing me, her skin glistening, soapy bubbles clinging to her breasts. She looks straight out of every teen fantasy I've ever had. "She thought I was drunk?"

"She implied it." I start shedding my clothes, unable to stop myself. Fuck it, I'm joining her. I won't try anything, but I want to touch her skin. Wash her hair.

"I had maybe two glasses," she mumbles, grabbing the bar soap and rubbing it over her body.

For once in my life, I'm jealous of a bar of soap. "I told her that too. She's such a bitch sometimes."

Jensen doesn't say a word as I open the shower door and step inside, the warm water hitting my skin and making me close my eyes. I scoot closer to the showerhead and douse myself, reaching out to grab her waist when I sense she's trying to leave. "Stay," I tell her.

"I'm sick."

I open my eyes to find her watching me, blatant hunger in her gaze. "Really? You still feel nauseous?"

She slowly shakes her head as she reaches out and settles her hands on my chest. "I think it was a one-shot thing."

"Yeah, it probably was." I touch her breasts. Thumb her nipples, making them hard.

"I'm probably fine now." She's touching my dick, stroking it, and I bite back a groan at her firm touch.

"I bet you are," I practically growl, grabbing her so I can

press her back against the shower wall. She goes with me willingly, her long legs wrapping around my waist, the heels of her feet digging into my ass. "Are you okay with this?" I ask her, my gaze meeting hers as I slowly thrust against her.

The water streams down her face and she bites her lower lip, looking sexy as fuck. "Definitely okay," she murmurs.

I kiss her, my tongue seeking and finding hers. She wraps her arms around my neck, her fingers sinking into my hair as I continue to devour her. We haven't had sex in a shower yet, and I've always thought it was overrated.

But sex with Jensen anywhere is pretty fucking great. Within minutes I'm slipping inside her hot, tight body, closing my eyes against the blissful onslaught of sensation. No woman has ever made me feel the way Jensen does. The sex keeps getting better and better.

She's ruining me for any other woman, I swear.

Once we're done in the shower, we towel each other off, and I notice how sleepy she looks. We climb into bed wearing nothing at all, the two of us snuggling in close, the lights off and the house quiet since Chad is gone for the holiday weekend.

It's barely nine o'clock at night.

"I could fall asleep just like this," Jensen says, her voice light, as are her fingers as she quietly strokes my chest. "Who knew having sex after getting sick is such a cure-all?"

"Sex cures all ailments," I tell her, stroking her arm. "Just call me Dr. Rhett."

"Oh God." She starts to laugh. "That was super cheesy."

"You make me super cheesy."

"This is my fault now, hmm?" She socks me lightly in my right pectoral muscle. "Whatever."

"Did you have a good time?" I ask a few moments later, once we start to grow quiet. I want to ask her before she falls asleep, before she has too much time and distance to really know how she felt about today.

"I—did?" She says it like a question.

"It was pretty bad, huh."

"Your dad was nice. So was Addie and Trent."

"I think Diane was trying," I venture.

Jensen actually snorts. "Please. More like she was trying to make me look like a fool every chance she got."

"You really think so?"

She lifts her head a bit so she can meet my gaze. "Absolutely. She was slinging very subtle insults my way."

Damn, how did I miss that? "She sucks."

"Yeah, she does." Jensen strokes my chest, her touch light as a feather, making me shiver. "Your brother is a complete asshole."

"Tell me all about it."

"No, I'm serious. He was terrible to me. He cornered me when I got out of the bathroom, told me some crazy story about your father sleeping with an old girlfriend of his, and then I made the big mistake of admitting I knew about him and Diane."

Oh. Shit. "You told him you knew?"

"I did mention his affair with Diane." Jensen makes a face. "He threatened me."

"What the actual fuck?" I pull away from her and sit up, running both hands through my damp hair. "He   you?"

She nods, biting her lower lip. "It was my mistake. I should've never said that to him."

"Doesn't give him the right to threaten you, Jensen. Jesus." I glance over at my phone where it sits on my beside table. "I should call him."

I'm reaching for my phone when Jensen lunges for me, batting my hand away. "Don't call him."

"Why the hell not?"

"Just—leave him alone. I'm sure he didn't mean to threaten me."

My ass. "Yeah, right. I'll text him then." I grab hold of the phone this time and she yanks it out of my hand, tossing it onto the floor. I glare at her. "Why the hell did you do that? You could've broke it."

"I didn't, you're phone's fine. Listen." She grabs my hands, staring into my eyes. "Don't talk to him about this. It'll just upset him more. Let's just—forget it ever happened."

The problem is I won't be able to forget it. And why should I? My brother is acting like a total asshole toward my girlfriend. He deserves to be called out for it. "Why are you letting him off the hook?"

"I'm not. Not really. I don't want it to be a bigger problem than it needs to be, you know what I mean?" She smiles, but it doesn't look real. "It's okay to let things go sometimes, Rhett. To be the bigger person."

"Clearly my brother can't do that," I mutter, shaking my head.

"Is it true what he said? About your dad having sex with his girlfriend?" Jensen asks hesitantly.

I stare at the wall, thinking, but I come up with nothing. And you'd think I'd remember something like that. It's pretty major. "Not that I know of."

"Could he have made it up?"

"Possibly. I wouldn't put it past him." Before all this blew up, I would've never said that about my brother. But now, it's like I don't even know him.

"Has your father…ever cheated on Diane?"

"Yeah. Quite often, actually. It's like this known thing with the family that no one ever talks about. But she'll never leave him. She'll never even confront him. I don't think she wants to lose what she's got, you know?"

"And what does she have, really? A lot of money, an unfaithful husband, a broken marriage, and the stepson she's banging on the side?" Jensen sighs heavily. "Sounds like one of my favorite TV shows."

I can't help the laugh that escapes. "Don't forget, this is my life we're talking about."

"I know." She pauses. "Mine too."

FIFTEEN

Jensen

For the first time since I don't know when, I feel…good. Strong. Confident. Almost carefree. And it's all because of Rhett. He's the first person in my life who's never given up on me. Having someone there, who stands by my side no matter what, is…amazing.

It's the best feeling in the whole world.

After that semi-disastrous Thanksgiving, Rhett and I talked. A lot. He told me more about the dynamics within his family, and how Park is struggling with their father right now. It made me understand Park's behavior a little better.

Kind of. He's still an ass, though.

Park hasn't reached out to either of us since Thanksgiving, and it's a total relief. We haven't seen Diane either. Or talked about her. If life could continue this way, I wouldn't have to worry about a thing.

Life isn't that way, though. She will come back up. After all, she's Rhett's stepmother. If I continue a relationship with Rhett, this woman will be in my life whether I want her to be or not. It's something I'm going to have to deal with, and I've come to one major conclusion.

I'll keep my one last major secret, but that's only because I don't know how to tell Rhett the truth. And is it really that important? What his entire family doesn't know won't hurt them, right? I won't reveal my true relationship to Diane to anyone. I'll keep it all to myself and that way no one has to know.

Perfect plan, right?

My biggest fear if I do tell Rhett the truth? His reaction. What if he feels betrayed? Used? What if he hates me? I can't bear the thought. Deep down inside, I know it's wrong to keep this from him, but I can't bear the thought of him not being in my life anymore. I just…

I can't do it.

We had a busy week at school. The semester is winding down, we're prepping for final projects, plus Rhett has practice and a game, so I don't see him as much as I would like. But I've pretty much moved into his house, much to his roommate Chad's displeasure. I took away their title of coolest bachelor pad, according to him. Rhett says that title's bogus.

It's Sunday night, and we've decided to go to dinner, then to the local bar where we very first met. A few of his friends from the team will be there in celebration of someone's birthday, and Rhett promised he would stop by. I go along with his plan because I want to be the supportive girlfriend. Plus, there's something so…exhilarating about walking into a room on Rhett's arm. It's like everyone pays attention to us. He has this certain kind of magnetism that draws everyone to him. He's special.

Yet he somehow chose "We won't stay long," he tells me as we head toward the bar's main entrance. "I'll wish Johnny a happy birthday, we'll have a drink, and then we'll take off."

"Why don't you want to stay long?" I squeeze his hand, smiling up at him. He looks extra good tonight in the black sweater and jeans, his dark hair a little longish on top and kind of messy, and there's a layer of stubble on his cheeks.

Sexy.

"Wouldn't you rather spend the rest of the night in bed?" His wicked grin tells me he's not talking about sleep, making me laugh.

"We'll stay an hour," I suggest.

"Thirty minutes," he counters.

"Forty-five."

He grins. "Deal." He brings our linked hands to his mouth, kissing my knuckles just before he opens the door with his free hand.

We enter the crowded bar, Rhett's friends cheering loudly when they spot us. Making our way over there, we're immediately enveloped into their group, Rhett and I each handed a beer. I watch as Rhett embraces the birthday boy and chats with him, his focus zeroed in on Johnny and no one else.

A sigh almost escapes me as I watch them. That's what's so great about Rhett. He makes people feel special. When he shines his light on you, you feel like there's no one else in the world. There's just you and Rhett.

At least, that's how he makes me feel.

Minutes later he's back by my side, slipping his arm around my shoulders and tugging me close. I go willingly, resting my hand lightly on his flat stomach, smiling up at him with adoring eyes. I don't even need a mirror to know that's how I'm looking at him. I can literally feel the adoration beaming from my eyeballs. I am so gone over this guy, it's unbelievable. It happened so fast, too.

What's even crazier? I viewed him as my enemy for the longest time. Thought he was awful. A snake. A phony. A womanizer. A spoiled rich boy who gets whatever he wants.

Well. He's rich. He's probably a little spoiled, though he's the first one to admit it. He's the most genuine, honest person I know. He's the complete opposite of awful. And he's all mine.

"Having fun?" he asks, dipping his head so his mouth is right by my ear.

I offer a little shrug. "I don't know anyone."

His eyes go wide. "I'm sorry, I didn't even introduce you to everyone. Hold on." He raises his hand like he wants their attention and I grab at his arm, pulling it down. "What? You don't want to meet them?"

"You don't need to do that for me." I'm still not used to drawing attention to ourselves. I'd rather lurk in the shadows. My relationship with Rhett still feels too new, too delicate. Like one wrong word or movement could have the entire thing unraveling in seconds.

"But I want to." He taps the tip of my nose with his index finger, his eyes sparkling as they meet mine. "I want to show you off."

"Please." I roll my eyes and laugh, but the sincerity I see in his expression makes me sober up quick. "Why would you want to show me off?"

Rhett lifts his brows, leaning away from me. "Are you being serious right now?"

"Um, yes." I'd rather show off. He's the big deal, not me. "I don't get it."

"Hmm, let me see." He taps his chin, like he's contemplating something very serious. "First up, you're sweet. Second, you're beautiful. Third, you're smart. Fourth, you're interesting—"

"Interesting?" I repeat, interrupting him.

"Let's just say life with you is never dull," he says with a grin.

I lightly sock him in the chest. "Right back at ya."

We drink our beer and talk and flirt. He introduces me to Johnny and eventually the rest of his teammates, and they're all friendly, a few of them even shooting Rhett appreciative looks, like they're somehow impressed with me? Just because I have a decent face doesn't mean I'm a decent catch. I realized that about myself a long time ago.

Rhett brings out the best in me. He makes me want to be a better person. I want to be good for him, and for myself. I've turned into a total and complete sap, but it's true.

"Let's get out of here," he whispers later, his arm around my waist, his fingers squeezing me. "I want to take you home."

A shiver moves through me at the promise in his words. "You're not drunk, are you?"

"Hell no. Even if I was, you could drive. You've barely touched your beer. Hey, remember that night I let you drive my car?" The private look he shoots me makes everything inside of me grow warm.

"Yes, I remember."

His knowing smile is cute. Cutely sexy. "You said some pretty amazing shit."

I laugh, my cheeks hot.

"You did some pretty amazing shit too." He pulls me to him, our lower bodies crushed together, and I can feel the effect I'm having on him. "Maybe we should try and reenact that night."

"I was sort of pissed at you that night," I remind him.

"Yeah, well, I was mad too. But I'm not mad anymore." He kisses me, right there in the middle of his friend group in the bar, and he takes it deep quick. His friends start yelling, one of them saying, "Get a room!" and I break the kiss, shoving him away from me.

"How many beers did you have?" I think he's a little drunk.

His lopsided smile tells me yep, he's feeling no pain. "Three? Plus I had one at dinner."

I don't know how he drank three beers in the short amount of time we've been here. "I'm definitely driving. Come on, drunk boy."

We say our goodbyes, and then I take his hand and lead him out of the bar and into the cold, dark night. We head for his car, Rhett trying to grab my ass with his free hand and I keep slapping it away. By the time we're both in his car, we're breathless. And he's handsy.

I let him get handsy with me as we lean across the center console and kiss. He touches me everywhere he can reach, his fingers sure, his breath hot against my neck when he kisses me there. We're steaming up the car and frustration starts to build.

"We could be at your house in less than fifteen minutes," I remind him in between kisses.

He smiles against my lips. "Then what are we waiting for?"

"I should ask that question, since you're the one who can't seem to stop kissing me."

"I don't hear you protesting."

Like he ever would.

Rhett kisses me again, this one long and tongue-filled. He's getting worked up, and so am I. I push him away and start the engine, readjusting the seat and the mirrors before I pull out of the bar's parking lot.

I drive back to Rhett's house, both of us quiet, me concentrating on the road, Rhett scrolling on his phone, checking his notifications. My mind drifts, imagining a life like this, with Rhett. The two of us together, living in our own home, Rhett taking care of me. He could go to work doing whatever while I stayed home and took care of the house. Maybe we could travel. Maybe we could move somewhere else, somewhere exotic, and live our own lives with no one around to bother us. Like Diane…

There's an unfamiliar car in the driveway and I hit the brakes, making Rhett's head jerk up. "Who's car is that?" I ask.

"I don't know." He's frowning. "That's a brand-new Porsche."

It's low and black and sleek, and looks very, very expensive. "Chad has a new rich girlfriend he didn't tell you about?"

Rhett chuckles. "He freaking wishes."

Since that gorgeous Porsche is blocking the garage, I pull the car to the curb in front of the house and shut off the engine. We exit the car, me locking it with the keyless remote, and Rhett takes my hand as he leads me to the front door since the garage is closed and I forgot to open it. The living room light is on—we can see the glow through the front window—so I'm assuming Chad is inside.

Hopefully he's not "entertaining" some girl, AKA the two of them writhing around, naked on the couch. That is the absolute last thing I want to walk in on.

Rhett tries the handle to find it unlocked, and he opens the door, leading me inside. The couch doesn't face the door, and I can see the back of two heads sitting there, both male, one of them Chad's. He whips his head around when he hears the door opening, a giant grin on his face when he spots us.

"Hey, Rhett, your uncle's here. We've been hanging out."

Rhett goes completely still, his fingers curling around mine so tightly it starts to hurt.

The man turns his head to smile at us, and it's like everything goes in slow motion, though I know it happened in a matter of seconds.

I know this man.

This man Chad said is Rhett's uncle is the same man who attacked me at City Lights.

It's Greg.

SIXTEEN

Rhett

S hit. I hold onto Jensen's hand, trying to keep her in place because…I don't know. I want to explain myself, but how? I kept this from her because I didn't know how to tell her and I fucked everything up.

She slips her hand from mine and raises it to her face, covering her mouth, her eyes wide open in shock. "It's—it's him."

Uncle Craig just sits there, his eyes a little wide, like he can't believe he just got caught, but that surprised look disappears in an instant and smooth, friendly Uncle Craig is back in place. He stands, making like he's going to approach Jensen.

"Please. Let me explain myself," he starts, but Jensen cuts him off.

"Shut up!" She's at the door, throwing it open, but then she turns to look at me, and all the hurt and misery and anger is there, swirling in her eyes, written all over her face. "You knew, didn't you? You knew all along, yet you didn't tell me"

I reach out to her, trying to capture her hand, but she jerks it away. "Jensen. Please. I was going to tell you..."

"When? At Christmas? When we're all circled around the tree, listening to carols and drinking hot chocolate while handing out gifts and you give me one from your dear Uncle Craig the rapist?" She's shrieking, her voice shrill, her entire body shaking, and I feel like a complete asshole.

A liar.

They say your life can change in an instant. One second everything's fine, the next, everything's in complete chaos.

I finally understand what they mean.

"What the hell?" Chad says, a nervous laugh escaping him. I almost forgot he was here, our lone witness to the craziness.

I send him a dirty look. "Get the fuck out of here," I tell him, and he does as I say without protest. I hear the slam of his bedroom door seconds later.

"I-I can't do this," Jensen says, her voice breaking on a sob, her eyes filling. My heart lurches as I watch her hitch her purse up higher on her shoulder, tears streaming down her face. Seeing her like this, I wonder how I could've ever doubted her before. She wasn't lying about my uncle. The hurt and shock and shame is written all over her face.

And then she's gone, pulling the door shut behind her. I chase after her, throwing open the door and running across the lawn toward my car, watching in disbelief as she climbs inside it, starts the engine, and takes off.

"Fuck!" I yell, clutching my head with both hands, fingers tight in my hair as I watch the red taillights get smaller and smaller until they disappear. I drop my arms and turn to find my uncle standing in the open doorway, his expression neutral. Completely unruffled while my whole world feels like it's crumbling around me.

"Did she tell you?" Craig asks.

I stomp back up the lawn toward him, my hands clutched into fists at my side. I'm tempted to beat his ass for hurting Jensen, but what the fuck good would that do me? I want to hear what he has to say for himself first. "Yes."

"And you didn't tell her about me?" He raises a brow.

"I—" Shame washes over me and I shake my head. I can't say the words out loud. And it's more like I didn't to believe her. Big difference.

But not anymore, not really. I messed everything up. How is she going to be able to trust me after I what I did to her?

"Listen, I did this all for you, son," Uncle Craig says. "To protect you."

"Protect me? From what?" I ask incredulously.

"From a money-grubbing little whore, that's what. She doesn't care about you. She's just after your money." Craig runs a hand across his face, his expression pensive. "We started hearing stories about you getting involved with a stripper and we wanted to put a stop to it. Can't have you destroying the Montgomery name, so I tried to—scare her out of town. Clearly, it didn't work."

I'm shaking my head, trying to comprehend what he's telling me. It doesn't make sense. Destroy the family name? I'm the cleanest one of the family outside of Addie. Why are they interfering in my life when we haven't done anything wrong? And who are they anyway?

"What do you mean, 'we'?"

Craig takes a deep breath, looking away from me. "I can't say. Just know that we all care for you and the family. We're protecting our own interests."

"This is such bullshit." I charge up on him, grabbing the front of his shirt and jerking on it, thrusting my face in his. "Who the fuck is telling you to attack Jensen, huh? Who?"

I think I know who, and I don't want to hear his answer. It'll devastate me. But I have to know the truth. I have to.

The faintest smile curls his lips, and he says, "Diane."

Okay. That was the absolute last person I expected him to say. I figured it would be my dad. I'd bet Park was involved before my stepmother, who usually acts like she hates my guts.

" "

"She's always watching you and Park, making sure you two are doing what you're supposed to. She's got Park under her thumb, but you, she has no control over you and it makes her crazy. So she has someone spy on you on occasion. Sometimes that spy is me." He at least has the decency to look scared when I pull on his shirt even tighter. "What the fuck do you think you're doing, getting involved with a stripper, Rhett? She only wants one thing."

"She's not a stripper." I shake him. "And she's not after my money either."

"Really?" Craig sneers. "Funny that she's not working anymore and living with you now, isn't it? I'm guessing you're completely supporting her? She's spending your money, driving your car, living her best life like a high-class escort, hmm? She doesn't have to strip anymore—she's gone exclusive."

His words are messing with my brain, making me doubt Jensen for the quickest second. But she'd never do that to me. I care for her. Hell, I'm pretty sure I've fallen in love with her. "It's not like that."

"I'm sure it's not like that." His tone is mocking and he has the nerve to laugh. "She's playing you so hard, Rhett. Can't you see? Or are you too blinded from all the good pussy you're getting day and night?"

I hit him. It's like an automatic reflex. I let go of his shirt, sling my arm back, and punch him square in the nose, so hard I hear the bones crunch beneath my fist. He doubles over, his hands covering his face, cursing loudly while I just stand there, my knuckles radiating with pain, my entire body vibrating with rage.

"Get the fuck out of my house," I tell him, my teeth

clenched as tight as my fists. I'll hit him again if he doesn't leave.

"You're really going to choose your whore over your family?" he asks incredulously, staring up at me. Blood streams from his nose and I don't feel one ounce of sympathy for him. The fucker asked for it.

"Get out." I don't bother answering his question. What's the point? Besides, my father actually likes Jensen. Maybe.

Maybe my entire family has me fooled.

I stay in the open doorway as I watch my uncle head toward his fancy fucking car, his face covered in blood. I don't bother offering him a towel. I don't offer him anything.

I just want him gone.

"What the hell just happened?" Chad's voice startles me, and I shut and lock the door before I turn to face him. "You always told me your uncle was so cool."

"Not anymore," I say bitterly, pulling my phone out of my pocket. No notifications.

No surprise.

"Did Jensen take your car?" Chad shakes his head. "You don't let anyone drive that damn thing."

"Yeah, well, she does," I mutter, staring at my phone screen. I should call her. But she won't pick up. And I don't want to distract her while she's driving. What if she's so upset, she wrecks? I don't give a shit about the car.

I care about her.

"I was watching from the window, Rhett. You freaking punched your uncle in the " He sounds downright giddy. "Isn't your dad going to be super pissed you did that?"

"I really don't give a damn."

Chad whistles. "Talk about family drama."

I don't bother answering him.

He's summed up my problems in exactly four words.

SEVENTEEN

Rhett

'm not surprised when I find the text from my father the next morning. I'm sure Uncle Craig ratted me out as fast as possible, the asshole. It's already close to noon and I slept through my first class since I was awake most of the night, unable to sleep, trying to reach Jensen. But she didn't respond to any of my calls or texts. No surprise. We've played this game before.

Only this time, she has my freaking car. Not that I really care. I just want to make sure she's all right. I'm actually thankful there's something still connecting us beyond the feelings I have for her. Bringing back the BMW is the perfect excuse to see her.

I'm sure she'll figure out a way to give me back the car and never see me again. She's good at that. Avoiding people.

Real good at it.

I decide I better respond to Dad before he starts blowing up my phone.

He replies immediately. Shit. That is the last thing I want to do.

His response is quick. I choose not to answer that particular question. Panic rises inside me and I sit up, my fingers flying over my phone as I type out my response. I'm sure I can convince Chad to give me a ride. Or any of my friends. Hell, I could call Addie and she could come pick me up in her new Jeep.

"Damn it," I moan as I fall back onto the mattress and close my eyes. I can't lie around for too long, so I crawl out of bed and walk through the house, double-checking that Chad isn't around, finding the house blessedly quiet. I glance through the window outside, wondering if my car magically appeared, but it's not there.

At least she hasn't run away, though I don't know that for sure. For all I know, she could be long gone by now.

I tell myself that no way did she leave. Not after everything we've been through, not without talking to me one last time.

When I'm finished with my shower and dressed, I head out only to hear my dad already banging on the front door. I hurry to the living room and open the door for him, surprised to see how serious and—sad he looks.

I expected him to be full on pissed, not sad.

"Son." He gives me a firm nod as he enters the house,

going straight for the kitchen. I close the door and follow after him, stopping at the counter so I can watch as he opens the fridge and pulls out a beer. He twists the cap off and takes a long drink before setting the bottle on the counter with a loud clink. "I have something to tell you."

He has a lot of bad habits, most of them falling under the or the categories, but he's not a day drinker, unless he's on vacation. And even then, he doesn't really like to drink too much. Always claims alcohol makes him feel too out of control.

So something major must be bothering him.

"If it's about Uncle Craig, I need to tell you my side of the story first," I say firmly, not wanting him to feed me a bunch of bullshit before I explain what really happened.

Dad tilts his head to the side, frowning. "What are you talking about?"

Dread settles low in my stomach. This has nothing to do with Uncle Craig and what he did to Jensen? "Um, what are talking about?"

"Let's go sit down."

We both sit, him at the head of my small dining table and me directly across, facing him. Nerves eat at my insides as I wonder what the hell else is about to be thrown at me.

I don't know if I can take any more.

"What I'm going to tell you is—shocking, to say the least," Dad starts out, then clears his throat. "I'm still reeling from the news myself. But I figured you were the first person I should talk to, since you deserve the truth."

"What is it, Dad?" I sound anxious, and that's because I anxious. I don't like being kept in suspense.

"I hired a private investigator to look into Jensen." He holds up a hand when my mouth pops open, ready to protest. "I do this with pretty much every woman you and your brother date, and your sister too. Trent and his family were fully investigated last year. That Veronica person Park sees on occasion, I had her background looked into as well, and that's how I knew about her three children from three different dads."

I clamp my lips shut, silent. Waiting for him to tell me what he found out about Jensen. Some stuff I already know, but there are still questions…

"Her name really isn't Jensen. She had it changed from Jennifer about a year ago. Jennifer Fanelli."

"I already knew that," I admit quietly.

Dad lifts his brows, appearing surprised. "So she told you."

"Yeah, she did."

"Well, there's more." He clears his throat again, rests his clasped hands on top of the table. He looks terribly uncomfortable, so I know this isn't easy for him. And this definitely isn't easy for me either. "Jennifer Fanelli's father died right before she legally changed her name. He was a single father, raising Jennifer from the time she was a baby."

"She mentioned her mother ran out on them when she

was little," I explain. "She said she doesn't even remember her."

"Well, I assume she knows who her mother is, and that's why she came into our lives," Dad says irritably.

Now I'm just confused. "What are you talking about?"

"Rhett." He levels his gaze on me, his expression serious. Too serious. "Jennifer, I mean Jensen…her mother is Diane. My wife. Your stepmother."

I blink, trying to comprehend what my father just told me. is Jensen's It's hard to believe, difficult to wrap my head around.

Yet if I'm being honest with myself, it's…

Not.

Memories swarm me. The things Jensen would say, how evasive she was, how she worried over what she had to tell me and how it could ruin our relationship forever. I don't know how many times I'd reassure her that my feelings for her wouldn't change. That she could tell me anything and I'd understand.

If she originally got with me to get to Diane, did her feelings change as we became closer? These last few weeks together—minus a few mishaps—she's been so genuine. Sweet. Thoughtful. Into me—totally into me. And I am totally into her.

Was that all a lie?

Jensen was very conscious of Diane's behavior toward her. How nervous she would always get while in Diane's presence.

It truly bothered her, how Diane would ignore her or treat her so terribly. She always worried about Diane, and I never understood it.

It all makes perfect sense.

"I'm guessing Jensen contacted you in order to get close to her mother. I assume she had ulterior motives, though I'm not exactly sure what she thought she would do once she became close to you and the rest of the family." Dad peers at me with his hawk-like gaze. "Did you really trust this girl, Rhett? Tell her things you probably shouldn't have? Have you ever left her alone in your house?"

"Why do you ask that? Of course I trusted her." Most of the time. God, I feel like an asshole for thinking that, even after everything Dad just told me. "I've left her in my house alone more than once, yeah."

"She could've searched through your private things, trying to dig up information." Dad sighs heavily. "I haven't told Diane any of this yet."

"Seriously?" I find that hard to believe.

Dad nods, his expression solemn. "I wanted you to know first."

"But Dad—she's Diane's " Jesus, which means Jensen is my stepsister and that's just…

All sorts of fucked up.

"A daughter she abandoned when the girl was just a baby and never saw again. A daughter she never once mentioned to me in all the years we've been married. What sort of mother does that to her child?" He sounds disgusted and secretly, I'm relieved. I was worried he'd be on Diane's side and believe Jensen was out to get us all.

Maybe that's not the case. Maybe this is all a total coincidence...

Yeah, no. This was planned somehow. But what was Jensen's motive?

"Where is Jensen right now?" Dad asks, his question pushing me out of my thoughts.

"I have no idea where she's at."

"Do you think she's going to use your car as some sort of leverage to find out information about Diane? Because if that's the case, she can have the damn car. I'll get you another one," Dad says bitterly.

"Trust me, that's not her plan." I can't imagine her holding my car for ransom or whatever. That's crazy talk. "She would never do that."

"You don't know this girl, Rhett. You might think you do, but how long have you two been together, hmm? A few months, tops? She can tell you whatever she wants you to hear and you'll believe it. I know, because I see just how enamored you are with that girl. She could tell you clouds are made of pink cotton candy and you'd totally believe her, as long as she still sleeps with you every night."

"Jesus, Dad." I scrub a hand over my face. I hate it when

he talks like this.

"What? It's true! Not that I don't have any faith in you, son, because I do. I sometimes think you might be the more capable son of the two, but I also know both of you are just like me. Always led by your dick." He waves a dismissive hand when he sees my grimace. "I'm just watching out for you. This girl is most likely after our money and hell-bent on revenge. You need to cut her off. Now."

I blink at him. "It's not—it won't be that easy."

He seems shocked at my answer. "Why not?"

"I'm in love with her." The moment the words leave me, I know they're true. I'm totally in love with Jensen. Yeah, our relationship has been down more than up, but I believe her. I believe her. I believe in I just need to talk to her, find out what she was doing, have her tell me she feels the same way. I'm sure she's just as in love with me as I am with her.

Thinking like this probably makes me a fool. Right?

Well, fuck it. I'm a giant fool then.

"Please. You're not in love with her," he snaps. "You're just pussy-whipped. You can find someone else easily, son. You're a catch. Rich. Good looking. You come from a good family."

Did he seriously just say that?"

"You've got it all," he continues. "You just need to find a respectable girl who'll understand her place in our family."

Understand her   Talk about barbaric.

"I don't want anyone else," I say firmly. "Only Jensen."

He sighs and hangs his head, staring at his still clasped hands resting on the table. "Son, you don't mean that."

"Yeah, I actually do." I study him, nerves making my stomach twist. I could tell him.

Tell him about Diane. And Park.

Tell him about his brother, and what he tried to do to Jensen.

There are so many things I could say that will change his perspective on...

Everything.

"Dad." He lifts his head, his gaze meeting mine. "I have something to tell you too."

We remain quiet for a moment, and I can see the silence, the not knowing, is already driving him insane.

"Go ahead," he says. "Spit it out."

EIGHTEEN

Rhett

"Diane is having an affair." I pause for a moment, trying to spill my secrets slowly so they'll be less painful, but he speaks up before I can continue.

"I already know." Dad shakes his head, suddenly looking weary. Older beyond his years. "She's been having little affairs off and on for years. Just like I have."

That he can let that slip so easily is mind blowing. "Yeah, but she's been having a long affair with someone specific," I say. "And it's—"

"My brother. Yes, I know about that too, but they aren't together anymore. Diane promised it was over."

My mouth drops open. Holy , that was information I wasn't expecting. "Diane's having an affair with Uncle Craig?"

He appears taken aback at the surprise in my voice. "Isn't that who you were going to tell me about?"

"No." A ragged breath escapes me. "Dad, she's been sleeping with Park for years."

"What? " His shoulders slump and he buries his face in his hands like a man facing utter defeat. "Are you sure?" he asks quietly.

"I didn't know how to tell you, so I kept my mouth shut for a little while, but it kept eating at me. Since Addie's dinner at Cheesecake Factory." Dad lifts his head, his gaze meeting mine. "Remember when they argued and then they both took off? When I went looking for them? I found them outside behind the building, in each other's arms. Kissing."

It hurts to tell him. I can see the flickers of pain in his eyes, the way he flinches when I say the word , like I just hit him. It sucks, having to say it, but he needs to hear the words. He deserves to know the truth.

"Did they see you see them?" he asks.

"Yes, and they both demanded I keep quiet and not tell anyone, especially you. Then they go off and make a big deal about Jensen working at City Lights, calling her a stripper that night during Addie's party. It was such bullshit and their lies could've blown up in their faces if they didn't watch it, but it was like they didn't care." I study him closely. "You knew Jensen worked there, right? I'm sure Diane told you."

"Before the investigator brought me that information, yes. Diane mentioned it to me. I always wondered how she found out," Dad murmurs.

"Through Uncle Craig." At my father's confused look, I continue, "Or maybe Diane found out on her own at first. Supposedly she keeps tabs on me and Park to make sure we don't do anything awful to mess up the family name." Isn't that ironic? Everyone in my family is messed up. Definitely more messed up than I am—save again, for Addie. "Diane sent Craig to the club one night to scare Jensen, and he paid ten thousand dollars to meet with her privately. Then he tried to rape her."

"Are you serious?" Dad's expression is horrified. "Craig paid ten grand to spend time with Jensen and then tried to her?" He reminds me of a parrot, but I'm guessing he's trying to absorb all the crazy.

I nod. "Jensen admitted everything to me, about how this man named Greg attacked her at City Lights. When we were leaving Addie's birthday party, we got separated, and when I went out to the car, she was waiting for me, in near hysterics. Telling me how she saw Greg inside your house. When she described him, and where exactly she saw him in the house, I knew who she was talking about."

I pause. This is the part I don't like admitting. "She was referring to Craig. I—I didn't believe her. Not at first. I didn't to believe her, didn't want to think my uncle, a man I'm related to, someone I looked up to my whole life, could do something so fucking awful." Now it's my turn to hang my head in shame. "But she wasn't lying, Dad. It's true. All of it. And now it's all a complete mess."

"Good Lord." I glance up just as Dad rises to his feet, kicking the chair back. "I should go."

I stand as well. "Where?"

"I need to talk to Diane. To Park. To Craig." He starts to laugh, but the sound lacks humor. "I don't know who I should start with first."

"I'd go with Diane," I suggest quietly.

We walk together to the front door, and he turns to face me before he leaves. "You should go find Jensen."

"You told me only a few minutes ago I needed to cut her off."

"I changed my mind. Talk to her. Find out the truth. That girl lacks the sophistication to pull off a giant revenge scheme, and you know it. If anyone is out to screw me over, it's my wife. And quite possibly my oldest son."

With that, he walks out of my house, shutting the door behind him.

♥ ♥ ♥

Chad came home soon after my dad left and he let me borrow his car. I drove aimlessly through town for a while, cruising Savannah's apartment complex looking for my car in the lot, then parking and marching up to their door so I could knock on it.

No answer.

No surprise.

I call and text Jensen, but she won't respond. I drive around campus, hoping I can spot her, but it's like I'm searching for a needle in a haystack. I always thought that old cliché was stupid, but now it's apt.

Jensen is nowhere to be found. But I don't know where to look for her, so that's part of my problem.

It's just past five and the sky is dark when I pull into the City Lights parking lot. There, parked near a light post, is my BMW.

Triumph surges through me and I park Chad's car, then head for the entrance. I push through the double doors and burst inside, the bouncer appearing directly in front of me, his thick arms crossed in front of his massive chest.

"Where the hell do you think you're going?" he asks.

"I'm looking for Jensen."

He frowns. "Jen? She doesn't work here anymore."

"Her car's right outside." I don't bother explaining it's actually my car.

He turns to one of the topless cocktail waitresses who just happens to walk past. "Is Jensen here tonight?"

"She came in with Savannah," the woman says before heading for the bar.

"It's your lucky night." He holds out a meaty hand. "That'll be forty bucks."

"Forty bucks?" Like a dumbass I reach for my back pocket

and pull my wallet out. "What for?"

"Cover charge." He laughs, the sound booming from his chest. "Rich dicks looking for their girlfriends gotta pay up."

Figures he would know about us. I slap two twenties in his palm. "Where're they at?"

"I don't know." He shrugs. "That's on you."

He steps aside and I walk into the club, thankful it's not crowded, but it's a Monday night so I'm guessing that's typical. I check everywhere in search of Jensen, or Savannah, but neither of them are anywhere to be found.

Deciding I need a drink, I go to the bar, where the older bartender offers me a sympathetic smile. "You looking for your girl?"

What, does everyone here know I'm with Jensen? "If you mean Jensen, yeah. I am."

He nods, grabs a shot glass, and pours me a drink without asking what I want. "She's a good girl. Sweet. Quiet. She doesn't belong here."

His words surprise me. "I agree."

The bartender pushes the shot glass full of amber liquid in my direction. "Take a drink. Then I'll take you to where she's at."

I down that shot so fast, I barely feel the fiery liquid slide down my throat. "What do I owe you?" I ask, my voice scratchy from the alcohol.

"On the house. Just—get her out of here once and for all.

Wish I could say the same for her friend, but she's a smart one. She's on her way out on her own. But yours? She'll get sucked in if she doesn't watch it." He nods once. "Good luck."

I appreciate the speech, but… "Where is she?"

"Oh, yeah." He chuckles. "Follow me."

NINETEEN

Jensen

"You can't hide out forever," Savannah says as she paces the length of the dressing room. Her shift starts in fifteen minutes and we got here early at my urging. I didn't want to linger at the apartment any longer than we had to. I didn't want Rhett to come around, and I definitely didn't want to have him stop by while Savannah's at work.

So I solved that problem and drove her to City Lights in Rhett's fancy BMW. Savannah oohed and ahhed the entire drive, running her hands over the leather interior, begging me to go faster. I sped up a little but not too much, scared I might wreck Rhett's car and then he'd really be mad at me.

Though truly I'm the one who's mad at him. No, I take that back. I'm not mad, I'm   He had to have known his uncle was really Greg. Yet he didn't tell me. I don't know how he could keep such a huge secret from me.

Ugh. I have no room to judge.

"I can hide out tonight," I tell Savannah, settling into a chair. "I'll stay back here while you work."

"Don will probably beg you to come back." Savannah wrinkles her nose.

"He's not here tonight; I already asked around." I smile, though it feels forced. "Dodged that bullet."

"Lucky you." Savannah's tone is heavy on the sarcasm. She plops into the chair next to mine. "You need to return his car."

"Tomorrow."

"You need to talk to him."

I wave a hand. "Tomorrow."

Savannah sighs. "You need to tell him the truth, once and for all."

Once I got to Savannah's apartment last night, I cried on her shoulder, and then I told her everything. All of it. Every last sordid bit of my true story, my connection to Diane, my reason for seeking out Rhett. How my original plan had been to destroy him, but then I realized he was actually a decent guy.

A sweet and sexy guy too.

"I will," I finally say, though I feel like I'm lying. I can't imagine telling him the truth. "When I'm ready, I will."

"Jen." We both turn so we're facing each other and she grabs hold of my shoulders, giving me a shake. "You will never feel ready. There will never be a right time. You just have to… gain some courage and tell him. It's the only way. Like ripping off a Band-Aid. The anticipation is killer, but once it's done, it's so worth it."

The tears spring to my eyes and I tilt my head back to prevent them from spilling. "I'm so scared he'll hate me," I admit.

"He won't hate you." Savannah shakes my shoulders again, and I glare at her. "I promise. He had a secret, and yeah, it was a shitty thing he did, keeping that from you. But your secret is pretty big too."

"Thanks for making me feel so good," I say sarcastically, and she shushes me.

"Let me finish." I press my lips together, remaining quiet before she continues. "I'm just saying I think he'll be understanding. You both have secrets. You found out his, and it's a biggie, I can't deny that, but I have faith you two can work it out. So now it's your turn to tell him yours."

"His secret was awful," I whisper.

"I know." She wraps me up in a quick hug before she pulls away from me again, her hands still on my shoulders. "And I'm sorry everything happened the way it did. But you should probably come clean with him. I know you care about Rhett a lot."

"I do," I admit, biting my lower lip.

"I believe he cares about you too. Whatever you tell him,

he's going to be understanding. You just need to be open with him, okay? Stop holding on to all this hate and tell him the truth," Savannah says.

I'm kind of irritated with her, but maybe I need this dose of reality. "Can't you just let me wallow in my misery for a minute?"

"I did that last night. Now you need to woman up and talk to your man. Make this work." Savannah squeezes my shoulders before letting them go. "Maybe you should go see him right now."

"No way." I shake my head. "I'm staying here tonight."

Savannah sighs and stands, resting her hands on her hips. "You're ridiculous."

"Thanks."

"I'm gonna go clock in."

"Have fun." I grab a magazine I snagged from Savannah's coffee table before we left the apartment, and open it. "I'll be sitting here waiting for you."

The moment she's gone, I close the magazine with a sigh, tilting my head back so I can stare up at the ceiling. I don't want to sit here all night, but I feel like I have no choice. Where else could I go? Sitting around the apartment, waiting for Rhett to possibly show up, sounds like pure misery.

Though I miss him. I miss him like crazy. I'm just scared to face him, scared to see his reaction to my truth, scared to hear his reasoning for protecting his uncle.

This entire plan was a huge mistake. I should've never gone after him. I deserve all of this and more for trying to get revenge on my real mother. It may look like Diane is living the perfect life, but she's absolutely miserable. Having an affair with her stepson, always fighting with her husband, unable to get along with her stepchildren, constantly trying to make herself look prettier and younger by spending all sorts of money on cosmetic procedures…it's awful.

I didn't need to ruin her life. She's already done that to herself.

"Hey." I glance over my shoulder to see Chuck the bartender standing in the doorway, a faint smile on his face. "You gals decent?"

"I'm the only one in here, Chuck." God knows where the strippers are tonight. Mondays are notoriously slow and they don't start the shows until closer to ten. "And of course I'm decent. I don't work here anymore."

Chuck laughs, shuffling his feet. "You got a visitor."

"Who'd want to see me? Oh…" My voice fades when I see who appears next to Chuck.

It's Rhett.

My stomach churns. My heart races.

"I'll leave you two be," Chuck murmurs before he ducks out of the room.

"Jensen." All he says is my name, and hearing his deep voice, seeing him standing in front of me looking so fucking miserable, makes my heart ache.

I glance down at the crumpled magazine in my hands and toss it on the chair next to me. "You found me."

"I need to talk to you. Explain some things." He scratches his forehead, tunnels his fingers through his hair. He looks unkempt, even a little sloppy, words I would never use to describe Rhett. It's like the guilt and the worry over me, over has put him through complete torture.

In the past, the old me would've thought this was great. I would've thought he deserved it. Instead, now I realize I'm just as miserable as he looks.

"You want to talk now?" "Definitely. If you'll listen to me."

I point to the chair next to me and he enters the room, scooting the chair a few feet away from me before he settles into it. I realize I have to do everything Savannah told me to do. I need to woman up, grow some courage, and tell him the truth. Pray to God and anyone else who's listening that he won't hate me when he finds out my real story.

"You look…" His gaze searches my face eagerly, and I decide to put him out of his misery.

"Terrible," I finish for him, making him smile faintly. "If you told me I look good, I would've called you a liar."

"I'm just glad you're here. Sitting with me." He looks ready to grab my hands, but he doesn't. "There's so much I need to tell you."

"Like what?" I can feel his warmth, his strength. We're not

even touching, but I can feel it all. I want more of him. I want all of him.

I probably want too much.

"I planned on telling you about my uncle. It was just—so shocking when you said you saw Greg in my dad's house, and I realized pretty quick who you were referring to. I just didn't want to believe it," Rhett explains. "It hurt me, to think my uncle was capable of something so terrible. And for a while there, I didn't believe you, because you've lied to me before."

The last part hurts, but I also understand. I lie to him. A lot. I deserve him not fully trusting me.

"Uncle Craig was going to my dad's for Thanksgiving, but he cancelled at the last minute. Said he made other plans." Rhett's gaze meets mine before it flicks away. "I was so relieved, but I knew I would still have to tell you eventually. I planned on mentioning it right before Christmas."

"You would've strung it out that long?" I ask incredulously.

He throws his hands up in frustration. "I didn't know how else to handle it. My plan was to talk to him, find out the truth, and then tell you that Greg was really Craig, my uncle. I realize now my plan made no sense. I should've just told you who he really was from the beginning."

Yes. He should've.

"Then he had to show up at my house and ruin the everything. And that made me realize I was the one who really ruined it all. I should've been open with you from the start."

I'm quiet, absorbing everything he said, turning it over in my head. There's only one thing bothering me about this story. "Did he tell you   he did it? Why he attacked me?"

"He claimed he was sent there by…Diane. That she kept tabs on me and Park, and she didn't want me involved with a gold digger who's only out for my money." Rhett exhales loudly. "He also said they wanted to protect the family name, and they didn't want me to ruin it by getting involved with a stripper."

"God, I wasn't even a stripper," I mutter irritably, making Rhett smile. Probably because that's the only thing I can focus on. "So Diane sent your uncle here to, what? Threaten me?"

"He claims he was only supposed to scare you a little bit. And convince you to leave me alone," Rhett says.

"Yeah, he scared me all right. If I hadn't fought him off, he would've   me. I know he would've." The memory still makes me sick to my stomach.

"And I'm sorry for that. I'm so sorry, Jensen. I wish I could take back what my uncle did to you. I'd do anything to make it so that never happened, and you never had to suffer by his hands." His earnest tone tells me he's sincere.

"My dad came to talk to me today," he continues. "I told him about Park and Diane."

I jerk my head so I'm facing him. "You did?"

He nods. "Turns out Diane was having an affair with my uncle too."

"Are you serious?" Oh my God.

"Yeah. He hit me with that before I could get Park's name out and I was in total shock." He reaches out and grabs my fingers, holding them loosely. His touch feels so good. So right. "She's been sleeping with my brother my uncle. My dad just… lets her do this to him, time and again. But he's no saint either, so they just keep cheating on each other, again and again. It's—awful."

"It's so awful." I squeeze his fingers, wishing I could reassure him better. "I don't understand her."

"I don't understand either of them," he agrees, then hesitates. "Dad told me some other stuff too."

"Like what?" The way he's looking at me makes me nervous.

"He mentioned things about…you. How he had a private investigator look into your background."

My hands, my entire body immediately goes ice cold. "Really?" My voice is shaky and I brace myself for the bad news.

"He found out that Diane is—your mom. Your   mom." He grips my hands tight, his gaze locked on mine. "Is it true, Jensen? Did you know she was your mother all along? Is that why you tried to get close to me? So you could get back at her somehow? Were you concocting some sort of evil plan to take down the Wicked Witch of the West and in the meantime ended up falling for me?"

My heart is racing so hard, I can hear the insistent pounding is roaring in my ears. I stare at him, my head spinning, relief flooding me that the truth is finally out there, lying between us like a living, breathing thing. I'm still intact, and so is he, and neither of us seem angry, which is a good thing.

A very good thing.

Wait a minute. He asked if I ended up falling for him. Does this mean he's fallen for ? I always thought my truth would be the end of our relationship.

But maybe it's the beginning.

TWENTY

Rhett

I wait for her answers, my fingers still curled around hers, our gazes still holding like we can't look away. There are tears in her eyes, making them extra blue, and when one of those tears falls down her cheek, I reach out, stopping it with my thumb.

"Why are you crying?" I ask.

She sniffs, closing her eyes like she can stop the flow of tears, but it's no use. They're really coming now. "I don't know. I think I'm just so relieved you know my secret, I can't help but cry."

"So it's true. You knew all along Diane was your mother."

She nods, her dark blonde hair sliding across her shoulders. Her face is pale and her hair isn't brushed, and she doesn't have a lick of makeup on. She's the most beautiful woman I've ever seen, and that's because she's mine. Despite everything that's happened, all the secrets and the lies and the bullshit, none of it matters.

All I care about is her. All I want is to hear her say she's in love with me, and she wants to be with me, damn the consequences.

"And when you first met me at the bar?"

"It wasn't an accident." She gives me a watery smile. "I planned to run into you there. I planned that night in the library too. And at the diner."

"Placing yourself everywhere I went."

"I semi-stalked you for months. I was so scared that night in the bar, and when you approached me, I was also mad. Mad that it worked. Mad that you were so charming. Really mad that you were so good looking." She rolls her eyes and I reach out again to wipe away her tears. "You frustrated me on an almost daily basis when we first started spending time together."

"You still frustrate me on a daily basis," I admit, making her smile. "What were you trying to do?"

"I don't know…it was so stupid. I wanted to lure you in, make you believe I was your girlfriend and then get back at Diane somehow, yet never knowing exactly how. I was more curious than anything else, I guess. Curious about her, about you, your entire family. And I did all of this, studied you, researched the family, put all this time and energy into my plan, into my anger." She hesitates, swallowing hard. "Once

I got to know you, my plan just…disappeared. I couldn't go through with any of it. I can't even explain to you exactly what I wanted to do."

She releases her hold on me and runs her hands over her face. "It was all so stupid, so fake. I can understand how you'd never want to talk to me again."

"That's the last thing I want to do," I admit, making her drop her hands from her face so she can stare at me. "It never felt fake to me."

"It never felt fake to me either," she confesses in a hushed whisper. "From the start, I wanted—more. I kept resisting it, knowing the deeper I got with you, the worse it would be. I felt so much guilt for keeping my secret, and I didn't know how to explain it to you. How could I get involved, fall for you, and never tell you the truth? I knew you'd never forgive me."

Damn, this girl. Her words are making me sad. I can sense her fear, her regret, her frustration. I understand it, because I've felt so many of those same emotions too. "Come here," I whisper, beckoning her, patting my knees. "Sit on my lap."

She frowns but still gets out of her chair, settling her perfect butt on my thighs. "What?" Her face is so close, I wish I could kiss her. But not yet.

"This entire situation started out…fucked up. We can be real with each other right now, okay? You lied. And I fell for it."

Jensen makes like she's going to leave and I tighten my grip on her waist, keeping her there. "But then I lied to you too," I admit, my voice soft. "And I felt terrible. Guilty. I didn't know how to tell you my uncle was the one who tried to attack you. And the longer I kept the secret, the harder it became for me to tell you the truth. Secrets are like a disease, Jens. The longer you hold on to them, the deeper they rip into your soul and churn your guts."

She wrinkles her nose. "That's sort of gross, Rhett."

"You get what I'm saying, though, right?"

"Yeah, I get it." She loops her arms around my neck, her hands sliding into the hair at my nape. "No more secrets."

"No more secrets," I agree.

"I'm sorry." She blinks up at me. "For everything."

"I'm sorry too." I kiss the tip of her nose. "For everything."

"There's more I need to tell you," she starts, and I almost want to place my hand over her mouth to shut her up. "But it's nothing major. Just, bits and pieces from my past, you know? All the big stuff has been revealed, though, so don't worry."

I actually laugh. "Okay, good. I don't think I could take one more big secret."

"Me either." Her expression turns serious. "That's all you have to tell me, right? Just about your uncle?"

"Yeah, though they were all working together behind our backs. Diane and Craig, maybe even Park. They had some sort of sick and twisted little relationship going on. One I will never be able to understand," I say.

"How's your dad taking this?"

"Not well. He knew about everything but Park and Diane." I pull her closer, my arms wrapped tight around her slender waist. She feels damn good sitting here. Like she belongs. "He's hurt. But he told me I needed to talk to you. Make sure you were all right."

"He didn't think I was after the Montgomery fortune?" She bites her lip before she continues. "At one point, I was. I can admit it."

"I appreciate the honesty." I brush the hair away from her forehead. "And no, he doesn't think you're after the Montgomery fortune. Not anymore."

She frowns.

"Trust me," I say gently. "He likes you. He was worried about you."

"Really?" The hope that lights up her face makes her extra beautiful.

"Really." I lean in and brush her mouth with mine, kissing her nice and slow, not too pushy. "I've missed you," I murmur against her lips.

"We've only been apart approximately twenty-four hours." She smiles.

"The longest twenty-four hours of my life." And that is the absolute truth.

Her smile fades. "Mine too."

I kiss her again, longer this time, though I don't take it deeper. Not yet. I still need to approach her carefully. "Come home with me," I say once I break the kiss.

"You want your car back?" she teases.

"I want back," I tell her.

Her eyes widen and she pulls away from me to look into my eyes. "You've got me."

That's all I needed to hear.

♥ ♥ ♥

"Are we accepting each other too easily?" Jensen asks once we return to my house. I drove the BMW home with Jensen, and Chad had a friend take him to City Lights to pick up his car. I have a feeling they're staying there for a while, which means we have the house all to ourselves.

"What do you mean?" We're in the kitchen and I'm grabbing us both cold bottles of water. I hand her one and crack mine open, chugging half of it in one swallow.

"Maybe we're being too forgiving of each other too soon." She sets the water bottle on the counter, bracing her hands on the edge of the granite.

"Are you saying we should suffer more?" I want to laugh, but don't. "Come on, Jens. Haven't we done enough of that already?"

"Maybe you're right." She taps the counter with her nails. "It's just—nothing ever comes easy for me."

"I know. Your life has been hard, and I hate that. But

maybe sometimes, you've also made the wrong choices."

She smiles at me. "Are you saying you're the right choice?"

"For you." I approach her, my hand going to her waist, slowly pulling her closer. "And you're the right choice for me. When you choose right, it's easy."

"I want to believe that so badly," she whispers, and I can hear the uncertainty in her voice, feel it in her trembling body. "My whole life has been filled with hard choices, most of them wrong. I don't trust my instincts anymore. That's why easy feels so foreign to me."

"Trust yourself, baby," I murmur, pulling her fully into my arms. I hold her close, my hand cupping the back of her head, her face against my chest. She fits perfectly like this. As if we were meant to be. I truly believe we are. "Go with your gut."

"What's your gut telling you?" she asks, her voice muffled against my shirt.

I slip my fingers beneath her chin and tilt her face up so she's looking at me. "That we belong together. That I've fallen completely in love with you."

Her eyes go wide and her lips pop open on a gasp. "Wait. Are you serious?"

I can't help but laugh now, not holding it back. "Not exactly the response I was hoping for."

"It's just that—no. I'm sorry." She huffs out a laugh, her gaze dropping down. "I'm messing this up." She clears her throat and returns her gaze to mine once more. "No one has ever told me they loved me before, beyond my father, and he only told me a handful of times."

"I'll tell you it again, every day, every hour if that's what you need to hear." I cup her face in my hands and kiss her, my mouth lingering on hers. "I love you, Jens."

She's crying again. I can taste the salt of her tears on my lips before I see them. "I love you too, Rhett."

Her words make my skin catch fire. I didn't know how much I needed to hear that until she finally said it. "Thank God," I mutter just before I kiss her again.

We stand in my darkened kitchen kissing for what feels like hours, but it's only a few minutes. I haul her up so she's sitting on the edge of the counter, her legs spreading wide so I can step in between them. She buries her hands in my hair, clutching me close while I let my hands wander all over her. Along her hips and waist, across her stomach, around her breasts.

She thrusts her chest into my hands and I cradle her there, my hands kneading, wishing the bra was already gone so I can really feel her. Our mouths are fused together, tongues tangled, lips capturing sighs and moans, sliding my hand down, down, down, until it's curving around her butt so I can haul her in close, our lower bodies touching as best they can, considering our positions.

"Take me to your bed, Rhett," she whispers against my lips, just before she starts to giggle.

I sweep her into my arms and carry her through the house, headed straight for my bedroom. She's slapping my chest, telling me to put her down, but I can tell she loves it. I'm trying to make all of her romantic fantasies come true tonight.

I'll spend the rest of my life trying to make them come true, as long as she lets me.

I kick my bedroom door open and barge inside, heading straight for the bed, where I deposit Jensen, dropping her right onto the middle of the mattress. She lands with a little bounce, glaring up at me for the briefest moment.

And then she starts to undress.

I stop and stare, enjoying the view. Savoring it. She removes her sweater and her jeans, making me smile when I watch her struggle to get them off. She rises up on her knees, wearing a plain black bra and matching panties, a coy smile curling her lips. Hot as fuck and driving me right out of my mind.

She continues driving me even crazier when she starts touching herself. Drifting her fingers across her chest, dipping into her cleavage. "Like what you see?"

"I always like seeing you," I tell her.

"You certainly have a way with words, Rhett Montgomery." She bats her eyelashes, her fingers going to the front clasp of her bra and undoing it. The fabric springs apart but not completely, offering me a teasing glimpse of her perfect tits.

"You think so?"

Jensen nods, toying with the open clasp of her bra. "Maybe

you should start undressing too."

Without hesitation I whip my shirt off, then start working on my jeans. I'm standing at the foot of the bed in just my gray boxer briefs in a matter of seconds, my cock already straining against the cotton. Her gaze drops there, lingering, and her eyes go wide.

"Eager to see me?" she asks.

"Eager to feel your hands on me," I correct.

Her smile is knowing, her hand slipping beneath her bra cup to toy with her nipple. "I know what you mean. I can't wait for you to have your hands on me."

"What exactly are we waiting for again?" I'm starting to sweat. I can feel it form on my forehead, and I know it's from watching her touch herself.

"Aren't you having fun?" She sheds the bra completely, exposing her upper body, and my gaze locks on her breasts, my mouth watering at the sight of her hard, rosy nipples. "Watching me?"

"I'd have more fun actually touching you. So would you," I add.

She laughs, her hands dropping to her waist, fingers curling around the waistband of her panties. "I'm really enjoying this."

"I bet you are."

Her expression turns serious. "A few hours ago, I believed I wouldn't be able to touch you ever again."

Her words sober me up, make me realize just how perilous

close to ending our relationship was not even twenty-four hours ago. "You've got me now. For as long as you want me."

She reaches out a hand, beckoning me to come closer. "Let's make that forever and you've got a deal."

TWENTY-ONE

Jensen

Rhett takes my hand, joining me on the bed. He's on his knees as well, his hands going to rest lightly by my neck, his fingers sprawled, gently stroking across my collarbone. "You are truly the most beautiful woman I've ever seen," he says reverently, just before he dips his head and presses his warm, damp lips to the spot where my neck meets my shoulder.

I toss my head back and close my eyes, reveling in the feeling of his hands on me, his mouth on my skin. I want to savor every moment of this. It hurts to think I could've lost it, lost him. I almost did.

He loves me. And I love him. Those confusing, overwhelming feelings I couldn't put a name on, they were love. My love for Rhett. How sad that I couldn't quite identify them, that I didn't know what was going on inside of me. It felt like a tumultuous storm, rising up and up and up, trying its best to take me over, sweeping me under. I fought and struggled at first, as if I was going to drown, and now I realize I went about this the wrong way.

I should've let the tidal wave of emotions sweep over me and take me under. I should've enjoyed the fall.

Rhett kisses his way up my neck, along my jaw, until his lush mouth is pressed against mine. Our lips connect, and the kiss turns carnal in an instant, wet lips and velvety tongues. He's leaning me back onto the bed, his big, hot body over mine, his hands braced on either side of my head. He shifts downward and kisses my breasts, licks and sucks my nipples, making me wet, making me restless.

Driving me wild.

"I wanted to make this last," he breathes against my skin. "But I can't wait. I want to be inside you."

"Yes, please," I tell him with a little laugh, and he lifts his head to meet my gaze with a smile. "We can make it last another time. Just…"

I don't get to finish my sentence. He's too busy pulling my panties off, then shoving his own underwear off. Until we're totally naked and he's thrusting his erection against me, teasing me. I spread my legs wider, reaching for him, guiding him toward me, and when he slips inside, we both moan at the sensation of our bodies forging together into one.

"I will never get tired of this," he says as he starts to move.

In. Out. A slow, delicious glide that makes me close my eyes, totally lost in the sensation of our bodies making love. I never thought it could be like this. Never thought it could be so good with someone.

With Rhett, it's better than anything in the world.

"Promise?" I whisper.

He's already increasing his pace, ramping up the friction, making the heat spark hotter, higher between us. "For you? Always."

I lose all coherent thought, my ability to form actual words, the harder he thrusts inside me. I wrap my arms around him, clinging to him, letting him sweep me away, and when the familiar tingles start low in my belly, I know my orgasm is close.

And so is his. Within seconds, we're coming together, a first for us, and when it's all over and I'm lying in his arms, both of us sweaty and exhausted and unable to stop touching each other, I am finally able to form sentences once again.

"That was fast."

He bursts out laughing, burying his face in my hair. "Way to stroke my ego."

"I wasn't trying to be insulting." I lift my head, resting my arm on his chest so I can study his perfectly handsome face. "I liked that it happened so fast."

He raises a brow, brushing the hair away from my face. "Why?"

"It shows that you can't control yourself around me. That you want me so bad, you have to have me right this second." I smile. "I like that I can make you lose control."

"I like that I can make you lose control too." His fingers linger on my cheek, caressing me there. "You know you're moving in here, right."

He doesn't say it like a question. More like a statement. "I am?"

"Yes." He nods. "No more staying at Savannah's house. I want you here. All the time."

His gentle command makes me want to beam with happiness. "What about Chad?"

"What about him?"

"I'm taking away your bachelor pad status for good." I bite my lip, trying to act like I care. I don't mind Chad. But I would love for him to eventually move out and for us to have the house all to ourselves.

"His lease is up in the spring. We'll kick him out then," Rhett reassures me.

"You own the house, right?"

"I do."

I'm not comfortable talking about finances with Rhett. And it's probably going to take a while for me to be comfortable with it. Or maybe I never will, who knows. "Is it the only house you own?"

"In my name? Yes. Once I graduate college and figure out

what I want to do, then I'll buy a house wherever we end up."

I love, love, love how he uses the word . That will never get old. "What do you want to do?"

"You know what? I don't have a clue." He chuckles and tugs me closer. "That probably makes me a dumbass."

"No, I think that makes you a guy with a lot of opportunities in front of you, and you're lucky that you can make a choice," I say softly.

His laughter dies. "You're right. Thank you for putting it in perspective."

"No problem."

We're silent for a while, Rhett playing with my hair, me stroking my fingernails lightly along his chest, making goose bumps rise. I could touch him like this for hours. For days. I wonder if he feels the same.

"Did you ever hear from your father?" I finally ask.

"Yeah. He texted me earlier, right before I got to City Lights. Said that he talked to Diane, and she denied everything. All of it. About Craig, about Park" He hesitates and my heart starts to pound. I'm scared of what he's going to say. "She said she didn't believe you."

"She didn't believe what?" My voice shakes. This is such a big moment, yet it also feels very, very small.

"That you're her daughter. She told my father she never had a daughter."

"She actually said that?" I thought it would hurt more, to

hear that she denied me. But for some reason, it doesn't. His words, her denial, it's all…

Meaningless.

Oh, I can admit I experience a small twinge, hearing Rhett say it, and it's frustrating, how she can so easily deny everything she's ever done.

But most important of all, her denial doesn't hurt. Diane will most likely deny my existence for the rest of her life. She will probably never want to be in a room with me again. That might make for some awkward family encounters, but for once in my life, I don't care. I don't care what she thinks of me, I don't care what she's doing, and I don't care that she won't be a part of my life.

That's all thanks to Rhett.

"Dad kicked her out of the house. Told her she couldn't live with him anymore and promised he would file for divorce by the end of the year," he continues.

"Is she going to take him for all he's worth?" I'm sure she will. She's greedy. Always has been.

"Nah. Dad had her sign an iron-clad prenuptial agreement right before they got married. She'll be paid well, but she won't take half of everything. He guaranteed that."

"Your father is a very smart man," I murmur against his chest.

He stirs beneath me, suddenly restless. Suddenly hard. "Let's stop talking about my dad."

I slip my hand downward, seeking and finding his erect cock. "Oh? Why do you say that?"

"Let's do other—things." He chokes out the last word when I stroke him from base to tip.

"What do you have in mind?" He's rock hard yet velvety soft. I smooth my thumb over the tip of him, catching the wetness there. "I can't believe you're ready to go again."

"It's all your fault." He moves fast, flipping me over so I'm on my back and he's hovering above me once more. "Maybe this time around I'll make it last."

"Please do," I murmur, closing my eyes when he shifts downward, his mouth on my stomach, his hands braced against my inner thighs, spreading me wide. I bite my lower lip, loving those tender kisses across my belly, sucking in a surprised breath when his mouth lands on my wet center. His tongue searches my folds as he slips a finger deep within me, and holy God, he's going to make me come so fast I might faint.

If it's always going to be like this between us, I'm afraid he might end up killing me.

But I guess death by good sex is a pretty great way to go.

TWENTY-TWO

Jensen

"I bet you didn't expect me to be here, did you?"

Diane whips around at my words, her expression one of pure shock for all of about a second before it's replaced with cool indifference. "What are you doing in house?"

I've been waiting for her, for this moment, for what feels like hours. Days.

Years.

And now here we are, alone in the Montgomery house, with no one around for either of us to hide behind. Everything blew up in her face only a few days ago, so the emotions are still raw. The family is broken up, in turmoil, Parker angry at his wife and oldest son, and Rhett angry at his brother.

Me? I'm trying my best to stay neutral, but it's difficult. I want to support Rhett, but I also want to get my digs in. That cliché rings true.

Old habits die hard.

We're in the living room, Diane and I. The curtains are drawn, the room is dark, even though it's early in the afternoon. I rise from the couch and start to approach her. She doesn't move, doesn't so much as flinch as I draw near, and I'm reluctantly impressed.

"This isn't your house anymore," I tell her, glee filling me at the flicker of irritation I spot in her gaze when I speak.

What I say is true. She doesn't live with Parker any longer. The only reason she's here is to pick up a few of her belongings while no one else is around. I saw texts between her and Addie last night, when I was hanging out with Addie at Rhett's house while he was at basketball practice. We were binge watching a show on Netflix, munching on popcorn when I noticed someone kept blowing up Addie's phone with endless texts. She caught me looking over her shoulder, and funny enough, she was the one who ended up feeling guilty.

"Diane wants her stuff," Addie told me with a defensive shrug. "So I'm letting her know when the house is empty."

"Won't your father be angry?" I asked her softly.

"Probably, but I don't know what else to do. She won't leave me alone," Addie confessed. "I figured this is the only way I can get her off my back."

That's why I'm at the house. The opportunity was handed to me, and I couldn't pass it up. The old me would've jumped all over this chance, yet the new me said I didn't need to waste my time. I didn't need to get revenge on my mother. She'd ruined everything on her own.

But guess what? The old me won.

Rhett doesn't know I'm here. No one knows, except Diane.

Who's she going to tell?

"It isn't your house either," Diane says snottily, and I shake my head, already frustrated by our conversation.

None of this matters. She knows why I want to talk to her. It's definitely not to go 'round and 'round over who belongs here. We have bigger things to discuss.

Like why I haven't heard from her for the last nineteen years or so.

"Why did you do it?" I ask, cutting right to the chase.

"Do what?" She blinks at me. Either she knows how to play dumb really well, or she's being purposely obtuse.

"Why did you abandon me? Why did you abandon my father?" I take a step closer, vaguely surprised that we're the same height. Though I guess I shouldn't be. I'm reminded that we do have things in common, now that I'm standing so close to her. We have similarly colored eyes and hair, though hers is brighter, thanks to expensive highlights. Similarly shaped nose.

She's not in her usual heels and elegant designer clothes, her hair sleek and her makeup perfect. Instead her hair is in a ponytail, and she only has on lip-gloss. She's wearing a black velour sweat suit, like the ones that were popular about ten years ago, though what she currently has on is definitely designer. I can tell by the J zipper dangling between her breasts. Of course it's Juicy Couture. High-end is the name of her game.

I wouldn't expect Diane Montgomery to wear anything less.

"I don't know what you're talking about." She lifts her chin, the very picture of defiance. "Now, if you'll excuse me, I have things I need to do."

Diane tries to push past me but I grab her arm, my fingers clamping tight. She struggles, which only makes my hold grow stronger. "There's no one here you need to impress," I tell her. "You can be real with me, Mother."

She yanks her arm out of my grip and takes a step back, her eyes wild. "Don't ever call me that."

"Truth hurts, right?" I wondered why Rhett didn't react to me saying my last name, and I just found out it's because Diane was using her maiden name when she first met Parker. Makes me wonder if I needed to change my name at all. Was that a waste of time? Was it a waste of time to try and get to her through Rhett?

Definitely not. Never in a million years did I think I'd fall in love with him, or that he would fall in love with me.

"You don't know what you're talking about," Diane says as she starts to make her way toward the staircase. "I don't have a daughter."

Her words enrage me, despite telling myself none of this matters. It does. It still hurts, what she did to me, and to my father.

I follow after her, our feet pounding as I chase her up the stairs. "Was it really that easy? To just forget about me and pretend I didn't exist? Because I never forgot about you. And trust me, I tried so hard."

At the top of the stairs she turns to face me, her expression one of pure fury. "I wouldn't have been a good mother to you."

I'm taken aback by her words. Her subtle acknowledgement of me seems to fly right over my head. All I can focus on is what she just said. "What do you mean?"

"Your father was always criticizing me. Saying I didn't love him enough, I didn't love enough. I would give and give and all he did was take and take. Same with you. Every day it was the same thing, over and over again. I didn't have a life. I had you and your father to take care of, and at the end of the day, there was nothing left for me. I always felt so drained and scared," Diane explains.

"Scared?" I ask incredulously. "Scared of what?"

"Of my life! I knew if I stayed there, I wouldn't amount to anything. Your father had no aspirations, no goals, no focus. He didn't want to better himself for his family. He liked his life just the way it was."

And my mother didn't. That much is clear.

"I knew I was trapped, but I had no one to turn to," she continues. "Your father isolated me. I had no other family. No friends. Just you and him, and that wasn't enough. It was never going to be enough. One night we got into a huge fight, and I couldn't take it anymore. So I did what I thought was best."

"You thought it was best to leave me behind?" My voice is shaking and I clear my throat, frustrated by my weak show of emotion. For once, I wish I were as callous and hard as my mother.

"I left your father. If I stayed there, he would've ruined me. I couldn't take the risk." She sniffs, like she's emotional or something, though I see no trace of tears anywhere. "You were just collateral damage."

Her casual statement should hurt enough to draw blood. But it's like her words trigger a realization deep within me. One I should've had a long time ago, but was too blinded by hate and vengeance to see it.

I don't matter.

I never mattered.

At least to her.

"Collateral damage," I repeat tonelessly.

She nods, her expression downright hopeful. "And look at you now. You've found Rhett. He's rich. Handsome. He'll be successful, just like his father. It's in their blood. If you play it right, he'll take care of you for the rest of your life. You'll be fine." She says this with total assuredness.

"Does that make you feel better? Knowing that I have Rhett? That he'll take care of me?" I ask. What a messed up way to think. Does she really feel justified in abandoning me when I was a baby, but now everything's okay because I have a super-hot, rich boyfriend who'll take care of me?

"Yes. Of course it makes me feel better. Just make sure of one thing." She leans in, as if we have a close relationship and she's about to share a bit of advice with me. "Never return any gift he gives you. Keep any cash he gives you too. Stow it away, just in case. And if you marry, make sure you have a solid prenuptial agreement, one where you get everything you deserve, which, by the way, is half. I'd suggest no prenup at all, but this is the Montgomerys we're dealing with, so that won't happen. Just—no matter what, guard your assets."

Her advice could be taken as somewhat caring, but really? When it comes down to it? It's all about the money. Everything's a business deal to this woman. There's no emotion, no love, no hate, no nothing. I almost feel sorry for her.

Almost.

She feels nothing. And being with her, talking with her, is making me feel nothing too. It's like my anger has disappeared.

"I'll let you get back to whatever it is you're doing," I tell her as I start walking toward the stairs. I'm halfway down before I hear her voice.

"Wait a minute."

I stop and turn to look up at her. She's standing at the

top of the staircase, her eyebrows furrowed, like I've totally confused her. "Is that all you wanted to say?" she asks.

I think about it for a moment, but nothing comes to me. There's nothing left to say. "Yes."

Diane makes a face. "Really? No raging confrontation or plans of revenge?"

Just thinking about my earlier rage and revenge plans leaves me mentally exhausted. "I'm over it."

"Over it?" She raises a brow.

"How can I care when you so clearly don't?" I wave a dismissive hand at her, at a total loss for words.

Seems like Diane is too. She says nothing. Doesn't stop me from leaving. Doesn't throw anything at me. We're just…

Done.

I turn and make my way down the rest of the stairs, stopping in the foyer to look back up one more time, secretly hoping she's still standing there. Watching me.

But no. She's gone. Probably in her giant walk-in closet rifling through her expensive belongings, our conversation already forgotten.

She doesn't care. She never has. She's selfish, only worried about her next move, concerned about who's going to take care of her, never thinking of anyone else. That's the realization I had only a moment ago. My mother doesn't care about me, but I shouldn't take it personally. She doesn't care about anyone.

Only herself.

I leave the house without a backward glance, quietly pulling the door shut. I walk down the driveway, headed for Savannah's car, which is parked a few blocks down the street. My footsteps are light, my mind clear. I glance up at the blue sky, smiling when the warmth of the sun caresses my face, and I actually laugh.

For once in my life I'm full of joy. It's a strange feeling, one I'm not used to. It's like those oppressive emotions I've carried with me all these years have evaporated into thin air. I'm finally free.

Free.

EPILOGUE

Jensen

"Fuck me, this is the life."

I take the straw hat off my head and smack Rhett with it. He lets loose a soft "ow" and rubs his arm, glaring at me. We're sitting out by the pool, the sound of the waves crashing against the shore nearby, the breeze rustling the fronds of the giant palm trees that loom above us.

He's right. This is definitely the life.

"Don't talk like that," I chastise. "There are little children nearby."

The "little children" are Addie and Trent, who accompanied us to Maui. We're staying in a gorgeous vacation home not far from Makena Beach for the next two weeks, thanks to an old family friend of the Montgomerys. Rhett's family has a vacation home in the Caribbean, so the two families like to trade a lot.

Ah, the perks of having a boyfriend who comes from a wealthy family.

"Those little children, as you call them, have worse mouths than me," Rhett mutters, completely annoyed but ultra-cute with it, especially with his newly sunburned nose. "Have you heard Addie lately? She curses worse than I ever did."

He's totally joking. Addie never curses. "She's a polite young lady," I tell him primly, my laughter immediately escaping me because it's pointless to pretend. "Fine, you're right. She curses like a sailor."

"You know a bunch of sailors, babe?" He lifts his brows, teasing me. It's been like this for the past six months. Easy. Lots of teasing. Lots of laughter. Lots of sex.

Lots of love.

We're here in celebration of Rhett graduating college, and I'm so proud of him, though I wish I still didn't have another three years until I can graduate. As a graduation gift, his father offered us an all-expenses paid vacation to Hawaii, but with one catch—we had to take Addie and Trent with us.

Not a hardship. We gladly got them out of California so Diane could come to the house and finally move all her stuff out. Parker kept his word and filed for divorce before the year was through. They've bickered, they've gone back and forth, Diane even trying to convince him to take her back at one point, but in the end, the divorce happened much quicker than any of us expected, and the final papers were signed the day we flew out for Maui.

And now, finally, Diane had hired a moving company to come collect her things. Parker said he was going to let her take what he wanted, but he was wise enough to get Rhett and Addie out of there so it wouldn't turn into a total disaster.

The rumor going around is that since they separated, Diane has been living with good ol' Uncle Craig. None of us know if this is true or not. No one has spoken to Craig for months.

But I wouldn't put it past her.

Parker cut Park loose and let him start his own business. Their relationship isn't the best, but Rhett has faith they can still make this work. They all feel snowed by Diane, and Park is even in counseling. I hope it helps him.

Addie seems to be thriving without Diane in the house. Parker is working less, so he's able to spend more time with his daughter. She only has one more year in high school and then she's off to college, so he wants to enjoy her while she still lives under his roof.

Parker isn't a bad guy. He's just made some bad choices, which I can totally relate. He's trying to rectify that now, and I can't help but admire him.

And then there's me and Rhett.

I glance over at him stretched out on the lounger, wearing a pair of blue Hawaiian print board shorts and nothing else, his tan skin turning a faint shade of red. They kept warning me the Hawaiian sun is intense and I should be using plenty of sunscreen, but it looks like Rhett isn't taking his own advice.

"Hey." I nudge him in the side with my index finger, making his eyes crack open. "You need more sunscreen."

He lifts up his sunglasses, squinting at me. "You gonna rub it on me?"

Yikes. He sounds and looks like a perv right now. But he's my perv, so I don't mind. "Oh yeah, I'll rub it on you."

I grab the spray bottle of sunscreen out of my bag and stand, walking over to him so I can start spraying. But before I even hit the button he's on his feet, knocking the sunscreen to the ground. His hand locked around my arm, he drags me toward the pool.

"Rhett, no!" I yell just as he pulls me into the water. We fall straight to the bottom, his arm snaking around my waist, holding me close as we slowly float back to the surface. When our heads break water, he's grinning at me, the water running down his face, and I sort of want to punch him.

Or kiss him.

"Why'd you do that?" I splash water at him and he splashes back.

"You're being a nag," he teases. "'Don't curse, Rhett. You need sunscreen, Rhett.'"

"You're an ass." I try to dunk him, but he's stronger than me, so that proves impossible. Instead he dunks me, sending me under, and I punch his shoulder once I break the surface yet again. "Ugh, I hate you."

"You do not." He scoops me up into his arms, both of us treading water as we stare at each other. "You love me."

"You're right. I love you." I kiss him to prove it.

"Hmm." He hums by my ear, holding me close, his hand wandering down to the flimsy waistband of my bikini. "This swimsuit is indecent."

"You should know since you helped me pick it out." I wrap my arms around his neck, smiling up at him.

"I was crazy. I should've never let you get it."

"No one else sees me in it. Just you," I reassure him.

He rests his big hands on my bottom, giving me a squeeze. "Me and Trent. Every time that kid spots you, his eyes bug out of his head like a goddamn cartoon character."

"Please. He's only got eyes for Addie." I lean in and kiss him. Once. Twice. Three times. "And I only have eyes for you."

"Good," he murmurs, trying to take the kiss deeper, but I won't let him. He growls in frustration. "Let's go upstairs."

I raise my brows, surprised, yet I know I shouldn't be. "Are you serious? Again? Really?"

"Yeah, really. It's already been a few hours."

Since we've come to Maui, we've been fucking like crazy. "More like it's only been an hour."

"Oh. Really? Well, damn. Guess I better learn some self-control then," he says with a smile.

"Please don't," I say as I try to climb up on him. I only

manage to wrap my legs around his waist. "I like you like this."

"I like you like this too, especially in the skimpy bikini." He slips his hands beneath my bikini bottoms, touching me between my thighs. "Aw, babe. This is ridiculous. Why do you keep denying yourself? And me?"

"Oh, fine. Let's go upstairs." I make an irritated noise, like this is such a hardship, but I'm putting on the best performance of my life. Because nothing with Rhett is a hardship.

Not one damn thing.

ABOUT THE AUTHOR

Monica Murphy is the New York Times, USA Today and #1 international bestselling author of the One Week Girlfriend series, the Billionaire Bachelors and The Rules series. Her books have been translated in almost a dozen languages and has sold over one million copies worldwide. She is a traditionally published author with Bantam/Random House and Harper Collins/Avon, as well as an independently published author. She writes new adult, young adult and contemporary romance. She is also USA Today bestselling romance author Karen Erickson.

Made in the USA
Middletown, DE
04 February 2019